SWEET FIERCE FIRES

Joyce Myrus

ZEBRA BOOKS
KENSINGTON PUBLISHING CORP.

ZEBRA BOOKS

are published by

Kensington Publishing Corp.
475 Park Avenue South
New York, N.Y. 10016

First printing: July, 1984

Printed in the United States of America

One

"But Mother, really! Even if I were to consider such a thing, whatever makes you think he will want to marry me? I don't suppose he even remembers me at all." Brigida Lydon stood at her looking glass in a camisole and flounced petticoat, vigorously brushing her shining pale hair and watching her mother's reflection flit in and out of her line of sight. Emma Lydon was moving about restoring order to the feminine chaos of her daughter's room, and with quick, birdlike gestures she replaced a string of pearls in their satin case, folded silk stockings, examined a pair of long kid gloves for a hint of soil.

"Of course he remembers you. How could he possibly forget? He was one of the family by the time he left us." Emma shook her head. "You were such a reckless little antagonist, always at him, and he, somber and serious, trying to pay you no mind. I don't suppose he succeeded in that, do you?"

"No, I don't believe he did," Brigida answered with a small smile, remembering an intense young boy with hard blue eyes, so fierce and so silent—at first. He had

5

talked to her, after a time, as he did to no one else, not to her brothers who were his staunch friends, not even to Emma, whom he loved so. Under huge, starry tropical skies he had spun out chains of magical words, a fairy tale for a little girl about a place called Silver Hill. There had been such immeasurable longing in his voice, Brigida could hear it, in memory, still.

"Of course I wouldn't think of suggesting an arranged marriage, not to you in this day and time," Mrs. Lydon went on. She stood in the center of the room with her head to one side, reminding Brigida, as always, of a sensible little sparrow. "It is eighteen seventy, after all. That would be a touch old-fangled of me, though I do believe that's still the best way, no matter the modern fashion." There was a hint of sarcasm in her tone. "But you know, Brigida, his mother is my dearest friend, and from the time you were born Elizabeth Hawkes and I have dreamed how wonderful it would be if her son and my daughter . . . Elizabeth is not at all well. I want a good long visit with her and, in any case, you've not been home since you were a little thing. It's time."

"Home? But that's always been where you and Father were, silly." Brigida stooped to give her mother a quick hug. Though not very tall, she hovered some inches over Emma, who was barely five feet. "Father's ship was home to me because you both were there . . . and the boys, and now San Francisco is getting to be. But Mother . . ." Brigida's voice came muffled from beneath the petticoat Emma was lifting over her head. "Mother . . . do you suppose I'll know how to behave properly in a really civilized place? I mean, after all the time we spent at sea

6

and in the Islands . . ." She was teasing but her words were not entirely unserious. The sophisticated East did seem a little intimidating. She turned back to the mirror to study her image again, delighted and still a little startled by the person staring back at her with mischievous large dark eyes. "Will I really do for Boston or New York? That is where Slade is now?" She pulled on a bed gown and curled into a chair to sip the warm milk Emma had brought. This was her favorite time, visiting with her mother after a cotillion in this charming room she'd done herself in pink and white with touches of lace everywhere. She yawned, content.

"Slade is in New York, yes, and yes, you will do. Anywhere. And you know it. You know the stir you've caused in the time we've been in San Francisco. I'll have none of your false modesty, young lady, nor this fishing for compliments, either. You receive all the adoration you need from everyone else." Emma was thinking particularly of her husband. Captain Lydon. Tom was a large, powerful man of such austere, commanding presence he could wither the rowdiest deck hand with a glance, yet he was soft as wax with this charmer. That was how it had been ever since she was born eighteen years ago and that was how it was with other men now, since they'd settled in San Francisco nearly a year ago. And Emma was enjoying it all nearly as much as Brigida was. She took deep pleasure in her daughter's unfolding young womanhood. While keeping off the despoilers who were always a danger to any blossoming young beauty, she was charmed by the ardent young men who came courting. Brigida, for her part, took up each new flirtation, each romance, with bubbling delight from the very first moment her imagination was touched by a clever turn of phrase, or a handsome face, or a noble history—or any number of other things Emma couldn't always fathom.

The first had been an aspiring young writer who had introduced Brigida to San Francisco's intellectual elite. He had been followed by a rugged, rough-hewn prospector who seemed perpetually surprised by his immense new wealth and at finding himself in Mrs. Lydon's very Victorian parlor. The most recent and most serious had been a slim young Spaniard down from the mountains on a dancing golden palomino. Exuding Old World charm and arrogance, he had offered to share his endless lands and wild herds with the whaling captain's beautiful daughter.

After the first flush of undying love, Brigida's interest quickly waned. Unfailingly kind, always more than polite, she refused him, refused them all.

Captain Lydon was relieved. Not one had been good enough for his lovely jewel, though the prospector came closest, being the man most like himself, a man who had wrested a fortune from nature's tight-clenched fist, taking gold from the hills, as the captain had plundered his own wealth from the ungenerous sea. He had found the rancher insufferable and the writer inscrutable, and he was pleased to see the last of the lot.

Mrs. Lydon, too, was pleased, though not particularly surprised that her exquisite child had rejected even the most attractive and eloquent of her suitors. Having grown up aboard ship in masculine company, Brigida wasn't intimidated by men as some other girls were.

Being clever, she quickly saw their flaws—the worst of which, Brigida decided, was a tendency to place her in the unacceptable category of delightful but inferior female. Behind Brigida's nearly perfect facade of confidence, her mother knew, there was still a vulnerable young girl, one blessed—or cursed Emma sometimes thought—with a quick intelligence and a streak of passionate stubborn pride that would make her a terrible handful for the wrong man. But for the right one? Emma had her own plan.

"I wasn't fishing for compliments, Mother, don't be short with me," Brigida said breaking into Emma's thoughts. "I still need you to remind me I really am all right. Everything is so suddenly different and fascinating . . . and a bit frightening sometimes."

"I know that, dearest," Emma smiled, "so you must keep in mind what I tell you. You are unusual, you know, freer in your thoughts and feelings than . . . you've been half round the world when most other girls your age have only been to high teas and coming-out balls. You've been places and seen things that proper young ladies aren't even supposed to think of. Please be cautious, though I know that's not your nature. Unless a man is strong enough to understand and let you be exactly what you really are, you won't be happy and . . . enough now! Don't fret." Emma smoothed the girl's puzzled frown with an affectionate hand, then pulled up the comforters as Brigida slipped into bed. "Your own instincts will lead you right, depend on it. And if you have doubts? Well, we're here, aren't we?"

Emma had no doubts. In six months, when Brigida was

finished at the Mercer Day School, when she herself had returned from a short cruise north with Tom and their sons, then they'd consider Slade Hawkes. "Tell me," she said briskly, "about tonight. You haven't said one word."

"It was the same as usual—the music, the people, everything. There was a new officer posted to the garrison here, quite attractive in dress blue. He's calling on me tomorrow, of course." Brigida was drowsy, her golden hair in a wild swirl about her lovely face. She yawned and stretched like a kitten. Feeling safe and warm and wonderfully tired, she snuggled deeper into her quilts. Sleep came to her quickly as it did to a child, Emma mused, as she tiptoed about extinguishing the lamps. Leaving the room, Emma stopped to straighten the bonnet of Brigida's last doll that still sat propped on the mantel. Before the next fateful six months had passed, this last reminder of her daughter's childhood would be banished to the back of a cupboard, and sleep would come to Brigida only in short, fevered fits and starts.

Two

"Where'd you come from, I'd like to know that? Such a pretty thing and so young, ain't you afraid, travelin' about all on your own?"

Brigida was sitting by herself at the captain's table of the *Bristol*, one of the huge new night boats ferrying between Fall River in Massachusetts and New York harbor. Earlier, she had spent some hours on deck, alone, thinking, as she watched the vessel's forty-foot paddle wheels, set amidships, churn the chill waters of Long Island Sound. Still lost in a wistful reverie of California sun and blue Pacific, she looked up startled to study the portly, pleasant-faced man who had spoken. He was attired in the simple woolen jacket and scarred and scruffy high-topped brogans of a country farmer.

"The steward showed me to this place," Brigida offered. "I hope I'm not intruding."

"Intrudin'? Not likely. This craft can carry near eight hundred passengers and maybe there's a baker's dozen makin' the trip tonight. On the eve of the New Year, folk tend to stay close to home and friends." The man

11

glanced about the spacious empty dining salon that was lavishly appointed and elegantly decorated with an ornate carved ceiling and glittering chandeliers. "Even a floatin' palace like this is no comfort if you're alone to see in the New Year. I'm Bill Squires, friend of Captain Halsey. He'll be right along." The man took a place opposite Brigida. "Well, I'd not have my girl sailin' about alone with two rogues like this pair on the loose," Squires said just loud enough to be heard by two young men approaching the table. He winked conspiratorially at Brigida.

"Mr. Squires," Brigida half smiled, "I've spent most of my life on the sea. I've no fear of it nor of such rogues as these, as you so uncharitably designate them."

"Oh, I'm just teasin' you, missy. I've known young Phil here since he was born. There's no sweeter lad anywheres, that's certain, though I can't vouch for his friend."

"Pay no attention to old Bill, Miss Lydon. He's a confirmed curmudgeon," one of the young men laughed. "Philip Carpenter at your service." He bowed. "And allow me to present Hollis Stancel."

Both gentlemen were well and expensively dressed. Carpenter was a barrel-chested, solid young man with silken whiskers, curly chestnut hair and smiling brown eyes that put her at once at her ease. He was got up rather as a dandy, showing a lot of immaculate white linen and muscular leg in well fitted boots and breeches. His companion, a thin, long-boned man with a narrow face and stick-straight dark blond hair, toyed incessantly with the watch fob dangling at his waistcoat pocket.

Gradually, the dozen chairs at the table filled, and Captain Halsey joined the small company of New Year's travelers. It was a convivial group, and after introductions were made, they talked of their reasons for being in transit on this last night of 1870.

When everyone had told some story, Captain Halsey turned to Brigida. "You are a young lady of Western provenance, I'm told. Will you tell us about San Francisco, Miss Lydon?" The captain had an abundant thatch of snow-white hair and very blue eyes lighting a tanned and weathered face. Almost hesitantly, Brigida looked directly at him and felt her eyes gently mist. They were so alike, she thought, these sailors, these men in command of ships. In some undefinable, wonderful way they all seemed to share a certainty of their own strength and worth and power. Suddenly she missed her father terribly, missed them all with a pain so sharp it seemed physical. Her last days in San Francisco came back in a confused memory of black bombazine dresses and black veils, of jet mourning rings on her fingers and black-bordered cambric handkerchiefs.

"I'm sorry," she said to a momentary silence around the table. "I was . . . thinking. Well . . . San Francisco . . . it's a community of fortune hunters. Wealth is the only real power there. Your coachman one morning could well be your landlord by nightfall. I found that delightful."

"Pardon, ma'am, but I've heard San Francisco described as a city of vulgarians. I heard San Francisco is a city of penny-pinching cads, a place where godlessness and prosperity are walkin' hand in hand?" Stancel's statements sounded like questions. He wore a cracked smile as Brigida flashed luminous dark eyes full on him.

"You're quite in error, Mr. Stancel," she said indignantly. "Penny-pinching? San Franciscans scorn that coin as too insignificant to bother with. We don't use it, and we use the new nickel with reluctance."

"I was just playin' devil's advocate, ma'am, you could call it," Stancel answered quickly. "And with such a charmin' champion as you, your city is safe from even the worst slander. You must have been born there, to defend it so admirably?"

"No one was born in San Francisco," Brigida bantered. "I lived there only a short time. I took my first breath aboard my father's whaler in the South Pacific."

"I used to work with the offshore whalers, as a lad, out east on Long Island," Captain Halsey said. "There'd be thirteen, fourteen of the monsters sighted in the space of five miles, more of them spouting farther out. There's still some offshore whaling, isn't there, Bill?"

"Sure, out to Amagansett, but oysterin' has grown a better business, I'll tell you, and there's none in the world so good as ours, practically jumpin' outa the bays for you. You can eat all the oysters you want in New York City for ten cent. They're even servin' Long Island oysters on them new Pullman trains out in the middle of the prairie! Can you beat it?"

Philip gulped down a mouthful of coffee in a rush to speak. "Hollis and I are thinking of taking a Pullman to California in the fall. It's quite the fashionable thing to do now. Everyone's going, and I've heard the trip is spectacular—wild red Indians, tunnels through the mountains, all that. I'll do photographs if we go. Tell me, Captain Halsey, did you never think to go to sea on a whaler?"

The captain answered, "I had thought on whaling, years ago, every Sag Harbor boy did, but I took to the Sound instead. I've no complaints. I've the best craft plying these waters. There'll be more like her soon, all up and down the coasts."

"If whaling ships were fitted with steam engines, Captain, if they had some power besides the wind, many a vessel would not have been lost to storms or northern ice," Brigida said softly. A recurrent cold tremor passed through her.

"Everything will be steam run one day very soon," the captain said, standing. "Enjoy your brandy, don't hurry. I'll get back to the wheelhouse now, but before I go, we'll drink to the New Year." He raised his glass and the others joined him. "To eighteen seventy-one," he toasted, "sure to be better than last and not as good as next. Here's to more . . . of progress, of machines, of fortunes made. You youngsters will see it all. This is a time to be young, the best time. Well, sail with me again, Miss Lydon. It's been a true pleasure dining with such a charming and beautiful young lady."

"Do you think the captain's right, about progress and all? I wonder . . ." Brigida asked when most of the guests had withdrawn to the saloon for cards.

"Of course he is," Philip interrupted. "Everything's new and changing. Think what's been done in just the past few years! The telegraph, the western railroads, steamships crossing the Atlantic in days only, the great

15

canal at Suez. Why, more progress has been made in this century than in all three that came before it!"

"Phil Carpenter spoutin' off again," Bill Squires grumbled pleasantly, "and with the papers so full of disaster and treachery, too. But never mind, I like things as they used to be. The future ain't what it once was, is what I think."

"I agree," Hollis Stancel spoke in his slow drawl. "I, too, prefer things as they used to be . . . before the war." He downed his glass of brandy and poured out another. "Tell us about you now, Miss Lydon, really. I think we've waited long enough," Stancel demanded.

"I've come round the horn from San Francisco. I had to pay a call at Boston. Now I'm going to Silver Hill Manor on the East End of Long Island. Now you know all about me," she stated with a short laugh. "Are you satisfied?"

Mr. Squires sat up straight in his chair. Philip Carpenter jumped to his feet and sent dregs of coffee splattering across the white tablecloth as he upset his cup.

"Extraordinary, you going there!" he burst out. "Silver Hill Manor is not far from our island. It's a place I know so well. I spent countless hours there as a boy when it was still all brightness and . . ." Then, after a pause, he asked gently, "How well do you know the family?"

"My mother and Elizabeth Hawkes were dear friends. She asked me on after . . ."

"And Slade? Do you know Slade Hawkes, Miss Lydon?" Phil asked.

She nodded. "I've not seen him for many years, though. I was a child when we last met and he was not

16

much older than seventeen or eighteen. I was madly in love with him then—the way only a little girl can be in love. Well, do tell me about him."

Her elegant fingers played about the rim of a glass as Hollis Stancel rose from the table, taking his snifter and the brandy bottle and, a bit unsteadily, made for a lounge chair. "Yes, do tell us about the renowned Captain Slade Hawkes, Phil," Hollis slurred a bit. "His reputation as a Yankee . . . officer, I'll say in polite company was . . . prodigious. I heard he was a pirate, with the soul of a shark, who'd exploit any situation for his own gain."

"Women always want to know about Slade Hawkes, blast him," Phil Carpenter told Brigida, ignoring his friend's outburst. "I'll tell you what you want to know. You remember 'forewarned is forearmed,' though I don't know how often that's true, do you? He's handsome, irresistible, women say, whatever that means. We'll start there. He's imperious, cold as ice. There is none of that backslapping and pawing so many go in for, and, of course, being Elizabeth Slade's son—the Slades are old New York society—he's a true aristocrat, lives by his own rules, looks on us ordinary folk with, oh . . . a certain disdain, I've always felt. Bill here knows Slade. The Squires' farm is only a few miles from Silver Hill. Do you agree, sir, with my description?"

"I verily believe Slade Hawkes to be a man of education and industry and civil enough—if you are not in his way," the farmer pronounced. "Well, go on, Phil."

"He's utterly charming," Phil continued, "when he chooses to be. Sharp, quick-witted, perhaps more ambitious than any man should be. He has more than doubled the fortune his father left him, and he's not yet content. He'd be richer still—talks in six figures, nothing less."

Brigida's look was skeptical. "From whaling? He's done that well from whale bone and oil? I knew his father had left him five . . . or was it six ships? But even so . . ." She leaned forward eagerly.

"Slade's not one of the colossal millionaires, not yet, rather one of the second rank, though he'd be furious being called second at anything," Philip laughed. "Only partly from whaling, a small part actually. He's got five ships. One was lost during the war. He's in real estate, too, and railroads . . . he's got dry docks. I don't even know what all else. He's much intrigued with machines, isn't that so, Mr. Squires?"

"Yes, 'tis. He takes up one inventor after another, I've heard. Slade puts up money for these inventors of his and makes it back times over, keeps on gettin' richer." Squires made use of a gilt-rimmed spittoon and lapsed back into silence.

"There's no more I can tell you, Miss Lydon. I haven't seen much of Slade since the war. He spends most of his time in the city now, but when we were boys we were thrown much together. We competed at everything, and Slade . . . he could do everything better, perfectly, with no fear. I worshipped him. I still do, a little. You know that sort?"

"Oh, yes, I knew him, too, remember," Brigida answered. "But who runs the manor if Slade spends his time away? Elizabeth?"

"No, Levi Phillips does. That's Slade's man. The two

are almost inseparable. Levi's an Indian, Long Island Shinnecock, former harpooner. There isn't much to run at Silver Hill, though. They only keep a few cows now, harvest a little marsh hay. They haven't put in a real crop since I can remember. Mr. Squires do you . . . ?"

"The place ain't been farmed since the old captain died. Jarred been gone near ten years, is it Phil? Nine anyways." The old man, looking weary, didn't wait for an answer. "But why did they ask you on, Miss Lydon, when no one but servants been up there in years?"

"Slade took his first sea voyage with us, Mr. Squires. He was my father's cabin lad when he came aboard. Three years later, when the cruise ended, he was boat steerer and sometime harpooner, no small accomplishment for a boy. He . . . they asked me to Silver Hill because all my family were lost at sea and everything we had sold off for debt." Brigida stated the last simply as the three men stared at her in surprise.

"All of 'em? How could such a thing happen?" Mr. Squires asked indignantly.

"Ice, Mr. Squires," Brigida answered.

"Beg pardon?" he asked again.

"Ice," she repeated. "The American whaling fleet remained north too late. They were trapped, caught in the Arctic Sea ice. Seventeen ships in all, crushed like . . . like eggshells. Only one managed to break away and pick up a few survivors. But that was after my brothers went off on foot for help. No trace was found."

"I saw a wreck once, on an Atlantic crossing," Philip Carpenter said softly. "Our vessel was threading a valley of ice floes, mountains really, at sunset. The sky and ice

19

were tinged pale pink, the sea was beautiful. Coming round a turning we spotted the wreck, a splintered hulk resting crookedly in an icy nest. We all felt very small and very lonely, thinking of the poor devils who perished in that cruel wilderness."

Brigida was trembling a little, and without a word, Carpenter poured her a snifter of brandy. Wanly, she smiled her thanks. "I'd have been with them if not for my studies. I was furious at having to stay at home." She shook her head. "My brothers and I did so miss the sea after just a few seasons ashore."

"A whaler doesn't seem a proper place for a lady, Miss Lydon," Stancel offered skeptically.

"Mother didn't think so either. We spent more and more time with missionary families in the Islands. Finally, she decided that it would be unfitting for me to remain longer among the rough sailors and heathen savages, as she called them, who comprised Father's crews. That's when he built the San Francisco townhouse for us. It was fine, of course. But I couldn't wait to be at sea again. Oh, don't look so askance, Mr. Stancel. Many captains do keep their wives and children with them. You must know that."

"I've heard some very sensational stories, ma'am, about the hard life on the boats. Haven't you, Phil?" Stancel looked to his friend.

"Some masters are brutish, it's true," Phil said thoughtfully, "but surely not all."

"My father was firm, but respected for his fairness; men were always anxious to sail with him. He had the reputation of being a lucky captain you see . . . until the ice. Well, his luck just ran out, that's all." The back of Brigida's left hand came to her lips. "A lawyer arrived to tell me, a Mr. Rand. I'd never even heard of the man before, I didn't know my father had debt." She took a deep swallow of her brandy, remembering an agitated, corpulent man, florid and puffy of face, wheezing slightly as he extended two heavy, blunt hands encrusted with jeweled rings. "Poor dear," Rand had said in a stilted, thin voice, "I bring you most horrendous news."

After that, dressed to the last detail as the mourning manuals dictated in dull black with no glitter of silk or leather anywhere, no jewel but jet, no lace, no trim but lusterless crepe collar and cuffs, she had politely received curious callers. Most were nearly strangers who spoke in hushed tones of everything but what she most needed to speak of. "Never mention death to one who wears the weed," the manuals instructed. No one did, and after a short time Brigida abruptly put an end to what seemed to her a parlor charade, a theatrical display of private pain. Long before the expected year was over, she gave up the trappings of mourning and decided to do as her mother had wished—go "home" to the East.

During the long voyage around the Horn, Brigida kept very much to herself, and she had almost come to terms with the tragedy by the time she boarded the *Bristol* at Boston. She was still, though, unwilling to talk much about it.

"Well, now everything is gone, sold off," she told her companions almost briskly. "And here I am and . . . oh! Whatever is the matter, Mr. Stancel? Are you ill? You look dreadful. Shall we talk of other things?"

Stancel filled his own glass again. Gradually he seemed to get his thoughts together and his agitation appeared to lessen. "I, too, lost everything, Miss Lydon. In the war. I came out of it with my pipe and pouch—no more, and I, too, impose on the kindness of friends. My family is dead, treasures gone, the plantation burned to ash and rubble. I have only one distant cousin—in the West—who generously did provide for my education. Phil here and I met at Yale some years ago. He has been gracious enough to invite me for a stay with his family on their island after our visit in the city. The Carpenters own a whole island, don't you Philip?"

"Father does. Yes . . . a small one off East Hampton . . . purchased from the Indians by a very great-great-grandfather.

"Do let's go to the saloon now. I'd enjoy a game of hearts or whist. Would you, Miss Lydon?"

Mr. Squires yawned and stretched. "I'm off to my quarters for a bit of sleep," he announced. "I been up since before sunrise. Now you come by the farm for a visit, Miss Lydon, and bring Elizabeth Hawkes, if you can get her away from Silver Hill. She and the wife used to be thick as thieves one time, but Elizabeth just kind of stopped going about. She don't have no visitors anymore, neither. Well, goodnight now. You young folks shouldn't be stayin' up too late. We'll be makin' Brooklyn Ferry about dawn, you know."

"It sounds dreary, Silver Hill, doesn't it?" Brigida asked pensively when the old man had gone.

"Once it wasn't at all that way, and you'll make any place bright enough, I can tell. I've an idea, besides. Just get settled in a bit and I'll ask my sisters to invite you to Carpenter's Island when Hollis and I arrive there in a few weeks' time," Philip beamed. "And then, who knows? Perhaps you can just sort of . . . stay on with us, one way or another?"

"But, I can't . . ."

"I'll brook no excuses, Miss Lydon, of course you will come to us," Philip said with feigned fierceness. "Is it whist or hearts, then?"

She hesitated a moment. "Hearts," she answered, taking his proffered arm as they left the cabin and wandered toward the *Bristol*'s grand saloon, Hollis Stancel following some distance behind.

Three

New York harbor was a forest of sailing masts and steamboat stacks early on the bright cold morning that Brigida viewed it for the first time.

With intense curiosity, she looked about her as she stood with Philip Carpenter and Hollis Stancel on the top deck of the *Bristol*. The magnificent steamer, its massive paddle wheels churning, navigated down the narrow East River, which was crowded with tugs, barges, and square-rigged packets. Fishing boats rocked off Fulton Street Pier near the new Market Building where a sign advertised ferry service half-hourly to Morrisania, Harlem, Astoria, and Highbridge. Floating wooden elevators disgorged their golden wealth of grain into the holds of ships bound for ports halfway round the world, and a floating oyster market—a string of barges laced together—was moored off South Street.

"Such a sight! I always get wild, coming into New York," Philip said excitedly. "There's a bridge being built that will connect Brooklyn Ferry with Manhattan Island. See the guy wires? Look, they're just doing the foundation stanchion beneath."

"It is wonderful. There can be no other sight like it." Brigida, too, was animated.

"We're making a landing. Come along, you two!" Stancel called nervously, heading for the bow, and his companions quickly followed.

When farewells were made and invitations exchanged, Brigida disembarked the *Bristol* and, followed by a porter carting her trunk, purposefully threaded her way along the noisy dock past sacks and crates and barrels piled everywhere. The exotic aromas of recently landed tropical fruits and spices, oils and baled leathers combined deliciously with the clean salt scent of the harbor. Shouting vendors hawked hot potatoes. Dray wagons, pulled by straining, steaming teams of heavy horses, rumbled past. Sailors moved with grace and speed along swaying gangplanks.

A little reluctant to leave the noise and excitement, yet anxious to reach her destination, Brigida hurried to make a train connection. She rode the South Side Railroad east to the end of the rail line, arriving late that afternoon. A row of carriages and wagons stood at the station.

A man with deep-set, expressionless dark eyes watched her progress toward him, and she studied him in turn. He wore a black suit over a stiff, high-buttoned collar. His skin was leathery of texture and shade, his cheekbones high and prominent, his aquiline features strong. From beneath a black top hat, straight black hair reached to his shoulders. He stood, Brigida surmised, some inches above six feet.

"I am Levi Phillips," he announced in a softer tone

26

than she would have expected from the look of him. "You will come with me now to Silver Hill."

"And you will collect my trunk, the brass and walnut there, with the straps, and my boxes, please," she replied, pointing, her tone of command sure, her expression as impassive as the Indian's, and she surprised a flicker of interest in his somber eyes.

The carriage, pulled by a fine pair of matched Morgans—with black points and straight black tails and manes—was distinguished by shiny black lacquer and polished brass. Inside it was red velvet and sumptuously comfortable.

Brigida, who had been awake into the small hours playing at cards aboard the *Bristol* and then had risen before dawn, curled into the soft plush upholstery, pulled a fur lap robe up to her chin and fell into a shallow, troubled sleep.

It was not quite dark when a sudden stop awakened her. Curious at what seemed an overlong delay in the middle of nowhere, she threw off the fur, stretched and opened a door of the carriage. Still drowsy and flushed, she stepped down into a dusty, deserted high road, lined in both directions as far as she could see by oak brush scrub and dwarf pines.

"Mr. Phillips?" she called, moving languidly toward the front of the carriage. A brisk wind took the hood from her head, loosing her untamed mass of gold-blond curls to fall about her shoulders and down her back. The wind caught at the hem of her cloak, held only by a clasp at the throat, and lifted it billowing out behind her.

"Mr. Phillips!" Brigida called again, "I've been

months journeying and now . . ."

As she came to the front of the horses, she found the driver engaged in talk with a mounted rider who broke off his conversation to look down at her. Brigida made no move to pull her billowing cloak about her as he made a slow, thorough appraisal of her slender figure. It was well defined in her black traveling suit, the jacket closely fitted over high, full breasts and tailored to a narrow waist. Her skirt draped softly, following rounded hips, and was molded along the length of graceful legs by the strong wind.

"Slade?" Brigida asked with a questioning smile, still a little vague with recent sleep. The sinking sun, tangled in stark branches, was at the man's back, leaving him in shadow but lighting her lovely face with a glowing warmth, glinting on golden flecks in her dark eyes, setting her hair ablaze in fiery gold.

"Well, Brigida Lydon, how nicely you've grown," the man said, dismounting a dark bay stallion. He paused, his hand resting on the shoulder of a huge dog, and Brigida recognized the grace and carriage of the man she remembered so well. In two long strides he reached her, passed an arm about her waist and bent to her lips, almost fiercely. Brigida's senses were flooded by his unexpected proximity. She felt awash in a faint aroma of lime and soaped leathers. Startled and confused, she made no rejecting gesture, she didn't even pull away, just stood stiffly, unresponsive, a vague weakness touching her limbs. His arm tightened about her. She felt herself crushed to his lean length. When his lips parted and his mouth on hers grew harder, more demanding, Brigida

28

wrenched away and with some effort broke free of his grasp. Slade stepped back to look down into her now wary eyes, which had become unfathomable dark pools.

"You are unmannerly, Slade Hawkes," Brigida said, her voice throaty and low. "Just as I remember. I'd expected you to have become something of a gentleman by now, or at least have learned to behave like one."

"And who the devil are you, St. Brigit? You look more like her wild Druid sister. The Celtic Brigit was a goddess of fire, did you know? Well, you could be all the pagan divinities in one from the look of you—Diana, Athena, Brizo—witches every one of them. Tell me what you've become—saint or witch. Are you virginal still as the winter moon?" His tone was cold and taunting.

As he spoke, Brigida stared at Slade Hawkes as brazenly as he did at her, studying every detail of his hard, handsome face. The strong features were perfectly chiseled. There was a suggestion of aquilinity in the nose and the high bones that shadowed his faintly hollow cheeks. Only his eyes were as she remembered, deep-set, piercing as those of a regal bird of prey, their color a chilling icy azure blue. "You've no manners to ask me such a question when we've only just met again." Brigida's tone was heavy with contempt, and Slade's mouth twisted into a cruel smile under her unblushing scrutiny.

In a slow, very deliberate manner he said, "You'd do well to keep a more civil tongue with me. I am to become your husband presently. That gives me every right to ask what I will."

There was a flinty light in his darkening eyes as he

stood glaring down at Brigida, his feet planted wide apart in black knee boots, his arms akimbo. As he frowned, irritated by the bold, elegant young woman before him, he could still see in her the golden tempest of a child he remembered—agile and quick as a boy climbing the riggings of a rolling ship or racing planked decks with her brothers. He remembered fine, soft yellow curls in tropical sunlight, pretty laughter rising in equatorial stillness, remembered even her painted rocking horse on a quarter deck. All had been comforting to a lonely boy gone, for the first time, from home.

"Come," he said, taking Brigida's hand, "I'll ride a little way with you now." Confused by his sudden change of mood, aware only of Slade moving with a quick, easy grace, she allowed him to hand her into the carriage. As he climbed up after her, he called to Levi Phillips, "I'll go as far as Beaver Dam with you!"

Undoing brass buttons, he removed his fur-lined greatcoat, and reached into a pocket of his leather jacket to extract a cigar and a metal match safe. He struck a light and puffed on the cigar repeatedly to get it properly burning. Brigida's glance traveled from his tawny hair and broad shoulders to thighs thick with muscle beneath close-fitting buckskin riding breeches. She looked up quickly.

"Captain Hawkes, don't look so . . . angry," she said as he continued to concentrate on his cigar, "I am sorry to disappoint, but I am neither saint nor goddess." Her softened tone was almost playful.

"That's not for you to decide," he said shortly. When their eyes met again, Brigida suddenly felt an almost wild exultation, and with a terrible clarity she knew she was in love with Slade Hawkes, and that she had been since they'd last met. Her little girl's infatuation had, in a single moment, become a woman's love. At the same time, a cold fear encircled her. She sensed instinctively that this man, staring back at her so fierce and arrogant, must not know . . . unless he first offered his love to her.

Slade drank in Brigida's startling, unexpected beauty while her extraordinary gold-flecked dark eyes sparkled at him boldly beneath thick lashes. He became aware of a faint perfume, light and fresh as a spring morning. He flung away his cigar and, moving to sit beside her, grasped her wild golden curls, gathering them to the nape of her neck as he pressed his lips to hers with a brutal fierceness that surprised them both. Wave after wave of a languorous sweetness flowed through Brigida's pliant body, and now she returned his kiss with equal passion. She felt his sure hands glide over her bosom and then loose the hooks of her jacket. As it fell open to the waist, he handled her round breasts, playing his fingers over their peaks as they rose against the smooth silk of her chemise.

"Well, goddess," Slade whispered as she moved against his touch with swelling pleasure, "I've had more women than I can count, but no respectable lady ever showed unveiled desire so readily as you." He laughed low. Before Brigida could answer, he undid her lacy chemise, then leaned to taste the pink crests of her breasts that had firmed so quickly to his caress, and Brigida gasped with surprise and delight. With devouring eyes, Slade leaned back for a moment to peruse her responsive form. Against the black of her jacket, the satin glisten of Brigida's skin was even more beautiful than he had hoped. Her eyes now were veiled by fluttering lashes, her delicate nostrils slightly flared. His hand moved beneath her skirt along silk stockings to soft, slender thighs. His lips at hers met no resistance, and his tongue plunged, exploring, while his hand went to the warm, soft center of her startled body. His fingers delved then withdrew, grazing lightly, then searched again in a way that made her cry out. He touched and paused and touched again, going a little deeper, pressing her harder, and she clung to him, her mouth eager and seeking, a new, strange, wild pleasure afflicting all her senses.

"Damn bloody springs!" he cursed when the carriage hit a rut and came down hard, jarring them both. He slid to his knees and pressed Brigida down on the velvet bench, sliding her skirt and petticoats to her hips. His mouth was strong on hers again, his hand, his fingers touching along her leg that was bent up against the seat back. Then his fingers were there again, working in and out, touching, pressing just where she wanted, in just the right way. His hot mouth was at her breast, moved down to her hip, and then she felt it along her thigh, felt his tongue flick, touching her now so that she moaned aloud, almost afraid of what she was feeling, until, after a time, he loomed up over her and she opened her eyes, waiting, questioning. "Christ," he whispered hoarsely, "you're like a peach, dewy, smooth and . . . firm flesh, like a perfect goddamn new peach."

"Why do you . . . stop?" she asked in a soft voice. She brought her arms about his neck, guiding him to her, her body arching against his, her heart pounding, until, through her soaring blind need, she became aware of his whisper in her ear, cruel and rasping now. "Witch," Slade was laughing softly, over and over, "witch, you're the same as the others, only the same, just another fallen angel easily tamed and cheaply won."

Brigida recoiled, horrified, a look of despairing bewilderment in her eyes, but she was held fast as if by steel bands. "No virgin goddess you, Brigida," he said, still playing her body, his blue eyes glowing cruelly as she fluttered in his grasp like a beautiful butterfly, pinned.

"Please!" she whispered. "I don't understand. Don't you want this? You're wrong, Slade, please. There was never anyone before." A rage was building in her, and in a nearly hysterical state of confusion and fear she groped about desperately for her fur muff and the small Colt pistol it concealed.

"It's well out of reach, goddess. You can have it back when you've taken control of yourself," Slade said huskily. "If unused virgin you truly are . . . you're a temptress, nonetheless." He looked into eyes that were wide now with fear and fury as she struggled beneath him. "Behave," he graveled, bringing his mouth hard to hers. "I could take you now if I wanted to and relieve your . . . distress," he said as he suddenly released her. "There isn't time. Get dressed, get yourself in order now. You're almost at Silver Hill. You can't greet my mother in such a state." His manner was completely cool and remote as he tossed Brigida a silk handkerchief.

When he moved to sit opposite her again, she violently flung it back at him.

"What? Not a tear to shed, goddess, over such a near

loss of your proclaimed innocence?''

"You'll never make me cry, Slade Hawkes. Never!'' she hissed, adjusting her chemise with trembling hands.

"Not even to wheedle and manipulate like so many of your duplicitous sex? I don't believe you.''

"You've a fine opinion of women, haven't you?'' Brigida demanded with sarcasm. "I don't weep. I don't lie either. I've never had to, you know, I've always gotten exactly what I wanted without resorting to devious devices.''

"And I've always taken exactly what I wanted,'' Slade said, reaching over to do up her jacket. "Your hands are unsteady, let me. . . .''

"Don't touch me. Don't you ever touch me again. I'll scream, the driver will . . .''

"Levi? He'd be in here quick enough, you're right. It wouldn't be the first time he and I shared a feisty bit like you. Scream all you like.''

Thrusting his hands from her, she reached out as though to scratch his taunting eyes with her long nails. "Oh, why . . . why did you ask me to come here? You . . . you're vile, monstrous!''

Laughing, he caught her hands in his before she could touch him. "Don't you, lady, ever again show me unsheathed claws. If you do, you'll suffer for it, I give you warning. I asked you here to silence my mother. Because of her endless pleadings, I agreed to a marriage with the penniless, orphaned daughter of her dearest friend; though you don't look much like a pauper.''

"What you see me in is almost all I own. My entire

34

fortune, such as it is, is on my back," she snapped.

"The manner of wealth doesn't so quickly fade as the means, does it goddess, nor the habits, either, of privilege. That your father lost his fortune and his life, that you come to me without wealth or property, I accept, as many would not, even though you are so perfect of face and form. And you will accept me as your husband," he went on, no longer smiling. "I will have you when I choose, and use you as I please, and you will learn to pleasure me. You will come to crave my touch . . . as others do."

"To the contrary, sir, it is you who will beg my favors before we are done. I shall exact a steep price, you may be quite certain." A smile began to play about Brigida's lips.

"I've found it doesn't do to treat women too well. To me, goddess, one skirt is much the same as another, it makes little difference. My mother must have grandchildren. You'll do as a bedmate and breeder. You'll be well used, I promise, and kept comfortably."

Brigida was neatly attired again, her hair brushed back from her beautiful face, but she was still flushed with anger and shaking. "You are a fool, Captain Hawkes," she said, her voice at least calm now. "We shall see who will play the tune and who will dance. I agreed to this . . . this union, only as a matter of practical necessity. I am used to comfort and luxury. It is I who will be using you, don't doubt it. I will never, without self-serving cause, cast a soft look upon you, nor will I find any real pleasure in your embrace. I will never come gently to your side or to your bed without some ulterior motive. You will try to win me to you and, in the doing, it is you who will be seduced, caught. I will simply take what I desire from you . . . and from others, as I choose. Heaven help any child born in the chill of our contentious lust."

In the half light, Brigida saw Slade recoil and pass a hand through his tawny hair. She watched him warily as he lit another cigar and the small flare of the match danced over his stormy features, his eyes reflecting points of light. The flame went out, leaving them again in the gloom of gathering twilight.

"A woman is the mouthpiece of the devil, I've heard. I believe it, too," Slade said. "Words flow from your perfect mouth as syrup from a maple, goddess, though not half so sweet. Good. A sharp-tongued, clever adversary enhances the pleasure of any contest, but just remember what I say to you now." His voice had become hard and fearsome. "No one uses what is mine unless I choose to share it. No other man will ever touch you except if I let him. But you won't ever want to seek pleasure elsewhere. I'll see worship in your eyes before very long, I promise. You will have no secrets from me. There will be nothing about you I won't know, no part of you I won't possess completely."

"Do your damnedest, Captain Hawkes," Brigida said with slighting contempt, "but you will never be sure of me, you will never really possess me. You will become obsessed with trying, though, and your obsession will put you in thrall to me."

There was a determination in her look that made him uneasy, but after a fleeting hesitation, he threw his head back and laughed. "Sure of yourself, aren't you? There you sit, a mere bit of fluff, a wide-eyed child, soft as a kitten and not much stronger. You presume to challenge me?"

"Yes," Brigida smiled sweetly, "and I will best you in this. I know."

"I warn you, when I choose to play, I never lose. Taking you to wife will be a challenge then, you're saying?" He raised an inquiring brow. "Good."

"It will be that and more, I promise," Brigida laughed icily. She felt his hands on her shoulders as he bent his bruising mouth to hers. Then she watched him drop lightly from the carriage.

In the early gloom of nightfall on the deserted, lonely road, he quickly mounted the stallion and rode off, the wolfhound gliding at his side like a silvery ghost.

Brigida sank back weakly atremble into the sheltering darkness of the carriage, all her fierce bravado deserting her, fear and anger and terrible loneliness mingling in its stead. "He will love me," Brigida swore to herself, pounding her clenched fist against the carriage window. "He will love me to madness, before I'll have done with the lordly Captain Hawkes!"

Four

A slivered moon intermittently illuminated two rows of twisted, aged oaks that tunneled the wide drive along which Levi Phillips urged the horses. He brought the brougham to a stop at the doors of a manor house, which was gradually being engulfed by a blanketing fog rising from the surface of a wide bay below.

"Wait," Phillips commanded as he disappeared into the darkness. Brigida heard him move away, mount several steps, and hammer loudly, the sound of iron on wood echoing in the thick dampness. There were two blows, then two more before the door swung open.

"Now come," the man called to Brigida. She alighted from the carriage and walked hesitantly toward the wavering light of a single candle at the threshold of the dark, silent structure. There, waiting, stood a small woman, an Indian like Phillips, round and thickly built with heavy dark hair pulled back from a plain moon face that was flat and immobile.

"Martha," Levi Phillips stated as an introduction. Then he left without another word.

Still shaken by her encounter on the road, Brigida was

suddenly very tired. She extended a hand to the woman and managed a weak smile.

"Brigida Lydon," she said.

"Yes, yes, come in. But do not stumble. Do not step on the door sill. You will bring us ill luck if you do."

"I don't believe in luck," Brigida answered wearily, careful, though, to step high over the sill.

Martha made no reply, just shook her head, and closed the door with a light slam. The woman placed a finger on her lips, indicating silence, then, sheltering the wavering candle flame with a thick hand, she beckoned Brigida to follow her up a dark staircase. On the second floor, where light spilled around the edges of a door, the woman tapped softly.

"Come in. Come right in, Martha." The voice was impatient. "It is Miss Lydon then, arrived at last?"

At the far side of a large room, with the light from a low fire playing about it, Brigida watched a woman rise from a chaise slowly, with obvious effort. As they drew close to each other, Brigida saw pain clearly etched in a thin face. She took the woman's cool, extended hands in her own.

"Mrs. Hawkes?" she asked.

"My dear," the woman said, "you are lovelier than even I could have imagined, who knew your mother at the height, the very height, my dear, of her own great beauty. I'm so pleased you have come to us. Warm yourself. Martha will fix you a tray. You must tell me about your journey. You saw to your affairs in Boston?"

"Yes, Mrs. Hawkes," Brigida answered, thinking of blue eyes so like those she looked into now.

"Well, you are here at last, praise heaven, and Silver

Hill is your home now. You will adore my son and he you, Brigida. I know it as a certainty. I've always known it. So did your mother. Slade will return tomorrow. Mr. Huntting will perform the ceremony then."

"Perhaps . . . Slade and I should become reacquainted before . . . perhaps your son and I shan't suit each other well enough, Mrs. Hawkes, what then?" In the silence that greeted her question, Brigida looked about the room, now lit by many flickering candles and lamps. It was a large chamber, done in gold, soft pinks, and dusty shades of rose. The pink silk drapery of a crown-canopied sleigh bed was open and askew, revealing a clutter of empty cups and glasses, books and papers amidst piled pillows appliquéd and ruffled with eyelet lace. A marble-topped dressing table with gilded lyre legs was strewn with Dresden jars and bottles and Limoge porcelain boxes of lotions and physics and medicinal salts. The crowded marble mantel held a collection of brass candlesticks, long-necked vases, oriental temple jars, framed pressed flowers—roses—set on little brass easels. Near a window, opposite the fireplace at the far end of the room, was a lace-covered oval table and two chairs all littered with paint pots, brushes, and rolled canvases. An unfinished oil, a painting of gray sky and water, winter oaks and dark evergreens, sat near the table on a wooden easel.

"It is a clutter, isn't it?" Elizabeth Hawkes asked. "I am much confined here, Brigida, plagued as I am with weak nerves and a stiffness and pain which no doctor has ever been of any help in treating. I have tried everything, my dear, from mind cures to hydrotherapy," she

41

said sadly, "but only your mother and one spiritual healer, both gone now, could ease one of my invalid fits, and they with only the touch of a hand."

Memory was busy in Elizabeth's eyes as Brigida waited quietly, studying the still figure that seemed almost oddly girlish and slim in contrast to her yellowed white hair, which was looped in a fraying coil. There were faint skeins of fine lines around Elizabeth's mouth and at the edges of her clear blue eyes. The intelligent face held more than a trace of a great beauty not entirely faded.

"The minister will come here to perform the service, in deference to my incapacity," Elizabeth said. There was a surprising strength in her voice, despite her frailty.

"Slade is widowed, Brigida, for about five years now. Your mother didn't know of his marriage. I never wrote to her about it. Slade never wanted . . . never expected to wed again. He agreed only to please me. But you will suit my son. He may seem moody and distant at first, but beneath the surface he is a man of cultivated taste and great warmth."

"Tomorrow! There's not time enough to form any attachment, let alone decide a life's course," Brigida said. She turned away from Elizabeth and extended her still cold fingers to the fire again.

"Come, Brigida, it has been decided. You have no choice. You have traveled thousands of miles to do this. There's no reason whatever for delay now. It was your mother's dearest wish, and mine, that this union join our families. Since her death, I feel more certain than ever that it is the right thing to do."

The woman stood, crossed the room quickly, and

turned Brigida to her, taking the girl's hands in her own.

"Slade is my only child. He was born late in my life, after many years of marriage. My son saw little of his father. They sailed together only once. Jarred Hawkes was at home perhaps five of the thirty years of our marriage, and I've long been in . . . frail health. Slade needs a wife, children, the real home he's not ever had. He needs you far more than you will imagine, seeing him for the first time, far more really than you need him. You must . . . make him know that, make him know he needs you."

"Why didn't he wish to marry again, Mrs. Hawkes?" Brigida asked as she extracted the pins from her hair and shook free her golden curls.

"You will call me Elizabeth, my dear. Slade returned from the war, when it ended, with a little waif of a bride, a southern girl, barely sixteen. That horrible war had done something to Bonnie—her name was Bonnie—affected her mind, I thought. Slade seemed to feel . . . he acted as if he were . . . oh, responsible in some way. I never understood it. The dreadful child was just not right, that's all, but after a year or so here, she seemed steadied, so Slade took the *Indian*, our flagship you know . . ."

Brigida nodded. "Yes, go on, Elizabeth."

"He took the *Indian* for a short cruise. He was to leave the ship and take a homebound vessel after a few months out." Elizabeth was nervously rummaging in her jewel case, holding up first one object, then another, and her voice grew more and more agitated.

"The nasty waif ran off soon after he had gone. She hated me, you see. Levi found her after a long while in one of those odd villages, a utopian commune, not very far from here. New Time, it is called. They use no money at all, they trade time for goods and services, I'm told. Well, be that as it may, the pathetic girl was quite completely mad by then. She thought she could control the sea, wind, fire. She accused other people—me—of stealing her thoughts from her, of planting their own in her head. Bonnie heard voices and spoke in strange tongues. She could sit for hours unmoving. The wretched girl would not come back here, so I sent the doctor to her. It was too late by then." Elizabeth shook her head.

Brigida was pacing the room in long strides, her fingers combing repeatedly through her pale hair. "How did Bonnie die?" she asked.

"Birthing," Elizabeth said quickly. "Of course, I wouldn't have . . . let her go and Slade would not have left her, if he'd known. But she never told me or him. He was wild, just wild when he learned of it," Elizabeth said softly. "He has never said her name to me again," she sighed.

"And the child?"

"I . . . I've never been absolutely certain in my mind. We were told the infant was frail and lived no more than a few hours. But I've wondered."

"Why?" Brigida stood absolutely still.

"We buried Bonnie alone." Elizabeth sighed deeply. "It was all just the wishful thinking of a foolish, lonely old woman to hope. . . . The child was lost. I should have accepted that long ago. Oh, Brigida, I am so glad you have come to us. You can help Slade. You have the same kind of strength he has, the same courage and confidence I've seen in so many whaling families. There's a rage in him that no one has been able to ease."

Brigida gazed into the fire, thinking of Slade's flinty blue eyes, of his lean, hard body pressing to her own, feeling again the waves of passion and fury that he had aroused in her, both at once. "I'll try, Elizabeth," she said with a calculated flashing smile. "I will surely try."

"Of course, and you will succeed, I'm confident. Here, I've something I want to give you." From the jumble on the bureau top, Elizabeth extracted a crocheted drawstring bag, its long fringe swaying as she held it toward Brigida.

"Elizabeth, there's no need. Your kindness is more than . . ."

A necklace spilled into Brigida's hand and, carefully, she held it to the light.

"How very beautiful," she breathed.

Signs of the zodiac in Wedgewood blue jasper cameos were set in gold frames that were linked by fine gold chain and beads.

"It's almost a hundred years old. My grandmother gave it to me the day before my wedding, for luck. Put it on," Elizabeth commanded when Brigida hesitated.

"Did it," Brigida asked, "bring you luck? It is magnificent."

"I ran off with Jarred Hawkes when I was seventeen. No one except Grandmother knew in advance, and she advised against it."

There was a soft knock at the door. Martha, carrying a tray, entered and crossed to the window. She cleared away the paints and brushes and laid the table for two. Candlelight shimmered on lacy pressed glass, Staffordshire china, a filigreed silver bread basket, and an unadorned silver teapot. Brigida, who'd had no food since breakfast, relished the simple supper.

Later, the room darkened and cooled as the fire burned low on the hearth. Elizabeth pulled aside curtains and heavy draperies to look out on the winter night. The clouds had broken and, as they ran, high and fast, the moon sent a curl of cold light across the still water of the bay.

"There will be snow soon," Elizabeth said absently as she and Brigida stood together, caught in unspoken thoughts of the future and of the man they expected would shape it for them both.

Brigida's eyes flickered open as she awoke from a deep sleep. Slowly, reluctantly, she let go the sensation of being rocked on some warm southern sea. She remained still, listening to whistling of wind in pines, and then she remembered all at once where she was and why she had come.

Snuggled into deep down, she closed her eyes and yearned to wake with the sound of familiar, lost voices in her ears, then she sighed and looked about the room to which she had followed Martha the night before. She had been too tired then to do anything but undress and crawl beneath the thick quilts of a wide bedstead with a gilded cornice and canopy of yellow silk.

Now, she saw at one side of the bed a commode of

mahogany trimmed with wreaths of gilded oak leaves, at the other, a Boulle clock—its carved cabinet inlaid with gold and platinum. The ceiling was beamed, the walls paneled and hung with small tapestries of garden scenes and hunts. At the far end of the room was a cheval long glass and a lace-skirted dressing table. A large rocking chair and a wing chair faced the hearth, where a blazing fire burned. Nearby stood a zinc tub, full and steaming. A woven Brussels carpet was decorated with swirls of yellow roses on a pale golden field.

Sunlight poured through diaphanous yellow silk curtains that moved at the merest touch of gentle air. Pulling on a wrapper and catching up her scrimshaw brush from the dressing table where it had been placed with her scents and creams, Brigida threw open french doors and stepped out on a small balcony into a perfect winter day.

Below, two cloud-white sheep wandered, cropping at faded grasses. Above wispy puffs of cloud rode in a blue sky that was reflected in the ruffled, sparkling waters of the bay. A small boat, its single sail stark white against blue water and sky, flew before a strong wind, toward Silver Hill. She watched the craft make a landfall near a weathered boathouse on the shore. Moments later, a brace of sleek hounds, followed by a horse and rider, crested the bluff and raced wildly across the wide lawn to the manor house. Slade Hawkes reined in and leaped from the stallion's back. He knelt to take a dog's head in his hands and shake it roughly from side to side.

"Go on Bran, go on!" Slade ordered, "get to the kitchen door and take your pretty bitch with you. Tell

Martha I said to feed you well!"

A stable hand led the stallion away, and Slade turned, as if feeling Brigida's gaze. When he looked up, his eyes were the sparkling blue of sea and washed in sunlight.

He nodded curtly. Brigida swung about on her heel and withdrew, slamming the terrace doors behind her.

"The man absolutely hates me," she thought bitterly, remembering his intimate handling of her and his effortless, cruel withdrawal as though she were just some object for him to use and discard at whim. "I'll not be added to his menagerie, one more of his adoring creatures grateful for a scratch on the ear." She stared at herself for a moment in the long glass. She slipped off her robe, wrinkled her nose and caught her lower lip in small, even teeth. Then, bending, she flipped her golden mane forward and began to brush furiously, setting it crackling.

She did not hear the door open but she did hear it close. She heard the key click in the lock. As she turned toward the sound, she threw her head back to fling the hair clear of her eyes.

Slade stood staring, his coat casually resting on his shoulders. He shrugged it off as he came forward.

"A beautiful sight, goddess," he said, "I particularly admire those inviting soft flanks so well displayed." He slid into a chair and pulled off his boots.

"Please do bathe, Brigida. Don't let me interrupt your toilette." He never took his eyes from her. He lit a black cigar and exhaled long and slowly. "I've come to examine the merchandise, to be sure the whole is of the same quality as what I've already seen."

"And is it?" she asked with more self-control than she knew she possessed. Brigida coolly pinned up her curls, displaying her splendid form to advantage. She presented Slade a view of her graceful profile and high pink-tipped breasts, as she daintily tested the tub with long fingers. She unhurriedly added several drops of rose-fragrant oil to the water, then stepped in and slid deep. She put her head back against the rim and calmly closed her eyes as the water's warmth caressed her. All the while, her heart raced so wildly, she was sure Slade could hear its pounding half across the room.

"Captain Hawkes, you must learn to knock," Brigida said with disdain, her eyes still closed. "It could be . . . unpleasant, surprising, even dangerous, entering a lady's chamber without warning." She began to move a soaped flannel along a graceful arm.

"In a few hours, goddess, you'll be my wife. There'll be no closed doors between us," he answered.

The varied views of Brigida's superb body—long legs and high rump, round breasts shifting as she moved—and the sight of her now, cool to his unwavering stare, made him impatient for her to be done. He watched her raise first one, then the other slim leg to lather satiny skin. Her face was flushed pink by the steamy water and pale blond tendrils clung damp to her temples and slender neck.

Deliberately, Slade crushed out his cigar and stood, stripping off his sweater and the shirt beneath it. The morning sun, streaming through long windows, wrapped him in gold, and to Brigida he seemed as awesome, as handsome, as a rapacious mythic god descended to rampage and ravish. "Oh, damn him! He will crawl," she swore to herself. Droplets of water in her lashes splintered light and haloed him in rainbows.

"The bath sheet, please?" she asked sweetly. It hung warming near the fire. She watched, shocked, as Slade stripped off the rest of his garments. Her eyes flicked over his naked form advancing toward her with controlled grace and surety. He was lean and spare, the muscles in his thighs and arms rippling beneath tanned skin. There was a strength and male beauty about him that stirred desire and fear at once, but she never averted her eyes.

"Do you like what you see?" he demanded, looming over her. "You are a brazen one. Any other virgin child might have flinched at the sight."

"I know what men look like," she said with smug contempt. "Living in the Islands, one can't help but see."

"What else did you see?" he questioned, suddenly angry. "Did you see what men and women do when they lie together? Did it rouse your own heat, watching?" Slade lifted her chin with a guiding hand, and when their eyes met Brigida was terrified at what she saw in his.

"I never looked, I . . ." her words trailed off in a whisper.

"You should have. The women of the Islands are the best I've ever had, anywhere. Now it's your turn. Get up." He didn't wait for her to respond, just pulled her to her feet, sending a flood of water across the floor. He lifted her and set her down before the glass, then ran his hands lightly over her glistening wet skin, fingering the puckered tips of her breasts, coming to rest at the pronounced in-curve of her waist, pressing her back against him hard. "Open your eyes now and you'll see a coupling you won't forget. A body so nubile and so sensitive as yours was made to be . . ." His leg between hers changed her stance so that her feet were braced wide and his hand moved down over her belly and between her thighs as he held her locked against him. "Look at you," he whispered, "look!" He shook her roughly, and through fluttering lashes she did look, in small furtive, frightened glances, saw her head thrown back against his shoulder, rolling a little, her golden hair tumbling to one side. She was captivated by the sight of her body undulating against his, sculpted ivory against umbred bronze, his hard, dark arm passed like a leather thong about her waist. She felt his legs flexed along the length of hers, felt the swell of him purposefully working against her.

"No!" she almost shrieked, tearing at the arm that held her, "don't, don't. I told you I don't ever want you to touch me, I don't want you to." She began to shiver violently, and he wrapped a bath sheet so tightly about her that her arms were caught rigid at her sides.

"It doesn't matter anymore what you want." He turned her to him and a strangled cry escaped her throat as of a small trapped wild thing. His hard naked body, like a sprung trap, held her. "Strutting little tease, you can't bounce and flaunt like a whore and then say 'no.' And you're lying, tease, you do want me to touch you. I was there yesterday, remember?" He turned in time to deflect her lethal rising knee, and when he dropped her across the bed, the barbarous ferocity in his face reduced her to rigid staring silence. He stripped off the toweling, which came away from her soft skin like a whiplash. "Don't scream or I might throttle you," he hissed, seeing the stony fear strong in her eyes. "If untried virgin you really are. . . ."

"You shouldn't force me. Please, don't." She slid up against the bedstead, bracing herself.

"I'll use you as I want, not as I should." He was kneeling over her, a hand at her throat. "You led me to this, enticer, now be easy, I know what you want." He pressed her down when she tried to scramble away, his fingers marking the soft skin of her arm. She closed her eyes, feeling his full weight along the length of her, and she trembled with fear and anger and something more she couldn't control.

"Let me go," she hissed, twisting helplessly. "Devil, demon! You must be Lucifer himself to use me so!"

"You're not the first to say so. You won't be the last," Slade answered to her anger. "But Lucifer, remember, is the star of the morning that brings in the day. Lucifer, goddess, is the light bearer. I'll ignite such sweet, fierce fires in you lady, those darksome eyes will shine with wonder."

His hands, his mouth moved with tantalizing, excruciating thoroughness over her body, and her nipples tightened to sensitive hard buds that he caressed with his lips and tongue and teeth while his slow touch went and stayed where she wanted it most. She began to whimper softly and to rotate her hips against him when he kissed her lips again, almost gently. Then his wide, hot mouth was at her temple, at the curve of her ear, moving to her slender throat. She felt his teeth along her swelled breast, descending the planes and curvings of her pliant body that softened and flowed and opened to him. He crouched between her knees, which he pulled wide, his hands under her lifting, exposing her softness, and she felt the rigid shaft of him touching, forcing into her a little, withdrawing and invading with quick, shallow thrusts again and again. Brigida, gasping, looked up wild-eyed into the glowing depths of his eyes hot as blue flame, and she writhed beneath him, beating clenched fists against his shoulders that were like a wall above her.

"Hold now," he whispered, his breath fire in her hair. "If you are a virgin, I'll be quick, I'll be easy with you." He trapped her hands above her head, pulling her breasts against his chest, and his delving hardness pierced her slowly, relentlessly, sending a scorching deep pain spreading until she screamed out.

"Hold, you witch, you make it worse struggling," Slade hissed, then he withdrew a little and looked into her accusing eyes with unmasked surprise and a flicker of cruel amusement.

"Chaste as the morning dew. Don't be so angry, little girl, I'll be quick, I said I would, didn't I?" He was in her again, pressing deeper in strong, rhythmic thrusts, smothering her protesting cries with his hard mouth until they both tasted blood and he pulled his lips away with a low oath.

Brigida's pain began to fade, to commingle with a strange, pulsing pleasure, and when her body arched up to meet his, Slade released her hands. Her arms twined around his neck, and she caught his lower lip in her sharp little teeth, again clinging to him desperately, wildly, moving with him, pleasure building until she thought she would shatter into whirling fragments of splintering surging light. . . .

Then Slade was still, quiet, looking down at her, kissing away salt tears that slid from beneath her tightly shut lids.

"It's all right to cry a little, pet." His rough voice was soft, almost caressing. "Next time it will be better for you. I won't hurt you at all. Now look at me," he demanded, losing patience. With her expressive eyes hidden, her face seemed a beautiful and blank mask. It began to crumble at her first words.

"Bloody tyrant! I am not crying," Brigida choked out, swallowing a sob. She needed him still, wanted more, wanted it to go on forever. She hated him and loved him terribly and felt tender and murderous and more out of control than she ever had in her life. And more extraordinary. She didn't know what to do or say or how to tell him any of it, or even if she should. She wanted him to know how unordinary she felt, to share the strange new wonder of it, but instead she just glared.

All Slade saw was a restive fury in her glittering eyes. He rolled away into a deep pile of pillows—the tenderness Brigida had surprised in his look now gone. The cold, half smile was there again. He lit a cigar and insolently watched her as she hurriedly rose and moved about the room.

She slipped on a black lace chemise and stood at the cheval glass brushing her tangled hair, pretending to ignore him as he reclined, casually smoking.

"You've been better served on your wedding morning, Brigida, than many women are on their bridal nights," he offered after a long silence.

"I wouldn't know, would I," she shot back, "as you're the first, and you took me by force. Perhaps when I try with others . . . comparisons can be instructive, don't you agree?"

With a low growl, Slade was off the bed. Before Brigida could move, he was standing behind her, coiling a hand in her silky hair, ripping her chemise from top to hem. It fell to the floor, a black pool at her feet.

"What the devil are you doing? That's all French lace," she protested as Slade brought his hand sharply against her bare buttocks, leaving its imprint on her smooth skin. Still grasping her hair, he turned her to him and forced her to her knees, pulling her head up until their eyes met, hers fearful, his chilling.

"There are times you should keep that lovely mouth shut or you just might find yourself choking on more than you can swallow. You're a bitch and a tease, but no fool I think, so listen carefully. Control your provoking pagan eyes and goading tongue, or they'll earn you more trouble than you can handle, I promise."

He released her and gathered up his things. His tawny mane and dark, hard body were sunlit again as he stood for a moment staring at her . . . his cold, regal face nearly expressionless. "Breakfast at nine. The marriage ceremony will be at four." Half dressed, he left the room, leaving her clutching the ripped chemise to her nakedness, unable to move, to speak, for fear of rousing his anger again.

Five

"Dear Brigida! In the light of day you are even lovelier than in candlelight," Elizabeth Hawkes sighed. "The sight of you quickens memory, my dear, of times long gone . . . long gone. Such sweet balm for a weary soul, Slade, isn't she?" Shawled and blanketed, Elizabeth was reclining on a settee in the library. "I've been telling Slade all about you again, my dear."

Brigida's smile was dazzling as she entered the room. The dress she had purposely chosen—a simple gray, with white collar and cuffs—lent a pristine, schoolgirl innocence to her appearance. Her hair, loose and brushed smooth, was held back by a narrow ribbon— very bright red against her golden blondness.

As she approached him, she seemed to Slade so entirely confident, so fresh and completely innocent, he was stunned. He stood also smiling in his almost sinister way, relieved, he had to acknowledge, to see her shining self-assurance undimmed. He despised sulking women.

Studying him, Brigida saw the small gash she had made on his lower lip, and a discernible swelling. He was freshly shaven. His tawny hair was damp, and there was about him the faint aroma of spice and lime. He was in buckskins, knee boots, and a white silk shirt open at the throat beneath a leather riding jacket.

"So, Mother, this is the woman . . . the girl you've selected for me? I remember little Brigida when she was so high." He held a hand parallel to the floor, flashing a wide, white mocking grin.

Brigida's color rose. She halted her progress toward him.

"Do not embarrass her, Slade," Elizabeth admonished. "Brigida, dear, do you remember my son? I know it has been a very long time."

"Captain Hawkes," Brigida said with a dip of her head, "I do have some memory, though only a rather vague one, I'm afraid."

"Don't let that trouble you, Miss Lydon, you'll get to know me well enough," Slade taunted. "She does bear all the marks of lineage and refinement, Mother. Tell me," he went on, circling about Brigida, "what are your qualifications for the position to which you aspire?" Out of sight of Elizabeth, he ran a hand down Brigida's back letting it rest a moment on a soft swell of flank.

"Captain, you are neither buying a mare nor hiring a parlor maid," Brigida hissed in a controlled voice, stamping an expressive foot. She pranced away out of Slade's reach.

"Spirited, isn't she?" he commented.

"Slade, please," Elizabeth said again.

"Well, Mother," he answered in irritation, "I'm the one to be stuck with her for the rest of my life. I hope she can do something well."

"Slade, please!" Elizabeth was becoming exasperated.

"For your information, sir, I attended the Mercer Day School in San Francisco," Brigida said, striding back and forth in front of him, hands on her hips, eyes flashing gold sparks of irritation. "I studied Latin, French, history, philosophy, the arithmetic, writing, and exposition." She counted out the subjects on her fingers as she spoke.

"All that? And what of the more feminine pursuits?" Slade's voice was honeyed.

"I sew. Plain and fancy. I've studied music, I cook . . . a little. I like to grow things, flowers and . . ."

"You'll do," he interrupted her. "Now, sit down, it's not ladylike, pacing like that."

The library was a comfortable room with an arched ceiling embellished with plaster medallions and a simple brass chandelier at the center. Glass-doored mahogany bookcases, fitted with finely wrought brass hardware and scrolled decorations, lined the two long walls. At one end French doors, draped in lime silk and set in an arched mahogany frame, gave onto a wide lawn. At the other, an arched mirror, into which the fireplace was set, reflected the wintery outdoor landscape. Brigida began to examine the books.

There were sets of encyclopedic works, dictionaries in several languages, and the modern novelists—Balzac, Hugo, Dickens, Hawthorne. Down low she discovered a whole shelf of penny dreadfuls with lurid, colorful covers.

"You've an interesting library, Captain, and so

varied," Brigida said, taking up a copy of *Gulliver's Travels*.

"Praise from one so well educated as you are, Miss Lydon, is praise indeed," Slade answered, removing the book from her hands, "but you'd best let me excise certain passages before you read this. Innocent that you are, you'll find it shocking."

"My brothers and I read it years ago . . . aloud," she glared.

"It's not proper reading matter for little girls," Slade teased. "Are you ready for breakfast? I'm unusually hungry, but then I have had an active morning."

"Yes, and you should keep up your strength," she said. "Where is the breakfast room? I could do with a cup of coffee, certainly."

Half listening to Elizabeth and Slade discuss matters of business, Brigida refilled her coffee cup. She sipped it in silence, her attention wandering to the paintings on the wall and to the patterned carpet reflected in the low under-mirror of a pier table.

"Barrat will bring the *Triton* into Sag Harbor within the week. I've been told by some who passed her at sea that she was heavily loaded," Slade said. The subject captured Brigida's attention. "If the barrel price holds, and if she is first in, before Del Carpenter's two that are homebound also, there'll be reason to celebrate. I cabled Captain Barrat at Baltimore, Mother, that should he meet a French or English merchant carrying cloth, he is to trade me several bolts of the best yard goods, now there'll be two of you to dress." Slade glanced at Brigida.

"I was told it's a very quiet life here. Homespun would do for me. I shouldn't want to be a burden to you. Not going often into society minimizes one's need for the latest styles and frills," she said.

His eyes went from her pretty hand, fondling the cup, up along her arm like a cruel caress, to a faint nervous pulse at the base of her throat, then traveled the row of tiny buttons down her bodice, his eyes leaving a path of heat.

The sensual assault in his look was so blatant, Brigida flushed and looked to Elizabeth, but she seemed to take no notice.

"I'll outfit you as I choose and as is appropriate to your situation, and you will dress for me—beautifully always, whether I am here or not. You will always wear the correct costume—morning dress, riding suit, dinner gown—as required. Your little schoolgirl outfits may be charming but they shall soon bore me, and you'll find I detest tedium." His smile was encased in ice.

"But when you're not here . . . ?"

"Whenever I choose to be at Silver Hill, whenever I arrive here, no matter how unexpectedly, you will be perfect, perfectly beautiful, like a moonstone, a pearl, secreted away in dark velvet, my private treasure. Understood?"

The menace in his look, in his voice, struck Brigida like a whiplash.

"Your private prisoner, you mean," she said.

He was unprepared for her directness in front of Elizabeth, and red anger shot through him.

"Have the sniffing gossips been at you already?" he demanded. "Who told you about the so-called quiet life here?" His expression was terrible. "What else have you heard, Miss Lydon, about Silver Hill?"

"That's all, Slade, really," Brigida said quickly. "And I'd hardly call your neighbor Philip Carpenter a sniffing gossip, would you? We met on the steamer coming down from New England. I found him quite charming." She was testing now, to find his flash point, the fatal edge of his control.

"Carpenter's a refined enough fellow, but a mere boy, a dandy, and something of a tame peacock," Slade stated irritably, controlling his anger.

"Really? How odd you should say so. I thought him a true gentleman and quite attractive." Brigida watched Slade's eyes. "He's invited me to visit at his island, once I've settled in here."

"You'll go nowhere unescorted, unless I grant you leave." Slade drank his coffee, and Elizabeth looked from one to the other of her companions with a puzzled expression.

"Well, then, Captain, perhaps Philip Carpenter would pay me a visit here." Hard as she tried, Brigida couldn't keep a show of anger from her own face.

"You tread dangerously, lady," Slade said before he pointedly turned away from Brigida. "Now, Mother, when I return from the city, we . . ."

"Slade, I thought . . . how long will you be gone? Brigida has just come and I so had hoped you would . . . ?"

"Would what? Moon about holding her hand? Play the

doting husband and never leave her side?" His manner now was gruff. "I'm no lovesick boy, and that was not the arrangement, was it? She's to be more your companion than mine, remember?"

"I had only expected you would at least introduce her to the local gentry." Elizabeth smiled at Brigida. "It's just that I do not want you to find it dull here, Brigida dear," she said, fluttering her thin white hands nervously.

"If you want her to meet the neighborhood gentlefolk, you'll have to take her about yourself. You know I've no patience for fools." Slade leaned back in his chair. "The polite society of the local fops and dull women with their endless silly chatter isn't to my taste, Brigida. The fisherfolk and Indians are more to my liking. As my wife, you'll have to find some other source of amusement here than the attentions of a flock of attitudinizing men and light-headed females, like yourself, hanging about filling your days with nonsense."

"Captain Hawkes!" Brigida exploded, putting her coffee cup down a little too hard, "You've no reason, no right to make such a . . . a narrow, unflattering judgment of me on the basis of our brief contact."

"Do you try to tell me that you are different from others of your dissembling sex who move only with indirection toward their true desires, who use artifice to take advantage wherever they can?"

Brigida's dark eyes flashed. "My greatest weakness, I think, is to be too open and direct, but I do learn quickly who is to be trusted and who not. I will surprise you. I am unlike those others of my dissembling sex, as you so erroneously designate us all. It must be that you've poorly chosen your female companions in the past."

"Watch what you say and don't challenge me, Brigida," Slade answered. "Contrary to your own opinion, I find you not at all unlike others of your gender; you think as much with your anatomy, it seems, as with your brain."

"How dare you speak so to me!" Brigida gasped, the color rising to her cheeks, indignation animating her lovely face. "If I am honorably treated, sir, not taken advantage of. . . ." She saw Elizabeth's stricken look and stopped.

"You mustn't worry yourself further on my account, Elizabeth," she said with genuine concern. "I shall be quite content here, all on my own, if need be. Those years at sea taught me a certain self-reliance. I wouldn't want your son put out in any way. It's quite enough that he so charitably offers me his name and a place in his home."

"I'll take Miss Lydon for a walk now," Slade said. "Have some of the first floor rooms opened, will you, while we're out? They'll need airing after being so long shut up."

Brigida watched him guardedly and Elizabeth nodded, pleased. "Yes, fine," she smiled. "A good ramble out of doors is just the thing, the best way for young people to get acquainted. Run up and get your cloak, dear, and your walking boots. It is rather cold out, Martha tells me."

Brigida hurried from the breakfast room past a high fire burning on the entrance hall hearth and rushed up a wide staircase that divided at a landing, becoming two narrower routes to the same destination. She paused a moment to look at the full rigged ship rocking on a blue ocean that was painted on the iron lunette of a tall clock just striking the hour of ten.

At the prospect of a walk in the bright sea air, her anger had quieted. Brigida was almost smiling to herself as she pushed open the door of her chamber to discover a girl, near in age to herself, polishing one of the many candlesticks that stood about the room. The heavy brass object fell to the floor with a loud ringing clatter as the girl looked up, her brown hair escaping in wisps from beneath a cloth loosely tied about her head. She had almond-slanted brown eyes, a blunt broad nose, and full lips that curled in a grimace as she retrieved the fallen candlestick. Self-consciously, the girl tried to push the escaping strands of her hair back in place.

"Sorry I startled you. I'm Brigida Lydon. And you are . . . ?"

"Nan Edwards, miss," the girl answered, looking down.

"Are you a member of the household, Nan?" Brigida asked hopefully.

"Heavens, no! I just come up from the village to help Martha about the place. My sister comes, too. She works in the kitchen and the dairy. We heard you was comin' here. Did you travel good?" she asked, smiling at Brigida for just a moment, then quickly looking away again.

"I did, thank you, Nan. Tell me, do you and your sister come every day to Silver Hill?" Brigida was rummaging for her gloves as she spoke.

"We do, miss. My father carries us to the gate and meets us again at evening. I'd not want to stay the night in this place."

Brigida was startled and a little amused. "Why ever not?" she asked. "What's wrong?"

"Now I've said what I'd not meant to! It's a terrible fault in me, my mother says. 'Tisn't nothin' wrong, it's just—I like bein' home in the village. It's too empty and quiet here, I'd be lonesome here, is all. I'm to get back to my work now. I was told not to bother you, miss, beyond a good day and so forth."

"Who told you—Captain Hawkes?" Brigida was lacing up a walking boot.

"Oh, no, not him. It's Martha keeps us busy. Martha wants everything kept exceptionally tidy. She's very demandin'. He never so much as looks at me, prefers my sister to talk to, she bein' the pretty one. He don't come here very frequent anyways, and he don't stay long when he does. It's like a black mood settles right on 'im when he walks through the door."

"Maybe he's always that way," Brigida ventured.

"No, Rose tells me he's a different man, very social like. Rose—she's one of the Carpenters' ladies' maids— she sees the captain in the city with all his drinkin' friends and lady loves, low women they are, mostly, Rose tells, and even some real ladies who'd have the captain to bed and not have to be asked twice. I'd be feared to take up with one like him. So wild as he is and changeable like, you'd never know what to expect. No, I want a lad steady in his ways." Nan went on polishing as Brigida listened in rapt attention.

"Captain Hawkes's wife . . . she steadied him some, it's said, but I . . ." Nan slapped a hand over her mouth.

"Oh, I done it again! I didn't intend to talk so personal. The captain's good to his people that works for 'im, you know. My brother sailed with him and there never was a better ship's master, Robin told us. Robin's third mate on the *Triton* comin' in any time, and . . . I have to stop chatterin' with you, miss. I'm not to waste your time talkin'."

"You must talk with me, Nan, you and your sister, or else think how lonely I'll be at Silver Hill. What is her name, your sister?" Brigida, peering into the glass, was fastening her cloak.

"Mary, my sister is Mary. She's older than me by two year. She been comin' on here longer than me, and there's rooms here even she haven't never seen opened once, it's that silent, not a'tall like a real home. Oh, we'll be happy to talk with you." The girl looked directly at Brigida for the first time, smiling. "We could play at cribbage sometime. Robin taught us."

The door opened just then and Martha came padding in. "Nan, please, come with me now," she said in a quiet, firm way. "We are to open the music room and the ballroom, because Miss Lydon has come."

"Martha, how lovely. Who plays?" Brigida asked.

"Elizabeth did, before her hands went stiff. I do. She taught me. When I play I know the notes have flown from some magic place to my fingers, the sound is so beautiful. Come Nan, there is much to do today."

Brigida stood a moment, lost in thought when the two had gone, until she heard Slade calling impatiently from below. Then pulling her cloak tight about her throat, she hurried down to find him restlessly pacing the hall, the huge dog at his heels. He hurried her out into dazzling sunlight that, in spite of her unsettled state, sent her spirits soaring. He took her gloved hand, almost crushing it.

"What are the outbuildings?" Brigida asked as he pulled her along, she trying with effort to match his long strides.

"Well house, icehouse, carriage house, dairy, carpentry, smokehouse, the usual . . . kennels and stables down the hill off to the east, cow barn and holding field to the north, orchards to the north, too."

They were walking away from the house and the water in a northerly direction.

"Why . . . is it called . . . Silver Hill?" Brigida was a little breathless.

"Do I go too fast for you?" Slade slowed his pace a little. "My great, great . . . four greats, I think it is, grandfather Jarred saw the hill for the first time on a summer night with a full moon shining. Every tree and blade of grass were silvered in its light. He planted the weeping silver linden you see from your room."

The centerpiece of the front lawn, the linden, spread limbs and branches high and wide around the massive double trunk at its heart.

"It's beautiful, Slade. And the pines, the birches?"

"Jarred's sons and grandsons. There has been a Jarred or a Jude in every generation, until now. They put in the white birch and white pine; Jude—my grandfather—the flowering dogwoods. My father nursed the white mulberry all the way home from the Orient. Every one of them added to the manor house. China tea and Arabian coffee built part of it, indigo and Sumatra pepper, too, but whale oil and bone is the most of it. After my father brought my mother here, a bride, he raised the two new wings for her."

Slade was silent for a while, hurling a stick for the wolfhound who raced about them like a puppy, then streaked off after a squirrel it sighted at the edge of a wooded copse.

"Elizabeth furnished Silver Hill?"

"Yes. She had years and years to do it in."

"It's beautiful."

"Of course. It's my mother's museum, everything under lock and key. Elizabeth is flawlessly well-bred, did you know? A lapse of taste would be impossible for her." The bitterness in his tone silenced Brigida and they proceeded for a way without speaking.

"That's the Good Ground Mill," Slade pointed. The structure stood derelict some distance from the manor house at the top of a rise, its sails tattered, its windshaft cracked, shutters banging forlornly.

"The mill is out of use?"

"There is not much in use at Silver Hill, you'll have noticed by now. I'm not interested in the manor or the mill."

"Why? You once loved this place—I remember what you told me."

"Never mind why. It doesn't matter. I'm going to sell off the mill stones. I've had an offer."

"Let me have it repaired and I'll run it," Brigida said, pulling him to a stop.

"You? What for?" Slade questioned skeptically.

"Just something to keep me busy. So I won't have to seek the company of other empty-headed women. Out of boredom. The winds and tides are second nature to me, Slade, I've spent so much of my life attuned to both. It seems a crime to me, to waste a breeze. It would please me, that's all, to see this mill's sails catch the wind again."

He studied her for a long moment, his eyes bright as blue jay feathers in the morning sun. "All right, fine, do it. Send for the sawyers and carpenters and joiners, hire a millwright," he said. "The idea intrigues me, you running my mill. We'll see how well you do."

They had turned back to the south and as they approached the house Slade pointed out the first and oldest construction.

"The glazing was bequeathed to the second Jarred by a brother who'd settled in Connecticut. Did you know they used to do that, leave the house to one, the glass to another? That's how valuable it was and costly to come by."

When they turned a corner and moved toward the water, Brigida looked back over her shoulder at the manor house, getting her first full view of it. All the windows on the ground level were six-over-six-over-six again.

"For easy comings and goings," Slade explained, following the direction of her eyes. "My father envisioned Silver Hill in eternal summer, with chains of children passing in and out at every portal."

"Oh, I see," she answered quietly. "How lovely a vision."

The newer wings of Silver Hill were built in the Greek style. There was a massive central portico, supported by six Ionic columns and flanked by two low wings with smaller columns. The addition to the west housed the ballroom and the one to the east formed a shady, roofed piazza that provided Brigida's room above with its small terrace. Her windows were thrown open, she saw, and so were those of the other room that also opened onto the terrace.

"Whose is that?" she inquired, pointing.

"Mine," Slade said.

"You'll be staying there?"

"When I'm at Silver Hill, yes. Where else?" he asked with a twisted smile.

"I thought . . . married couples sometimes share a bed. It's warming . . . in winter, I've heard. You'll leave me in peace, then?"

"I've no intention of leaving you in peace, nor of taking up residence in your chamber. I've yet to find any woman I'd want to have in my bed longer than necessity required. There's no possibility of mutual comfort here, you swore so to me yesterday. I'll never be one to wake to a cold embrace or worse, to a shrew's sharp tongue."

"Thank you," Brigida pulled away from him to stand at the edge of the bluff. She needed a moment alone. The sky had begun to cloud over. A gust of cold wind nearly took her breath away. She watched a gull roll its wings perpendicular to the water and sail across the bay in a long, curving arc.

"What is the strip of land where it's headed?" she asked as Slade came to her side.

"The barrier beach. At night when it's quiet and the wind is right you can hear the sea pounding at the far shore. Come now. We'll go through the wood a way here before we go in." She pulled her cloak close about her and he turned up the collar of his greatcoat. They entered a shadowy grove of large trees and followed a track dappled with cold, fading sunlight. Remnants of summer weeds and wild flowers were scattered about—goldenrod and Queen Ann's Lace. Kneeling, Brigida found, half hidden, little green rosettes.

"These will spring into daisies and buttercups on the very first warm day," she said, delighted. "Oh! Here. Look. Untouched by winter. The immortals of the glade." She fingered a growth of fork moss at the base of a tree.

Slade found to his mild surprise that watching her gave him a certain pleasure. She moved along the wooded path with an agile, easy grace and, like some wild creature, she seemed attuned to everything, seeing tiny hidden things he hardly knew existed. They emerged from a small glade and walked along the edge of a meadow bordered by a weathered stone wall.

"Is this all your land, Captain Hawkes?"

"And more," Slade answered, watching Brigida from beneath a faintly furrowed brow. "As far as you can see. More than a thousand acres. It's a lot of land in this part of the world, but it's ten years since it's felt a plow. Now we just grow what's needed for our own stock."

"Could I put in a kitchen garden and flowers, do you think?"

"As you please. I've never been a farmer. Now that I

don't go to sea, I've other interests."

"So I've been told." Brigida shivered.

"Are you chilled? We'll go in," he said, absently bringing an arm about her shoulders and turning her toward the house. She let her head rest against his shoulder, feeling for a moment how easy it would be to put her fate in the hands of this man, so sure of himself, so certain of his strength and power. She tensed and pulled away.

"Relax, goddess, I only meant to shelter you from the wind, is all. Well, you'll soon be in at the fire." The hard edge returned to his tone. "Just shiver until you get there." Slade quickened his stride and Brigida hurried after him toward the manor house.

The ceremony was brief. Slade Hawkes took Brigida Lydon to wife and she promised to stay by him until death did them part. When they turned toward each other as man and wife, the minister, the Reverend Mr. Huntting, was disturbed to see neither love nor softness in the look that passed between them. Rather, it seemed that each hurled an unspoken challenge at the other. The groom's eyes were icy blue and hard, the bride's smoldering coals. The open sensuality of their kiss and the tight bending together of their bodies further confused the minister and caused him to turn away in embarrassment and to peer out at a white-capped bay some distance off.

Snow, which had been threatening for hours, had begun finally to fall. Large, heavy white flakes brushed against the library windows, swirled like feathers about the house and thickened the boughs of pines along the crest of the bluff on which the manor house stood.

The young couple had moved apart, he to lean at the mantel, staring moodily into the leaping fire, she to coolly ponder some mystery in the swirling snow beyond the leaded window panes.

As the day darkened, Brigida watched the blurred reflection of her husband take shape before her, mirrored in the blackening windows. Noticing the faded empty shell of a summer moth caught frozen in the casement, she shivered, wondering at finding herself in this cold and somber place wed to the distant, brooding man who seemed to her now a total stranger.

Brigida sighed and turned from the window to help Martha with a tray of fluted glasses and delicate tea sandwiches arranged on little silver platters.

"Martha, how lovely," Brigida whispered, but the Indian woman seemed distracted.

Turning to the minister, Brigida cast her full, dazzling smile upon him. "Mr. Huntting, you will sample Martha's delecacies and take a glass of my husband's champagne?"

"Yes, indeed, Mrs. Hawkes," he said. "Martha's culinary skills are well known to me; I used to enjoy her fare regularly in the past, though not of late." He cast a chagrined look about the unresponsive company. "And Slade's wine cellars," he went on quickly, "have no equal on the East End, not even at Carpenter's Island. Am I right, Slade?"

"Are you ever wrong, Mr. Huntting?" Slade turned from the fire as Brigida took his arm to draw him into the company. The two stood still together for a moment, hand in hand, Brigida in a rose silk day dress with a waist band that emphasized her soft, full curves, Slade strikingly handsome in dark wool and white silk.

"Slade, darling," she said, looking up at him with a glorious smile, her dark eyes mischievous. "Our union is now to be toasted. You must stand by me! Why, whatever will Mr. Huntting think, with you scowling so?" Her small fragile hand in his was as soft as rose petals. Of the assembled company, only Levi Phillips heard the tinge of scorn in Brigida's voice and saw the cool look of teasing amusement in Slade's face.

"Come then, goddess, drink up," Slade answered, passing an arm about her waist. She stood to just below his wide shoulders, looking for all the world the happiest of brides. "Even Mr. Huntting, minister that he is, will understand, looking at you, that I am anxious to be alone with my new wife."

"It's not seemly to speak so, Slade. You embarrass Mr. Huntting," Brigida chided. The minister was blushing, and for a moment his eyes could find no comfortable place to light. Then he nodded with a twinkling smile.

"You are a lucky man, Slade," he said, "and I wish you and the beauteous Brigida all the joy and contentment that a loving pair will always find in wedlock." Raising their glasses, the small company echoed his words.

"You'd best knock on wood to deafen the devil." Martha shook her head. "How do you know there are not demon lovers lurking about to carry off a happy bride? Too much happiness, the devil gets jealous—it's true."

"You needn't worry about this bride, Martha," Brigida

answered with a meaningful look at Slade.

"I'm more than a match for any . . . any demon lovers the lady might take up with." Slade fixed Brigida with a telling look.

"But the bride had no maids to attend, and no veil either, to hide behind to fool the devil." The little woman pushed her spectacles higher on her flat nose and shook her head again.

"Martha, you worry too much. What you need is more champagne. That will get your mind off demons and devils." Slade refilled all the glasses but Mr. Huntting's, which had remained untouched.

"Some say just the opposite, Slade, about drink," the minister commented. "But I'll toast you, and your bride, and your future, and the next generation at Silver Hill." Mr. Huntting raised his glass and sipped, then went to sit near Elizabeth at the fire.

"You know, Mr. Huntting," she smiled, "I, as others, have had measures of both happiness and pain in my life. The one joy left me still is the thought of this silent old house filling with children."

Brigida's eyes met her husband's. Mr. Huntting again sensed a heat between the two that seemed more audacious than loving. He cleared his throat nervously once more, and stood, leaving his glass half filled.

"I will take my leave," he announced, "before the snow prevents me going altogether."

"I'll walk you to your carriage, sir," Slade offered, guiding Mr. Huntting to the door, "and Levi will ride with you as far as the mill. By then you'll be halfway home at least."

Left alone in the library after Elizabeth, exhausted, had retired, with the drapery drawn against the dark and the fire leaping, Brigida waited, impatiently anticipating Slade's return. She felt an unsettling, almost sweet agitation that set her pacing the room. She was actually yearning, she admitted, for everything she had feared a few short hours ago.

When she heard his step in the hall, she snatched up the first book that came to hand. Slade found her deeply engrossed in reading. She barely looked up until he knelt to stoke the fire. Then she watched him furtively. He flicked back a lock of tawny hair, rested a hand on the head of the drowsing wolfhound, placed a cigar between his teeth. He struck a light and casually dropped the spent match into the fire. He uncorked a new bottle of champagne, crushed the cigar, poured out two glasses and gave one to Brigida, first taking the book from her hands.

"Drink up," he said. "I'm not a patient man."

"I could teach you to master your impetuous nature, Captain," Brigida answered.

"I've no desire to learn," he said shortly.

He led her to the windows. The snow had stopped and the curve of the moon was just beginning to show above the horizon of a clear sky.

"There'll be boisterous weather tomorrow. A large star in the moon's wake always tells it." Brigida was gazing at the still bay, its dark waters, like the velvety heavens, holding a million candles of starlight. The world was white in new snow, the trees iced and glistening like glass.

"How can you be long gone from this place?" she said

softly, entranced by the loveliness of the scene before her.

"It's not home to me anymore," Slade said. "It hasn't been for . . ."

"But why?" Brigida asked. Then she heard the first strains of music. She glanced questioningly at Slade.

"Come," he said.

He led Brigida across the hall and into the ballroom, which was brilliantly lit by candles glowing in stands and sconces and in a glittering crystal chandelier. When Martha, at the piano, began again to play, he took Brigida in his arms and whirled her round and round to the lilting melody of a waltz, his lithe form graceful, hers slim and pliant, her golden curls catching light.

Suddenly, Slade stopped still and lifted her in his arms to carry her from the room and up the wide staircase to her room. He kicked the door to behind him. Without pause or word, he undid the fastenings at the back of her gown. Brigida let it fall to the floor, then bent to remove silk stockings, spilling her breasts forward to Slade's fierce eyes.

"You are something exquisite," he whispered roughly, pulling her to him. Slowly he unlaced her camisole and unhurriedly kissed the crests of her freed breasts to firmness, his lips and tongue hot on her cool satin skin. He held her locked against him, leaning back a little to look down at her. Brigida played her hands over his shoulders and along his arms, her mouth upturned, sweet and smiling.

"I'll change," she said.

"Don't dawdle." His voice had that smoky quality—

threatening and seductive both—she'd heard this morning.

"Patience is one of the virtues," she recited, her eyes lit with taunting bits of golden light, but she did exactly as he asked and when she stood at the fire again in the gown he had given her—a sleek fall of white satin and lace—he reached out and nearly closed his hands about the sharp lovely curve of her waist. He had pulled off his shirt. His hair was in tumbled disarray, his upper body coppered in firelight. He heard and understood the gasp of breath in her throat at the moment she realized how much she wanted him, how much she craved the perfect bulk of him in her encircling arms, longed to feel the hard plowing surge of his strength. About to move toward him, she hesitated, the savage look of him frightening her, and she froze like a startled doe ready for flight.

"What . . . are you waiting for?" she asked, her left hand at her lips, her words nearly inaudible.

"For you to tell me what you want." He had to turn away from that child's gesture he remembered in her and add a log to the fire while Brigida watched him in silence. When he faced her again, leaning casually on the mantel, she looked up at him, flushed and unsure.

"But you . . . know," she almost stammered, swaying a little like a graceful delicate reed. The uncertainty, the entreating gentleness in her look put Slade into a simmering rage. Her softness threatened to weaken him, to make him responsible for her in a way he refused even to consider. His angry magnetic gaze prevented her looking away as she longed to.

"Tell me what you want me to do to you. Ask," he

demanded, trying to savor her increasing discomfort.

"Just the same . . . as before," she managed, and her flush deepened. Then she did pull her eyes away, twisting her slim, pretty hands. A knifing, capricious stab of pure lust caught Slade unawares. He cursed, almost staggered by it, and by her innocent seductive radiance, which made him wary and cautious. The knot of anger in him pulled tighter. He snorted a harsh laugh, and she saw the cold, cruel look she was learning to dread come into his eyes.

"The same? As before? That was nothing, an expeditious ribbon cutting, to dispose of a small obstruction to your full participation."

Nearly devastated by the indifference of his words, she responded with controlled, gentle malice.

"There are men who would have valued most highly the gift of that small obstruction," she said.

"Gift?" He glared into her dark, troubled eyes that seemed to be light and shadow all at once and were so beautiful he had to look away. "I did you a service. You abused me for it. Now ask for what you so obviously want."

"But I don't know what I want except . . . the same. I don't know how to ask." Her voice was unsteady. She turned and walked a little away to lean on a bedpost. Watching her, watching the soft, satiny body moving beneath satin, her hair sunlight and moonlight blending, flowing down her back, Slade's body remembered all the warmth of her, the sheathing narrowness giving way, parting to him.

"You do know. You know more than you think, but I'll

teach you just the same," he relented, the smoke back in his voice. "And you'd best be damn quick to learn."

Looking over her shoulder, Brigida saw a nerve jump along his cheek, watched firelight finger the tensed muscles of his arms and chest. "I do already know that you can touch me, just touch me, and . . . have me craving and reckless and . . . I have learned that much from you already." She tried a small smile.

"Come here," he said, the shade of a threat crossing his face when she hesitated again, and then she was in his arms, bending back under the strength of his kiss, his thumb pressing the hard points of her breasts, circling over them until she crushed herself to him. Her arms went about his neck and his knee came up between her legs, lifting her to ride as she clung hard to him.

"Such a lewd little schoolgirl, a shameless child wife." His words hissed against her slender throat, and then his hands beneath the swells of her buttocks lifted her so that he looked up into her dazzling eyes before he let her slide slowly down along his hard length, let her feel his full heat and power, which made her soft and fragile with a quickening voluptuous greed.

When she lay stretched on the bed, her hair smoothed over her shoulders like golden silk, he traced the lace insert of her gown from one taut breast to the other, and she watched him, first his hand, then his eyes, her own eyes narrowing as he went over her body carefully, his slow, endless caress making her feel nearly transparent under his lambent eyes.

Her touch went instinctively to the hard swell beneath his belt.

"Don't press me, brazen, hot little . . . because I'm going to teach you to curb your impetuous nature. I'm going to play with you until every inch of you burns and shines with needing me. That overexpressive pouty little mouth will say all the words I want to hear."

"But I can't," she protested. "I can't say such things as you want." She shook her head and closed her eyes, feeling him stretch out beside her and, with deliberate, slow precision, with care and unwasted mastery, set his hands, his mouth, the whole hard, controlled length of him to playing her slender form, which was so perfectly desirable, so incredibly responsive, that she astounded him again. Her passion had seemed to burst into flame at his renewed touch, and he felt that his every nerve focused in his dilatory fingertips. Watching her move, hearing the soft, small sounds she made, a violent surge of his own need assaulted him again, but he held back, waiting, prolonging it, testing her, wanting to push her to her utmost limits and turn her to pure heat and light and longing in his hands.

His first touch separated Brigida from time and place and words, and she came to feel gradually, under his malingering hands and mouth and his blazing eyes, clear as glass, open and clear as a flooding tide pool dredged of shadows and mystery. She became insubstantial as breath on a looking glass, as wisps of cloud shredding in high hot summer wind. And she became, too, at the same time, all flesh and nerve, all sensual heat and feeling, more than she had ever been, more than she could have ever imagined. When he found that enfolded secret point at the soft core of her undulating body, Brigida made one formless cry and arched to grasp the bedstead above her head. Parting her long legs, she silently implored, willed his invasion with every gesture of her articulate body, while she floated on a rush of pleasure so intense, so crystalline, that it became a beautiful torment spreading to every cell of her radiant body.

After a time—a time that seemed to her long, eddying eons of timelessness, of space—she lay with her eyes half closed, close to weeping for him, breathing deep, and almost gasping, she spoke in a hushed flow of words that broke from some last shady secret place, some secret corner of her spirit. And then he was straddling her hips, ripping away satin and lace, stripping her twisting body bare before he slammed up into her as she was asking, begging him to with pretty, proper words and vulgar ones, all the crude, low, mean words she had ever heard that were now perfect and right and, somehow, almost beautiful.

"Dirty sweet little bitch," he whispered, "dirty . . . sweet . . . bitch, I am in you now." He pulled her knee up, the strength and depth of his driving thrusts increasing, and their bodies flowed, working together in a siege of unrestrained carnal heat that left Brigida, finally, speechless and weak in Slade's arms after the tremors shook her first, over and over, then passed to him, as she clung with all her strength, still riding the billowing, long, slow-cresting wave with him.

Brigida awoke to hear the landing clock strike three. She slid carefully from the bed, stepping over the ravaged gown on the floor and, shivering, found a warm robe in the armoire, a pale yellow silk lined in white fur, with fur-lined bed shoes to match it. She added a log to the fire, and when it caught and flared she turned to look at Slade.

He slept facedown, his upper body bare, the sheeting rising over the swell of flank and following his long legs. His left arm extended down over the side of the bed, his right cradled his face, which was turned toward the fire. Even in repose, Brigida thought, there was a hard tension about him, like a sleeping animal ready to spring. His mouth was clenched shut. A muscle jumped along his jaw. Long lashes cast shadows over high cheekbones. His lids flickered a little, and there was about him then a hint of the boy Brigida remembered from long ago. A wind whistled about the chimney. The fire flared, throwing a dancing pattern of light and shade on Slade's face, deepening the shadows about his eyes, etching clearer the strength of mouth and chin, the flare of nostril, changing him for an instant to someone alien and frightening, almost demonic.

"Lucifer," she thought. "Dark, gleaming Lucifer and his witchwife bride. You'll see whose magic is really stronger."

She went to pull a thick quilt up over his bare shoulders. It was then she saw the scars that striped his muscled back. She knew at once, as any sailor would, the cruel mark of the cat; the brands might fade with time, but they would never be gone completely. Brigida stared down disbelieving that the powerful, regal Slade Hawkes could ever have been so cruelly used. Hastily, she covered him with quilts and left the room.

Slade was awake, propped against the pillows and

smoking when Brigida returned. She cast her most glorious smile toward him. He regarded her steadily, surprised again by her devastating loveliness, as he was each time he saw her.

"Yours is a dangerous beauty, Brigida. It sets the blood to dancing every time," he said.

"I told you so, didn't I?" she laughed softly.

"Where were you?" he demanded.

"Now, just where does it look as if I've been?" she teased, setting a tray in the middle of the bed. "I thought you'd be hungry. We never did dine last evening."

She climbed up onto the bed and sat cross-legged, pulling her robe and a quilt about her. "And what will be your pleasure, sir?"

"We'll eat first. What have you got there?"

"Blood sausage, white cheddar, a loaf, apples, and a pitcher of ale. Good enough?"

"Good enough," he answered.

"I saw the markings on your back. How did you come by those?" she asked when they had finished and she had removed the tray and slid beneath the warm quilts.

"There are some questions polite little girls wouldn't ask," he said, pulling her to him, and she stiffened in his arms.

"I'm not a little girl, and I never was overly polite. Tell me, Slade?"

His mouth on hers was sweet and tart at once, with the taste of apples and strong ale blended.

"Tell me!" she demanded. "I know practically nothing of your life, of you, since we last met. You seem very . . . changed."

"You know all you need to. I'm rich enough to keep

you comfortably and well enough endowed to gratify any of your . . . desires." His look was one of irritating complacency. "That is what interests you. You told me yourself."

"You, braggart, forced yourself on me. Surely you didn't expect me to graciously thank you?"

"What I expected was a modest and prim New England lady. Then I saw you there, in the blustery highroad, moving with all the sinuous grace of the wildest Island girl who ever seduced a sailor with her brazen invitation. It was your own fault." Slade was looking sullen, watching Brigida warily.

"Brazen!" she flared, sitting up, appalled. "I'll remind you I was virginal, as the snow that's falling outside this very instant! Perhaps I'll just deliver a handful to you, in your warm bed, so you'll be able to appreciate its purity for yourself." But before she could move, Slade's arms were holding her fast.

"You forced yourself on me, outrageous rogue. How was I to know you for a rapist? I trusted you."

"Your mistake. I trust no one except myself, and Levi Phillips. Be still witch, stop fighting me."

"I can't help the way I walk, can I?" Brigida was furious but too cold to leave the warm bed. She ceased her useless struggling and flailing about. "I lived for months at a time on Ponape, you know? Perhaps I was influenced—a little—by the Island girls and the ease of life there. But still . . ."

"And I could not have been expected to know that the free spirits of the Pacific Isles had gifted you with their enticing spontaneity. You'd no cause to rely on my restraint."

"But you were my betrothed. You asked me here." Her voice became almost wistful as she looked into his hard face. "Do you offer love to no one?"

"Be careful, Brigida. I've heard that tone before. Every lady thinks she will be the one to succeed where others have not. Well, don't think you'll make me love you . . . don't even try. You'll only come to tears if you do. Just pleasure me, and I'll do as much for you, for whatever time it is a pleasure. But then, that is all you want of me, you've said so." His lips were at hers and then his breath was warm in her ear.

"Exactly," Brigida answered. "But are you sure you can trust even Levi?" she asked sarcastically, probing for a weakness, some vulnerability.

Slade pushed her away from him and reached for a cigar.

"Levi brought me home. After my father was killed. I was half mad when they marooned me . . . Levi . . . he jumped ship, stayed with me when I was so crazed I hardly remembered his name, and neither of us knowing if we'd ever again see Silver Hill." He puffed his cigar, his head thrown back.

"I'm sorry, Slade." Brigida softened, moved by the pain and rage she saw come into his eyes. "I didn't know . . . about any of it." She refilled his tankard and waited.

"It was during the war, early, on my first voyage ever with my father, after I'd left you. A Confederate warship, a steam cruiser and armored, was hunting down the Yankee whalers to cut off the North's oil. The *Shenandoah* was British built for the Confederacy, and when she overtook us in the Caribbean, we were trapped, helpless against her guns and armor and speed. We tried but we couldn't . . . we couldn't outrun her. They boarded. The mate was in charge. That bloody pirate, Captain Waddell, was safe in his ship relieving captured men of their money while his boarding crew stripped our vessel of instruments and stores. My father was on the quarterdeck with a whale gun cradled in his arms, and when that mate claimed the *Eagle* for the South my father wouldn't move. He damned them all, and the whole Confederacy besides. That mate, Root"—the name sounded evil on Slade's tongue—"Root had the rest of us taken off in the longboats, and then they rushed him, tied him alone to the foremast. . . ." Slade's voice was barely audible. "That foul black smoke rose in the air, the blaze . . ."

Brigida felt the violence that shook him, waited for him to go on.

"You fought them," she said finally.

"Yes!" His answer was biting, but the cold rage in his eyes had turned to anguish.

"You were one man . . . a boy of what, eighteen . . . ? against so many. You shouldn't be blaming yourself, certainly not all these years later," Brigida said very softly.

"I'll carry Root's scars on my back, and the vision of that blaze in my memory, forever. I can still hear his thin drawl, still hear it just as plain . . . I'll never forget it. Root left the *Shenandoah* not long after that, and I joined the Union Army and went to look for him in the Shenandoah Valley, where he came from. I didn't find him . . . and when I didn't, I fired his plantation. I set up the house with my own hand and watched the flames consume it. I was like some madman possessed when I went to torch the stable . . . I found her, not him." There was a heavy pause. "But I will," Slade said in measured words, "I surely will find that devil. My crews, my captains . . . I've agents in every port from here to the Japans, and one day I will find him and I will kill him." The brutal hatred in Slade's face was terrible.

"Who did you find? You said . . ."

"Bonnie . . . Bonnie cowering in a stall I was about to torch. I saw the madness come into her eyes with the flames I set . . . she was his sister. Root's sister . . . ! Damn!"

A blue wreath of smoke unraveled and slid across the room toward the hearth.

"I couldn't ride off and leave her the way she was. I stayed a while. Then I quietly married her and I carried her home, here. I thought she was mended in her mind by the time I heard that Root was in the Falklands and . . ."

"Oh, good God, Slade, what a desolation of emptiness . . . nothing but tides and gales there in those islands. Not even a tree grows in the wretched place."

"Any vessel damaged rounding the Cape will make for the Falklands first. It wasn't impossible he'd be stranded there and then think it a good place to hide. Well, there were the hulks of more than a dozen ships rotting in the harbor, but no trace of Root. He wasn't there, never had been. I left Bonnie alone here with my dear mother, and before I reached Silver Hill again, my wife was dead, and so was my son."

Shivering as if with cold, Brigida rose to add more wood to the fire. She remained kneeling at the hearth, keeping her back to Slade. She was frightened by the untrammeled emotion she had seen in him, and overwhelmed by her own jealousy of his past, even of his fierce hatred of this man Root. She wanted, needed, she realized with a shock, to be the center and pivot of his entire life, his single passion, his only obsession.

A log burned through, and still Brigida stayed as she was until Slade's low voice broke into her thoughts.

"Come here now," he ordered.

She stood and stretched, composing her thoughts, erasing any traces of them from her face. She turned slowly, undoing the sash of her robe, letting it fall open, then slip off as she neared the bedside. She smiled, and Slade pulled her down over him, her light body's length resting on his, her satin breasts soft against his muscled chest. He wrapped her to the shoulders in down as if the soft comforters were lush pelts of ermine. He tangled a hand in her hair and forced her lips to his as he rolled over and surged into her welcoming softness.

When Brigida half awoke in the early dawn, she found herself alone. A shutter banged somewhere. A flock of geese, honking, moving upland away from the water, told her that the day would bring rain. She snuggled deep in the warm bedclothes to escape again for a while into sleep.

Six

The library mantel clock chimed delicately as Brigida carried a tea tray to the fireside. The house was winter-still, wrapped in misty fog. A steady, icy rain drummed against the windowpanes. Slade, it seemed, had gone out; Elizabeth had not come down, and the servants kept to the kitchen and pantry.

Wrapping herself in an afghan throw, Brigida, feeling very lonely in the silent house, curled into the sofa and began leafing through a stack of newspapers and maga-zines—*Country Life, Horseman's Friend, The New York Times.* In *American Woman's Home*, a housekeeper's manual done by Catherine Beecher and her famous sister, Mrs. Stowe, there were plans for a kitchen sink with water drawn from a hand pump indoors. This so engrossed Brigida's attention as she pored over it that when the library door opened, she barely looked up.

"Are you Mary?" she asked the young woman who smiled at her. "Your sister told me about you yesterday. Do come here, Mary, and see this. A kitchen where the water runs right in."

The girl crossed the room and eagerly looked over Brigida's shoulder. "I'd venture they've got 'em already, rich city people, wouldn't you think so, missus? Sounds just the thing for the captain, taken as he is with new gadgetry. Not pullin' and haulin' water from the well . . . it seems almost wicked, havin' life so easy as that."

Brigida laughed and looked up with curiosity at the girl. "You're very different, yet somehow, I'd know you and Nan for sisters, anywhere. Do people always say so?"

Both girls had brown hair and eyes and there was a similarity of body and facial structure—almond eyes and upturned noses—but where Nan was thick and broad in limb and feature, her sister was delicate refinement.

"Nanny tries, missus," Mary said, "but she's always been a mite clumsy. Martha's teachin' her about housekeeping, Martha is that patient. A chatterer, Nan is, I'm sure you noticed."

"I found her delightful. She told me you're the dairymaid."

"I help out in the house, too, but I'm mostly with the cows. I'm the best milker. They all give for me easy, and ours is the best milk, the richest. Slade don't keep but three cows now, just enough for Silver Hill and for some others that needs it."

There was an awkward silence. "Captain Hawkes, I mean, missus. Now, I'll have to remember."

"Speak of him as you always have, Mary. There's no reason not," Brigida smiled. "You're finished, now, with your milking? Sit and visit then. Tell me, do you have a young man? A lover?"

"Tom Sayre, missus," Mary said with a special intonation. "We'll marry when we've enough put by for a bit of land. No marriage before means, Tom says. He's a carpenter workin' over to East Hampton now, but we want our own farmstead."

Brigida clapped her hands. "I need a carpenter! Will you ask Tom Sayre to come and see me when he's able? I'm rebuilding the mill. I shall need a man to oversee the work. Do you think he'd be interested?"

"Tom's father and grandfather, on his mother's side, were millwrights. There's no work he'd prefer except farmin'. He'll be done this job in a month maybe. I'd be pleased to have him work so close by me. Now, my brother Robin . . . he's a joiner. He just come home this morning on Captain Hawkes's *Triton*. Four years and more gone, but Robin will not go again to sea. He'll stay at home and work with Tom. They're of an age, and though not alike in temperament, they've always got on well together."

"How are they unlike, Mary?" Brigida poured out two cups of tea, then wriggled back into a corner of the couch, her legs curled under her. Mary settled, a bit tentatively, into the opposite corner.

"Well, Tom's shy, real quiet, steady and quiet, and Robin's like a spring afternoon, all brightness and noise and full of promise. His tongue's so sweet and glib, he'll charm you that fast." Mary snapped her fingers. "They both will turn twenty-five in fall, and that's when Tom and me would marry, if we could, when all the folk could come and be in a mood to celebrate after harvest. But I don't know. . . ." Mary's voice trailed off.

"I should have liked such a wedding, too, with everyone there," Brigida said, subdued for a minute. "Why will Robin stay ashore now?" she asked.

"Oh, 'tis a bit sad, missus. Slade says he must, now Robin's leg got broke. He walks real stiff. It pains him."

"Have you been out to Sag Harbor already today?" Brigida was surprised.

"Yes. The Cedar Island lightkeeper sent word. Slade kindly came for me and we went to watch the *Triton* come home in the dawn rain so pretty, even with her ragged, patchy riggin' and her hull all crusted over with barnacles. Robin will be getting a share of the haul. Her holds are full to burstin', it's said, with bone and oil. And spermacetti to make the finest candles, you know?"

"Yes," Brigida nodded, "and creams for the skin. I used to mix it with the coconut oils the girls in the Islands use. Oh, that must be Slade," she exclaimed, springing up when she heard a carriage roll toward the front doors.

"Oh, talkin' so much, missus, I near forgot to tell you what he bade me say! That's the seamstress now, up from Sag Harbor, to fit you. The captain has gone to the city and won't be back for a time."

"How long gone, Mary?" Brigida tried to mask her disappointment. She smiled stiffly, toying with a curl that had fallen forward over her shoulder.

"He didn't say, missus. He never does say, but usually he's away a fortnight at a stretch. It's said he does like the night life in New York."

"Who said, Mary?"

"Why, only Rose. She's Julia Carpenter's dresser, acquainted with a parlor maid in the captain's city house. Rose—well, she don't know everythin', though she likes

94

to let on she does. Rose says there's streetwalkers and real low entertainment. Oh, don't it sound like the devil's own place, that city? I won't speak on it more. I see in your look it upsets you."

"It's best I know about such things," Brigida answered. "Come, watch my fitting? You can tell me which styles you like and which not."

"I'm to help Nan, now, missus, hemmin' linen, but later?"

"Yes, come to me later, both of you. We shall have a game of hearts or cribbage. Everyone needs company on such a dreary day."

Ann Overton, the seamstress, was a woman nearing thirty. Her dark hair, already shot through with streaks of steel gray, was swept up from a small face that was quietly beautiful, though world weary, with faint dark circles under large, dark, jaded eyes. A small, bowed mouth that turned down at the corners lent a faint look of displeasure to her rather bored expression. She wore a plain dress of rich, dark wool, crafted with a striking simplicity of style that heightened the elegance of her tall figure.

The seamstress's movements were easy and languorous, conveying a total absence of energy as she cast professional, appraising eyes over Brigida.

"Here, glance at these," she said, extracting a tape from her pocket and handing Brigida a *Demorest's Monthly* and a *Frank Leslie's Ladies Magazine*. "But first, disrobe, just to your chemise." The seamstress's voice was a low purr.

"I'll only have to take your measure. Slade has selected the fabrics and picked most of the gowns. You are allowed to choose one or two more from the illustrations there. If you wish."

"Do you design the things yourself . . . Miss Overton, is it?" Brigida, standing at the cheval glass in her room, worked diligently along a row of tiny jet buttons at her right cuff.

"Mrs. Overton. I'm widowed. Yes, my own designs. In a way. Usually, I go to Paris and bring back originals to work from. Slade pays for it all, and I do a display at a salon in New York. I make copies, or variations, to order. I repay him at the end of the season. We've been very successful, but this year Paris is out of the question. The war . . . the Franco-Prussian War . . . the siege of Paris . . . you know, interferes with everything. We started touting American fashion this season and the *Herald* took up our position. Why, whatever is taking you so long, Mrs. Hawkes?" The woman yawned as if the tedium of it all was too much for her.

Brigida had now started on her left cuff. "Had I known to expect you, I'd not have worn such a dress. You and my husband are well acquainted, then, Mrs. Overton?"

"Yes, yes. I've been a friend, shall we say, of Slade Hawkes for some time. He was most helpful when my husband passed over. I've always dressed Slade's ladies. He's done exceptionally well in you, though. You will wear my things splendidly." And though Ann Overton had offered a compliment, she seemed to Brigida to do so almost grudgingly.

"Are you done, finally? Good. Now be a sweet child and don't fuss," the woman said, deftly slipping her measure about Brigida's waist. "Fine, fine, and no lacing at all," Ann commented.

"Does he have many?" Brigida asked.

"Many what?" The seamstress was making notes on her cuff.

"Ladies."

"Well, he's impossibly handsome, very rich . . . what would you expect? He's capable of great, if short-lived, tenderness, besides." A hint of a smile touched the woman's downturned lips.

"I've heard him described as vain." Brigida made a half turn at the dressmaker's gesture.

"Mm? I wouldn't say vain so much as . . . aloof, remote. I've heard him described as irresistible by some women, as a blackguard of overweening pride by others. He's probably broken more hearts than he can count." Ann Overton paused at her work, leaving Brigida standing with outstretched arms. "Slade is a restless man, you'll find, full of a quick energy. He tires easily of what he's mastered and moves on to other . . . challenges. Oh, please, do put your arms down. It makes me tired to look at you. I'm through with your bodice."

Brigida stretched and turned again. "How many gowns will you be making for me?"

"Dozens. Slade always dresses well, and so must you, of course, if you should ever accompany him to town. You will find that away from here, in society, he is a man of elegant manners, though deferential to no one. He's outrageous with women, of course, but I find your husband, Mrs. Hawkes, quite the most fascinating man I have ever met."

"Were you born on Long Island?" Brigida asked, abruptly changing the subject.

"It is best we talk of other things, you are quite right. Yes, I was born here, but Mother is French, a Parisienne. It's the usual story—a good-looking sailor, a pretty barmaid, *et voilà*! Love at first sight. They say it happens, but I don't believe in it." The woman laughed dryly as she stretched a tape from Brigida's waist to the floor. The girl smiled at her own image in the long glass, tossing her hair and pursing her lips.

"I do believe in it," she stated. "How did you learn your trade, Mrs. Overton?"

"Maman, like so many French, you know, has a certain sense of style and originality. She gave that to me, and I have facile hands and a quick eye. I started with the superb paper patterns from *Demorest* and *Butterick*. Hold still one more instant. I only must do the right shoulder to the wrist—there. Now, would you like to see what Slade has selected for you, Mrs. Hawkes? Shall we be on first-name terms, or do you prefer formality?"

"I . . . I shouldn't want to hold myself distant, Ann," Brigida said, slipping on her furry wrapper. "May I order you a tea?"

"Brandy, please. It's warming, on such a damp, cold day. But first, look. He bid me give you this, carried from the Imperial Court of the Romanovs. Magnificent, yes?" With a great, slow flourish, Ann pulled a Russian bashlyk from her large tapestry bag and displayed it full on the rug at Brigida's feet. White velvet with deep fringe and scarlet satin trim spread out for yards. "We're making you a gown specifically for it, it's such a rarity. The dress will be shot silk crepe de chine, wine red, glorious with your coloring. I smoke, though not in public. Do you mind? Will you join me?"

"I don't, I won't. Just do whatever you want!" Brigida laughed. She had snatched up the long cape and, wrapping it about her shoulders, pranced back and forth before the glass, alternately smiling, then looking over her raised shoulder very seriously and regally displeased. "Oh, I love it, I do! Should it have white boots, Ann, or red, do you think?"

"Both, of course. Now sit down and look." The woman pulled a sheaf of sketches from a flat case and took a chair near the fire as Martha arrived carrying a decanter of amber liquor and several glasses on a silver tray.

"Martha and I always have a good smoke together, don't we, Martha?"

"Every time, yes. But it is a secret." Martha stood near the mantel while Ann rolled two cigarettes, sealed them, pulled a flat silver match safe from her pocket and struck a light. When she and Martha were puffing happily, all three women turned their attention to the matter at hand, the sketches, each of which had a swatch or two of fabric and bits of lace and ribbon pinned to it.

There was exquisite lingerie—petticoats to be made up entirely of fine chantilly lace, silk pantalettes trimmed in lace, matching camisoles with slim straps.

"This is beautiful!" Brigida breathed, extracting a swatch and drawing of a narrow form-fitting fall of white China silk, low cut, with thin straps at the shoulders and blooming with hand-painted, pale pink roses. "Is there a peignoir to go with it?"

"Of course. Next sketch." Ann nodded, sipping.

There were ball gowns and day dresses, walking costumes and riding suits. Flaming silk brocades for grand evenings, and soft, flowing chiffons with touches of ruching and piping, for summer.

"What is this? I can't possibly wear such a thing!" Brigida was incredulous.

"Whatever do you mean? Am I to take offense? It is the most dramatic gown in the entire collection." Ann Overton glared at Brigida. "You'll be moving among the wealthiest, most sophisticated people in the country, my girl. I hope you can rise to the demands of your position. You're not married to some ribbon clerk, after all."

The item under discussion was a brocaded ball gown, bordered with black chantilly lace, embroidered with tiny black pearls. The gown shaded gradually from black at the revealing neckline to silvery gray at the hem. The bustled skirt was to be cut *en traine* and worn over a specially made petticoat styled exactly like the skirt, but of gray glace silk covered with puffs of chantilly lace and black pearls. It would show where the gown was looped up almost to the waist, on the left side.

"It just seems so, so . . . grandiose, don't you agree, Martha?"

The Indian woman nodded seriously. "Yes, but you won't wear it more than one time. Don't worry."

"One time?" Brigida looked to Ann.

"You couldn't wear such a magnificent thing twice. Everyone would remember. No, no! If you dress plainly, in black, you may repeat a gown. But this? It is out of the question. I almost forgot, one more measure. I'm to finish lace fillets for your brow. In every color of the rainbow."

Ann flicked what was left of her cigarette into the fire and reached for her tape as Brigida come to the last sketch, a very full black taffetta skirt and a short jacket of red velvet with dangling red velvet pom-pom trim at the waist, neck, and cuffs.

"This one is different, somehow," Brigida said, looking questioningly at Ann Overton.

"It isn't for you." Ann lifted the picture away. That one is for Lydia Worsley. Slade's . . . friend, you know? Oh, I'm sorry, you don't know, I see," Ann said. "Now listen, you can't expect the man to change just because he's taken you to wife. Yours is an arranged marriage of convenience, I'm told, so if he continues his other liaisons, there's no harm done, is there?"

Brigida made no reply.

"Oh, I see again how it is with you. I should have guessed, knowing him as I do," Ann sighed. "But isn't it better to hear the truth than be shocked later? Besides, we all know the male drive is so much . . . stronger. You should be relieved he won't be unleashing all his baser passions on you."

"Baser passions?" Brigida echoed, "But I thought . . ."

Martha interrupted before she could say more. "There is a charm I know that will not fail. Gather up his footprint from the soft earth, in spring. Plant marigolds in the soil you collect. As the flowers grow and never fade so will his love." Martha was positive.

"It won't," Brigida said petulantly. "He's already gone off to what's her name. Did you know his first wife, Ann? Did you know Bonnie? Was it this way with them, too?"

"Martha, give this girl a brandy. Get yourself in hand, Brigida. It'll do no good to take on. Of course, I knew her. For almost a year he never left her side." Ann rolled and lit another cigarette. "There was something between them, surely. He treated her . . . like a broken doll." Ann shook her head. "They troubled me." The seamstress began to gather up her things and Brigida wandered to the window.

The rain had stopped and most of the fog had blown off, but the sky was still full of hard-edged, inky clouds, low and ragged. "More rain coming," she commented distractedly. Ann downed the last of her brandy and Martha withdrew, taking the tray.

"Did my husband's ship carry all these exquisite goods, Ann?"

"No, no. A British merchant, off the China trade, put in for a repair at the harbor. I thought Slade would buy up the entire cargo and . . . gloves. I'm to measure you for gloves, too. Well, that's not much," Ann said, taking Brigida's hand. "I'd have thought he'd give you a real jewel for your finger, not a little skimp of gold. Come to me for a fitting. A week today. My place is off Main, Levi knows where."

"So soon?" Brigida was rebuttoning her dress.

"It's all to be done in a few weeks' time, Slade insists. I've a machine to do it with, a new Howe he gave me, with all the special pieces—it hems and ruffles and braids, and one part even does as well as Kensington hand stitchery for embroidery."

"Mother told me they used to show them at fairs, those machines, for six cents the look. Imagine, now you've actually got one."

"Yes, and soon I'll buy more and open a salon of my own in the city, with porters in blue uniforms like Mr. Constable has. One day, I might even have a steam elevator like the one in the Lord and Taylor emporium on Grand Street."

"But will you really go away from here, Ann? Won't you miss this countryside?"

"No, I won't miss it," Ann said, looking out into the overcast day at the still pines and the bay beyond. "I belong in cities. Besides, the summer colonies creeping out along the beaches are getting closer each year. It will all be different soon. Silver Hill, though, will be wild and beautiful forever, I think. I'll leave you now."

Brigida began pacing the room as soon as Ann Overton had gone. After a few minutes she changed into her warmest things and left the house, pulling her hood close, as the clock at the turn of the stairs began ponderously to toll the hour. The light musical notes of the library mantel clock chimed, and from other parts of the still house the striking of clocks reverberated together—measuring out the heavy quiet of a country winter noon.

Seven

Formed by the last glacier to come roaring down the wide Hudson Valley, the south shore of Long Island is an outwash plain cut jagged by inlets and channels and tidal streams. A slender strand of barrier beach parallels the island for a hundred miles, forming a protected chain of salt marshes and bays.

Along the upland northern shore of one of the chains, Brigida walked, a child of wind and ocean, an intimate of tides and moon, seeking comfort in the timelessness of seascape and sky, as she always had done. There were ducks on the water—Labrador, sheldrake, and scoter. A flotilla of gulls rose over and over only to settle again, calling loudly. The tide was low. It had left a ridge of broken shells and eel grass and colored pebbles high on the bay beach. Those Brigida found especially pretty she slipped into the pocket of her dress. She moved slowly, only glancing up occasionally, lost in thought, devoid of all sense of time or place. There was no color in the sunless winter day—water, sky and land were all somber shades of gray. Only the wind, shredding low clouds, seemed alive, blowing wet and cold on her face. Her mood was desolate.

"The very first day," she said to herself again and again, "to just leave, and not even try to make a secret of the reason." She began to hurl the pebbles she had collected out over the water, listening to them splash unseen off in the mist that hung over the bay. "How could he . . . and buy her gifts besides . . . and Ann Overton and everyone else in the world knowing." Brigida began to walk more briskly, flinging a handful of pebbles with all her strength. Suddenly, hissing like serpents, a pair of swans rose up out of the fog, startling her so that she stood trembling for some minutes before she began to laugh aloud. Her sadness turned to bubbling anger.

"I will not be brought low by that blasted, devilish man!" she shouted, striding along, shooting pebbles now in rapid fire. "I will beat him at his own game. I will goad his jealous nature, and leave a chain of broken hearts wherever I go."

Exquisitely made as she was, Brigida knew her power. She was used to the attentions of men and boys, to their imploring glances and flirtatious smiles. Slade Hawkes never would have a moment's peace of mind, except when she was in his sight.

Only gradually, as her mood lightened, did Brigida notice the changes that had been taking place about her for some while. She had marked, but ignored, the wind's shift, the rushing sound of turning tide, but now she could ignore them no longer. Ducks and gulls were moving upland again, and the bay, dotted with whitecaps, would soon send its waters high into the creeks and ponds and across the narrow band of beach behind her, to crash against the weathered dune bluff.

There was no returning the way she had come. She hurried on. It wasn't much further that she came to a wide inlet that prevented her proceeding further. Cold winter rain had begun to fall again, the wind to rise. Brigida knew by the sound of its scream that a raging northerly was in the offing. To go back through the marsh meadow and woods would be treacherous for one unfamiliar with the land. A northerly gale could blow for two or three days; to be lost in it would be dangerous. To make matters worse, no one at Silver Hill knew where she had gone or even that she had left, alone.

Brigida turned inland, watching the cattails and faded marsh grass bend to the wind, the bracken and beach plum cling stubbornly along the bluff. Higher up, great wind-winnowed, twisted oaks and flailing swamp maples grew and, to her relief and surprise, sheltered a solitary cottage that was almost hidden from sight. It was shingled and thatched, a fisherman's dwelling, she decided. A curl of smoke rose from its chimney.

Brigida struggled up the steep incline of the bluff, grasping as she went at the gnarled roots of aged trees unearthed by wind and water. She pounded frantically at the door. After a moment there was a shuffling within and the door swung open. An old man and woman greeted Brigida with astonishment.

"We thought it must be the grandson. No one else in 'is right mind wanders the shore when a northerly's blowin'. Well, come in and warm yourself, for glory sake," the woman said, drawing Brigida forward while the man pushed the door to behind her.

The cottage was small and snug—the shutters were closed, a fire burned, and a kettle was simmering. A large iron clam rake and several woven wood baskets hung on pegs from the heavy beam that spanned the room. There were an oak table and benches near the fire. A candle flickered in a corner near a spinning wheel and a quilting frame, and on it, almost done, was a cotton quilt, the pattern a sunburst in reds and pinks and shades of green bordered in purple and lilac.

"Give me that sodden cloak before you've caught your death," the woman said as Brigida admired the handiwork.

"It's the most beautiful one I've ever seen and I . . . do you have others?"

"I been quiltin' for fifty years, since I married John and come out here to live with 'im. John, he been fishin' and clammin'. He sells his catch to the boats goin' to the city and I trade my quilts at the fair for what's needed here, that we can't get ourselves, just salt and nails mostly."

"I sometimes nets menhaden and sells 'em for fertilizer. To farmers," the old man said. "Who are ya?" he asked bluntly. "We don't see a lot of strangers here. Curious when we do."

"Don't be pryin', old man. Is it your business? Give 'er a cup first," the woman snapped.

Brigida laughed at the fiesty pair and told her story briefly.

"Do you expect you'll be liking it up to Silver Hill?"

Sarah Hand wanted to know. She had gone to work at her quilting and had to shout to be heard over the rising roar of the wind.

"Oh, I expect so," Brigida answered noncommittally, watching the woman set her needle to a corner of the star. "It's very . . . lonely, though. Slade's gone already this very day away to the city."

The old man, tall and thin and stoop-shouldered, bent his weathered face to a net he was repairing. A boy who had slipped quietly into the cottage sat silent on the chimney settle regarding the visitor in awe. He had red hair, light eyes, and a quick, shy smile. He wasn't much younger than Brigida.

"I know Levi Phillips communes with no one 'cept Slade and the old Montauk Indian George Pharoh who lives over t'other side. Well, Island people are awful closed up," Jonathan Hand said, puffing on his pipe.

"Yes, but once you get one of 'em goin', old man, you might hear more'n you'd care to," the woman said. "But Levi Phillips is about the tightest I've ever met."

Mr. Hand paid scant attention to his wife and went on speaking. "Not many come now to settle away out here so remote from the city, and those few that have come on of late, in the past twenty year or so . . . it won't be till their grandchildren are growed they'll be accepted here."

"I've found the Edwards girls—Mary and Nan—very friendly," Brigida said, lifting a painted toy horn from the mantel.

"Oh, but you've a way 'bout you, don't she Johnny, and a whaling man's daughter? You were one of us before you ever got within a hundred mile."

Sarah rethreaded her needle and paused at her work. "Now, the Hawkeses been here a long time. They have prospered in worldly goods, but they was never easy in their ways, they never been content. Think of it! Jarred Hawkes takin' a young girl like Elizabeth from her home, against her father's wish, mind. They was city society folk. Though what was wrong with Jarred Hawkes for a husband I'll never know, 'cept for him being a sailing man. But anyways, he took her, and then he left 'er alone. Built that grand mansion and left 'er all alone in it." Sarah Hand shook her head in disbelief. "No wonder, is it, she was always goin' off. We all give up on there ever bein' young of that union, and wouldn't you know, there's Slade born after ten years, she near thirty and flittin' all over the neighborhood and the city and back to that Paris again, leavin' Martha to raise up the boy and her own baby too. Levi and Slade are the same age by a few weeks.

"Way back, 'tis said, the Hawkeses had a witch amongst 'em, and I always thought she did put a pall over that house."

"Oh, gad, Gram, what you sayin' now?" young John asked, chagrined. "Them silly old stories wouldn't interest such a clever lady." He looked horrified at the old woman who stared him down without a word of reproach. She went to make a pot of tea, rising to her full four feet looking like a ruffled hen.

"The witch was Jerusha Hawkes," Sarah plunged on undaunted. "She went over to visit one of the Carpenter ladies, Jane it was, on the little island. Jane had wed a Johnson boy that Jerusha always wanted her own self.

110

There was a girl child just born to Jane, and the poor woman took sick the very minute Jerusha's foot touched Carpenter Island soil. She got the childbed fever and swore, Jane did, that Mistress Hawkes put the devil on 'er . . . she passed in a terrible agony, it's said." Sarah shook her head, picturing the scene. "That was just about the time the white deer was seen about. Beautiful it was said to be, but fearful and so fleet no hunter could touch the creature until Selah Edwards ripped the silver buttons offn his soldier's coat, put 'em in his gun . . ." the old woman paused for dramatic effect while her audience attended breathlessly.

"Put 'em in his gun and waited, waited out in the woods there near Silver Hill, and finally it come along shining in the full moon's light on a midsummer eve. Selah shot . . . and he hit it, but only to wound, and that devil deer rushed away like the wind." Sarah tucked her needle in her apron and clapped her hands. "Rob Edward's gram tells the tale just the same, don't she Johnny? How Selah followed that deer to the manor house and found Jerusha in the entryway bleedin' from a wound in 'er side?"

"Yea, she tells just like you," Johnny said, eyes wide, caught up in the story. "She tells how that Jerusha Hawkes mended and they sent her to Connecticut or Massachusetts maybe for a trial."

"We never had but one or two of them so-called witches out here, you know," old John interjected, "so we didn't know how to deal with 'em proper. 'Tis said she never did admit to doin' the devil's work, poor lovesick girl, but she was hung for it just the same and died with a curse on her lips for the Carpenters and her own people, too, for not savin' her. None of the Hawkeses of Silver Hill, down all the generations of time, Jerusha swore, would find peace or contentment on the land, but would all be driven to roam the world seekin' something they'd never find. It didn't do the Carpenters harm, that curse, but the Hawkeses. . . ."

There was just the howl of wind for a while, and the crackling of the fire. "I don't . . . I won't believe in such things," Brigida said very softly, but even as she did, she felt a slow prickling along her spine.

"Nor me neither," the boy said boldly.

"Oh, children, it's just an old story, it's not meant serious. But that little southern wife of Slade's?"

Brigida nodded, her nerves suddenly taut.

"Some say she had the devil in 'er when she died." Sarah came to sit in the rocking chair near the hearth.

"But she . . . she was mad, Elizabeth told me so," Brigida insisted, pacing.

"Some call it one thing, some another. Some say Slade caused it, some say it was Elizabeth's doin', but I never listen to that talk."

"Old woman, hold your tongue or I'll be callin' you a witch. Now listen darlin'," John Hand said to Brigida, "Slade may be changeable as winter wind, but he's a noble, princely lad, for truth, always remembers us way out here, sends all manner of things—fresh milk, spring lamb, pheasant when he hunts. Now, I see something's amiss with you, so hear me out; no matter what you may think, no matter what you may hear about 'im from anyone, remember I told you that lad is straight as a string and no fool a'tall. If you're patient, he'll warm to you."

"But I don't know if I am patient, and I didn't know my feelings were in my face to be so easily read," Brigida said, her eyes luminous.

"Gram, you must do somethin'! She's settin' to cry tears," Johnny said, standing, then sitting, then standing again.

"John, look what you done, makin' the child sad!" Sarah scolded.

"What, me? You're the one said about all them terrible things." Old John was affronted.

"Pig stupid, that man sometimes. Now dear, don't get yourself weepy, that won't solve it. How would you like to make Slade a quilt? I'll teach you, I'll help you. You come down here to me whenever you can and before long you shall have something beautiful of your own hand to gift him with. Would it please you?"

Brigida nodded. "I will love to come quilting with you, Mrs. Hand. I didn't mean to upset you all. It's just that so much has happened in such a little time, and everything's so new to me and . . . I just don't seem to belong at Silver Hill, or anyplace, now. I mean, I have no home, no people to belong to and . . ."

"You have a place. You come right along to us whenever the fancy moves you," John said, lighting a pipe with a straw at the fire.

At that instant the door opened, and Slade Hawkes, streaming water from an oiled skin cape stood with Bran at the threshold.

"I've come to take Brigida home now," he said.

"How did you find me? They told me you had gone

away." Brigida turned from him, but he had seen a pellucid sparkling of recent tears in her eyes.

"There is no other place, lady, for you to have gone from Silver Hill," he said, the timbre of his voice low. "In the opposite direction, the beach ends just around the bend at an inlet." He came to stand near her. "It's five miles you've walked, and it's even longer home through the woods. Only naughty children run off without a word to anyone."

"You'd gone away and not said a word to me. They told me you'd be gone for weeks, as usual." She glared up at him defiant. "What are you doing here?" With the fire behind her, Brigida's hair flamed like a torch.

Slade brushed a curl back from her temple.

"I was kept late at Sag Harbor. Too late to make the city journey today. Tomorrow will be time enough to go. Do you propose to question me about my comings and goings?" A quick anger passed between them like a lightning flare.

Johnny Hand went out muttering to see to the stallion, and old John took Slade's slicker to hang on a peg near the door. The dog shook, spraying water about and went, as was his habit, to the hearth.

"Slade Hawkes, I've known you all your life and I'll not have any of that famous temper in my house, you know that. You mustn't trouble your pretty little wife so. I'll give you a tea to warm you and the old man'll pour you a rum."

Shooting a glowering look in Brigida's direction, Slade drew something from the pocket of his jacket.

"The *Triton* came in today, Sari, I've this for you and

something for John as well. Open it."

"It's a musical box! I thank you, Slade," she said, placing it carefully on the mantel.

"And look what he give me—a match safe." John Hand displayed a miniature violin of shiny copper. He opened and closed the lid, snapping and clicking it several times. "It's real fine. Got one of them Kentucky burley smokes with you, Slade?"

"There's a hidden compartment, John, for coins and such," Slade said, passing the old man a black cigar. "We'll be going. I've brought you a slicker, Brigida."

"Taking a lady out in such a blow. She'll catch her death, and you could wait for the storm's end just as well. Bran there knows I'm right, don't you boy?" The big dog raised its head and thumped his tail, waiting.

"You, Sari, who wander these woods and shores in all weathers and seasons, to say such nonsense."

"But I been walkin' out in the worst weather all my life and she ain't," the old woman scolded.

"We'll be fine, Sari," Brigida interrupted. "And thank you for the shelter."

"You are to come and see us now, often as you can. The boy there will always be glad to walk 'er home, Slade," John smiled.

"I shall soon know my way about." Brigida kissed the old man on the cheek and then as the door opened young Johnny fell into the room, scowled at Slade, and resumed his seat on the settle.

"And thank you, too, Johnny," Brigida smiled at the boy.

He looked up at her, entranced by the exquisite,

shining creature suddenly plummeted into their midst as if by magic.

"Oh no, thank you, miss," he stuttered. "You'll visit again?"

"You've made a conquest of young John, I see." Slade helped Brigida to the stallion's back. "You'll have to ride astride," he said mounting behind her.

"I don't mind. It's the western way, actually," she said as his arms came about her. She rested back against him, feeling his legs flex along the length of hers, engulfed in the scent of spice and lime and soaped leathers.

"Bend," Slade ordered leaning over her as they rode out of the Hand's small shed and moved north from the cottage and the bay along a woodland path with the dog leading the way.

"Storm's over," Brigida said.

"Just gathering strength for a stronger blast," Slade commented. He urged the stallion to a quick trot. The dappled light of the moon fell through bare branches to light their way.

"Don't toy with him, Brigida. He's a true innocent, unlike you, with no experience in the world."

"Young John?" Brigida laughed at Slade, looking back over her shoulder. "When I decide to engage in a . . . flirtation, I'll surely find more worldly company in the neighborhood, won't I?"

Not gently, Slade pulled off her hood. "You are not at liberty to engage in flirtations," he said against her rose-fragrant curls.

"And you, sir? Are you at liberty?" she snapped, stiffening in his arms. "Just for appearance's sake, couldn't you have waited a decent interval before announcing to the entire world your intention to be off to . . . to the city?"

"Were you missing me so soon, goddess? I promised you would, didn't I?" he teased, bringing an arm about her waist, his lips to the nape of her neck. His hand slipped beneath her cloak and Brigida responded to his touch with mixed stirrings of desire and irritation that her overmastering passion was roused by his merest touch.

"Is it much further?" she yawned.

"A good way to go yet. You're here but a day and see the trouble you've put me to already?" he complained.

Despite the accusation, Brigida relaxed against him and was soon asleep in his arms. Looking down at her storm of blond curls and her beautiful profile, Slade marveled at her, so trusting and almost childlike as she slept.

"Mawkish tripe!" he said aloud. He dug his heels into the stallion's sides. As the startled animal leaped forward, snorting indignantly, Brigida came wide awake with a start.

Silver Hill manor stood dark at the top of the next rise, barely silhouetted against a dark sky. Snow, small, serious hard flakes of it, driven by a north wind, swirled in whirlpools powdering everything, thickening the air, muffling sounds, transforming the familiar world to a strange, alien place where horse and riders seemed to be the only living things.

Eight

Brigida awoke shivering. She rose, put three logs on the grate, and added kindling to recapture what fire still burned. Methodically, she moved about lighting lamps and candles until the room seemed to be ablaze. Then she lay on pillows piled so near to the now flaming logs that the heat was painful on her face. The clock showed two. A clamorous wind shrilled about the house and echoed thundering and hollow down the chimney. Her soft yellow wrapper closely followed the lines of her curving form. Pale curls flowed like liquid silk over the sleeve in which she hid her face. She lifted her head just enough to look up at Slade over her arm when he entered, her large, dark eyes wide and pleading.

"Stay with me a little?" she asked in a small, quivering voice.

He nodded, surprised by her again, this time by her weakness, her appealing need of him . . . or someone.

"I saw your lights."

"I dreamt I was in a strange house, all bits and pieces of many places I remember. It was dark and gloomy and cold, but sunlight fell though chinks in the shutters. I was buried there and I had to get out into the sun. Nothing else mattered, but the doors and windows were all sealed with ice and I . . . everything outside is green, summer-green and very far away. . . ."

Brigida was shivering again. Slade brought a down comforter from the bed to wrap her in, and sat in the rocking chair holding her. Then all was quiet but for the crackle of the fire and the howl of the wind.

Snow fell steadily all night and into the next morning. Slade, caught by the storm, had to remain at Silver Hill. He took refuge in his study.

Brigida was driven by the cold from her lonely room, and she passed her time in the big, silent kitchen, with Martha, who baked, and with Levi, who smoked, and watched the fire leap up the wide throat of the cavernous chimney. He set up a steady creaking from an old rocker that stood at the hearth. At regular intervals, he rose to cut himself a piece of sugar from the cone set at the center of the long table and to pour a mug of cider from the hogshead he'd brought up from the cellar.

"It is no usual thing, such cold and snow in this place. It's soft, watery country here, usually kind because the ocean current warms the land all winter, though many a time my gravy was hard as stone before the meal was served," Martha offered hesitantly.

"My mother used to tell of her dish towel freezing in

her hands when she turned away from the fire, and of keeping pies frozen half the winter in a northern bedroom. But that was New England, though." Brigida smiled, relieved to have someone to talk with.

Martha was using a massive rolling pin on dough she took from a wooden box. "Did Levi carve that for you, Martha?" Brigida asked.

"Slade did, from one piece of wood." Martha said. "Can you cook? Please stir the soup, if you're of a mind to."

Brigida took a long-handled wooden spoon to a kettle suspended from a lugpole over the cooking fire.

"I can . . . a little. Simple fare. For a stretch at sea, we had no ship's cook." Brigida rested the spoon back on the mantel among candle molds and snuffers, grid irons, trivets, and wrought iron toasters.

"The cook took sick and got put ashore to mend, and Mother did for cabin and fo'c'sle too, and I helped her. When we put in at an Orient port, we took on a Chinese man. He came home with us and stayed as Mother's cook until . . . I left San Francisco."

"We spoke aboard your father's ship once, when Slade was sailin' with you. I was with Captain Jarred. You were too young to remember," Levi said unexpectedly.

"I do remember," Brigida announced. "I remember Slade never came on deck to see his father and they sent me to get him. Slade was so angry. I thought at me but . . . I always wondered why he was with us, not his own father."

There was no answer, and quiet settled again as more snow fell, insulating Silver Hill from all the world.

121

When the pie cabinet was full, the quail fried, and the soup, in its iron kettle, ready to be served for the midday meal, Slade, in a great cape and knee boots emerged from his study. He strode through the kitchen to the fireside.

"You must be freezin', man, in there. Nicer in the kitchen," Levi grunted.

"I've work," Slade answered brusquely, coming to stand over Brigida. "Has Martha been letting you cook?" he asked. "Here, your apron strings have come undone."

"A sign her lover has been thinking of her," Martha pronounced.

Levi stood and stretched and Martha spread the fare— black bean soup, freshly made bread, squash filled with molasses and sausage. Tankards were set about for ale. To everyone's unspoken surprise, Elizabeth came down from her chamber unassisted to join the group in the kitchen.

Over the meal, Slade and Levi decided that the storm was growing worse and that no end was in sight; measures would have to be taken to further insulate the house against the biting cold. The foundation had been banked with leaves and straw in the fall, and now all but a few essential rooms would be closed off and keys left in their locks to keep out cold draughts.

"You may have to set up our beds here in the kitchen, if the cold gets worse," Elizabeth told Slade.

"And you all will have to share the warmth with the stable boy and a litter of terriers just whelped. If I don't bring them in to the fire they'll be lost," Slade replied.

"I have had such company before. I have had chicks hatch in the chimney cupboard," Elizabeth said. "You and Brigida will keep to yourselves upstairs, is that it? Just use the bed warmer," she instructed. "There is one in your room, and use extra down. Then, if you take some hot mulled cider up to bed with you, you will be very cozy indeed."

There was silence until Martha went back to the soup kettle to refill the bowls again. "Slade told me you will plant herbs and flowers in the spring," she said to Brigida. "I will be pleased."

"I will also be pleased. Among the cabbages and gourds I'll put chamomile and lavender, tansy, too. When I was in the Pacific Islands, I learned to make creams and scents and preparations for the hair. I use a chamomile rinse to make mine paler."

"And what have you for me?" Elizabeth asked, touching her faded tresses.

"Cornflower! It will make your hair pure white and so lovely, Elizabeth!" Brigida clapped her hands delightedly, and when Slade paused to look at her, her laughing eyes met his. She looked away quickly and jumped up. "I'll help you clear, Martha, and then I'll take Elizabeth up her tea," she said.

"Not up, but in the library, dear. When you have done here, join me. It is too cold upstairs. Besides, I do not want to be alone today. The snow . . . the snow changes things, somehow. I think today I shall show you all the rooms at Silver Hill when we have done our tea. Do you think that a good idea, Slade?

"Yes, before I lock them again. If you feel up to it, of course."

Soon the others had gone their ways and only Martha

and Brigida were left tidying in the kitchen.

"Martha?" Brigida ventured, "She . . . Elizabeth, what's wrong with her? She seems quite strong today."

"You'd best touch wood or you will be calling up the devil. I was thinking just the same myself, but I'd not say it out. Elizabeth is a puzzle. Nothing is ever enough for her when she has got it, and when it's gone, she pines for what's lost. It is a curse to be ever vexed and dissatisfied. She has been invalided with this nervous prostration for many years, on and off, since . . . since Slade was born. She used to have fits as a girl, too, she told me. She just took to her bed once for two years, 'til some healer was brought to lay hands on her and then she got right up. Maybe you have got the touch? Today she is almost as I remember her when I first came to Silver Hill." The Indian woman fussily rewiped the table after Brigida.

"How was that?" Brigida asked.

"She was the prettiest thing, going about all over with the other ladies. There were so many people about, she was like a light drawing moths, then. I remember your mother, too, visiting when you were a babe—Emma Lydon, another beauty, not troubled like Elizabeth. They were close, those two." Martha vigorously rubbed the frost glaze from a circle of window and looked out.

"The snow won't end for a good time yet. They'll have to shovel again to get to the cows this night. Well, the woodbox is full, the cellar, too. The snow could fall for a month and we'd want for nothing, knock on wood." Martha fed the fire and settled into the rocking chair to darn. "I used to carry a bundle of reeds on my back, long years ago," she said, "selling from farm to farm, reeds for

124

the caning of chairs. Elizabeth and Captain Jarred, they made me stay at Silver Hill. Later, when it was all over with them, she and I were here together, the long, silent years alone with just her boy and mine, and after they'd gone, too, to sea, she taught me many things."

"Your husband? Where is he, Martha?"

"Drowned," Martha quickly answered. "I suckled Elizabeth's son with my own, she too weak with the quinsy to do it, not wantin' to, besides. Oh, it all seems such a long, long time ago," Martha sighed, "nearly thirty years gone." Then she smiled, almost shyly. "You will bring a light to Silver Hill again," she said. "I can tell it."

"And a noise as well. It will not be silent here, ever again, it will not, I promise you," Brigida declared, flourishing a bit of linen she had used to dry the dishes.

"Martha, music! Come! This instant. You must play the piano for me!"

Brigida propelled the protesting, laughing little woman along the hall to the ballroom and settled her on the claw-footed piano stool, then stood on a chair to light the candles in the crystal chandelier at the room's center. She took up a table organ, pumping it with one hand, running its keyboard with the other, while Martha, giggling, did scales on the piano. The room was filled with discordant notes that floated through the house. Their breath hung in white puffs in the frigid air of the unheated room, their fingers were clumsy and stiff with cold but they played until the others were standing in the doorway, Elizabeth startled, Slade scowling, Levi impassive, as always.

"That piano is a Gibson and Davis, in a Duncan and Phyfe case, the best ever made. I have only the best things. Come now Brigida, I want to show you something," Elizabeth said, drawing the girl away from the others.

"I've been collecting silver and pewter and other things, as well, since I first came here with Jarred, and one day, not too far off, it will all be yours, my dear, yours and your children's. You must care for these things properly, when I'm no longer here."

"But why are you talking this way, Elizabeth? You're a young woman still, Mother's age, and she would not yet have been . . ."

Elizabeth was unlocking a door at the end of the center hall.

"I'm an old woman, dear, and not at all well. My life is mostly behind me now. Now, I live only to see my grandchildren. They are my only future, those innocent angels you will give my son."

The two women entered the banquet room. Brigida lit an oil lamp while Elizabeth unlocked a massive sideboard and began to caress the objects within it.

"This is a Revere you see, dear, the pellet mark on the bottom shows it." Elizabeth displayed an elegant silver pitcher with a bulbous body and a simple, ear-shaped handle. "The style is adapted from Liverpool pottery, do you see?"

"I don't know very much about these things. We were at sea so much and Mother . . ."

"Emma's life was too full for her to concern herself much with objects, as I did. I know, though, that she had

nice things. I shall have to educate you now, my dear."
Elizabeth took another key from her pocket. "I will show
you a true treasure that I acquired only in the past year
from Tiffany. The chasing is all hand done. Some silver,
these days, is not. Remember that." She lifted the lid of a
large chest that contained a set of flatware elaborately
scrolled in a shell motif of great intricacy. "The place
settings are seventeen pieces each, my dear. There is
service here for twelve. It makes quite a collection, but if
you will offer seventeen or eighteen courses, as you
should, it is the only way." Elizabeth was intense and
very engrossed.

"This is something very, very special, dear," the older
woman went on, unlocking a smaller case. In it, in the
same pattern as the full service, were several complete
silver settings perfectly miniaturized. "For the children," Elizabeth sighed. "The food pusher," she smiled,
handing Brigida a little hoelike implement. "To help the
mites get food on the fork, you see. But whatever is
wrong, dear? You aren't listening at all."

Brigida sat at the dining table, toying with the
diminutive hoe, a troubled expression on her face.

"I don't know anything about babies, Elizabeth.
What if I'm not good at it?"

"But you won't have to be." Elizabeth was amused at
what she thought a ridiculous question. "You will have a
nursemaid like everyone else of your station who
will . . . oh, dear, that's not what is disturbing you, is it?
Now, Brigida, we all know that decent women are not
troubled by . . . passionate feelings as men habitually
are. I know Slade will respect the purity of your nature,

my dear. He'll not inconvenience you any more than necessary."

"If he doesn't 'inconvenience' me, Elizabeth, what will he do?"

"Brothel women, degraded as they are, serve us very well, drawing off what could be very destructive energy."

"Are they so different than we, those women?" Brigida tried to hide a discomfort that Elizabeth took for modesty.

"They are of a lower order, Brigida. They are less moral than we, more . . . animal, but they are a necessary evil."

"But what if a respectable woman—you or I—had such cravings?"

"My dear, well-brought-up young ladies are carefully sheltered and shielded from anything that might stimulate them that way, but if a perfectly normal, respectable girl develops . . . needs, medical surgery can cure an overly passionate nature. Brigida, my dear, you are upset by such talk. I think the subject is too delicate for you, we shall not pursue it further now. Come, I will show you the other rooms and more of my treasures."

Elizabeth led Brigida on a tour of parlors and sitting rooms, sewing rooms and bed chambers, pulling open drapes and curtains as they went, flinging shutters wide, letting light fall where it hadn't in years, then sealing the rooms again behind them to shut out the cold. Bundled in cloaks and scarves and gloves, they wandered from room to room, passing the winter afternoon.

"I've collected clocks too, you see," Elizabeth said proudly at the entrance to a small sitting room off the library. "Mostly American cases with movements from

England, only the best, the best. Now, one thing more, my dear. This way."

The conservatory was off the kitchen, and the fragrance, when Elizabeth unlatched the door, almost made Brigida giddy with delight. "Roses! Oh, Elizabeth! Look at the roses," she sighed, inhaling deeply. "They are my very favorite."

"I know, your mother wrote that to me. They are my favorites, too. I do worry about them in this weather, even in the glasshouse. Now, you must not tell Martha I brought you here. It is another of her bad omens, roses blooming in January, so don't breathe a word."

"When did you . . . how long have you been cultivating them?" Brigida asked, wandering the fragrant narrow pathways.

"I was in London one July. A friend took me to the first National Rose Show there. The British are mad for roses, you know, and so have I been ever since. In front of you, dear, is perhaps the most beautiful rose in the world, the Madame Hardy, pure white and exquisite, you agree, do you not? Near her is Robert le Diable. He does look like a devil, all purple and violet and splashed with scarlet. I prefer the older roses, large and straggling on their untidy bushes, their scent unequaled, all mixed with ramblers and wild roses I've brought into the garden for color the summer long. The glasshouse is here for the tea-scented roses and the Noisettes, mostly. There's a little delicacy there, you know. I could spend my life here, could you?"

Looking at Elizabeth, Brigida saw her for the first time happy.

"Yes, Elizabeth, I think I could too," she smiled, "but

we've both other affairs to tend to, haven't we?"

"Not both, my dear," Elizabeth sighed, "only you."

The day darkened early as snow continued falling. Lamps were lit, drapes and shutters in the few open rooms were drawn against the elements. Brigida read aloud to Elizabeth in the library.

Slade, half listening, puffed a cigar and went often to glare out into the flying snow.

"Are you always so restless," Brigida asked him later, "or is the weather keeping you from something of particular importance?"

The very air about him seemed charged by his restlessness. They were alone after supper, the others having retired early, and Brigida had followed Slade to his study. Beneath the baluster of narrow, turning back stairs, a low door led into a room that appeared almost unchanged since colonial days but for a comfortable horsehair settee and woven Indian hangings on the walls. There were a plain table with several stools and a combination bookcase and pigeon-holed accounts desk of pine. The low ceiling was heavily beamed, the floor was oak.

"Sherry?" Slade asked.

"You didn't answer my question," Brigida said, nodding. "Are you always so disquieted?"

"I'm not at ease here."

"Are you anywhere, or is it that you're more attuned to the amenities of city life? Would a game distract you?"

An hour later Slade sat back, regarding Brigida with

skeptical interest. "Chess is not a woman's game, but you do respectably well at it," he said.

"I had a good teacher, a very patient man, a writer who came courting me in San Francisco. You're not too bad at chess, either," she answered matter-of-factly, stretching, her hands laced behind her head. "Perhaps next time your game won't be quite so flawless. Shall we do it again, Captain?"

"I've other inclinations." Slade's darkening blue eyes traveled from her laughing face to high breasts thrust temptingly forward. "You won't win against me, goddess, you know that."

"Perhaps not at chess," she said pointedly. "Do you keep the household accounts in here? I could look after them for you, if you'd like." She stood and walked to the desk.

"The manor accounts are minimal. My other affairs take considerable time and manipulation and . . . Brigida, do you see the letter on top there, addressed to B. Rand, Esquire, the San Francisco lawyers who settled your father's estate? I'm having your affairs looked into, to be sure all was handled properly. Knowing your father, it doesn't seem right that he'd not made some provision for you; he wasn't a man for debt, that I knew of."

"And of course, what is mine is now yours, Captain Hawkes, isn't that your purpose in this inquiry? You wish to be certain you've not been cheated of anything due you?" Brigida turned on Slade heatedly, reading from the letter in her hand. "'Inexperienced girl, who perhaps, didn't understand . . .' how can you infer I was so foolish as to lose everything? Why, perhaps I didn't really have to seek refuge here at all or rely on your charity."

She tore the offending sheet in two and crossed the room to fling the pieces into the fire, when Slade swung her about and lifted her quivering chin, forcing her to look up into his hard eyes.

"I don't need what's yours, Brigida, do I?" When she didn't answer and tried to pull away, his grip tightened and he shook her. "Look at me and answer."

"No," she admitted, her eyes still averted from his.

"You're angry because I've discovered something you've worried over yourself, isn't that so? Isn't it?"

"Yes," she snapped. "Let me go."

"There are some things you will learn to let me deal with, understand?

Her beautiful eyes held his. "Yes, you are right. I'm sorry," she said. The tigress became gentle as a kitten, her surprising smile so dazzling that Slade went silent. Then he leaned and kissed her, crushing the softness of her against him.

Quickly he led her, almost pulled her after him, through the silent sleeping house, as he snuffed the lights, secured doors and windows against the wind, built up the kitchen fire to hold off the bitter cold.

The intensity and seeming completeness of her surrender to him had been in his thoughts through the slow, silent day, and the memory of it drove him now to test her again, to press her, to take her farther. He needed to know if her rare generosity was as artless as it had seemed or part of her devious schemings.

He locked the door of her room behind them and, in his fierce impatience, ripped the buttons from Brigida's gown, his hands gliding over her until she stood in all her profligate, perfect naked beauty. He extracted the pins that restrained the wild glory of her hair, letting it flow about her face and shoulders. Firelight burnished her ivory skin to palest rose, and she saw his eyes widen with pleasure, as they had each time he viewed her. He saw her lips part with readiness, heard again her faint intake of breath as they moved toward each other.

"What will you teach me this time, Captain?" she asked in a low, tremulous voice. There was a faint pretty flush under her eyes. She turned away and felt his looming muscled strength behind her. His breath was hot at her ear, his hands moving over her supple body, which followed the curve of his. As she swayed back, the firm swell of him began searching, pressing in a way she had never expected, and she twisted to face him, a trace of fear in her eyes even as her distracting lips parted and her arms reached out. He took her hand, guiding it down to close her fingers about him, and she felt the throb, the rigid hardness beneath petal-smooth skin.

"Now you do know what you want?" he said softly.

When she lay spread beneath him, he came into her quickly, and when he turned, she held him wrapped deep and tight so that she became the one moving above, her small, hard nipples brushing his chest, and she was smiling down at him, nearly laughing with the surprise and delight of it. Her undisguised pleasure, her complete unpredictability sweetened their passion and almost made Slade smile. She leaned to kiss his mouth again and again, keeping him deep as she rode. His hands on her flanks directed and moved her, then went to her shoulders, lifting, forcing her up until she was leaning backward. He brushed her raised breasts lightly, and then his hand went between their thrusting bodies and her dark, shining eyes went darker and softer and warmer.

"How does it happen you're such a skilled instructor?" Brigida was curled against Slade's long back, her lips often brushing his shoulder, her hand playing along his arm.

"I do nothing at which I don't excel," he answered, only half teasing. He rolled, trapping her arm beneath him, sliding a leg between hers.

"Yes, but how is it you're so . . . I've heard—" she gave special inflection to the word, teasing in turn—"I've heard other men are not all as . . . generous. Or as knowing." She tried to extract her arm, but he didn't move.

"I've been with some of the best courtesans in the world. They're good teachers themselves, when they take an interest."

"Best?" Brigida frowned. "What do you mean, 'best'?"

"Ladies of notorious beauty, renowned for certain of their special skills. Kings have been known to crawl for the favors of some."

"And is that what you're teaching me to be?" Brigida finally pulled her arm free and leaned on an elbow, looking down at his face very seriously.

"You?" he laughed. "You've only begun, my lewd little schoolgirl. We'll just see how far you want to go, and how long I'll want to be bothered instructing you." He met her steady stare and saw her flinch at his words. "I'm just trying to relieve the appalling dullness of this place, Brigida, by teaching you to please me a little."

"But what if I use elsewhere what I learn from you? Or worse, use what you teach to have you crawling at my feet like those kings you mention? Or what if I don't want to be bothered, first, what then?"

That quick anger was in his face, and he moved with the fatal swiftness of a plummeting hawk, pinning her down, locking her wrists above her head, and Brigida went rigid and silent under the cutting barrage of his words delivered in a low voice, cold and quick as a knife thrust.

"You'll never tire of me, you teasing little witch. Before I've done, I'll have you besotted with lust. I'll have you following me about like a damned spaniel; the more you're punished the more you'll wag your pretty little tail and beg. I know what a natural harlot you are, I know your appetites. When you gave that away, you gave me all the advantage. I also know that when I'm not here with you, you'll spend all your nights and your days in a wet, misty haze of indecent craving. You'll direct the servants, visit with dear Mother, walk the shore, sew at the fire—all in a hidden agony of heat until I choose to come back here and serve your need."

He had risen and put on a silk robe that clung to his wide shoulders and small hips.

"You'd best keep your eyes open all the time, else

you'll never know whose child you might be rearing."
Brigida reclined, smiling strangely, knowing what he said
was true, and hating him for saying it.

"There'll be no confusion of paternity here, witch, no
other lovers. If you ever threaten that again, I'll beat
you."

Brigida kept a growing black rage hidden beneath her
now coldly exquisite exterior as Slade looked hard at her
for a moment before quitting the room.

Slade rode the stallion Blackhawk away from Silver
Hill before dawn.

The air was cold. The dampness coming up off the bay
chilled him to the bone. When he passed the sleeping
manor house, he hesitated to look up at Brigida's
windows, knowing she was there for him—soft and
enticing beneath warm quilts. If she had materialized on
the terrace at that moment, with her gold-flecked eyes
and seductive smile, he might not have gone. For a while.
As it was, he turned his collar up against the cold and put
his mount into a canter, leaving Silver Hill behind. But
during his long, solitary ride, his thoughts remained
there, images of Brigida haunting his imagination—dark
eyes and glimmering smile in the delicate, beautiful face,
throaty, soft voice teasing, small white teeth, like a
child's, catching her lower lip as she bent concentrating
intently over chessboard or card table. Most of all it was
her body he thought of, so unchildlike in its ripe perfection, glowing in firelight like warm ivory, and the feel of
her when she was ready and eager in his arms. And every-

where she was . . . the faint scent of her rose perfume.

Something nagged at Slade as he rode, something vague and unsettling preyed on his mind. At first he thought it was the threats she'd made, and jealously curled in him like a viper. But he knew almost at once that it wasn't that, wasn't anything so simple and transparent as her angry-child's chatter of chilly lust and lovers, as if he'd give a tinker's damn about it, or pay her any mind at all if it weren't for Elizabeth's blasted heirs.

And his own, he had to admit after a time. He'd not have some other man's ill-begotten brat inherit what he'd made, to say nothing of Silver Hill, and his own father's grudging legacy.

Slade came to the place on the high road where they'd met that first day such a short time ago, and he slowed the stallion, hardly realizing he did it. He remembered sunlight blazing in Brigida's hair—the fire goddess aflame. Well, Levi would have to be the one to watch her. He'd be damned if he'd hover like some nervous cuckold now, or wonder later whose eyes were staring back at him from his own sons' faces.

But there was something more, too, something he hadn't quite got hold of, that kept Brigida in his thoughts through the long, chilly day as he rode, his concentration intense and complete. By the time he was narrowing his eyes against the early cold winter sunset, he knew, knew she had already deceived him, had already spun the first silken strands of her tangling web by giving in, giving over so fast and so easy, by seeming to offer him all there was to have. Women like her . . . treacherous, submerging themselves in a lover completely, bending softly, ready to give up everything they were before, everything else they ever dreamed of being, to make a man feel like a god, an irresistible living god. Slade laughed, then leaned to pat the stallion's neck as the animal, startled, danced. "And what do they ask in return for bestowing this . . . this immortality?" Slade asked aloud. "Only your life." Your life and love and passion, exclusively and forever. And unless you're very quick, very sharp, you never discover she's given only the most insignificant part of herself, just a body so soft and willing, so beautiful, it can haunt a man's dreams forever after. And all the while she's kept free, kept her spirit, her . . . heart, untouched behind the locked gates of her scheming mind. It would take infinite patience and cunning, over time, to breach those gates.

I'll have it all, damn her, all, whatever it takes, Slade promised himself, putting the stallion into a full-out gallop, the silver wolfhound loping along beside them.

"It's of no moment to me, Slade, is it? You'll leave her there in the country, you'll spend your time in town as usual." Lydia Worsley had taken the news of Slade's marriage with complete equanimity, total unruffled calm. The two had dined together at the graciously appointed Worsley townhouse on Fifth Avenue. Dinner had been superbly prepared by Lydia's chef, and afterward she had rung for the butler to bring coffee and cigars to the drawing room.

"Your new child bride," Lydia went on as they waited, "unlike the last, may be capable of giving you the house-

138

ful of whelps you and your mother want. I've other things to offer to you, if not to your mama."

Slade made no reply. He had been silent through dinner, and now he scowled into the fire, his habit when preoccupied.

"What is it concerns you?" Lydia persisted. "You've done well in your business dealings today, I know, and we are making progress after all this time in our own special project. You've been sumptuously dined and wined, and here am I ready to do your bidding. Some women would take affront, Slade, to be so ignored." She awaited his response standing at the drawing room windows, which overlooked a steady parade of carriages moving along the gaslighted avenue below. She was a tall, stately woman, no innocent child, with pale skin and calculating slate-gray eyes. There was a natural hauteur of expression and gesture about her as she stood, a beauty still, exquisitely groomed, with not a single dark hair out of place. She traced a jeweled hand with long lacquered nails over a perfect chignon. "Would you prefer to go out for a while, Slade, before we retire? You've remained too long in the country, that is what ails you. It's too dull and stultifying for you there."

"You're right, the damn storm caught me and . . . I'm going right back, Lydia," Slade said, never looking up from the fire at the fastidious, polished woman who showed no sign of impatience or temperament. His mind was flooded with the golden vision of the unadorned beauty of Brigida that was dancing in the firelight before him. "Tiger eyes," he was thinking, awaiting Lydia's answer with mild interest, "tiger eyes like gemstones, dark and flecked with gold."

"Can't you stay the night at least?" Lydia asked. "I'll arrange a party for you, the sort you like. You know how pleased Angelique always is to be . . . to be with you. Did I tell you I've taken on her brother Raoul as butler? He's wonderfully skilled and remarkably well endowed. You'll enjoy seeing them together, brother and sister, and with a friend of theirs from the same town in France— Veronique. She's seeking employment, by the way. I thought you might need a new parlor maid or even a scullery girl at Washington Square? She's more than accommodating, I promise you. No? I see in your face your answer is no, for tonight at least. Well, go then. Get her out of your system, like all your other decorative, delicate little blondes. You, of course, know, dearest, that with physical passion, possession is nothing— enjoyment is all. She is yours to enjoy at whim, and you will keep her guessing, if I know you, have her fearful and restless and longing for you. It won't take much to have her waiting like a slave. Then, she'll simply bore you, like all the others. When you're ready, when you're thoroughly tired of her, come back, bring her to the city with you. I'll arrange something very special for your little bride. Better yet, bring her now. You can always send her away if she interferes."

"I want no confusions of paternity, Lydia, as I already told her . . . I left Levi at Silver Hill to . . . watch her."

"Darling, wouldn't you enjoy seeing her with Angelique? Angelique is so slow and thorough she will know just how to handle your little innocent, and Raoul can assist, shall we say, without actually causing any confusion at all, you know that. We'll invite Levi, as always, and whomever else you like. Billy? Pretty, is she?" Lydia asked, not really expecting an answer. "Raoul," she commanded the butler, "Captain Hawkes is leaving. Get his coat. And order up the carriage for me, as well."

"She is very pretty, and you are right, as usual." Slade kissed Lydia's lips quickly, remembering the fragrance of windblown summer roses. "I'll soon be ready to bring her to New York, to one of your events. You'll enjoy her. I'll take my leave now."

Raoul, a lithe young man with dark, smooth hair, held Slade's greatcoat ready, evaluating his mistress's special guest with curious, shrewd dark eyes.

"May I drive you somewhere?" Lydia asked Slade. "I'm off to the theater. An evening alone here would be maddening." She exchanged quick glances with the young butler, who half bowed, holding the front door wide.

"I'll walk. I've got to see Billy McGlory. He has some information for us, I think."

"Take care, Slade, and if anything comes of McGlory, which I doubt, he's such a braggart, you will let me know? She extended a long gloved hand from the carriage window after Slade helped her in. The bobtailed hackneys pawed nervously and jingled silver harnesses.

"Of course," Slade said impatiently, turning up his collar. Then he smiled. "Don't I always tell you everything, Lydia?"

Nine

"It was a very special time, these past days, Slade will soon be back, he will not stay long away from you." Elizabeth was already in the breakfast room when Brigida came down.

"You're so early, Elizabeth," Brigida said, as she picked at the plate Martha had set before her. "Do you mind if I open the draperies?"

"Just as you like, my dear. Brigida? Brigida, I . . . I want to go with you today, to the harbor, but I haven't dressed in so long, or done my hair or . . ." The woman's hand shook as she raised her cup. "Perhaps I shouldn't. The doctors, after all, say . . ."

"I'll help you, Elizabeth," Brigida said quietly. "Let me? We can manage a short outing together, I know we can."

"Yes, an outing. We shall go to the harbor today, to Ann. It's been years since I left Silver Hill, but with you. . . ."

From the chaos in Elizabeth's armoire, Brigida selected a dark silk that Martha hurriedly pressed.

Despite Elizabeth's frequent protestations, Brigida did up her gray hair in a flattering sweep, chose a simple cameo and bracelet from the jewel case, found old but serviceable kid gloves at the bottom of a drawer. The nearer the moment of departure grew, the more uneasy Elizabeth became, until, pale and shaking, she stepped over the threshold of the manor to await Levi and the carriage. Shivering in her warm cloak and fur-lined boots, she smiled at Brigida, who left her long enough to dash upstairs for her own things after racing from one room to another opening shutters and draperies until the whole house was flooded with sunlight. Returning to the portico, she noticed a pair of wintering cardinals sitting on a near branch, the male burning bright as fire against a last clinging patch of snow, even his drab mate almost showy in her white setting. Brigida went off to the pantry, gathered a handful of dried corn and scattered it about just before leaving for town.

"Tea or brandy, ladies? This way please." Ann Overton beckoned, leading Elizabeth and Brigida into the front parlor of her tiny cottage. A discreet sign in front read *Stitcher*. She had met them at the white trellised gate when Levi brought the brougham to a halt on the quiet, narrow street of small, neat houses with postage-stamp gardens and picket fences.

"Neither, thank you, Ann. We're to lunch, when we're done here, at the inn. Mrs. Hawkes has broken her retreat," Brigida glanced at Elizabeth, "at least for today. We intend to celebrate. Join us and make a party of it?"

The dressmaker rolled her world-weary eyes skyward. "Happy as I am and amazed as I am to see Elizabeth, I'm not at leisure, as you ladies are, to fritter away my days and hard-earned dollars." A tentative smile touched her lips. "Thank you for asking."

"Oh, Ann, don't pretend poverty with me," Elizabeth said, a touch irritably, removing her gloves. "Even you could go to lunch if you chose to. No, no, it's pure avarice and ambition that enslave you, that's all. Admit to it."

They had relinquished their cloaks and Brigida was examining the sewing machine that occupied an exalted place in the room under the front window.

"Elizabeth, my dear friend," Ann Overton half laughed, "I am enslaved to nothing and to no one. I will be rich by my own efforts and have more freedom than you, or our little Brigida, ever will. You admit to that. Besides," she went on, shaking out a crimson silk for Brigida to slip into, "what if I didn't finish your lovely daughter-in-law's collection in timely fashion? I've no wish to rouse her husband's famous temper. Come, into this, please, Mrs. Hawkes, so I can get to the final finishing and be done in a week's time. The lingerie you may take with you today."

Brigida changed from one costume to the next, Ann sipped a brandy and nipped and tucked and pinned deftly, while Elizabeth watched with an appreciative eye, and when the fitting was completed, the dressmaker asked for her impressions.

"Magnificent, quite the best work I've ever seen from your hand, and Brigida does the collection full justice," Elizabeth pronounced.

"Elizabeth has always worn my things better than anyone, until now," Ann explained with a nod of her head to Brigida. "She has got an artist's sense of color and style, Elizabeth has, you'll see. I'm running up several new things for her also. Tell me how you managed to shake her free of Silver Hill."

"Actually, she does me a great kindness. I was needing company and . . ."

"He's gone already," Ann said knowingly. "You mustn't fret. It's just his way. He'll not change." Elizabeth scowled at the seamstress, and Brigida smiled with effort as they took their leave of her. "Are you up to walking, Elizabeth? It's so pretty and crisp, and I'd like to see more of the village. It reminds me of other whaling towns I was fond of."

"Perhaps so, dear, the inn is close," Elizabeth answered, waving the carriage off and taking Brigida's arm. Drays and wagons loaded with barrels of oil rumbled up from the docks over narrow, cobbled ways. "Now, you must not listen to the things Ann says, you must not take her too seriously. I do dearly love her, but if anyone can always find the most discouraging word to offer, it is she. Her marriage was brief and unfortunate, Overton was a weakling and a drunk, and she's not had a good word to say for any man since. Except Slade, of course. Look! That is Philip Carpenter. He was such a lank lad, and now see, quite the young man, I'd say, as his father was."

They had just turned the corner into a busy thorough-fare and the excited young man was hurrying toward them, waving wildly and calling.

"Ladies, what a delight to find you here!" he said

breathlessly, raising his hat. They stood still on the busy street in the midst of the town's activity flowing past them.

"I will be at Squire's farm near you, with my friend Mr. Stancel, on Wednesday next. We're purchasing a bull, a Holstein, actually, for Father, and we planned to stop at Silver Hill, Elizabeth, to see how your charming house guest is getting on. We three met on the Boston Ferry, did she tell you? Will you be at home to us?"

"When have you ever been turned away from Silver Hill, Philip Carpenter? I've only known him since he was born," Elizabeth told Brigida. "Brigida and I will be delighted to receive you. Slade is away. And how is all your family, Phil?"

"Never better. But you, Elizabeth! I'd heard you were ill, incapacitated, and here you are looking perfectly lovely. I must tell Father."

Abruptly, Elizabeth extended her hand. "Day after tomorrow, Philip, for late supper."

"See you then, in a few days, Miss Lydon," he nodded, smoothing his full mustache, beaming at Brigida happily.

Brigida spent most of the following day with Sarah Hand. She walked early along the beach to the cottage and they began on Slade's quilt. Old John would build another frame for Brigida to use and, until it was done, she would do templates and then appliqués on a small embroidery frame. She began with a wreath of red and yellow flowers, and they talked and worked the day away so happily that Brigida didn't think of the time until the sky began to darken and Old John and Johnny came in from a day's ice fishing on a nearby pond. They stood at the fire huffing and stamping and blowing on their cold fingers and, after he was well warmed, Johnny shyly offered to walk Brigida home along the beach to Silver Hill. Though barely a word was spoken all the way, she was comfortable with this boy who seemed to her as much a part of the salty bay world as the mallards flying into the setting sun, as the slender reeds of the marsh.

Their eyes were bright and their cheeks were glowing red with cold when they reached the manor. Brigida sent Johnny to the kitchen for warmth and refreshment and when she came down for dinner, considerably later, she found the boy still visiting with Martha, Mary, and Nan.

Next day, Brigida went again to the Hands', but she returned early, in midafternoon, and went up to look for Elizabeth. The bedroom, to Brigida's surprise, was orderly and neat as a pin—but deserted. She called out several times, hearing only faint answers until she wandered along the corridor toward the older part of the house. She descended a few steps to a back hall, then climbed a half flight to the third floor, emerging into a large, low-ceilinged room that spanned the old wing. A skylight and windows decanted northern brightness into the room, illuminating paintings, sketches, etchings, drypoints, and lithographs—hundreds of them hanging on every inch of the walls from floor to ceiling, standing four or five deep, resting against tables and chairs. The subject of every work was exactly the same, one particular view of the bay and sky, the beach and trees fronting the manor house.

"I used to work above, in the cupola, where the vantage is best. This was my gallery before I . . . gave up. Elizabeth stood in the center of the room smocked in unbleached cotton, arms folded across her chest. "Well?"

Brigida pivoted slowly, looking at pictures of wind-raked reeds, tawny maize and marsh hay, pale against pale fall skies. In some of the paintings, the edges of color and form stood out vividly in distinct long lines—sky and water boldly blue, sand white. In other of the paintings the lush colors of spring and summer were blurred and moisture-laden. Those done in the clear winter light were stark with the brown lawn in front of the house and the black tree trunks ominous against glinting cold winter skies.

"They're extraordinary," Brigida said, walking slowly about the room as Elizabeth watched her.

"This, Brigida, is where many of my years have gone."

"Who's seen them? Has Slade?"

"Ann, and Del Carpenter, long ago. That's Philip's father. He wanted to take several to a dealer in New York once but I never wanted to part with even one." Elizabeth laughed.

"You must show them. You've done things with light that are extraordinary, and they're too beautiful to keep hidden, Elizabeth."

"I think not. They're only landscapes, after all, and very private ones, full of things I felt and thought about alone all those venomous years in this place. The rim of the bay was the edge of my universe, and the wind played such sad tunes in the pines." Her blue eyes were wide and distant, and she seemed to float, slowly turning in the middle of the airy room.

"Now, I want to start again, do a portrait," Elizabeth said, "of you and Slade. I'll sketch in the figures first, do a few studies. The sittings could be few."

"Do you think Slade could sit at all? He's . . . it would be like asking a wild lion to pose for a picture."

"He'd do it for you, Brigida." Elizabeth pulled off her smock and folded it over the back of a chair.

"You're in error if you think some argument of mine would move him," Brigida said with a little laugh. "He's already left me for . . . other interests."

"No, you are the one in error, my dear," Elizabeth said kindly, with a sadness in her eyes, "you are in error . . . to give up, to think you are of little moment in my son's life. That is the illusion I had about his father, when he went away to sea, and my weakness destroyed any happiness we could have found together."

"I never give up, Elizabeth," Brigida said, startled.

"I hope not, I hope not," Elizabeth sighed, and then she began to fuss nervously at her hair. "It is time to dress. Our guests will be here quite soon now."

Philip Carpenter and Hollis Stancel reached Silver Hill at dusk and were shown into the library by Levi, who left them a tray, glasses, and a decanter of bourbon. "Mrs. Hawkes will be down soon," he said.

"Fine, fine Levi . . . and Miss Lydon?" Philip asked.

Levi regarded him silently, nodded and withdrew, leaving the two men alone.

"Arrogant brute," Hollis Stancel commented, browsing the library shelves. He stooped, squinting pale eyes to read the titles on the bindings before him.

Philip splashed bourbon into two glasses. "Drink?" he offered his friend, who had moved to the windows and stood, thin and a little round-shouldered, looking out at a cold winter sunset.

"Of course, a drink. Where does he come from?"

"Levi? He's Indian, Long Island Shinnecock. He sailed for years with Jarred Hawkes, Slade's father, until he was killed," Philip said, pacing the room and casting impatient glances toward the door.

"And where is the notorious Captain Hawkes, do you think?" Hollis asked, fondling his watch fob. "Does he often travel without his man?"

"No, not as a matter of course, not usually. Usually Slade takes Levi to the city with him to pull him out of the Greene Street dives and bawdy houses he favors when he's had a few too many. He needs Levi to put him to bed. Bran can't do that, you know." Philip shook his head.

"Bran?"

"The dog, the wolfhound. Slade always has the monster at his side. Best protection in the world."

"Has the good captain always been so wild?" Hollis asked, paging through a copy of *Horseman's Friend*.

"Worse since his wife died. Bonnie. I hardly knew her," Philip answered thoughtfully.

Hollis downed his drink in one swallow and poured himself another.

"He was so loving and devoted a husband, was he, that he was crushed by her death?" Hollis asked in an ironical manner.

"I suppose, Hollis." Philip studied his companion thoughtfully. "What's it to you that you should scoff so?"

"Me? I'm curious, is all. I've heard so much about the man—his brilliance, his fortune, his poor, mad wife— I'm just curious about my absent host, that's understandable, isn't it?"

"How'd you know Bonnie was mad?" Philip demanded as the library doors swung open.

"Mrs. Hawkes," Levi Philips announced almost formally as Brigida swept into the room in a rustle of mist-green silk, her golden hair swept up softly, and the faint scent of roses was delicate in the air. She was all sparkling smiles, extending her hand first to Philip and then to Hollis as the two stood transfixed and speechless.

"Well, why won't one of you, at least, say something and not stare at me so oddly? Have I left buttons undone?" She glanced down at her décolletage, which revealed just a hint of the soft swells rising above the modest neckline.

"But y'all are not Miz Hawkes," Hollis said, falling into a thick drawl.

"But I am, surely. What is the matter with you both?" Brigida asked. "Didn't you know?"

"Brigida, we hadn't an idea you'd be marrying the man," Philip said, sinking into the couch.

"Your husband does acquire the most exquisite creatures, I've heard, Miz Hawkes. His blooded Arabians and Virginia breds are among the finest horses in the country, his huntin' dogs are superbly bred and trained."

Now he's added another expensive bit of livestock to his holdings, it would appear." Hollis Stancel made a formal half bow to Brigida.

"Mr. Stancel!" she gasped, her color rising.

Philip sighed. "Hollis expresses himself a bit harshly, but a scorned suitor must be forgiven certain indiscretions in the face of sad disappointment. Brigida, why? Could you . . . you couldn't have fallen in love with him overnight." Philip's look was pained.

"No . . . I think I've always been," Brigida stated simply, turning toward the fire as the mantel clock counted six.

"Why didn't you say, on the ferry, you came to marry him, and not lead us both to hope? Oh, damn!" Philip exploded.

"Mr. Carpenter, whatever is the matter with you? Good evening, gentlemen." Elizabeth Hawkes entered the library unannounced, leaning on Levi's arm.

"You've surely kept it a secret, Elizabeth, that Slade has married again and to the most enchanting lady in the entire world. I had designs upon her myself until moments ago, and so did Hollis. It's not fair, you know," Philip bantered, regaining his composure.

"This is Mr. Stancel?" Elizabeth asked, pressing Philip's hand in passing. "You seem somehow familiar, young man. Where is your home? Do sit gentlemen, please."

"It was in Virginia, ma'am," Hollis answered. "I've never before been in this particular part of the world. It's unlikely we've been acquainted unless you've been South?" He smiled, nervous fingers busy at his watch fob. "I've heard a good deal about you, ma'am. From Phil. And about your son. I look forward to the pleasure of meetin' him, too, before I quit the neighborhood."

"From Virginia?" Elizabeth echoed distractedly. Then she turned to Brigida. "Tell Martha please, dear, we shall sit down directly the gentlemen have finished drinking."

"Elizabeth?" Philip hesitated. "My father's to stop here."

"Oh? Shall we wait on his arrival, then? When is he due?" Elizabeth secured a lace handkerchief tucked into the narrow sleeve cuff of her dark silk dress and a faint color touched her cheek before she paled noticeably.

"Now. Do you mind?"

"And if I did?" she said softly, in a low voice, her blue eyes a little sad. A silence settled over the gathering, until Brigida began to pace from window to hearth and back again, her silks rustling furiously.

"I'd not describe this as a very gay company," she announced finally. "Philip, shall I tell you more about San Francisco? When will you go?"

"It's definite. We'll take a Pullman Palace across the country in the early fall. We saw a lantern slide show while we were in New York, pictures of the West. It's . . . well, wild, free, magnificent beyond description. And we saw paintings, Elizabeth, by a landscaper, Bierstadt, who makes the Sierra Nevada mountains look as if God had walked through there and graced the earth at every step!"

"Do you know what Phil will travel with?" Stancel asked. "Three hundred pounds of equipment, and not one ounce less—camera and lenses, tripods, glass plates, tubes, funnels, trunks . . . more. He'll require his own Pullman Palace."

"I've talked to a chap name of John Powell who's going down the Colorado River taking photographs. I might join up with him."

"It sounds glorious, Philip!" Brigida's eyes were bright. "I shall ask you to look up someone for me if you go to San Francisco. Will that be all right?"

"There's nothing I'd deny you Brigida, ever, even though you've jilted me so cruelly," Philip teased. "Elizabeth, if I may, I'd like to bring my camera here to Silver Hill. On a wagon I've had made, with a dark tent. I'm doing portraits now."

"I had decided just today to paint my first portrait, one of Slade and Brigida," Elizabeth answered. "Now there'll be no need."

"But it isn't at all the same," Brigida interjected. "It is true that the likeness of a photograph may be exact, but the feeling is not the same. Do you agree, Hollis?"

He had wandered off to the window and stood with his back to the room. He turned, and Brigida caught a look of scorn, a furtiveness in his eyes that disturbed her. It vanished in seconds.

"I can't say. Make a comparison," he replied.

"Elizabeth, what do you think?" Brigida smiled.

"Philip's work will take no time and mine . . . it could be months before . . . oh, I hear a carriage." Elizabeth looked upset.

"It must be Father," Philip said, standing, and Elizabeth stood too and moved with suppressed agitation toward the entrance hall. The fine lines at the corners of her eyes and mouth vanished into a strange smile when her expectant eyes met Brigida's. In an instant, a tale was told that needed no word of explanation.

Adelbert Carpenter had gray eyes and steely gray hair—the same shade as his neatly trimmed, small beard. He was a big, bluff, jovial man with a hearty laugh and a sunny temper. Though he was inches taller than his son, there was a striking resemblance between the two, more of manner than of form; a similar warmth radiated from both, and their gestures and inflections were almost identical.

"Del, you've the same light in your eye I so well remember." Elizabeth smiled graciously as he kissed her first on one cheek, then the other. "The years have treated you kindly. How long is it since . . ."

"Too long, Lizzy, since you stopped going about in society. But now you've a charming guest to entertain— that's brought you out of seclusion, I hear."

"Brigida Hawkes, my old friend, Del Carpenter. Brigida is not a guest, Del, she's Slade's wife," Elizabeth beamed as Mr. Carpenter searched his son's face for an instant before he wished the beautiful young bride an eternity of wedded bliss. Then he turned his full attention back to Elizabeth.

Martha had prepared a fine dinner—shepherd's pie, pear jelly, pheasant and rutabaga—that was served by Mary Edwards and a well-favored young man whom Brigida took to be her brother Robin. There was a good deal of laughter and lively conversation blended with the clink of silver and glass, and when they were done Brigida watched Elizabeth and Del leave the dining room, her hand on his arm as he guided her toward the front parlor.

"Well?" Brigida turned questioning eyes to Philip.

"I don't know," he shrugged. "It goes back before my time, but clearly it pleases them both—so why worry?"

"I'm consumed with curiosity, not worry, aren't you? How can you be so . . . so disinterested?"

"I've interests of my own," Philip answered with a sigh. "Or at least I had until you dashed my hopes."

Hollis coughed nervously. "We'd best be takin' our leave. It's late and growin' colder."

"Stay the night. I'm sure Elizabeth would be pleased. I know she will, and so will I, and then we'll not have to cut the evening short. We'll have a brandy and a good fire and a game. What would you like, chess, whist, hearts?"

"Hearts it will be. I told you I'd never deny you anything you asked of me," Philip announced as Brigida went off to speak with Elizabeth.

Later, settled at the gaming table in the library, Brigida dealt out the deck to herself and the three men, while Elizabeth, professing a disinterest in games, reclined on the sofa.

There was silence but for a log hissing on the grate, the rustle of pages turning as Elizabeth read, the snap of cards being shuffled and dealt. When Brigida totaled out the scores at the end and found she had won, she couldn't subdue her natural gaiety nor hide the spice of mischief in her eyes.

"Don't gloat so. It isn't at all ladylike. In fact, it's not ladylike for you to have won. You should know better than to do that," Philip laughed.

"You're brilliant at cards. I think she remembers

every damn deal, gentlemen," Del said approvingly. "Tell me, have you played with your husband? I think you're as good as he is, and he's among the best I've ever sat down with."

"Not yet, Mr. Carpenter, but thank you for warning me. I'll be on my guard." Brigida stretched, and the others stood, and when they had gone up to bed at the striking of the midnight hour, she and Philip were left alone. They sat at opposite ends of the long sofa, Brigida with her legs curled beneath her, and they enjoyed a sherry together as the fire faded.

"You aren't like any woman I've ever known before, Brigida. When I said before you weren't ladylike, I meant it as a compliment. You've broken my heart, you realize," Philip said, only half in jest.

Brigida shook her head, loosing a coil of gold that curled along the fine line of her cheek. "I don't believe you, really," she said, "but if it is true, I'm sorry, Phil."

"Oh, it's true enough, but there's nothing to be done about it now, is there?" Philip was watching her very closely.

"No, there isn't, there never was."

"Well . . . friends?"

"Of course." Her smile was bittersweet and very kind.

"And if you ever change your mind . . ."

"No, don't" she said, standing. "I'm awfully tired. I haven't been sleeping well. May I show you to your room, or will you remain here for a while?"

Brigida extended a hand to pull Philip up from the couch, and as he took it, Slade Hawkes came striding

158

through the french doors, Bran at his heel, bringing a gust of sharp, cold wind in with him.

"Philip. Brigida." He nodded to each of them in turn, moving with easy, long strides to the fireside. He undid his greatcoat, tossed it over a chair, and stood with arms folded across his chest, leaning against the mantel, in riding breeches and boots, the collar of his leather jacket turned up against tawny hair.

At the first glimpse of him, Brigida froze. She kept hold of Philip's hand and, unaware of what she did, clutched it tighter while Slade looked on coolly, his face stony in the fading firelight. He smiled crookedly, and his eyes, Brigida saw, were deep lazuline blue, the only visible sign about him of anger. But it was enough. With a start, she pulled her hand from Philip's as if she held a hot coal.

"Congratulations, Slade," Philip said, standing. "Your wife is an altogether lovely and amiable lady. Her freshness is enchanting and she plays a wicked game of hearts, besides. Did you know?"

"That's not the only wicked game she plays." Slade's eyes were flinty and narrowing. "You can find your own way up, can you Phil?"

"Yes, yes. I know my way about here almost as well as you do, friend. All those long-ago hide-and-seeks weren't for naught. Goodnight. Thank you, Mrs. Hawkes, for a truly splendid evening."

"Couldn't you bear to stay away?" Brigida said when Philip had gone. She walked to Slade slowly, silk rustling over satin petticoats. It was not in her nature to shrink, despite the fluttering of fear she felt. She searched his

159

face for some sign of tenderness.

"You wasted no time, did you, luring your admirer here?"

Brigida pulled the pins from her hair and shook her head, sending soft waves flowing down her back. Her eyes were teasing, her tone bantering.

"No, and we didn't expect you at all, nor did we hear you approach. Were you hoping to surprise me?"

"I went to the stable, Brigida, to put up the stallion myself. It's too late to wake the lad." He took a cigar from his jacket pocket. "If I had wanted to surprise you, goddess, be sure I would have. You're not as clever at games as you think," he said, sinking into the couch. Brigida bolted the french doors and pulled the drapery to. She came behind Slade and combed through his hair with gentle fingers, then massaged his neck and shoulders with firm hands. After a few moments he leaned back and looked up, and she bent forward to kiss his lips, her fragrant hair falling to tent their faces. He stretched up his strong arms, locking them round her narrow waist, and effortlessly he pulled her over onto the sofa in a swirl of silk and satin and curls and lace, her burbling seductive laughter rising, and his mouth was hard on her lips before she could speak, her small flicking tongue meeting his as it probed and she felt sharp curls of desire twist deep and strong. His mouth moved down the length of her throat.

"If I ever find you with Philip again, he'll be sorry and so will you." Slade's voice was a menacing whisper. "Now, tell me, did you think about me when I was gone?" he asked, pulling back to see her face and her tiger eyes, like gemstones dark and gold, looking up at him sparkling, her full, sweet mouth open, pointy little tongue playing quickly over parted lips.

"I did not," she answered, and her voice quavered almost imperceptibly.

"You're lying," Slade said roughly. "Tell me what you thought when I was away."

"Nothing at all, about you," she whispered, her cheeks going scarlet.

"So that's what you thought about, is it, goddess? Well, then get up to bed or I'll have you right here," he said huskily as he stood locking her against him, his hands moving until she captured one in her own and led him toward the hall.

The sound of the key turning in the bedchamber lock behind Slade was enough to set Brigida's blood throbbing. She looked away from her mirror to seek those azure eyes, smiled as they caressed her, extended graceful arms, standing with her hair newly brushed, falling like molten gold along bared ivory shoulders to her waist. Unbuttoning his shirt, Slade came to her slowly, relishing the view of her satin pantalets and camisole, anticipating the taste of her glistening lips, the delicious softness of her in his arms. Unhurriedly, his lingering eyes reading her face, he unlaced the camisole. Brigida stood with her hands at her sides until he had done, and when she lifted soft arms to encircle his neck, her velvet breasts rose against his chest.

His voice was languid, caressing. "Now, pet, you will assist me," he said.

When he sat at the dressing table bench, she bent to a

boot, breasts spilling free to his view. "Much as I delight in such a display, you'd better turn around. It's easier that way. And quicker."

And when she showed him her back a booted leg came up between her thighs. The lace-edged pantalets closely followed swelling curves as she tugged off first one leather boot and then the other.

"This prospect, goddess, is no less enticing." Slade pulled her back onto his lap and slid off her loosened camisole. He carried her to the bed, her golden hair fanning out beneath her. The pantalets came away easily in his hand, exposing all Brigida's alabaster beauty to his glowing eyes.

They were still for a fleeting moment, unmoving, each dazed by the heart-stopping beauty of the other. Then Brigida lifted her arms, inviting, beseeching, and she welcomed the warmth and weight of him, the hard, fierce power. Her body rose to his with an instinctive, wild joy as ancient as time, as primal as the wind and the swell of the sea.

When Slade slept, Brigida knelt at his side in the moonlight that washed the room. Her glance went from wide shoulders to narrow hips, and she shivered a little with a tremor of delight, remembering. Leaning to brush back a wave of hair from his brow, she touched the peak of her breast to his lips. His eyes fluttered open, and the mouth that so cruelly smiled did so almost sweetly, and his hands moved to caress all the in-curvings and swells and narrowings of her satin body poised close to him. Shadowed reflections of firelight danced about her like flickering leaves in a bower, rustling leaves in a summer breeze, and her gold-flecked eyes gleamed as from lush, shaded depths.

"Wild wood nymph you could be, Brigida, curled in some umbraed glade," he said, pulling her to him again.

"My son has got a hole in his pocket, I'm afraid; his money just runs away." Brigida heard Del Carpenter's booming voice as she came down for breakfast. "Philip is fair game for every flim-flamming, silver-tongued devil and glad-hand, gambling blatherskite in the country! He'll soon be shot of the inheritance from his mother, playing with such thieves. He won't have a cent from me if that happens. I've told him."

"Come on, Phil," Slade was saying as she entered the breakfast room, "Jayson Gould and his associate Fisk are too shrewd and crooked for a country boy like you to get involved with. They wrecked the Erie Rail Line and hurt a lot of people doing it. You should know that as well as I."

Brigida poured some coffee and filled her half-empty cup with cream.

"Morning, Mrs. Hawkes," Del smiled. All three men stood.

"Don't get up, gentlemen," she said, about to take a chair near Slade's when he abruptly pulled her to his lap and went on speaking when she started to protest.

He had caught up Brigida's dress and crinolines and, sheltered by her gracefully draping skirts, he swung his knees wide, spreading hers. She felt his hand under her, between her thighs. She was speechless.

"What about Dr. Durant? Would you go in with him, Slade?" Phil asked.

"He might just be the worst of the unsavory lot."

"Do you know about Black Friday, Brigida?" Phil asked politely, to bring her into the conversation.

"Oh, when the gold market collapsed?" she said with more apparent interest and control than she felt. "How did that . . ."

Del shook his head. "They almost toppled the whole U.S. government with that ploy, but Slade—Slade did fine, as always. Your husband's a clever lad, Brigida. He sold short at a hundred and sixty and picked up all he needed to deliver at a hundred forty-two. Slade's always right about these things, Phil. You steer clear of that bunch."

"Next it will be the railroads. What we know about that corruption is just the least bit of it, I've heard," Brigida said, neither her tone nor expression altering at all as Slade continued to play and probe, touching in a way he knew would agitate her.

"That will out too, before long, young lady," Del huffed, finishing off a platter of steak and eggs and beginning on a serving of wheat cakes. "The Army Engineers and even Grant himself, some say, are in on that one."

"Lealand Stanford and Mr. Huntington are reputed to own every judge in California," Brigida said coolly. "More coffee?" She extricated herself from Slade's grasp to refill the cups. And when she was seated again beside him, his hand traveled the inner curve of her leg. She sipped her coffee, and rested her hand on his thigh.

"Invest in Pullman—I have," Slade told Phil. "He's

honest, ambitious, a real perfectionist. His rolling stock is unequaled in quality, except for Abbott Downing coaches. He never stints on decor or service, feels Americans are willing to pay for the best. The profits come from cutting inefficiencies of manufacture. Carnegie has backed Pullman, too."

Brigida's hand was now caressing the bulge beneath it, and she smiled up at Slade, feeling him begin to stir and swell to her touch.

"Carnegie?" Del questioned between bites of a corn muffin dripping butter. "I hear he's one of those characters like you, Slade, who can always see the drift of things. Not like my son."

"I may surprise you one day, Father," Philip said quickly. "Slade," he continued, "we're going West, I told Brigida—Hollis, my friend, and I. He left early to take the bull and wagon, but you'll meet him soon. Come with us in the fall, you two, we'll make a party of it. People are rushing here from all over Europe to ride West, so surely we should go too."

"I might have business in Chicago," Slade answered, touching one of Brigida's curls down her back. "That's where Pullman's shop is. Why not go sooner?"

"Father insists I help bring in most of our harvest before we go," Phil stated irritably. "But I don't know . . . I mean farming . . . really!"

"Perhaps we could become farmers?" Brigida asked, turning a pretty, questioning look to Slade. He brought the back of his hand to her cheek.

"I'll think about it." She felt his leg against hers, and his hand, and though still outwardly cool, her eyes went soft as they met his.

"I'll send you a travel book, Brigida, a little dated, but the best still—*Beyond the Mississippi*," Phil interrupted with a self-conscious cough. "I'll send you guide books, too, about training West. They tell you what to take and all. We must be off now, Father." Phil rose from the table.

"Already? Elizabeth will be sorry to have missed you," Brigida said. "Shall I see if she . . ."

Del smiled. "Don't bother. We took our leave last evening."

Slade was close to Brigida, holding her back against him when the Carpenters left the breakfast room.

"You'd best shelter me a bit or cause some embarrassment to your guests, brazen tease. You're a natural deceiver," he whispered harshly in her ear, "the perfect thimblerigger, or is it horse trading you'd be best at? You dissemble as though you'd ice in your veins."

"Am I not to be trusted? Is that what you really think?" she giggled as they went after Del and Phil to stand waiting in the cold for the horses to be brought up from the stable.

"Your lady, Slade, is not only beautiful, but clever as well. There's an old saying—the three glories of a man are a beautiful wife, a good horse and a swift hound. You, my lad, have got them all." Del shook Slade's hand vigorously.

"If I'd known she was about to marry you, my friend, I'd have given you some keen competition. Has she told you I'm madly in love with her?" Phil said, kissing Brigida quickly before mounting up. "I almost forgot,"

166

he said, adjusting his sealskin hat and turning up the fur collar of his coat. "When shall I come with my camera? I'm going to do photographic portraits of your wife, Slade, and of you, too, if you'll hold still for a few minutes."

"No one mentioned anything. We'll send word to you, Phil, about the photographs. My plans are uncertain at the moment. Good trip home."

Del tipped his hat to Elizabeth, who waved from the drawing room window, then father and son rode off down Silver Hill drive toward the high road, and Slade turned on Brigida.

"There'll be no pictures. I told you I'd best not find you with him again. I don't share what's mine with any man, unless I choose to."

"And you'd best not threaten me," Brigida snapped, her own quick temper flaring. She turned to stalk off toward the house and grimaced when his hand closed hard around her arm. He swung her about and they stood face to face, the wind whipping about them, tossing Brigida's skirts and ruffling Slade's hair.

"I won't be responsible for what happens to you, or to him, if ever I do find you with Philip Carpenter." Slade's eyes were darkening.

"You bloody fool, you . . ."

The ferocity of Slade's look stopped Brigida's words, and she brought the back of her hand to her trembling lips as she glared up at him and stamped her small, slippered foot in frustration, a little gesture that brought a reluctant half grin to his face. "Remember," he said, propelling her indoors.

"That . . . that churl can't be civil two hours together," she thought, rushing up the stairs to get her cloak and boots. As usual at such times, Brigida sought the freedom of open sky and brisk wind and wide watery vistas to soothe her and, once dressed against the elements, she slammed out of the house to follow the curve of beach to the Hands' cottage.

At first, she moodily worked at her quilt, but after a while Sari wooed her out of her dark humor, and the two chatted happily, as usual, through the afternoon.

Before dusk, Brigida left, declining Johnny's offer of an escort home. She turned toward Silver Hill, feeling better able to face the growling lion in his den.

She increased the quickness of her long strides as the chill of evening came into the air and water lapped rushing at the land, the tide beginning to turn. The eastern horizon had already darkened and, behind her, rays of the sinking sun flamed at the edges of high-mounted clouds. It was her favorite time, beautiful as sunrise, and even more magical as inky darkness crept across the sky.

About two miles from Silver Hill she saw a horse and rider coming at full gallop along the shoreline where land and water met, hooves sending foamy droplets of spray high into the air. Though she knew at once it was Slade, for an instant she could see Poseidon thundering down upon her, powerful sea god, tamer of waves, gentler of wild horses.

The stallion passed at full gallop, then swung about and stopped. Brigida stood looking up into Slade's unreadable eyes, lightly resting her small gloved hand on

168

his knee, a tentative smile on her lips. He leaned down without a word and lifted her to sit astride the saddle facing him and pulled her close and kissed her, his open mouth hot on hers, the blaze of setting sun firing her hair, reflecting yellow points of brightness in her eyes when she looked up at him. Brigida undid the fastenings of Slade's great dark wool cape, slipped her arms around him beneath it, and he folded it about her. The rich salt smell of the sea swirled about them on the damp air, and the water lapped louder at the shore as he started the stallion at a walk toward home.

Their lips met again, and desire swept them, strong as the turning, rising tide, and no more to be deflected. Placing her hands on Slade's shoulders and her slim booted feet atop his in the stirrups, Brigida rose against him to return his kiss.

There was a flurry of wool and tearing of lace and then she felt the warm saddle leather smooth against her skin. When Slade put the stallion into a full gallop he bent Brigida back over the flying mane, and his thrusts matched the rolling rhythm of the surging animal beneath them as their bodies melded in an exultant joining under the darkening sky.

Ten

Two days later they left for the city. Slade and Levi went ahead on horseback, and a coachman from the New York house, in blue livery and monogrammed brass buttons, took a place on the driver's bench of the carriage. By evening, after several rest stops, the brougham was ferried across the East River—the beckoning lights of the city twinkling and reflecting over the water.

Fifth Avenue was crowded with carriages and coaches, some elaborately decorated with paintings of the Swiss Alps . . . of American Indians . . . of storm-tossed, full-rigged ships on raging seas.

"There is so much new money about, since the war," Elizabeth said, "very showy, bright as newly minted dollars these people are. They have a taste for luxury and the time and money for endless self-indulgence. Look at these garishly painted carriages!" she said disapprovingly.

The brougham slowed to a crawl and stopped in a crush of landaus, Victorias, and four-in-hands waiting to discharge passengers at a house off the avenue.

"The traffic is becoming impossible, Ann is right. She says a little social visit consumes hours, the streets are so congested. Look, there, Jim Fisk the financier, has a brownstone on this street. He is an acquaintance of Slade's. The vulgar man was once a carnival barker and he looks it still with his pomaded hair and dagger-point mustache."

"Slade said he would never have dealings with Fisk or Gould or any of that set," Brigida said with surprise.

"Oh, my son is scrupulous in his business affairs, Brigida, but Slade, you'll learn, drinks with many and gambles with most, and an evening out with . . . the less respectable elements . . . pleases him. He is probably in this crush now. Fisk has set up a new mistress here who plays hostess for him, open as you please. I would not be at all surprised if it was one of their little events causing this delay."

Brigida peered intently along the street of new townhouses as the driver finally maneuvered their carriage past the corner.

"That's Delmonico's," Elizabeth pointed. "Slade will take you there, I am sure. It is the best restaurant in New York. We are almost there now, thank heaven. I am weary. You must be also, dear."

"I'm too excited to think about being tired," Brigida smiled as the carriage entered Washington square, an open, treed haven that seemed remote from the frantic crush of streets they had just passed through.

Gaslight illuminated narrow, graceful houses. Iron-railed stone steps led to gleaming brass knockers on double doors with traceried transoms. On the west side of the Square the brougham came to a stop and the door of a house flew open. A white-capped and cuffed parlor maid tripped down the steps to unlatch the front gate.

"I am Veronique, mesdames," the girl said in heavily accented English as Elizabeth and Brigida stepped to the sidewalk. "Monsieur le Captain Hawkes requests that I make you welcome."

"He's not at home?" Brigida asked, regretting the note of disappointment she'd let slip into her tone in front of the maid, who seemed to be evaluating her critically.

"No, madame, the captain, he is not at home, but I am to show you the house. Perhaps you'd enjoy a rest before dinner?"

Brigida followed Elizabeth and Veronique into the narrow house, so different from Silver Hill on its grand scale. Here, a small vestibule was lit by a hanging stained-glass lantern, and through the inner doors, with their fan windows and sidelights of leaded florals, was an elegantly simple reception hall, with stenciled walls and a black-and-white-patterned floor.

Slade's city house was a perfect jewel, decorated with the finest objects and furnishings the continent had to offer, and supplied with the latest conveniences. Unlike Silver Hill's sprawling old colonial kitchen, the one in the English basement at Washington Square was modeled after a ship's galley, with a long counter, drawers and cabinets beneath it, and a modern cast-iron hooded coal stove with two ovens. In the dining room the table was laid for two, with Beleek China and fine English sterling. The drawing room was upholstered and draped in pale yellow satin brocade and brocatelle. Slade's office, near the billiard room, was furnished with dark woods and rich leather. An Aubusson tapestry was mounted behind the desk, the walls were hung with Landseers.

The bedroom to which Veronique finally led Brigida overlooked a charming trellised garden lit by bands of light shining from the rooms below.

"Madame, would you like for me to draw a bath? The *salle de bain* is there." Veronique gestured toward a closed door.

"Thank you, I'll see to it myself. Did my husband say when I might expect him?"

"No, madame. Ring if you require me," Veronique said, hurrying out.

As soon as she had gone, Brigida went to have a look at the bath chamber, where she found a zinc tub, sleek as silver, encased in polished mahogany, and a washstand, its brass faucets with white porcelain caps set in an oval marble basin. She lightly fingered Slade's shaving brush, the bristles still damp from recent use. In the mirrored mahogany cabinet above, she found his pewter-backed brushes, a gold collar stay—small, personal things she hadn't seen before. They brought Slade's presence to her senses with a longing for all the close, everyday intimacies of a shared life and love. In her reverie, she unstopped his East India aftershave, the strong fragrance of spice and lime engulfing her. She returned it to its place with a sigh, and went to look in at the door of the water closet at the opposite end of the bathing chamber. She reached up toward a dangling brass chain, curious.

"I had an English engineer come and build it for me.

They're more advanced over there in some things than we are. This does away with chamber pots and carrying hot water from the stove. Do you like it?"

Brigida whirled about to find Slade leaning in the doorway watching her.

"Nice. All very convenient," she said, suppressing a desire to fling herself into his arms. She offered neither smile nor greeting, just followed him back into the bedroom.

"The whole house is charming, perfect really, but it feels so . . . so unlived in, somehow. It's too perfect. If you keep Silver Hill half closed up and this place so . . . untouched, where on earth are you at home, Slade? Where do you really live?"

"Nowhere in particular," he said evasively. "Hurry and dress. I hadn't expected you so early, but now that you're here you'll join me."

They stood facing each other near the mantel, and Brigida found Slade awesomely handsome in evening attire—black tie at starched white collar, discreet flashes of gold at white cuffs. He carried pearl-gray gloves and a black pellise lined with dark fur. His tawny hair was brushed smooth and his glorious eyes, as they studied Brigida, seemed to beckon. Involuntarily, she moved toward him, smiling just a little, and he dropped the cape and gloves and caught her to him as she came into his embrace with a sharp intake of breath and parted lips.

"Now get dressed. This will be an important evening," he said after a time.

"Yes? How so?" Her low voice was soft as a gentle rain. She went to turn the tap in the tub as a footman, followed by Veronique, brought her trunks and boxes into the room and the maid laid out Brigida's lingerie, then took several evening dresses away to iron.

When they were alone again, Brigida came and stood so that Slade would unfasten her dress. He followed her about the room to do it as she crossed to the gilt dressing table near the fireplace. The other furnishings of the room were all ebony, some pieces inlaid with ivory. The upholstery was black satin brocade. The thick black carpet was embellished with woven gold and emerald foliage. There were porcelain medallions of Greek figures set into the ebony headboard of the bed and on the backs of the chairs at a breakfast table that stood near the windows.

"This will be a debut for you in New York's polite society, so-called, and in some other circles. Social distinctions, since the war, are becoming less clear. You're aware?"

"No, not really, though Elizabeth told me a little about it all," she said, slipping off her dress. "In San Francisco, it's different. There are no old families except for the Spanish grandees, and they mostly kept separate."

"In New York it was the Dutch," Slade said, tracing his hand along Brigida's marble-smooth neck and soft shoulder, "but when Caroline Schermerhorn married an Astor, she lent that whole clan of fur trappers a respectability they didn't have before. It's Mrs. Astor's ballroom that defines the Four Hundred."

"The what?" Brigida called from the warm depths of her scented bath. She had left the door ajar so they could talk.

176

"The Four Hundred, the best people, the chosen circle, the socially desirable. She's got room for four hundred bodies exactly in her damn ballroom, and whomever she invites to her annual ball is New York society."

"You, Slade?" Brigida called.

"And you, too, now you're my wife. Hurry. We've got a box at the Academy and a table at Delmonico's and a nightcap at the Schuyler's after. What will you wear?"

"Would you prefer black or white?" Brigida asked, emerging from the bath wrapped in a towel.

Scowling, Slade lifted one of her scent bottles from the table and inhaled its fragrance.

"Wear white. I'll send Veronique up to help you dress and do your hair. If I don't leave now, I may never."

"Will you admit, sir, that you might need me just a little?" She saw his eyes go blank and hard as he turned to the door.

"I don't need anything. I do make use of what's available. I'll be waiting for you in the drawing room."

He was pacing when Brigida made her entrance nearly an hour later, and he stopped, eyeing her progress toward him with critical expertise, struck again by her beauty and now by a sleek sophistication he hadn't seen before.

"What gown is that?" he asked, his eyes going over her thoroughly. "I don't remember selecting it. You are full of surprises."

"Ann Overton kindly conveyed your message that I might have a choice or two all my own," Brigida answered sarcastically. "Well, what do you think?"

She pirouetted slowly just in front of him. Her hair was

swept up in a full curve all around her head and coiled in an elaborate French twist at the crown. Her silhouette was willowy and supple, encased in white satin. Gracefully trained, her dress was lightly bustled in the latest fashion, to accentuate rounded curves below a tiny wasp waist. The gown was barely sleeved, draped at the bosom, and low-cut back and front, revealing the upper swells of Brigida's high breasts, which faintly undulated when she moved. She wore long white kid gloves and carried an evening case of gold and mother-of-pearl.

"Well, what do you think?" She repeated her question, enjoying Slade's attention.

"You'll do," he answered as he extracted a flat velvet box from his pocket. He snapped it open, handed it to her, and waited.

Inside on the satin lid were the words Tiffany & Co., and below, shining like the Milky Way against dark satin, were a hundred small sparkling diamonds covering a gold chain of large square links. A square-cut emerald pendant glowed against the satin and, nested beside it, was a ring with another large emerald surrounded by baguette diamonds.

"Extraordinary," Brigida said coolly.

"The tools of your trade," Slade answered, fixing the clasp at the nape of her graceful neck.

"And what exactly does that mean?" she asked warily, moving away from him. "One might have thought you were trying to buy my affections."

"I'll remind you why you're my wife—to give me sons. Until that activity engages you, you will help earn your expensive keep by lending certain graces to the business dealings I engage in. The presence of a decorative woman of even modest intelligence can be useful in these matters. You'll find the wives of some of my associates excruciatingly dull, no doubt, but you will entertain them nonetheless, keep them out from underfoot, send pretty gifts on appropriate occasions, give charming dinner parties. Investors are put at their ease in domestic settings, I find, and sooner part with their money. You, goddess, are a very showy piece, sure to attract attention. You have to be appropriately jeweled . . . and draped for your work," Slade finished, folding a full length of white fox caping about Brigida's shoulders.

"I was told you were an opportunist and an adventurer, I was told you would exploit anyone, anything, to feed your rapacious ambition, but I didn't really believe it, until just now." Brigida gathered the cape close about her, her expression one of cold contempt.

"My ambition and your taste for luxury—a perfect combination," Slade laughed. "Do you like the fox? You should, it suits you."

"Being thrown into New York Society, innocent that I am, to play this whorish role you've devised for me, I just may be drawn to . . . some other man, some more gentle, courtly man who could keep me as comfortably as you do. What then?" Brigida taunted.

"You're more naive than I thought. I'm asking no more of you than any man in my position would of his wife. Pity you aren't up to the role," Slade answered with a derisive laugh, gripping her shoulders hard through the deep fur. "If you'd really like to play the harlot, be used like a real whore, I can arrange it."

"There's no part I can't play to perfection if I set my mind to it, Captain, no combination of roles I can't juggle should the need arise to do so . . . take care."

"Threatening me, witch?" he snorted. "You never will want any man but me, gentle or no." He brought his mouth to hers fast and hard, forcing her resistant lips to part. "The carriage is waiting. I'm interested to see you center stage."

When Brigida took Slade's arm, they were both smiling just a little, and when their eyes met they mirrored an identical challenge.

"Do sit down, darlings, you're holding up the entire performance!" Brigida heard a lilting, accented voice as she felt a tug at her hand. She and Slade had entered his box at the Academy of Music during the first intermission and, even before they had removed their wraps, a perceivable stir passed through the hall. Opera glasses fixed on them quickly: he, darkly handsome, his tawny mane just inclining to curl; she, a glittering, snow-blond beauty wrapped in lush white fur, then revealed in her slender, bejewelled beauty when he swept the fox cape from her shoulders as if undraping a work of art. There was about them both an almost primitive elegance that each heightened in the other, and they both sensed this as they stood a moment side by side, the focus of hushed attention.

"*Très distingué*, darling, handsome as always, even more so tonight. Tell me, is the child tight-laced, or is she actually made this way?" the laughing voice continued.

180

"There's no artifice about her appearance, Mireille," Slade answered. "Brigida, this is my good friend Madame Manceaux, Mireille, Miri, looking lovely as always," he said, kissing the woman's cheek. She had a pretty, pixieish face with doll-like features. Her hands fluttered and gestured and clasped and unclasped as she spoke, words rushing from her in torrents, her accent musical, her intermittent faint lisp charming.

"*Mon Dieu, ma petite*, there are women here zis evening who regularly risk fainting, who do indeed faint, *absolument* bizarre, they are, to have such a waistline as yours. Slade, *mon cher ami*, you do always find the most extraordinary young things. Zis one I can perceive, will be establishing fashion, not following it. See the attention she attracts, and from both sexes equally?" Mireille bubbled, passing Slade her opera glasses. "She has style."

"Her anatomy is her style," he snapped.

"There's more to any woman than just that," Brigida frowned, "even if you don't know it. But then, your view of the so-called weaker sex is not a flattering one, don't you find that's true of the captain, Madame Manceaux?"

"Slade, you'll find," Miri laughed, "adores women, don't you darling? Now, I'll brook no dispute, I must have Brigida, I simply must take her about, *cher*, she's the find of the season. This one will interest you for more than a day and a night, I predict. Longer perhaps than a year and a day."

"Do you think so? She's my wife, Miri," Slade said matter-of-factly.

"No! *C'est vrai?*" the woman gasped at Brigida, who,

not able to get a word in, nodded.

"I am joyous! I'm delighted for both of you! Who else knows of this, you wicked man? Does Lydia know? Have you told her yet, Slade?"

There was a moment of quiet when the conductor tapped at the podium as the gaslights were dimmed and Brigida heard Slade answer Miri's question in the affirmative.

"And?" Miri pressed, leaning toward him, but his answer was lost to Brigida in a soaring rise of melodic notes, and she gave herself over reluctantly to the lush, romantic music that filled the hall.

When the lights came up again, Mireille plucked at Slade's sleeve. "You will bring the new Mrs. Hawkes to our next small evening. Such innocent charm and beauty will inspire at least a dozen young poets and painters to extraordinary heights."

"Miri gathers ardent young men about her, Brigida," Slade explained, "all passionately devoted to an art or a craft, but mostly devoted to her. They're all noble and high-thinking, not one of them is indifferent about anything. Am I right, Miri?"

"But of course you are, darling," Miri smiled. "Our little evenings attract the most fascinating people. Alain is a professor, Brigida, of languages, and his idealistic young students, among others, flock to us. Will you come?"

Brigida looked to Slade.

"I won't have my drawing room cluttered with mooning fops, which is what will happen once those poets have ogled her in your drawing room. There'll be no romantic idiots turning her head, thanks all the same."

Mireille turned to Brigida. "Oh, he bellows like a roused bull, doesn't he? Your husband is showing possessive signs that I never would have expected in him, of all people."

Brigida laughed. "Why does it surprise you, Miri?"

"The invulnerable Captain Hawkes, darling, seems to be human after all."

"If you talk about me as though I weren't here, I'll deprive you of the pleasure of my company," Slade said, brittle with annoyance. "You two can enjoy the rest of the program without me." Grabbing up his cloak, he strode angrily from the box, leaving Brigida near tears.

"Always before, darling, Slade took his amours with great sang-froid, *très* cool but . . . oh, *chère petite*, he has upset you! I do dearly love him, but he can be a most difficult man. You must learn to handle him firmly. You mustn't let him play on your feelings so. Besides, he detests the music of Offenbach, he would use any excuse to go out for a brandy and cigar. He'll be his most charming self at supper later, believe me, *petite*. You take him too seriously; he is only a man, not a god, no matter that he is made like one. Smile and look about while I'll give you some advice from Stendahl, darling. It is quite impossible to put a stop to love, except in the very first stages, and I see you are beyond that, so listen to me. Slade will always try to give you a little doubt, to cause you a little fear, just to keep you in control, you understand? You must be the perfect woman, and you must arouse his jealousy, just a little, carefully, don't go too far, you understand? That will give you power over him. Probably you know all this I am telling you, just because . . . just because you are a woman, *oui*? Keep him off guard, never show you care too much, always surprise him and, most important of all, never let him imagine you are jealous one little drop. Don't ever accuse, no matter what you suspect. You will wear him down. No buts, darling," Miri stopped Brigida when she started to protest.

"Now I'll tell you all the gossip you'll need to be a success in the *haute monde*. In the box opposite directly? Take the glass and look. In pink? Alice Demorest. That's a wig, darling. She had all her hair cut right off, zip, zip, and had that yellow monstrosity made just because someone told her that golden hair was all the rage in Paris. It seems that women like Alice who live the most drab little lives are the most showy in their dress and self-adornment. Now look two boxes to her left, see there . . ."

"Oh, Miri," Brigida threw her head back and sent lilting laughter out over the auditorium, "you make me breathless just listening to you!"

"*Chère enfant*, can you imagine going to your grave without having said absolutely everything? I cannot! Actually, I am rather tired this evening." Mireille smiled, hiding a yawn behind a gloved hand. "My little girl was awake in the night with a touch of colic, poor baby. Ah, but see the person I direct your attention to now? It is Vienna Lennox. Vienna buys forty Worth gowns—every season without fail—and furs and lingerie and laces and jeweled combs, and on and on. Of course, this season the

Germans and French are fighting; the war prevents her usual soujourn to Paris, poor dear."

"This is the time for Ann Overton to open her New York salon," Brigida said, studying Vienna Lennox through the opera glasses.

"Oh, yes, I quite agree. I met your exquisitely bored Miss Overton only once or twice, but I see her creations often on certain very well dressed women here in town. Oh, there, your country neighbor, Philip Carpenter, a much sought-after young bachelor, darling, but a bit of a dandy, too fey for my taste, and there are . . . rumors about his spending, his debts. There is a new face with him this evening I see."

"It's Hollis Stancel, a house guest of Philip's," Brigida told Miri.

"What! Here am I instructing you about New York Society and you know more than I. Why do you laugh?"

Brigida was amused to find Phil Carpenter staring back at her through his own glasses, and they waved and gestured.

"He throws you a kiss, I see. You will have Slade terribly jealous, I predict," Miri tittered. "Good!"

"Those are the Miss Carpenters in the box near their father?" Brigida asked, lowering her glasses and fluttering her fan. The concert hall was growing uncomfortably warm.

"Pretty things, aren't they?" Miri nodded. "Their mother died of the ague when *les enfants* were all quite small. Del has been very devoted to them, but now the girls are about to fly the nest. They will go to school in Switzerland."

185

Brigida moved her opera glasses about the crowded hall filled with carefully barbered men in well-cut clothes who had the full, florid faces of the leisured rich. The women, exquisitely groomed and expensively dressed, were bedecked with diamonds and jewels that glinted everywhere in the gaslight. Playing the glasses over the orchestra floor, Brigida discovered Slade's broad shoulders and tawny mane with a pleasant shock of recognition, and her eyes lingered on him caressingly, following him as he moved through the crowd, stopping often for a word or two as he went. He was easy among these people, she saw, yet somehow different—he was hard and lean, and there was in his manner a constrained power, a restlessness where in others Brigida saw only smug contentment. Slade had stopped and was looking down, listening intently. He leaned forward, appearing to whisper conspiratorially, then he laughed, and the warm sound drifted up to Brigida above the low hum of voices, bringing a sympathetic smile to her own lips. She moved the opera glasses about, curious to see who so engaged his attention, and though his shoulder shielded from view all but a red-tasseled sleeve and long pale hand, Brigida knew it was Lydia Worsley.

"Now, look there, Brigida," Miri directed suddenly. "It is Miriam Squirer—with the bronze hair at the back box? I am quite mad about Miriam. She has become editor of Frank Leslie's *Gazette*, and he is quite mad about her, too, but, sadly, quite married. He may divorce his wife for Miriam. Isn't that a delicious allegation? You will meet all of them, before very long."

After a cursory glance at Miss Squirer, Brigida moved

the glasses to search out Slade again before the lights dimmed. He was gone, and Lydia Worsley's seat was empty.

At the concert's end, while the soloist took repeated bows under a barrage of roses, silk handkerchiefs and wild bravos, Slade still had not returned to the box.

"Don't concern yourself, darling. He's unpredictable, that is all, impulsive, restless, absolutely unreliable, but so charming, so romantic, so . . . oh, I adore him."

"You and every other woman he's ever met." Brigida protested.

"He'll be waiting for you in the lobby or at Delmonico's, you will see."

"With or without Miss Worsley, do you suppose?" Brigida's irritation was apparent as she and Miri moved through the red velvet curtains, out of the box and into the crowd flowing toward the marble staircase. As they went, Miri stopped frequently to introduce Brigida to friends and acquaintances, all of whom regarded Slade Hawkes's wife with great interest.

"They are curious to know the woman who has caught Slade, Brigida," Miri whispered. "Young ladies were constantly thrust upon him, as you can imagine, and now their mamas want to know how you did it."

"Caught him? You exaggerate. I've not caught him nor he me, and if he is waiting at Delmonico's as you suggest, Miri, he will go right on waiting. I'm going home."

"What—to sulk? That's exactly what you must not do if you wish to hold his interest. You must learn to be more . . . designing, darling, more subtle, not so like a petulant child. But how did you recognize Lydia? You amaze me!"

"The dress, Miri, I saw it at the stitcher's," Brigida answered. She had caught a glimpse of Philip Carpenter's dark head in the crush at the top of the stairs and was moving toward him.

"Now, don't anger Slade overmuch," Miri whispered in Brigida's ear. "You must be blemishless, even if you flirt a little. Don't get tangled in your own snare. It could be a dangerous thing to do. Please, darling, just accept what I tell you now. What Slade does, he does with good reason."

"Run off with that woman in the middle of the evening? What reason could possibly be good enough?" Anger set a glow to Brigida's cheeks that heightened her stunning looks, and she attracted considerable attention moving quickly through the crowd, the floor-length fox cape flying out behind her, open to show a flash of diamonds.

"Slade and Lydia, darling, have a . . . history," she heard Miri say, and she stopped still as the crowd separated around them like a branching brook.

"You know about it all then, Miri, about our arranged marriage, about . . . ?"

"Yes, all, and you know little. Ah, Monsieur Carpenter! *Comment allez-vous*? I've not seen you in some months," Miri effused a bit breathlessly, taking Philip's hand.

"Ladies, are you alone?" he asked, his eyes on Brigida. "You must join us then, for a light supper."

There was a pause, until finally Brigida spoke. "Thank you Phil, but we're to meet Slade. Where has Hollis gone? Miri was hoping to make his acquaintance."

"To the carriage, with Father and the girls. Miri doesn't miss a new face ever, do you, dear? Miri is the social hub of New York, perhaps of the world. There's no one she doesn't know."

"Quite right," Miri said. "You will bring your friend along to one of our evenings?"

"Miri collects eccentrics, Brigida—writers and artists, students, theater people from all over the world, even an anarchist or two is allowed to track up her carpets."

"But Phil, darling, I'd perish of boredom if I had to rely on polite society for my company," Miri laughed. "*Allez*! We must go, or we shall be late and Slade will be unhappy."

"It was Miri who suggested I do photographs of the western trip," Phil told Brigida. "You're astonishingly lovely tonight," he said softly. "Has anyone told you?"

"No, no one has," she answered, taking his arm.

"I did, darling, when you first arrived and—ah, see, there's Slade," Miri bubbled happily.

He stood leaning casually at the curve of the marble balustrade, the familiar teasing half smile on his lips, his depthless blue eyes dark, almost expressionless, fixed on Brigida. He moved to relieve Philip of her hand.

"Philip. Brigida." He nodded to each in turn, flashing a white, razor-sharp smile. He leaned close to brush Brigida's lips with his.

"Have you a new aftershaving concoction, Slade?" she asked with icy hauteur. "Gardenia, is it? It doesn't suit you at all."

Outside the air had turned bitterly cold, and flakes of

hard snow fell through the yellow shafts of the carriage lights. Ladies pulled furs close about jeweled throats, coachmen in brass-buttoned coats and curly brimmed hats quieted blanketed horses that snorted plumes of steamy breath as the line of elegant carriages advanced, filled, and drove off one by one into the winter night.

Eleven

"I'll dice you for the blonde, sailor, I've a taste for lively blondes," a thick whiskey voice graveled. It was dusk. Lamplighters went from post to post like fireflies. Slade was guiding Brigida along a narrow, thronged street, through a crush of people hurrying home or to the taverns and pubs.

The work day was ending and there was almost a carnival feeling in the air. Cartmen shouted at their nags and at each other, ragpickers moved slowly, bowed under the mountainous burdens on their backs, and cindermen with sooty faces leered at streetwalkers who waited out of the wind in sheltered tenement doorways for the evening's business to begin.

Slade turned to the man who had spoken, and Brigida peered round his shoulder to view a ruddy face with pouchy, bloodshot eyes.

"Ho, Captain! I didn't know you, dressed like an ordinary seaman as you are. What you doin', anyways?"

The man appraised Brigida, who now stood in the protective curve of Slade's arm.

191

"I see what you're up to, Captain," he said with a lewd smile. "That's a real sailor's dream you got there. Find her in this street? This is my street, so when you're through . . ."

"This one's mine, G.W., but when I'm done with her . . ." Slade crooked his arm about Brigida's neck and kissed her open-mouthed. She flushed.

"Remember, honey," the man addressed her, "when he gets tired of you like he done them others, you come find me, G.W. Pluckett. I'll set you up nice, keep you dressed fancy, like y'are now."

Brigida wore a tight red velveteen suit with glass buttons and dangling rhinestone earrings. Her hair was pulled to the crown of her head. It fell in long ringlets, and wisps of curl twined about her face.

She flashed the man a smile. "I will remember your offer, Mr. Pluckett," she said, glancing at Slade, who brought a hand hard against the curve of her bottom outlined in the close-fitting suit, and she protested and fussed with the feather boa at her throat to cover her amusement.

"Buy you a drink, Captain Hawkes?" Pluckett invited. "Come round the corner to old man Flood's. He'll let us use his velvet room even with the girl; it's early yet."

"A fast one," Slade agreed. "We've an appointment around the corner at Volet's."

The night before, after the concert, Miri's husband Alain had joined them for supper at Delmonico's and offered an invitation. "You must let us entertain you and Brigida, Slade, at a bistro in the French Quarter that is as unlike Delmonico's," Alain had glanced up at the large crystal chandelier above their table, "as day from night, though the food there is superb, too, French peasant fare at its best. Besides the cuisine, you may see things . . . hear things that will interest you. Will you come?"

"To dine at the Restaurant de Grand Volet, darlings," Miri had instructed, "you must dress like people of the street—a shopgirl, a drayman, whatever. Don't forget."

Now, turned out very much like a lady of the street, Brigida found herself at a worn table in a dim back room of a place called Flood's Bar.

"Why in the world is this called the Velvet Room?" she asked with distaste.

Pluckett pounded a fist on the table, startling a cat sleeping beneath it, and the animal slithered away, shivering its crooked tail. "Hear that? Solid oak."

Brigida nodded. "Yes?"

"It feels soft as velvet to them swillbelly bottlesuckers comin' in here to finish the night. They get a bowl full a alky for a nickel, or all they can down without takin' a breath, straight from the bottle. It puts 'em to sleep good; it don't matter that the swill's thinned with prune juice and hotted up with cayenne, it puts 'em under for the night, and that's all they're lookin' for. Don't go gettin' uppity, honey. That's life, ain't it? Where you been? She don't know a whole lot, does she, Cap? She just off the farm, maybe? You her first?"

"So she told me, G.W.," Slade answered. He grasped Brigida's hand as she stood looking toward the door.

"Sit down," he ordered, "or you'll really be in trouble, honey. A woman alone in this part of town, in an outfit like yours, is fair game for any man on the prowl."

"There's not a street in the world I'd not walk to get away from you! How can you talk about me to this . . . ?"

Slade pulled her onto his lap. "Watch what you say, goddess, I warn you," he whispered, nuzzling her ear.

"Well, don't she talk fancy for her station in life," Pluckett said indignantly. "Don't put up with any a' that temper from 'er, Cap. Break 'em in right—no matter if they're pretty like this one—or they ain't never no good to any man."

"I'll beat her as soon as I get her home, G.W.," Slade said wincing as Brigida's long heel came against his shin. He planted her firmly back in her chair and downed a glass of Irish whiskey. "What've you been up to, G.W.?" he asked.

"Well, as you know, Cap, I went into politics," Pluckett said, leaning his elbows on the table and rubbing his hands together gleefully. "I already made a small fortune and I'm getting richer every day!" His tone was one of pure surprise. "I only go in for honest graft, no blackmail or nothin', like some I know. Me, I got an inside tip, so I bought some land. I just take the opportunities when I'm showed 'em, that's the whole of it, same as your rich friends, ain't it?"

"The same, G.W.," Slade agreed.

"I do the best I can, but I'm not so smart as you are, Cap. I heard you bought land north of Forty-fifth Street years back when they first laid out that grid up to One Hundred Fiftieth Street. I never woulda believed anyone would live way out there, but when that Central Park is finished, you'll make a killing. Whereabouts do you own?"

"A block at about Sixty-fifth Street, it will be. Got any news for me, G.W.? We have to be going."

"Yeah, I got somethin' all right. A guy come into town a few weeks back, Bet-A-Million Bates, the Coal Oil King. Ever hear of 'im?"

Slade nodded. "At Saratoga. He never bets less than ten thousand at a throw. What about him?"

"Yeah, nice fella, just got lately rich. He bets on everything all the time. He's lookin' for some whoreson swine same as you are, same one, too, from what Bates showed me. He ran into the cur a few years back, when he got pressed into servin' on some merchant ship. His back is cut up terrible, worse'n yours."

"What did Bates tell you exactly, G.W.?" Slade's voice went hard as steel.

"Bet-A-Million says the bastard may be at a fight tonight under the Ninth Avenue elevated. Bet-A-Million says this fella is breedin' horses. Before the war, this guy was a breeder in Kentucky or Virginia, maybe. His stallion is training on Long Island now. Bet-A-Million thinks this fella is gonna have the horse ready to run at Saratoga this summer comin', a Virginia-bred name of Blue's Revenge."

The Restaurant de Grand Volet was a flight above the street. A heavy old woman with wild hair sat in a rocking chair at the top of the stairs and glowered at Slade with hostility, while two parrots, perched to either side of her, began to screech loudly in garbled, raucous French.

"Tranquil! Tranquil!" the old woman shrieked at the agitated birds, her rocking chair thumping loudly on the wooden floor.

When her beady-eyed pets quieted, she demanded suspiciously, "What is your business here, monsieur? I don't know your face." The crowded candlelit room became absolutely silent.

"We are to dine with friends," Slade said, glancing about. "They should be here."

Brigida saw Alain Manceaux rise and hurry toward them through the hushed room. He was a man of average height and a muscular, beefy build. His full, round face was almost cherubic beneath sandy, close-cropped hair, and his hazel eyes were lively.

"Oh, with Alain? *Mais oui*, madame, monsieur, you are welcome," the old woman smiled, showing a few yellowed teeth. "Pardon," she said to Brigida. "The birds are good French revolutionaries, but they use vile words when they shout the slogans. My son taught them, I try to keep them quiet but . . ." The parrots again broke into a loud squawking at Alain's approach.

"Tranquil! Tranquil!" the old woman shrilled as he led Brigida and Slade away to a table near a window where Miri waited.

"Madame DuBow is a really gentle soul, would you believe it?" Miri asked, kissing Brigida's cheek. "Whatever is wrong with Slade?" She lowered her voice to a whisper. "He looks . . . there's murder in his eye, I'd swear to it, *oui*?" She shivered. "And if ever he drinks anything but his favorite, champagne, something is not right."

"He's learned about the man Root," Brigida answered, fingering the length of feathers she wore.

"I had hoped that obsession of his would fade." Miri shook her head sadly.

"Apparently it has not, and its object is reported to be training a horse on Long Island somewhere," Brigida answered softly. "He's to be at a sporting match later this evening."

Slade had already downed one glass of absinthe and was starting another.

"I must tell you all something very important," Alain announced excitedly. "I brought you here for a particular reason." In his intensity he hadn't noticed Slade's clenched jaw and furious eyes. "I have already ordered dinner, veau à la marengo, ragoût de mouton aux pommes—*d'accord*?" Everyone nodded.

"Now, listen, you are, of course, aware that France accepted peace with the Germans?"

"Yes," Slade said. "Go on."

"Well, the bloody Prussians are claiming Alsace and Lorraine and they are demanding a billion-franc reparation from France."

Slade had relaxed some after his second drink, but his expression was still remote.

"What did you expect, Alain, when your emperor gets captured in the Sudan and lets a hundred thousand men be taken with him?"

"Ssh! Slade, keep down your voice. People here have very strong feelings about this." Alain leaned forward. "There will be another Commune like before. Paris will refuse to disarm. Money is required, weapons, food . . . I've given all I can." Alain looked at Miri, who was staring at him with incredulity.

"You were investing, you told me—badly," she said.

"I'm sorry, Mireille, I didn't want to involve you, but now . . . I was investing but in a good thing, in the freedom of France. But now I've exhausted my resources and . . . here is Madame DuBow's son, Jean Paul. He will tell you more, my friends."

"The instructor of parrots, is it?" Brigida smiled, extending her well-manicured hand. Alain introduced an intense, wiry young man wearing a chef's white apron.

"*Oui*, Madame Hawkes, just so." He barely brushed her hand with thin lips. Pulling a chair to the table, he settled near Brigida. "Do you know the story of Volet, madame? He was one of the grand masters of the *haute cuisine*, a true artist. One day, it is told, his fishes didn't arrive in time for a banquet he was serving. He fell on his carving sword and made an end of it then and there, and ruined the pudding to boot."

"No!" Brigida gasped, her eyes wide as saucers.

"Well, perhaps not exactly that way," DuBow laughed. "It is one of those tales one hears in certain circles. But we did name our restaurant after him. Sword or no, Volet was notorious." DuBow became serious, turning to Slade. "Alain tells me, Captain, that you may be sympathetic to our cause."

"Your cause?"

"Alain and I both march under the banner of anarchism. We believe that all power must come from below, from the people, the workers. If you agree, or even if you do not, we hope that your experience, Captain, as a spy and infiltrator in your own recent war of liberty could be put to use on our behalf."

"You've a reputation of your own, Monsieur DuBow, as a more than competent assassin. Cigar?"

DuBow nodded, and soon he and Slade were wreathed in fragrant curls of smoke.

"You view me as one of the dark angels of anarchism, as a terrorist, but we do what we must, as you did," DuBow smiled. "I require information. I've located a cache of weapons available for . . . a price, a price that keeps elevating. We have now bid to the limit of our resources, a half-million dollars in gold. Someone is bidding against us. Will you find out who?"

Slade continued to study the soft-eyed man opposite him, puffing thoughtfully. "Will you . . . eliminate your competition, Monsieur DuBow, when you know who it is?"

"I would hope that wouldn't be necessary, Captain. Once shown the error of his ways, a sensible man is usually willing to bargain. Haven't you found that to be true?"

"Sensible men don't play at these games, DuBow. If you'll tell me who's selling, I'll find out who else is buying. But why don't you go to Remington or Colt and buy direct?"

"Too long a wait. Besides, these guns, Captain, were . . . how shall I say, available at a very advantageous price—at first. Because the owner—the possessor is a more appropriate description—can't sell to just anyone. He needs money *rapidment*, fast, and the purchaser must be most discreet. We would not want it known that we are shipping such a cargo to France any more than he would want it known he had sold. You understand?" DuBow's eyes never once left Slade's face.

"Yes, I understand better than you might think. When is your deal to be made final?"

"There is a yacht leaving New York sometime in March, Captain, about five weeks from now. The guns must be on board. Many of the French here in New York are interested . . . one way or another. There are those who would interfere, if they could, and side with the Prussians. I will soon have the information you ask for. My lady, Janine, is getting close to the real owner. Until now we've dealt with an agent. And you, Captain . . . ?"

"And I will make inquiries on your behalf," Slade agreed. "DuBow—I'll want your man when the deal's done."

"If all comes off as I hope, Captain, I'll serve him to you carved up on a platter. I'm not a sentimental man. *Au revoir*. We shall meet soon again." DuBow smiled, unbending his long frame from his chair. "I'll bring Janine to visit soon, Miri, if I may?" He hovered near the small table for a moment as if anxious about something, then moved off toward the kitchen.

"Is he an assassin, truly?" Brigida whispered. "He has such gentle eyes."

"Did you like him? He's a disarming boy with his pretty eyes, Jean Paul, and good at his job. I've heard he smiles with those seducer's eyes even as he plunges home the knife."

"Slade, don't be so hard on the boy. His cause is the same as mine," Alain said slowly.

"How can anyone as charming as you are, Alain, be an anarchist?" Brigida asked, placing a hand on his arm.

"Ah, Brigida, how well your name suits you," Alain sighed. "It is from the Celtic Brigit, which is from the Greek *brizein*, to enchant. Perfect." Alain kissed her hand. "You don't understand, *petite*. You just hear of the bombs and so on, but we believe in peace."

"This shipment of guns for Paris . . . tell me . . ." Slade broke in.

"You won't interfere, Slade? Why do you want to know where they come from?"

"Professional curiosity. I was looking for some particular weapons hijacked during the war. They were never found. I'd like to neaten things up by finding the thief now. You be careful, Alain, you've done all you can. Leave the rest of this to those who know how these games are played," Slade said. "Drink up. We'll stop back at Washington Square for Levi. Then I'll take you all to a good fight."

"Blood sport now, is it? Many as your faults are, I'd not have expected you to engage in anything so cruel." Brigida extracted a tortoiseshell comb from the small fringed tapestry purse dangling on a gold chain from her wrist and began to smooth her hair.

"I don't engage. Blueford Root does. We are here to see what could be a fight to the death, the opponents are that well matched, I'm told. This is touted as a really big event. Root could put in an appearance."

"And if he does?" A quick fear heightened Brigida's attention.

Slade was smiling a little, a cigar stuck in the corner of his mouth, his collar turned up against the night wind. He lifted Brigida from the carriage and held her against him, their eyes on a level.

"If he does, I'll kill him," Slade said. "You can wait here if you have not got the stomach for a dog fight. Miri and Alain were sensible not to come."

"I expect I can take it if you can," she answered with seeming composure.

Nearly two hundred toughs and a few fancy women were gathered in a large shed when Brigida, flanked by Slade and Levi, moved toward the hub of activity, the pit area, demarked by wooden fencing. A man Slade described as a well-known New York sport had been selected to referee and was using his boot heel to mark a scratch line in the dirt across the center of the arena.

"The winner's purse is twelve hundred," a shaggy old man answered Slade's inquiry. "There's odds of one hundred to sixty dollars on Skip of Long Island. Are you a taker?"

The crowd parted in Brigida's path as she came to stand at the pit rail between her silent, serious escorts. Only the challenging dog, Jack of New York, was in the ring. He was a stocky muscular white bull terrier with the flattened face of all his kind. His ears were tattered, his eyes mere narrow slits.

Slade roamed away to scan the faces in the crowd, while Levi remained discreetly vigilant at Brigida's side. "Do you know what will happen here?" he asked her gruffly.

"I saw a cock fight in California . . . once. What on earth is he doing?"

A man in a checkered suit with a black bowler pushed back on his head, had entered the ring with the second bull terrier. Kneeling, he proceeded to methodically go over the dog's entire body with his tongue.

"To show there's no poison," Levi said.

The preliminaries done, time was called. There was an expectant rising hum from the crowd. Brigida moved closer to Slade, who had finished a turn of the place and come back to her side.

At the signal, the eager dogs sprang from their handlers with ferocious spitting snarls and bared fangs to rush at each other, savage and fierce, and when the first blood was drawn—one dog fastening his teeth in his opponent's jaw, to drag him down—the backers and bettors became louder, cheering on their favorite. The violence increased. There was the sickening crunch of bone and wet snarling growls as the dogs lacerated and tore at each other brutally. Brigida hid her face against Slade's arm until the animals broke apart for an instant. One of the handlers quickly snatched up his bloodied dog to end the round.

"Is it over?" she asked grimly.

"No, they'll tape up the broken joints and bones and

put them right back in. These things can take a long while, and get very ugly, goddess," Slade said. "If you want to wait outside, you'll be safe with Bran." Before Brigida could answer, the crowd roared again and both dogs were back in the pit, one floundering on a badly cracked front leg, the other bleeding profusely from the mouth, gurgling and panting hard.

"Collapsed lung," Levi commented.

The match continued, and the dogs slowed with exhaustion, stumbling and falling until finally one managed to get a grip on the other's throat and hang on, shaking him roughly, violently, as he might a rat. The shouting crowd surged forward into the pit as the handlers tried frantically to separate their broken, mangled animals. Brigida clutched at Slade's hand to avoid being carried off by the now roaring mob.

"Is it over now?" she shouted above the din. "Is it over, Slade? I don't want to see any more." His arm was about her, holding her against him as he guided her out of the frenzied crush.

"I should never have let you in here," he said with irritation. "You aren't such a strong little lady as you like to pretend, are you? Levi, take her out. There'll be trouble." Another roar went up from the mob of toughs and gamblers.

"What happened? Why are they all shouting again?" Brigida stepped over a recumbent form, a man with a bottle, propped against a wall.

"The dogs—they're both about dead. The referee is calling it a draw. The crowd's crying foul. There's a lot of money bet on this."

A general fight seemed to erupt spontaneously all through the place, and when a heavy figure, cursing, hurtled into Brigida, Slade swung out fast, sending the dazed man crashing through an unopened door. Then he lifted Brigida through the splintered portal and, looking back in from outside, they saw knives flash in the half dark. In the hush that followed, a man lay sprawled and writhing on the damp dirt floor, an ugly stab wound in his back.

"That will prove fatal to the dupe, you'll agree? Evenin', Miz Hawkes. This must be the captain? Good fight, wasn't it, sir?" Slade and Brigida turned to find Hollis Stancel standing near, small beads of sweat on his brow, his rheumy eyes gleaming unpleasantly.

"Tell me, do you often attend these bloody contests?" Brigida asked. She had taken Hollis's arm, after introductions were made, and was leading him toward the carriage, Slade and Levi coming after.

"I do. I love a real good fight, like tonight. In fact, I just bought a little bitch sired by the dog Jack you saw fightin'? That Jack won fifty matches and killed three dogs before tonight. I'm going to breed my bitch to a Staffordshire bull terrier just brought over from England."

"Slade, Hollis has just purchased a bull terrier bitch to breed for the pit," Brigida threw over her shoulder. "How much did you pay for her, may I ask?"

"Fifty dollars gold." Stancel toyed with his watch fob, observing Brigida fall back to take Slade's arm.

"I'd like to buy her from you if my husband has no

objections. How much will you take, Hollis?'' Brigida's smile was its sweetest as she gazed into Stancel's sallow face.

"Now, I don't know. I have plans for her, as I have said and . . . well, for you, I'll let the bitch go for the same I paid, fifty dollars. And costs—another fifty."

"Done," Slade said, peeling a single bill from a roll. He and Levi had remained silent throughout the transaction. Stancel observed them uneasily.

"Not many ladies take to this sort of sport. I'm amazed to find you interested," he said to Brigida.

"I'm not interested in the least," she answered. "This is the first and the last such event I ever hope to see."

"Well, what you want with my bitch, if I may make so bold as to inquire?" Stancel asked, his nervous eyes flitting from one to the other of his companions' faces.

"I just want to keep her out of the pits, Hollis. Besides, she will give a good feisty temper to our own terrier lines when she's old enough to breed. If we ever farm Silver Hill, we'll need ratters. Well, goodnight, perhaps we'll see you with Phil before too long."

"Mon Dieu, madame, you are dressed so . . . garish! What did the captain say to such a costume?" Veronique complained late that night as she helped Brigida to undress.

"The captain picked this suit for me, Veronique, I am so sorry you don't approve. We went to the French Quarter for dinner and he thought it best we not be too formally attired."

Veronique was moving from armoire to dressing table and back again, putting Brigida's things away. "At what establishment did you dine, madame?"

"At Volet's," Brigida yawned. "Do you know it?"

"*Oui*, Volet!" the girl said quickly. "It's late. If you require nothing further, madame, I'll go. I also am quite tired."

Brigida's tub was almost full and was steaming invitingly. Left alone, she stepped in and leaned back, letting her long hair fall loose over the rim in a golden curtain that almost brushed the floor. She yawned again and closed her eyes and thought of Slade, as usual.

The fine gentleman could become the companion of thieves and assassins without a moment's hesitation. He was as much at home in a bohemian dive as at the Astors', and yet . . . he was not really at home anywhere. And where had he gone now, at three in the morning? she wondered. Her pretty mouth set in a pout. Her eyes opened wide and she stared at the ceiling. They had arrived at Washington Square to find a note on the vestibule table. Changing quickly, Slade had left again at once.

Much later, when he broke into her troubled sleep and moved beside her to take her in his arms, Brigida was instantly wide awake and aware of the cloying, sweet fragrance of gardenias. With an exclamation of rage, she attacked him, her long nails flashing out to rake his angry, startled face.

"What the devil's got into you now, pagan witch?" he growled, effortlessly fending her off. He caught her to his lean frame, trapping her arms at her sides.

"Let me go, you whoring beast!" she commanded. "You'll have no pleasure of me tonight."

"Your verve, lady, is admirable," he whispered against her ear "but I'll have my pleasure, and so will you have yours." His mouth descended the length of her marble throat, his tongue and teeth played at the roused peaks of her creamy breasts as, furious, she writhed against him violently. Pinioning both her hands above her head in one of his, he let the other wander down over her belly to slide between silken thighs. His mouth on hers was cruel when he kissed her again and again, and she shuddered and sobbed beneath him, feeling him prying, then plunging, hard and hot, deep inside her. She yielded then, gave everything. surrendered completely, and when later they lay still, entwined, she cried again, help-lessly, against his shoulder.

"Brigida," Slade whispered, catching her to him when she started to rise, "why do you fight me? You never will win."

She twisted away and, pulling the satin sheet up to her throat, turned, burying her tear-stained face in the pillows.

"Just leave me alone you . . . you rake-hell libertine! Go back to your stews and dens of vice and let me be!" her pillow-muffled voice came to him angrily, and his hand landed with a resounding slap on her upturned bottom.

"I told Pluckett I'd beat you, and I swear I will if you don't learn to behave, witch. I'll leave you alone, if that's what you think you want. I'll leave you so alone, you'll come to me begging; it won't take long."

The pillow she hurled after Slade hit the door harmlessly as it closed with a slam behind him.

Before noon the next morning, Miri was at Washington Square, inviting Brigida for a skate on Beekman's Pond near the East River. Elizabeth joined them, but she remained blanket-wrapped in the carriage, enjoying the view of the colorfully dressed skaters flashing past.

When Brigida, lovely in a fur-trimmed mulberry plush skating costume, skated back to the brougham to warm herself, she did a graceful Dutch roll. Her colorful petticoats flashed as she neared the edge of the pond, a long scarf playing out behind her. As she came to a stop, she found Slade leaning back casually in the corner of the brougham and puffing on one of his black cigars.

"I meant to ask before," he said, by way of greeting. "Where'd you learn to skate so well?"

"A young man taught me. He was from Wisconsin. He struck it rich in the California hills. We visited a mountain lake once that reminded him of home and . . ."

"You're getting a lot of attention, as usual," Slade interrupted, offering Brigida a leather-gloved hand to help her up into the carriage.

"Of course," she smiled, withdrawing her own small gloved hand from her muff and placing it in his. "That's nothing unusual; you'll get used to it. Did you come to join us?"

"No, I've business elsewhere. I'm on my way to see about . . . some horses," he answered. "I stopped to say we're having guests to dinner. If I'm late, you'll have to be gracious. Elizabeth tells me she's off to the theater with Del Carpenter, or else she'd be hostess in my absence."

"It is right, Slade, that Brigida be mistress in her own home. She is equal to the position and always gracious, I know." Elizabeth pulled a fur carriage robe closer about her.

"I've known my wife to be less than hospitable," Slade said pointedly, blue eyes moving slowly over Brigida's glowing face and neat figure.

He opened the door and lightly jumped from the carriage, turning to lift Brigida down. His hands almost circled her waist, and when her arms closed about his neck for balance, their lips met. They stared, startled, into each other's eyes. Brigida's expression was one of demure, charming confusion. When he set her down, his furious eyes lingered on her upturned face, and she clung to him, unsteadied.

"Go back to your skating," he hissed through clenched teeth, "or I just might rape you now and to hell with . . ."

"You're leaving me alone, remember? Besides, such unseemly behavior would startle my companions, to say nothing of your man there, Philips."

The Indian waited at some distance, collar up, wide-brimmed hat low, mounted, holding the stallion's bridle for Slade. His usually impassive expression had given way to impatient glances and occasional deep coughs.

"Why, I do believe he's jealous of the attention you pay me. Best be off now and tell him he's got nothing to fear. Haven't you explained that I'm no more to you than a bedmate and breeder, and since last night, not even that?"

Brigida pulled free of Slade's arms and stepped out onto the ice, throwing a lilting laugh over her shoulder, and went gracefully gliding in among the whirl of skaters flashing around the pond.

Central Park Drive was crowded with coaches and carriages when the black brougham arrived there later, and elegant ladies peered out of every one.

"I would enjoy riding here, I think," Brigida said, observing a couple canter past, the young woman side-saddle on a dappled mare.

"That, Brigida darling, is Tennessee Claflin with one of the Vanderbilts, and here comes her charming sister, Victoria Woodhull. They are quite notorious and delightful, Ann Overton tells me." Elizabeth smiled. "She dresses them, you see."

"They surely do like money, those two, and men," Mireille clucked with a touch of mischief.

The brougham had reached the end of the unfinished drive and turned to go south in the direction from which they had come.

"See! The red landau?" Miri asked as a quickly moving carriage passed them. Brigida caught a glimpse of smooth, dark hair and dark fur.

"Lydia Worsley," Miri said. "Did you see the woman with her?"

"I didn't see even her, really," Brigida answered,

turning to stare after the red carriage.

"Madame Restell, an abortionist by trade. Her clientele is *la crème de la crème*, darling, society's best. You have seen those dreadful licentious advertisements of hers, haven't you . . . Madame Restell's Female Monthly Pills. If that doesn't work, there are her foul nostrums and her private 'respectable' board and dreadful devices one might expect to find in a medieval torture chamber."

"But dear Miri, remember the poor victims of passion madame has helped to avoid disgrace and ruin," Elizabeth said with an odd look.

"Yes," Miri smiled, "think of the vast wealth she has accumulated . . . from the abortions, and the little *chantage* she does on the side."

"She does what?" Brigida wanted to know.

"Blackmail, darling. Her profession puts her in a unique position to extort. She and Lydia are close. Madame really is Ann Lohman, English, like her friend, Miss Worsley." Miri shrugged and her bowed mouth pursed, her baby-doll eyes sparkled wickedly. She asked, "Anyone hungry? I am absolutely starving!"

"It's the skating that does . . ." Brigida stopped in mid-sentence as the red landau came abreast the brougham again, and she found her curious stare met by a pair of slate-gray eyes that narrowed when Brigida nodded with a faint smile and a barely perceptible tilt of her head. Lydia Worsley turned away, showing her haughty profile— aquiline nose and pale cheek.

"That's . . . ?"

"Quite!" Miri bubbled. "Intrigue is so enticing, isn't

it? And I think she is as curious about you, darling, as you are about her."

"Miri! I am not at all," Brigida flashed. Elizabeth and Miri exchanged glances.

"We shall lunch at home. Roland is expecting us, and then we'll do the Ladies' Mile, Brigida. You'll enjoy that," Elizabeth said, taking the girl's hand. "It is all the best shops along Broadway. It's where Ann will open her salon."

Brigida looked away and just sighed, trying to put taunting images of the pale and beautiful gray-eyed woman from her mind. She concentrated instead on arrangements for dinner, the first she would hostess for Slade.

Twelve

"Gold standard? But I just do not understand," Mireille was sweetly complaining to the gentleman seated beside her. "Why not the bean standard, monsieur? A commodity is a commodity, *non*?"

"Dear lady, I'm in banking. Let me explain. . . ." Brigida heard and turned her attention back to the man to her immediate left.

"You are an architect, Mr. Liverance?" she inquired. "You've business with my husband?"

"Yes, ma'am. I'm working on the captain's new block of French flats he's building. It's a grand opportunity for me, ma'am. There aren't many who'd trust a young architect with such a big project," he answered, glancing down the table at Slade.

"I'm sure he wouldn't trust you if you weren't entirely competent, Mr. Liverance. French flats?" Brigida dabbed at her lips with a linen napkin.

"Like in Paris, ma'am. They're very popular there. In New York City working people must take lodgings in rooming houses or live in hotels if they cannot own a house, which few can. Our flats will be modern and comfortable," the young man said enthusiastically. "Two stories, gaslights, and gas kitchens." John Liverance was so taken with Brigida and so flattered by her interest that he readily joined the ranks of her conquests. "We—the captain—decided that brick and stone, even some copper, were better suited to housing than cast iron—more . . . homey."

"And clerks and shopgirls with their factory furniture and cheap ready-made clothing are to occupy your French flats, sir, is that it?" Hollis Stancel asked. "It all sounds a mite tainted and tawdry to me. I mean, sir, what respectable woman would live in something called a French flat?"

"It is an economical means of accommodating a good number of people graciously and efficiently," John Liverance protested.

"An inefficient man is like a bird that can sing but won't sing, sir."

Brigida's eyes flicked over the man who spoke, Frederick Taylor, seated to her right. Then her glance went to Slade at the far end of the linen-covered dinner table that was set aglitter with slender fluted glasses and fine Irish china. Earlier, before the guests had arrived, Brigida had seen that the silver was well polished, that the flowers she had ordered were attractively arranged in a low centerpiece. She even tasted the champagne to be sure it was properly chilled, and when Slade returned with just enough time to dress, he found everything perfect.

"Yes, Mr. Taylor, do go on," Brigida encouraged.

"The purpose, Mrs. Hawkes, of my work, my research

216

in scientific management, is to increase surplus. For example, I have fully evaluated pig iron workers."

All other conversation at the table stopped as Fred Taylor's voice rose, demanding attention. He was a heavy-set man with receding hair, and his wife, a large-boned, large-featured woman, was plainly turned out, free of any frill or sign of cosmetic improvement. Her adoring eyes remained fixed on her husband as he spoke.

"I have found," Fred Taylor went on, "that a pig iron worker is merely a man more or less the type of ox, heavy both mentally and physically. Like an ox, he must be correctly worked in the most efficient way to assure greatest profits to his employer."

"Sir, you can't mean we are to use men like oxen and think of them as of no more consequence than beasts?" Brigida protested. Slade, almost imperceptibly, shook his head, silencing her. She let Taylor go on.

"No, not like beasts, madame, like machines, well-regulated machines are more what I have in mind. Take shoveling coal," Taylor said, then paused as a servant moved about the table pouring champagne.

"Now a worker," Taylor expostulated, "uses any shovel that comes to hand; he picks up a load with no thought at all and heaves it. Some of those brutes, ladies and gentlemen, can lift as much as thirty-eight pounds each heft but, I asked, how quickly do they tire? Are they consistent? I decided to experiment. First, I changed the length of the shovel handle. Then, I specified the weight load to be lifted. My results were surprising but sound."

"Tell them, Fred, what you discovered," Mrs. Taylor

said reverently.

"At the end of a month I established absolutely that you get several tons more from a worker held to exactly twenty-one and a half pounds per balanced shovel load than from the same worker lifting thirty-eight pounds. They are like machines, Mrs. Hawkes, to be tuned and adjusted for the long view and best possible profit."

"But, Mr. Taylor," Brigida said, "I can't think of men as machines."

"The trick, dear lady, is not to think of them as men at all," Taylor answered smugly.

"Attitudes like yours, monsieur, will help us spread the communalist movement all over the world. A man's labor is worth far more than any wage or profit," Alain Manceaux said with agitation.

"I've known ship's captains, Mr. Taylor, to cause mutiny, treating men as you suggest." Luther Crowell, a quiet, long-faced man with hazy brown eyes and an almost diffident manner spoke for the first time.

The butler was beginning to offer to each guest in turn a silver serving platter of roasted lamb prettily garnished and dressed.

"I do appreciate your approach, Mr. Taylor, but a man must have pride in his work. Would you agree?" Crowell asked.

"What exactly is your occupation, Crowell?" Taylor shot back.

"I've just been licensed a ship's master like my father and grandfather. The sea is our life, but it's the atmosphere that interests me even more. I'm designing—trying at any rate to design—aerial devices."

"Do you mean to fly, then?" Philip Carpenter was

delighted. "That is fine, Crowell!"

Lucy Crowell, a pretty, dark-haired woman with a charming southern lilt in her speech, tried to smother a giggle behind her napkin, but her tinkling laugh escaped and set the others smiling—all but the Taylors, who regarded her unamused.

"Like your bird, sir, that can sing but won't, my husband would fly but cannot. Would y'all pronounce him efficient or inefficient, Mr. Taylor?"

"I would pronounce him merely silly, madame," Taylor answered with a scowl.

"But some good has already come of my silliness," Luther Crowell said mildly. "While trying to build my balloon, I invented a device that makes these." He pulled from the breast pocket of his jacket what appeared to be a piece of brown butcher's paper.

"A piece of paper? You're showin' us a piece of butcher's paper, Crowell?" Hollis Stancel asked with disdain.

"Open it, please," Crowell said, handing it over to Brigida.

"It has got . . . it has got a sealed bottom. Why, it's a little bag of butcher's paper," she laughed. "How clever! How efficient, how very, very efficient." She smiled wickedly at Taylor. "Now clerks and shopgirls will save eons of time, not having to tie parcels with string. And think of the savings to be made on the string, besides!"

"That's just the sort of thing I have in mind, the kinds of devices my experiments are sure to lead to. Scientific management will make all work more profitable," Taylor nodded.

"But if Mr. Crowell had been restricted like one of

your mechanized pig iron men, he would never have dreamt of aerial balloons, and he'd not have made this." Brigida handed Taylor the paper bag.

He examined it closely. "Is your machine patented, Crowell?" he finally asked.

"Of course it is, suh," Lucy Crowell answered for her husband. "Luther may take to great flights of fancy, but I am very down to earth."

"People will travel in my balloons. You won't laugh when I've done it," Luther smiled good-naturedly.

"*Peut-être*, Monsieur Crowell, perhaps, but isn't the train more than adequate?" Alain asked.

"You can't hold back progress," Brigida said. "Don't you find it all wonderful?" Her eyes fairly sparkled with excitement. "I do."

Philip enthused, "My father took me to view some sketches for a mural that will go into the Grand Hotel in Saratoga soon. It shows the United States as a cornucopia, simply pouring wealth out on the entire world."

"A little of that wealth should be spilled at home," Hollis Stancel smiled crookedly. "You Yankees destroyed the southern economy, you left us burned out, left us with nothin'."

"But it's over now, Hollis," Philip said with an anxious look at his friend. "Let's not . . ."

"Over for whom?" Hollis's words were slurred and his drawl had thickened. "It will never be over for some of us, will it, Captain Hawkes?"

"Why, Mr. Stancel, where is that winning southern charm we're known for?" Lucy Crowell asked kindly.

"Gone like all else I had, Miz Crowell, but you, as the wife of a Yankee, wouldn't know. Now the captain here, our fine host, he was with Sheridan's elite corps, weren't you, sir," Stancel turned to Slade, "when they burned the Shenandoah Valley?"

"I was," Slade answered. "And you, Stancel?"

"You turned our green valley into a wasteland." Stancel's clenched fists rested on the table. "If no ladies were present, Captain, I would tell y'all what I really think of your Yankee burnin' and plunderin'," he said very slowly, his eyes red with drink, his narrow face ghostly white.

"All wars create terror, *mes amis*." Alain's tone was sad. "In Paris, even now as we talk, there is suffering, great need for . . ."

"Paris, mister, is a city of monkeys and whores," Stancel said, swallowing the last of the sparkling wine in his glass. "Why should I care about a passel of Frenchmen when I've nothing left of my own? The captain here, well, he didn't come out so bad, did you Hawkes? You are a rich man, I'm told, got this pretty new wife . . ."

"Shut up, Hollis." Philip looked helplessly at Slade. "He's drunk, I'm sorry. . . ."

Slade was regarding Hollis now with cold, evaluating eyes. "Take your friend home, Phil," he said after a long, tense moment, "and give him some Seidlitz powders for the headache he's going to have tomorrow."

"Throwin' me out of your fine home, Hawkes? Never mind, I'm leavin' anyway." Stancel stood, upsetting his chair, and staggered from the room.

"I'm terribly sorry," Philip announced to the table at large, but he looked only at Brigida. "He's . . . he drinks."

"Tell your friend for me please, suh," Lucy Crowell said, "that many young men lost far more than he. This is a time for those of us who did survive to be rebuildin', not wallowin' in self-pity."

"Oh, Phil, do go help him. We understand," Brigida said, and when Philip, too, had fled, she guided the conversation quickly back to pleasant talk while the table was cleared of dishes and cloth, and coffee and dessert settings were placed out, following fashion, on the rich, polished wood.

Slade took the gentlemen for brandy and cigars and, with the pleasant clink of glasses and billiards in the background, Brigida entertained the ladies in the drawing room. When the guests were about to leave, Del and Elizabeth arrived, and Brigida insisted on serving a nightcap before letting anyone plunge out into the late, cold New York winter night.

"Did you enjoy yourself?" Slade was in a chair near the fire in Brigida's room, hands laced behind his head, his silk waistcoat unbuttoned.

"Oh yes, I did," she answered, "except for Hollis Stancel. What's wrong with him, do you suppose? Not all Confederates are so . . . angry."

"A lot of them are, but they try not to show it. There is usually a certain gallant effort made at civility. It's not easy to lose with grace."

"The Crowells were delightful and John Liverance,

but Mr. Taylor! What a pompous ass."

Slade watched Brigida remove pearl drop earrings and a circle of tiny pearls from her wrist and place them carefully in a jewel case on the bureau.

"Will you finance him, do you think?" she asked.

She moved to the long glass, looking as fresh as she had at the start of the evening hours before, her golden hair pulled back smoothly from her face and twisted in two looped braids behind her ears.

"No, I don't appreciate his way of thinking. Pullman might fund him, I think." Slade watched Brigida as she proceeded through the steps of her bedtime toilette. This perfect vision of demure sweetness, this image of propriety with her hair bound up, slender figure draped in a flowing pink silk gown was, he knew, about to be transformed.

She uncoiled her looped braids and wavering liquid gold shimmered about her lovely face. Humming a little, mindful of her every gesture, she kicked off silver slippers and quickly undid the tiny pearl fastenings running down her curving bodice. After she had stepped out of three layers of lace-frosted petticoats, Brigida went about in pantalettes and camisole, a narrow pink ribbon and cameo at her alabaster throat. Fully aware of the effect on Slade, she moved about with seemingly unselfconscious ease from bathing chamber to armoire to dressing table, and the enticing scent of her creams and lotions hovered in the atmosphere.

She felt Slade's eyes on her, felt his heat in the very air between them. She turned to smile at him, inviting, teasing, her deft fingers working at the laces on her bosom, and then Slade was dazzled, as always, by the shimmering perfection of her naked beauty. The tingling tips of her round breasts were thrust forward, her lips were parted. Flecks of gold danced in the dark lambent pools of her eyes, flashing with an audacious invitation. He came to her slowly, savoring the vision of her proud sensuousness. Taking her extended hand in his, he completed her transformation, undoing the slim ribbon at her throat.

"Ask," he demanded.

"No!" She shook her head.

Then, without another word, he turned on his heel and left her standing alone in the middle of the room.

Before dawn that morning Brigida awoke wanting Slade desperately. She rose and went along the hallway to his study. The room was empty. Uneasily, she entered and looked about. On the desk she found a buff card protruding from an envelope, the dry red wax of the seal crumbling, an odor of gardenia clinging to it. Scripted in a firm hand, in black ink, was a single sentence: "I need you now." The last word was emphatically underlined. Below was the letter "L," drawn in great, sweeping, balanced curls. Brigida, stunned, stared hard at it as the undeniable actuality of the situation came clear to her. Slade had left her and gone to Lydia Worsley—that was the fact of it, and it was not to be denied.

With smoldering anger she tore the card in half and then in half again and again. She showered the confettied pieces into the fire, staying to watch them blacken and curl and the larger cinders float up the chimney with the rising smoke.

"I'll destroy that bitch," she swore aloud, stalking from the room.

Those first days in town set the pattern for the weeks to follow. Slade was in his study early to receive a succession of lawyers, architects, and engineers involved in the construction of the French flats and in his other projects. Inventors, some holding miniature models of fascinating devices, often waited in the reception hall with local politicians and salesmen. Sometimes a mate or captain from one of Slade's ships was to be seen among those shifty-eyed drabs—faceless, shabby men who could have but one purpose at Washington Square; they had come with information, available for a price, about Blueford Root. With one clerk scribbling away at a tall, narrow desk and another always at his elbow ruffling sheafs of paper, Slade guided his callers in and out, sometimes greeting Brigida's guests in the process. She was "at home" mornings to the wives and daughters of New York society and to not a few admiring gentlemen callers, too: most frequently, Philip Carpenter.

In the afternoons, she promenaded the Ladies' Mile, served innumerable teas, did Central Park in the black brougham with Miri and, less often, with Elizabeth, who was spending her time with Del Carpenter. Brigida almost envied the easy intimacy the two shared as Slade's remote manner grew more infuriating with each passing day.

They were in demand in society, invited everywhere. Through a whirl of theatres and concerts, skating parties, sleigh rides, Astor balls, and Delmonico dinners, Slade was correct and cool. Though distant with her, he was charming with their guests when they entertained at home—a succession of brokers and bankers and industrialists accompanied by their expensive wives. His advice and opinions, Brigida saw, were valued by these powerful men, and his attentions were solicited by their polished ladies. Always handsome in black evening dress—white silk and linen against tanned skin and tawny hair, blue eyes intense and calculating—Slade looked into every woman's eyes, kissed extended hands slowly, always had a smile, an intimate comment, while Brigida inwardly fumed.

For her part, everything she did—the dress she wore, the hairstyle she chose, every word she spoke, each gesture and smile and sigh—was meant only for Slade, though she pretended aloofness to wound his vanity. As she became more confident of her powers, she became so artful, in the beautiful bloom of young womanhood, that she could bring any other man to his knees with a glance. With consummate skill she flirted blatantly, while charming her many admirers with a gentle wit and warm manner, but all the while she would be surreptitiously watching Slade from beneath long, shadowing lashes. She always knew his exact place in a room, noticed to whom he spoke, with whom he laughed. Oddly often, he would look up to catch her eyes fixed on him and offer a thin, taunting smile.

"If I may take the liberty, I think you are too free in

your manner," he complained irritably to Brigida one evening at a ball where many gentlemen danced attendance upon her, as usual.

There was a flash of triumph in Brigida's look—she had attracted his attention—and then her irrepressible gaiety bubbled into seductive, low laughter.

"Would you prefer, my noble gallant, that I were less free in my manner and kept concealments from you?" she teased, gliding away on the arm of a gentleman who claimed the next dance.

They were rarely alone until well after midnight, and often, when they reached home, a buff envelope waited on the entrance hall table. Finding it, Slade would leave again at once, and Brigida would go angrily up to bed, showing him no hint of her true feelings.

What astonished Slade most about Brigida, he decided as he waited for her to weaken and give in, was the way she greeted him each morning, always perfect, radiant with smiles, full of projects and plans. She went about the management of his house and servants with faultless taste and ease, imposing a graceful order on the now lively household.

The rooms were kept bright with baskets and vases of cut blossoms that she brought from the flower market and charmingly arranged herself. When no fresh flowers were to be had, there were bowls of dried petals and porcelain boxes of potpourri freshening the air. Effortlessly, it appeared, she continued to charm his associates and amuse their wives, too, with harmless bits of choice New York gossip. But she never betrayed a confidence, and though some women were envious of her extraordinary looks, most found her as delightful as their husbands did.

But night after night, alone, her longing need of him became a torment as she listened to the household quieting, curled beneath her quilts trying to read a dime novel in the light of an oil lamp set near on the bedside table. She counted off the servants making their way, one by one, up the back stairs to rooms under the eaves, and waited for Slade's key in the lock, his step on the stair. Only then did she fall into a troubled, lonely sleep.

On one windy, wet night in March, as she half drowsed, half dreamed, floating on sea meadows blue as sky, feeling Slade's fingers on her skin, moving, caressing, going gently to the pulsing nub of her needy, warm body, there was a knock at the bedroom door. Brigida called out with a welcoming cry, her eyes flickering open, smiling, acquiescent.

"I didn't mean to awaken you, my dear. There was a light and I . . . I had to see you."

Coming awake slowly, Brigida flushed, as if Elizabeth could read her thoughts. Then she saw there was a special glow about the woman, a lightness in her step as she crossed to the bed, moving with an ease and grace she had never shown before.

"You are looking absolutely beautiful," Brigida smiled.

"I'm having a very, very wonderful time, my dear. And you?"

"Yes, fine," Brigida answered, closing her book over a lace marker.

"Your answer is so . . . abbreviated, it makes me

wonder." Elizabeth was standing with her back to the fire, regarding Brigida curiously.

"Slade is . . . a very distant person, Elizabeth. Secretive," Brigida said quickly. "It's . . . hard."

"My son, Brigida, is a prince of fortune, a force in the world—we both know that—a man to whom women have always recklessly offered their very souls, and yet he holds his own true feelings tightly like dollars in a fist, and perhaps that's for the best. He can be . . . violent, as his father was. Well," Elizabeth sighed, "even as a small child, Slade's eyes were completely unfathomable. Try to be patient, Brigida. He will show himself to you, I know. You two are so perfectly matched, a mating made in heaven—everyone says as much who has seen you together. There's that same strength and stubbornness in you both; your fathers were made in the same mold, you know that."

"Yes, I know, Elizabeth. But why are you telling me this now?"

"You both trace your lineage back to the Irish cattle drovers and Welsh rebels transported to New England long ago. Such proud and arrogant people they were. I see it in you both now clear as day, when I watch you together, I see . . ."

"Elizabeth!" Brigida breathed, sitting up and wriggling back against her pillows. "Whatever is the matter? Do tell me!"

"Matter?" Elizabeth laughed, clasping her hands in front of her and bringing them to her chin. "No matter, it's just Del and I . . . he's a fine man, Brigida, and . . . Brigida, we are going to be married and we are going to

Europe, to Munich. It's a great center now of modern art and literature. What do you think?''

Elizabeth stood in the center of the room, hands still clasped beneath her chin, blue eyes dancing. "I never hoped to be in love again; I never even wished it, I don't think. I lived all those years, my dear, with such sad memories and regrets. I almost let my life go by, without doing what I wanted to.''

"Elizabeth, I am so happy I can hardly say. When will you announce it?''

"Shh, not a word to Slade, not yet. I'm not . . . I'm not ready for that,'' Elizabeth whispered as they heard his tread on the stair.

The door opened and Slade stood on the threshold, shirt and waistcoat half unbuttoned, jacket slung over his shoulder. "I heard voices. Up late, aren't you, Mother?'' he asked.

"I was out helping Ann get ready. She is doing a fashion show tomorrow. Goodnight! Goodnight! I'm just leaving.'' Elizabeth pressed Brigida's hand. And then she was gone, closing the door behind her.

"Isn't she looking beautiful?'' Brigida asked Slade as he crossed with long strides to add a log to the fire.

"I didn't notice,'' he answered, crouching for a moment, then standing and stretching, examining Brigida warily to get some sense of her mood.

"What do you notice?'' she snapped.

"You, taunting every man that comes within a mile of you,'' he said, undoing gold cuff links.

He was agreeably distracted by the intimacy of feminine disorder about the bedroom—white silk stockings draped over a chair, a kid glove, a hair ribbon curled on the table, the delicate lace marker protruding from the book at Brigida's fingertips.

"Oh, how can you be so blind? Here is Elizabeth well and happy after all this long time, and you don't even notice!" Brigida was indignant.

Slade's chin set stubbornly. "You're out of sorts because I don't pay you more attention. Well, don't preach about Elizabeth. You didn't know her during all that long time. You weren't here. She took no notice of me then, just ruled the world from that room of hers, always too sick or too tired to come down. She drove my father away, from her, from me, from Silver Hill, and then she withdrew to that damn room." He turned to look down into the fire.

"I used to wish as a boy that she was a warm, homey woman, the kind who loves ribbons and flowers, who hums baking in sunny kitchens on winter days. She never did."

Brigida held her breath, waiting, wanting to comfort the hurting boy she glimpsed in the man for a fraction of a moment.

"Perhaps there was a reason for Elizabeth's distance," was all Brigida offered. "Sometimes children can't make sense of . . ."

"Don't make excuses for her. She was weak, that's all. And selfish."

"I'm sorry," Brigida said very softly.

"No, you're not, but it doesn't matter. I don't expect anything much of you, either."

Thirteen

"Will you come to the dock with me? You'll find it interesting, and I value your assistance." Ann Overton was dressed for business in a short, ankle-length black silk day dress and a sautoir of pearls that reached nearly to her waist.

"The show was wonderful, Ann. Did you take many orders?" Brigida, in a Watteau morning gown of scarlet wool, was stretched on the chaise in her bedroom listening to Ann read aloud from the morning paper. A friendship had flowered in recent weeks, enriched by their similar sensibilities and dramatically different personalities.

"I did well, thank you, and so did you. You dressed my mannequins superbly, and their hair has never been so nicely arranged. You've a talent for this sort of thing. If you ever want a job . . . that's why I'd like you to come with me. There's a Liverpool packet due this morning," Ann announced with weary interest, "and the cargo for sale is: 'flannels, cashmere, tartans,'" she read, "'Norwich crepe and calico.' Also: 'ribbons, flowers, feathers, plumes, waterfall curls of French manufacture, fine leather trunks, dressing cases, and parasols.' And more— 'silk cloaks, ready-made boots and a thousand yards each of military hat cord and braiding.' I'll make this a season of epaulets and soldierly trims. I will declare braid the very newest and most fashionable touch in European couture, what with the war and all. Well, will you come?" she asked, her weary dark eyes mildly inquiring.

"I can't," Brigida sighed. "Today I must take one of the Murray girls, Viola, to tea after a turn round the park. I am so very tired of it all."

"Viola? Poor thing. She uses bosom pads. Nothing helps." Ann noisily turned a page.

"Aren't you breaching some couturière's professional rule of etiquette giving out such personal information?" Brigida queried.

"You, Brigida, are too well bred. That can be a great drawback in fashionable circles," Ann scoffed, her tone heavy with irony. "All women talk too much and still don't tell half of what they could."

"Really? Well, guess what I heard?" Brigida asked, stretching.

"Yes? Well what?"

"I heard from Mireille Manceaux that Viola puts lemon juice and soap in her eyes to make them shine."

"Oh, too shocking, isn't it?" Ann actually laughed aloud. "You must be having a really ripping time here in New York if that's the level of gossip that titillates you. Don't be so naive, Brigida. They all do that, and eat lumps of sugar soaked in cologne to achieve the same effect."

Brigida went to the dressing table to shape her long

nails with a file. Ann went on reading.

"Audubon's 'Birds of America' plates sold for old copper. Hmm, here's a good one—'Darwin—Is Man an Inspired Monkey'—stupid! Ah, Victoria Woodhull is at it again, free love and the vote for women." A page turned noisily and Brigida looked up from her nails.

"Do you want a vote, Ann?" she asked, looking thoughtful.

"I do not give a fig for the vote. The dollar is what matters. If women ever do get to vote, it will only be because they have money. Want to hear about an accident on the Hudson River Railroad?"

"Ann, you're too cynical, really. I don't at all agree . . . there's the milk wagon. I won't be a moment."

"Let your servants see to such matters," Ann remonstrated. "Surely some one of them is capable of acquiring dairy products from the milkman?"

"Oh, I always give his little girls a treat. Mr. Kier carries them with him; they look forward to it, and they're so pretty in their bonnets. I'll only be a moment. I slipped out earlier and bought bake shop rolls. Will you have a hot chocolate with fresh cream?"

"Chocolate!" Ann seemed almost to choke on the word. "Café au lait and a brandy if you please, Mrs. Hawkes. And why do you go to a shop? Can't your cook bake?"

"Oh, Ann, I get so restless. I like to get about on my own; I like the smell of the bake shop. I like to watch the baker's wife counting out the warm rolls."

*　　　*　　　*

"My, there's been a death, and it has got to do with Madame Restell," Ann announced almost energetically when Brigida returned with a white lacquer tray of cups and glasses. "A body found in a trunk at the railway station."

"Restell? The 'ladies' doctor? I saw her once, out riding with Lydia Worsley. What happened?" Brigida settled opposite Ann to pour.

"An overdose of savin. That's the juniper oil madame prescribes for certain . . . conditions." Ann shook her head. "Bad for business, this sort of thing. The victim seems to have been a servant of some sort, Janine D'Arcy, not one of Restell's rich customers. Still, madame never makes an error. She's a brilliant business-woman. Her salesmen on the road cover the country selling her pills and referring clients to her clinics. She's opened them in Boston and Philadelphia, too, and she spends a small fortune advertising in all the respectable papers and religious journals, fifty thousand, even sixty thousand a year to advertise. Imagine, that much in a year and she . . ."

"But it's not a decent profession, and one reads so much about . . . about the mistakes like Janine D'Arcy."

"You'll not meet madame at any respectable dinner tables, true, but she has rescued many a poor soul from an early grave and saved more than one drunkard's woman from Lord knows what torment. What she does is legal and, of course, madame's clientele is only of the better classes now, refined women who can afford her services. By the way, that reminds me," Ann said, rolling and lighting a cigarette. "What do I hear about Del

Carpenter and Elizabeth? Is it true? Elizabeth left Silver Hill so . . . suddenly and completely, like a convict fleeing a solitary cell. She took everyone so by surprise, there's bound to be gossip. Tell me."

"Tell you what? That they go about together all the time? Yes," Brigida answered. "What else did you hear, Ann?"

"Nothing. How very nice for them both, after all these years." Ann refilled her brandy glass.

"Tell me! I've been dying to learn since that first evening at Silver Hill, but I'd no one to ask. Philip denies knowing a thing and Slade is impossible."

"Del introduced her to his good friend, Jarred Hawkes, and the handsome captain—it's said he looked just like Slade but with dark eyes and black hair—swept her away. It had been expected that Lizzy and Del were about to announce their engagement. They were both old society, they traveled in the same circles, fortunes on both sides. Del made a civilized match later, a quiet marriage, no great passion, but it was a comfortable thing. But Elizabeth! She railed at her fate, I'm told, through all the years she was married to Jarred, except the first."

"And after Jarred Hawkes's death, Del wasn't free?"

"Actually Del's wife passed young. Her gravestone was already green with moss by the time Jarred was killed. But then Elizabeth put all the world away from her. Except Martha, of course." Ann sighed and exhaled a long plume of smoke. "I'm pleased for them, Del and Elizabeth, having this time now. It's you who really brought them together again."

"What a waste of years they weren't together. How

sad." Brigida's eyes were pained.

"And you?" Ann asked. "And Slade?"

"Oh," Brigida sighed. "I don't know. It's all so . . . he's always polite—in company—but he's so pointedly interested in other women. I mean, he can't pass a shop-girl or a parlor maid without turning on his charm. All his grace and warmth is for everyone but me. He dances with the raving beauties and the wilting wallflowers, and they all adore him, of course, and . . . and Ann? He goes out. Alone. Every blasted night. To that woman. Ann, I can do everything just as I want to . . . except handle Slade Hawkes . . . I had to tell someone and . . ."

"Have you ever thought to be a little less perfect? Try to befriend him, not just take him to bed."

"Everyone has had advice for me since the day I came to Silver Hill. He doesn't . . . I don't take him to bed." Brigida blushed. "I said I didn't want him and he hasn't touched me since. That was weeks ago. I told you, he goes to that woman every night. He said once that I'd miss him horribly if . . . when he went away from me, but this is worse than I could have dreamed."

"How so?" Ann asked quietly.

"Seeing him, knowing he's there, and not being able to touch him . . . oh Ann, what seemed natural, beautiful feelings with him now are . . . shameful." Brigida rested her brow on a hand, avoiding a glance into her mirror or into Ann's sympathetic eyes. "Elizabeth said . . . you did too, proper ladies aren't supposed to have . . . certain feelings, but I want him all the time. I can hardly think of anything else. If I were less than a flawless paragon, if I didn't hide behind my shell of perfection, I'd lose control. He'd know my despair."

"He'd help you if he did. You are a little fool, but such a sweet one. Invite him back to your bed; you've nothing to lose."

"I've everything to lose," Brigida said stubbornly.

"I warned you from the first, women find him irresistible. He's not the one lonely now, is he? My *maman* once told me never to marry a handsome man, they're too much trouble, but then *maman* is a fool about many things. This can't be as bad as you think. You are the reigning beauty this season. Your success in society is unequaled. Slade is behaving quite respectably, sober, hardly ever seen in the worst places anymore, and that is very odd, you've no idea . . ."

The newspaper rattled again. "Perhaps there's something here that will distract you," Ann offered. "They are widening Broadway, did you know?" she asked, and then she came slowly to her feet. "Listen, my spring collection is reviewed." She cleared her throat, fingering her deep collar of pearls, " 'She'—that's me—'is a true American fashion leader.' How'd you like that? I'll go on. 'Mrs. Overton's designs are unique and original as she is herself; whether dressing her mannequins or graciously tending a crowd of eager customers, she moves like a countess who . . .' "

"Who is this man," Brigida smiled. "You must look him up."

"I'll drop him a note."

"Why not invite him to call?"

"You, my little friend, are trying to foster a romantic entanglement for me, isn't that so? Well, I've no interest, none at all. I see to my own needs, thank you. Unlike you, I prefer to sleep peaceably in my own bed without the agitation of a burdensome *affaire d'amour* to distract me from my work. I'd rather walk the streets than marry again. At least a streetwalker can refuse a man's attentions. A wife has no such right. Brigida, there are perhaps a dozen men in New York even worth talking to, and half of them can't be admitted to polite society in any case."

"But this one might be different, Ann, really. He knows about design and . . ."

There was a knock at the bedroom door, and Veronique entered carrying a silver tray.

"Is madame at home?" she asked. Brigida reached out, then pulled back her hand as if from a coiled serpent. On the proffered tray was a buff card with one commanding sentence: "Lydia Worsley requires a brief interview with Brigida Hawkes."

"Tell her to wait," Brigida said sweetly. "I will not see her," she whispered through gritting teeth when Veronique had withdrawn. "I won't!"

"You haven't yet made her acquaintance? Preposterous and uncivilized," Ann said with mild indignation. "Brigida, don't be the wounded wife; don't play the wilted flower now. Do you need a little lemon juice to spark your eyes? Shall I come and hold your hand?"

"If you don't I might strangle her." Brigida roamed the room like some exotic wild cat newly caged. "He came to me reeking of that gardenia scent she wears. He prefers her!"

"I doubt that's true. From a distance Lydia seems very elegant, very grand, but when you get to know her you find that she's shallow and cold, a weak woman of a certain fussy delicacy that passes for taste. Slade never loved her. She's available. And useful. She arranges . . . parties of a sort, for him and his friends. Her friend, Madame Restell, is in a unique position to provide willing young girls to engage in a variety of activities. I'm sure Slade tired of Lydia herself long ago. You just must learn to accept these things. Elizabeth never did and it nearly destroyed her. Now go on.''

The scent of gardenia was thick in the air as Lydia Worsley moved toward Brigida with a stately grace, arrow straight and tall. There was an unusual beauty about the woman. Her black hair was pulled straight back from a strongly contoured, pale face. Her features were sharp—prominent nose, wide mouth, and large slate-gray eyes that fell on Brigida with a disarming hauteur. Her voice, when she finally broke the silence, was pure ice.

''Mrs. Hawkes,'' Lydia Worsley said, with emphasis on Brigida's title. ''I thought it my duty to pay you a call. I'm a long time . . . family friend.''

''You needn't have,'' Brigida said, nodding the woman to a chair, pulling the cord to summon Veronique.

''Tea? A magnificent dress, Miss Worsley.'' Brigida flashed her brightest smile and took a place in the corner of the sofa, tucking her legs up under her. ''I saw it in the sketching stage, and now I see how well it suits you.''

''We share the same *modiste*, Mrs. Hawkes, among other things. Red and black has always been a favorite combination of mine." Lydia Worsley, examining a long nail on her right hand, didn't see Brigida's eyes flash with outrage. "Yes, Slade's eye for style and for the feminine form is unerring, don't you find?"

"Tea, Miss Worsley?"

"Yes, tea, thank you. How do you like our city? You're a Westerner, I'm told. It can be unnerving coming from a backward . . ."

"Actually, I'm growing rather bored of the life here, all the endless dressing and shopping and gossip."

"But Mrs. Hawkes, the music, the theatre. At Niblo's Garden the performance of . . ."

"We have seen everything, Miss Worsley, even the half-naked girls in The Black Crook at Niblo's; we have heard the Philharmonic Society present Offenbach at Steinway Hall; we've been to the Metropolitan Opera and to the minstrels and entertained every stockbroker and banker in the city and some from Europe besides. We've been drinking in Hoboken on a Sunday when you can't in New York, and we've been to hear your most dramatic minister, Mr. Beecher, at his Plymouth Church in Brooklyn . . . care for a pamphlet, Miss Worsley?" Brigida pranced to the desk and scooped up a handful of sermon pamphlets. "It is all exciting, of course, but we do have the country manor where the sea and the smell of the earth are soothing to the spirit. We'll be returning there any day now," Brigida fabricated. Her words tumbled out in a nervous rush.

"Do you mean to drag Slade back to the country, then? I know you won't hold him there very long," Lydia Worsley predicted with a hard laugh. "Ah, Veronique, be a good girl. Fetch me a glass of that plum wine the captain keeps in the sideboard.''

"*Oui*, Mademoiselle Worsley. Anything else?" Veronique inquired, placing a tea tray.

"Just the wine. Shall I pour, Mrs. Hawkes?"

"No," Brigida snapped. "This, in case you forget, is my home, not yours; Slade is my husband, not yours. I'll not discuss him with you except to say this: You seem not to know him very well, despite gossip I've heard about your long liaison. No one drags Slade anywhere."

"Gossip? Monstrous, isn't it, the way people go saying things behind one's back. In this instance, poor child, everything you may have heard is absolutely true."

"Really, Miss Worsley, why did you come here today?" Brigida asked as calmly as she could. "Sugar?"

"Milk only, thank you." There was a soft rattling of cups in saucers and a clicking of spoons as the two women viewed each other frigidly.

"First of all, I came to get a closer look at you than our previous passings have provided, and to tell you something. For your own good, of course. I will speak plainly."

"Don't," Brigida snapped. "Certain proprieties should be maintained."

"I will speak plainly, nonetheless," Lydia Worsley insisted. "Be prepared to fail with Slade as all the others have. Oh, you've a quick tongue, yes, and a certain . . . *élan*, I admit, but despite your protest, you are merely a child. There have been other pretty little things before you; you are not his first, and he always comes back to me. He will this time, too." Lydia Worsley watched

Brigida hostilely over the rim of an octagonal Japanese teacup.

Brigida set down her own cup and stretched with a slow sigh, then curled in her place again like a contented kitten pretending disinterest. "But you don't seem to understand," she laughed. "I am Slade Hawkes's wife. Could anything be clearer?"

"Yes, yes! I know all about that," the woman exploded, standing suddenly and upsetting the contents of her cup on the drawing room rug. She walked the length of the room and pivoted when she reached the windows. Her face had a hard, dry, anxious look, and all traces of beauty were gone.

"He married you only to please her, to please his dear mother, Elizabeth. It was the one way to secure her fortune, but you, of course, know that."

"What do you mean?" Brigida asked, taken aback.

"You don't know?" Lydia made soft, cruel, clicking sounds with her tongue. "The Slade family wealth will pass directly to Elizabeth's grandchildren, but only if she approves her son's choice of a wife. Your husband isn't one to let a fortune slip through his fingers, you know." She turned her back on Brigida and talked on in a deliberate cold tone.

"A man can be tolerably happy with a woman he doesn't love as long as he has got his freedom. Marriage for a man, you know, can become a convenient, unobtrusive little habit. But you! For a woman to do what you have done . . ." Lydia Worsley choked out her words in a voice tight with hate. "Marrying just for a home, as you have, is the most despicable of all means of obtaining a

244

livelihood. I'd hold a common streetwalker above you, Mrs. Hawkes. It's much the same, selling yourself to one man in marriage, or to many outside it. It's just a different kind of whoring, that's all."

Brigida was stunned, but when she stood, her voice was vibrant. "The cardinal virtues are not exactly abounding in you, Miss Worsley. I know you for a procuress, a female panderer, and an adulterous fornicator, but thank you for coming here today. You've told me something I've needed to know."

"Oh? And what might that be?" Lydia Worsley waited, still as a statue.

"That you are not at all sure of your position with my husband. If you were, you would not have come here to insult me as you have."

"Not sure? But you know Slade always comes whenever I send for him, no matter what the day or the hour."

Brigida had no answer. "Good day, Miss Worsley," she said sharply as she rang for Veronique.

"Before I go, and gladly, let me tell you the other reason for this visit. Slade asked me to invite you to one of our . . . parties. He'll be there, of course, as will some other gentlemen of your acquaintance."

"Invite me?" Brigida gasped. The invitation completely unnerved her. "Why didn't Slade ask me himself?"

"He's been detained. He won't be seeing you until tonight, half after eleven at my house. You look ill, Mrs. Hawkes. Will you come or are you afraid?"

"Afraid to be . . . debauched for the amusement of my husband? To the contrary," Brigida smiled. "You may tell him, Miss Worsley, that I will certainly be there. I intend to enjoy myself. Fully."

At midnight Brigida was at the door of the Worsley mansion. Apprehensive, she hesitated. Her brougham was just turning the corner. She could stop it still and go home alone to her safe bed.

A tall man of erect, military bearing, flourishing a walking stick, came bounding up the stone steps behind her. He grasped her arm and pounded the door impatiently with the brass head of his slim cane. "We'll not tell Raoul you were contemplating flight. At the very least, he'll withhold your reward," he said, to Brigida's complete mystification. The door was opened by a sleek, dark young man in an unbuttoned waistcoat and loosened collar.

"Ah, Raoul," Brigida's companion smiled coldly. A lean-jawed, narrow face beneath steel-gray hair made him seem, in the dim light, lupine and dangerous. "Have this one prepared for me in the usual fashion," he instructed, "unless she's been spoken for tonight."

"I'll ask Miss Worsley, Count," the butler said, smiling at Brigida. "She may be special."

"See to it. Let me know," the man commanded, striding toward the drawing room. "There'll be something for you, Raoul, of course, if you deliver her."

"This way please," Raoul gestured politely, his manner smooth and rather too familiar, Brigida thought, as he took her fur.

"Is Captain Hawkes arrived?" she asked, following

him up a wide staircase, in a whisper of silk under a lush blue velvet gown, her knees feeling a little soft, her warm hand riding the cool, carved marble balustrade. Gardenias, scenting the air, floated in silver bowls on the landing, where the walls were painted in imitation of Gobelin tapestries.

"The captain sent word he's been delayed. You are to enjoy yourself."

"Raoul, bring her here," an imperious voice called. Composing herself, Brigida entered a well-lit boudoir, where Lydia Worsley, perfectly groomed as usual, and another older woman waited.

"You told me Slade would be here," Brigida accused her at once.

"He will, he will. Don't be so childish and impolite. Say hello to madame, have a seat, have a drink. Raoul, a brandy for Mrs. Hawkes."

"The count has expressed an interest in her," Raoul said. He crossed to a sideboard and half filled a bulbous glass. Then, rolling it, warming it in his fine hands, he came to Brigida, leaning close as he proffered the drink. "What shall I tell the count?" Raoul had a disarming smile.

"Tell him . . ." Lydia hesitated, "not tonight, another time. Now leave us. See to my other guests."

"You seem agitated, Mrs. Hawkes." The older woman spoke in a whiskey voice. "I used to see frightened little things like you all the time. I found a nice talk and a toddy does a world of good."

"Are you a schoolmistress, madame?" Brigida asked ingenuously, knowing exactly whom she addressed, and

Lydia convulsed in mocking laughter.

"Let me introduce you properly. This, Mrs. Hawkes, is Ann Lohman, perhaps known to you as Madame Restell? She often attends our special evenings."

"Do you participate, madame?" Brigida studied the woman over the rim of her glass.

Smoothing a modest black taffetta dress, Madame Restell went to refill her own glass. "Not anymore," she said. "Now, I watch. You'll soon learn for yourself who does what here."

"When will Slade come?" Brigida demanded.

"You are tiresome," Lydia snapped.

"But I'm not sure he wants me to play in your games. He never said . . ."

"Sit down. He wants you here but he wants . . . hm, how did he put it? 'No confusions of paternity,' that's what he said exactly."

"Go on," Brigida said quietly, recognizing Slade's words, feeling betrayed and exposed.

"We'll see to it there are no confusions, I promised that to him. Now, I want you ready when he arrives, else my little surprise will be spoiled."

"Surprise? How clever of you, Lydia. What fun," Brigida smiled acidly.

"I didn't tell him when exactly I'd bring you into our circle; just that I would. Visit with madame now until I come back for you."

Brigida paced in a swirl of velvet, and Madame Restell watched her for a moment. "What you are doing, coming here, may help to stimulate your husband's interest in you. When he sees you with others, then . . ."

"What on earth are you talking about?" Brigida demanded. "I came here for my own pleasure, not his."

"Really?" Madame looked skeptical. "Well, that is fine. You know, some of my regular customers are married ladies whose husbands haven't touched them in years."

"You help them, madame, avoid the embarrassments of adultery with your witch doctoring?"

"What would you prescribe, abstinence? Looking at you, I think not." Madame frowned. "And I do nothing old-fashioned—no hellebore potions or blood-letting at my clinics—though I do pull a tooth on occasion, to get things started. To alleviate obstructions, so called, I prescribe a cocktail of tansy syrup and gin, black cohosh and bloodroot. It's often very effective for young ladies who have taken cold."

"I thought savin was the preferred nostrum. That's what Janine D'Arcy died of, isn't it? An overdose of savin?"

"Janine did not follow her instructions," Madame Restell said very coldly. "Juniper oil is potent; she knew that. She was an insolent young woman, as you seem to be. She swallowed more medicine than she should have in the hope of avoiding some of the prying mechanical tools I've perfected, and the syringes of penny royal and brandy. There are other ways, too, to treat the sort of cold Janine D'Arcy had—extraction pumps, galvanic shock . . . why, Mrs. Hawkes, are you taken ill? Lydia, the lady doesn't seem herself," Madame Restell said as the door opened. "And just as well. She's rather too outspoken for her own good. I think you should turn her over to the count at once. I'd enjoy it immensely."

"Tempting, but Slade may not be ready for that yet. What did she say to you, madame, to so arouse your ire?"

"You know the little maid we . . . treated? She intimated Janine's unfortunate death was my doing. Take her away. I'll be down after a while. Oh, and be sure, Brigida, to tell the other Mrs. Hawkes that madame asked after her. Elizabeth will remember me, I know."

There was an explosion of masculine laughter and then a hushed, expectant silence as Lydia opened sliding doors to the drawing room. In the gloom of deep chairs and dark wood, Brigida could just see several figures, three or four men, and the bare, fat white breasts of a heavy woman leaning casually over a chair back. All were fixedly watching two girls undress in the dancing light of the fire. One reclined amidst satin pillows on a wide velvet chaise. The other, her long brown hair hiding both their faces, was leaning to help her companion roll a black stocking down one pretty extended leg, then the other. Silk pantalettes slid over cooperatively shifting hips, small, pointy breasts were freed from a silk camisole.

When the supine figure on the chaise was stripped but for a filmy, lace-frothed shift, the two girls changed places. Brigida caught her breath, recognizing Veronique, who was herself left, after a long exhibition and sensual display, wearing just a satin corselette and embroidered stockings. Brigida watched, captivated and repulsed at once, feeling stirrings in her own body when Raoul, naked and smiling, gracefully stepped into

the circle of flickering light. Then, to the encourage-
ments of their attentive audience, Raoul lay on the chaise
and began to play with them, first one, then the other.
They were cautious, it seemed at first, and very slow,
kissing and caressing him each in turn, using their lips
and limbs and hands and darting tongues until, after a
time, their twisting, turning bodies seemed almost
fevered. The girl in the shift, her blue-black hair flung
back, her smooth olive skin aglow, knelt smiling, moaning, her body swaying, and Raoul, sliding her shift up to
her waist, took advantage of her exposed position.
Veronique rolled free to mouth and taste his body in a
way that made Brigida look away. She caught a glimpse of
Lydia raptly watching, sipping champagne, of the count's
silvery hair and glinting eyes, and then she discovered
the vulturous angular features and stooped shoulders of
Hollis Stancel—who was staring intently back at her.
Mortified, she turned to the chaise again.

There was a fine mist of sweat glistening all over
Raoul's wiry body as he lay beneath the lovely dark girl
who was riding him now and staring down into his face
that could have been a mirror image of her own with its
beautiful dark sloe eyes and wide, white smile.

"Such a comely pair, *oui*? They are so beautiful
together, you will want to join them I know. It will be
incroyable, your fair hair and skin with those two. Raoul
is very skilled, madame. Very . . . adventurous. He will
perhaps help you discover deep-seated pleasures you may
never even have imagined. See how well he serves his
little sister?" Veronique, wearing nothing still but the
corselette and one stocking, extended a hand to Brigida,

who shrank back in her chair.

"No, Veronique," she hissed as Lydia began to push her forward.

"What you've seen must have roused something in you, little fool. You can't be as cool as you appear. Do as you're told or I'll turn you over to the count now, or would you prefer Stancel there? He has left his distinctive mark on several of our reluctant ladies."

"You said Slade would be here," Brigida whispered.

"And he will. Go on!" Lydia's eyes were very bright.

Veronique pranced ahead, accepting intimate caresses and lewd laughter with swaggering ease. "Come, Madame Hawkes," she said, pulling at Brigida. "I undress you just as at home, *oui*? The captain, he's not been to your bed in such a long time, you will enjoy yourself with us, and no harm done."

Brigida stood still at the hearth, holding hard to the one thought that would keep her calm in the madness swirling about her, turned one theme over and over in her mind—her fury at Slade for abandoning her to this. Proud and remote, she watched as if from great distant heights as the layers of her clothing came away and fell like wilted, drifting rose petals, watched until she stood shivering a little in her last sheer garment, feeling the room draw closer about her, the silence seeming loud as thunder.

The count, shrugging thin, regal shoulders, stood at the mantel, his lips in a cruel grimace, his eyes going over Brigida's body methodically.

Raoul, on the chaise, languidly extended a hand to Brigida. "This will be a pleasure for Angél and me," he smiled, "serving such a lady as you. Don't look so frightened."

A lamp, blinding in the dimness, bloomed into light, then crashed shattering against a wall. The room went silent, the figures at the hearth froze, like an eerie waxworks display. The texture of Slade's voice when he finally spoke struck something near terror in Brigida.

"My wife is the very perfection of ladylikeness and virtue, isn't she, Raoul? Gentlemen? And the perfection of beauty, you all see that, don't you?" He moved about the room easily, quickly, lighting the lamps one after another, coming toward Brigida obliquely, his thin smile menacing. In her turbulent agitation, Brigida's own smile flickered like a candle, then went dead. Slade's voice when he spoke again, this time to her, was dry as dust.

"Would you like me to watch you with Raoul, Brigida? Raoul is good, but Levi is better. Try Levi and Raoul, or better yet, have them watch us, you and me. Would that excite you?" He stood in front of her, beginning to undo his shirt, and when she extended a hand to stop him, he crushed it painfully in his.

"I'm only here because of you!" She could barely speak. "That woman said . . ."

"She's fabricating, Slade. When she came to the door looking for you we just didn't know what to do. You must send the silly child back to the country where . . ."

"Shut up, Lydia," Slade ordered. "I want to introduce my wife to some of the folks, to some of your good friends. I want her to know what fine company she's chosen to pass her time with. You have met Stancel, Brigida. Shake his hand, come on. Feel that ring? Feel it!

It's burned his initials into any number of soft white thighs, hasn't it, Stancel? And black ones, too. Ah, and this, Brigida, is Everett."

A beefy, balding man rose, nodding and smiling politely. "Everett has a predilection for pederasty, don't you Everett? Boys, girls, it doesn't matter to Everett. Angélique enjoys his attentions. So does her handsome brother. Am I right, Raoul?"

"Right, Captain," Raoul grinned.

"Slade, stop please," Brigida whispered. "They don't know you're angry. I only came here because . . ."

"Here is Madame Restell, Brigida. She treats female complaints and private disorders. Perhaps one day she may be of service to you." He bowed deeply.

"The unfortunate must have some sanctuary, Slade, mustn't they? Calm yourself," madame rasped. "Nothing has happened." He shrugged the woman's hand from his arm and dragged Brigida toward the door, then stopped and laughed terribly.

"I almost forgot. Count, have you met my wife? Yes? Did you tell her how your tastes run? Take a good look at him, Brigida; perhaps you can guess. No? I'll show you then."

She felt a kind of pent-up madness in Slade's violent gestures as he dragged her stumbling after him from the room and down the back stairs through a dark kitchen to a wine cellar below it. Still crushing her soft bruised hand, he lit a candle, then reached overhead. A pair of chains and cuffs descended from a beam, and he secured her to them, then dropped to his knees to cuff a rigid steel bar between her spread ankles.

"The count designed that," Slade growled, seeing Brigida's frightened stare fixed on a chaise lounge that flowed like a wave, cresting in the middle. "Tied down to it, your perfect little backside would be raised just the way he likes. He usually starts with a riding quirt."

"I'm only here because you wanted me to be," Brigida said softly, watching him with disbelieving eyes. "I thought that; she told me."

Silent, cold, Slade ripped away her shift and circled her immobilized naked body, fingering the silken skin of her taut breasts, which were pulled high, resting a hand on the swell of soft buttocks, smoothing her hair down her back, and circling again before he violently took her trembling lips. "I only share when I choose to. I told you that, witch. Would you like to begin on her now, Count?" he said, still staring straight into Brigida's dark eyes. The figure lurking in the doorway stepped briskly forward, his narrow stick whistling as he tested it in air.

"With pleasure," the count said, just before he folded to Slade's blow, just before Brigida began to cry, to weep with a terrible desolate fury, her head thrown back and rolling from side to side as she wrenched against the cuffs, her golden hair flicking like flame, convulsive sobs shaking her so violently, that Slade was moved even in his anger to try and calm her. His own rage nearly spent, he watched hers with dispassionate, hard, possessive eyes as she fought against the restraints and, watching, awed at her frenzy, he wanted her. More, he realized, than he had ever before, wanted her just as she was at that instant—raging and struggling . . . and helpless. For an instant she was a wild, beautiful bird, tethered, hurling itself at the sky, a mountain mare roped and plunging, and then he was standing in front of her, devouring her mouth, tasting her throat, the tips of her breasts, one hand sliding down her back to her flanks, pressing her against him, the other working between her spread thighs, playing her lunging body until she began to move differently and the sounds she made changed. He knew then she wanted him, too, there, in that place, caught and powerless and vincible as she was.

"Say it," he growled, "or I'll use the stick on you myself."

"I want you now, I want you now," she whispered over and over. "I do, I really do, I want everything, whatever you want, whatever you ever wanted. Damn you, it's been too long, I need you. . . ."

He took her there, standing, swirling lost in the sound and scent and feel of her perfect body, her arms still caught, her legs freed to tighten about him, and he would have again if Levi hadn't suddenly filled the low doorway holding her white fur, might have anyway if the dark, impassive Indian eyes hadn't softened and fixed, for a fleeting instant before they turned away, on her beautiful tremulous body that was pink-tipped and ivory and so ready again—still. Cursing, Slade deftly undid her bonds, then covered her in fur.

"I'll take her home," Levi said. "You stay."

"I'll see to her." Slade roughly shouldered him aside.

"NO! NO, don't either of you come near me. He was watching and you . . . let him, and when it's his turn, you'd do the same. You both stay; you belong in this brothel!"

Brigida broke away and ran free, out of the hated house into the stunning cold of the wild March night.

It was almost dawn when Slade found Brigida, still wrapped in her white fox, its collar turned up high to frame her face, and she looked at him blankly when he came into the garden. There was an odd palor about her, a limpid, frightening glisten in her eyes.

"We looked for you in some damn odd places, Brigida. Are you ill?" Slade asked. He approached her cautiously to bring an arm about her shoulders and brush his lips to her brow to test its warmth. "Your eyes have . . . a glow."

"Of madness, do you think? Don't worry, I've been rubbing them with lemon juice, like Viola Murray, to achieve a special sparkle that turns men's heads." Her laugh was hollow. "You know, you can't really see the sky from here." She looked up.

Between the rows of four- and five-story gray stone houses and the stables in the mews behind them, the little gardens, separated one from the other by brick walls, seemed buried at the bottom of a well.

"I'm surprised anything grows at all, but the crocuses do. How did those trilliums get here?"

"I brought them, Brigida, snow trillium I found growing along the road one autumn. Do you like it? It's always first to show." Slade had never seen her so subdued, and her odd listlessness and the glisten in her eyes made him uneasy.

"What were you doing so late, while I was there?" she

inquired dully.

"I didn't know you'd be at Lydia's tonight. I was seeing to contracts. I'm selling off the whaling fleet."

Brigida stared at him. "But why?" she asked with some feeling. "How can you?"

"I sold two ships some months ago, to the government. They're outfitting the *Indian* now and the *Triton* soon, for steam. The rest of my fleet will go to a merchant for a very handsome price. Brigida, I didn't know about tonight. Lydia wasn't expecting me."

"You're cavalierly selling off our whole way of life, our history, just like that," she said, ignoring his last words, "to count dollar bills and push papers about?" Brigida brushed at the edge of her fur. A distant look came into her face. "I wanted my sons to know the sea as you and I did," she said, not looking at him.

"I'll take you and your sons to sea . . . if there ever are any sons," he said caustically. Then seeing the crazed, pained look come back to her eyes, he went on angrily.

"I'm being realistic, and so should you be. Kerosene is better than whale oil for lamps. There are fortunes to be made in petroleum now."

"I only agreed to this marriage because you were supposed to be a man of good seafarer's stock. I'll have to reconsider the whole thing, I'm afraid."

"Too late for that, lady. Besides, it's about over—the whaling, I mean. The herds have been nearly destroyed for some years now. It takes longer and longer a time at sea for a ship to come home with a full hold. I'll still be in oil," he said, watching her, talking on now just to keep that desperate look out of her beautiful eyes. "I've got refining stocks, I own a pipeline, did I tell you? A two-inch pipe—steam run—that goes from Pit Hole in Pennsylvania to the rail head at Titusville. I can make two thousand dollars in a day from that alone."

"That's a wickedly easy way to wealth. It sounds like thievery," Brigida criticized in a toneless voice. "Whaling at least is honest work."

"Brigida, don't be naive. I'm rich enough; that's not it. It's the play, the power, the winning at a rough game that appeals to me and . . . come in now," he ordered, passing an arm about her waist.

"I want to go home," she said, violently pulling away. "I want to go home."

"Home . . . ?"

"To Silver Hill, right now." She stamped her foot. She hadn't said San Francisco as he'd expected.

She came and leaned to him, hiding her face against his chest. "Could I go home please, Slade?" she asked in a small, plaintive voice.

His arms came about her, enfolding her slim, shivering body in the soft fur, and he brushed her hair with his lips. "Since you've asked so nicely, yes. . . . I thought you were ill."

"And what if I were ill? It would hardly affect you." A little color was coming back into her cheeks. "When can I leave?" she pressed. "This instant?"

"Tell me first," Slade demanded, lifting her face to look into her eyes, "why in hell you want to waste your time in the bucolic countryside? You're more valuable to me here."

"I'll make my time pay you then, damn it," she

answered, pouting up at him. "I'll farm the place. Or is that beneath Slade Hawkes's wife? It's almost spring, the willows in the park are going green, there's a cardinal wakes me every morning now. Slade, it's just . . . I want to go away from here. I need the sea, I need to hear the wind's music in the pines, I need to see the sky, not this paltry patch of blue. It is a dome, you might be interested to know. The sky is a dome. This is not the sky," Brigida called out, her voice echoing along the cavern of small stone buildings.

"Ah, *oui* madame?" Veronique called from a high window.

"Get rid of her," Brigida hissed at Slade.

"No."

"Why not? You saw . . ."

"I've reasons of my own for keeping her on."

"I bet you have," Brigida answered.

She was standing in the center of the garden with her head thrown back, fur clasped close. "I will wilt and fade, Veronique, if I don't smell the earth soon, if I don't stand in a real shaft of sunlight!" she shouted.

"*Oui*, madame," Veronique called, withdrawing her head and pulling the window shut.

"She thinks you're mad," Slade scowled. He turned up his jacket collar and dug his hands deep into his pockets as the first reflected morning sunlight touched the garden. "Come in!" he ordered again.

"Should I care what that whore thinks? Do you think I'm mad?" Brigida was laughing in a wild way that made him uneasy again.

"I think you're a strayed wood nymph, a pagan

Druidess reincarnate, is what I think, and you will be carried away to some forested glade to watch the leaves grow green, if that's what you want. Don't stare at me that way, goddess. You're the one that's mad, remember?"

She was watching him, amazed at his words as he came near, and she sheltered against him, almost content until he said again, "I didn't know about tonight. They won't trouble you again. I've seen to it. You don't have to go away."

Brigida began pacing the narrow garden paths gesturing wildly and speaking quickly.

"I do have to go or else spend all my days with vacuous ladies who do absolutely nothing but discuss bonnets and other inconsequential nothings and change their gowns constantly, and I must do the very same. I have morning clothes and day clothes and riding costumes and skating outfits; I have gowns for informal evenings and gowns for ceremonial evenings, for formal dinners, for balls, for theaters, and who knows what all else? If I should depart one fraction from the correct costume . . ." she paused, staring at him blindly, "I will be disgraced thoroughly and what's more, so will you. I am no more in this place than a peg for hanging clothes upon."

"That's not the term I'd use to describe you. Stand still." Slade, relieved at her frothy, more spirited manner, followed as she stalked the paths from end to end of the little garden. "Come here," he ordered.

"No, keep off, you," she shouted. "I'll never come on command like your well-trained dog. I'm not the bloody hound." They were glaring at each other across a flower-bed.

"He, at least, is smarter than you are. If I have to come and get you . . ." Slade's hands rested on his narrow hips and a muscle jumped in his jaw.

"Don't you dare!" Brigida's eyes flashed. "Lucifer! You threw me to those sharks and betrayed me to that . . . bitch and let Levi watch, oh . . ."

Her tears started, and in one long stride Slade reached her and lifted her in his arms and held her against him, glaring down with bright, cold eyes. "Levi wouldn't watch. He saw nothing. He only wanted to take you home, away from that place. I wanted you to know what sort of company you were in."

"Put me down, you damned bloody liar," she exploded.

He carried her up three flights of steps and she struggled and cried in his arms until he dropped her ungently on the horsechair settee in his study, where she remained a few moments in icy, tearful silence.

"What are you doing?" he asked when she stood and stalked toward the door.

"Leaving. To dress for breakfast. And you?" Brigida flung over her shoulder, wiping her eyes.

"Next time you come when you're called," he growled, catching her arm and turning her toward him. "Now stand still." Brigida felt a flutter of fear as his broad shoulders loomed over her.

Her tears were stopping, giving way to a flustered, pretty agitation, and she brought the knuckles of her left hand to her lips, the child's gesture Slade knew in her from long ago, and he paused.

"May I help you off with your wrap?" he asked softly,

undoing a hook, dropping his hand to slide it beneath the fur where it came in contact with the silken skin of Brigida's hip.

"I didn't ask you to touch me," she whispered, smiling a little wickedly, teasing. She let the cape slip off bare shoulders that were warm ivory against the lush white fur she had gathered about her low enough to expose the cleft of her breasts.

"Not with words you didn't, but you're asking all the same." Slade's eyes went dark as his exploring hand followed Brigida's roundness from hips to waist, up along her ribs to the swell of her bosom, and then she was in his arms, their lips wide and hungry, the kiss growing deeper and stronger as the white fur fell to the floor at their feet.

Fourteen

Brigida was at home to no one the next day. She spent the morning helping Veronique pack trunks and boxes for her solitary return to Silver Hill. Elizabeth would be remaining in the city with Slade for an unspecified time.

"Madame will leave the silver ball dress for the Astors' tonight?" Veronique inquired, folding lingerie into a straw trunk. Brigida eyed the maid uncomfortably. The girl had been so abjectly contrite after the affair at Lydia's, had wept and begged so pathetically not to be thrown into the streets to earn her living, that Brigida had agreed, reluctantly, to keep her on for the few days she'd remain in New York. After that, Slade could do whatever he damn pleased about Veronique, about Lydia, about all of it. At least she wouldn't be there to watch.

"Yes, and the tartan traveling suit for tomorrow."

"*Oui*, madame," the maid sniffed. Veronique's nose was still quite red, her eyes puffy from crying. "Ah, zut! The door again. The footman has gone round to the mews to see to the horses. I'll be only a moment."

Veronique had been turning away callers all the

morning, but this time Brigida was surprised to hear two
sets of footsteps mounting the stairs, and when the door
flew open, Miri Manceaux burst into the room in a flutter
of fur and flyaway fringe, her bonnet slightly askew.

"*Chère* Brigida! I heard you were on your way to the
country, and now I see it is true! But what magic, darling,
did you work, to get Slade to let you go before the season
has ended?" Mireille was breathless.

Brigida was examining gray kid gloves critically. "I'll
wear a new pair to travel, Veronique," she said, handing
them to the maid who had gone back to work and was
packing one of Brigida's hats into a copper bonnet box.

"That's very pretty. I never saw you in it," Mireille
said, touching a ribbon streamer before Veronique
lowered the lid.

"I don't like bonnets on me, but on you . . . Miri,
whatever is wrong? You're all . . . heated." Brigida led
her to a chair. "Give me your wrap."

"No, no, I can't stay. I must ask you a favor, Brigida.
Alain went out early this morning, before dawn, to con-
clude that business we talked of, remember? There's a
yacht at South Street waiting for . . ."

Miri glanced at Veronique, who continued her work.
"It doesn't matter for what. He's not yet returned. He
even missed his morning student, which is unheard of,
absolutely unheard of darling, and now I must go to look
for him. Getting involved in such madness with
DuBow—it is absurd, absurd! I shouldn't have let him; I
should have insisted on going along. What am I to do
now?" Mireille threw up her hands. "May I have a cup of
tea, darling? It always calms my nerves."

"Veronique," Brigida said. "Veronique!" she repeated more sharply, and the maid looked up, apparently pre-occupied and startled.

"Oui?" she responded slowly.

"Please fetch a pot of tea for Madame Manceaux."

The girl hurriedly left the room.

"I am sorry, darling. I don't trust anyone anymore since . . . since Alain told me about the girl at Madame Restell's."

"The one murdered? What about her?" Brigida felt a slow prickling along the length of her spine.

"She was DuBow's lady and working with him. Restell gave her the medication that killed her. The girl definitely was not *enciente*, DuBow swears it. Janine learned that the arms shipment for Paris was to be diverted—but by whom, why? That she didn't know yet. Oh, those evil guns!"

"Alain and Jean Paul went ahead with this, Miri, knowing there might be trouble? Can Alain deal with this sort of . . ."

"Darling, no! Alain is not Slade Hawkes. Alain . . . he can hardly harm a fly. DuBow told him only this morning why the girl was murdered. It was too late for Alain to back out. Besides, he believes in the Commune, do you understand? Alain believes the Commune is the only hope for France, so he has gone along today to do the deal and be done. He and DuBow took the gold and . . ."

"Wait, Miri, you go too quickly for me, and . . . it sounds such a serious matter, I think Slade should . . ." Brigida had begun to pace in her special way. "Shall I try to find him?"

"Darling, one doesn't try to find Slade Hawkes; that's impossible. He doesn't lunch at his club or at the Hoffman House as other men of his acquaintance do. I did come here hoping . . . Veronique told me he was out." Miri covered her face with her hands. "How long has that one been in this household? Who employed her?"

The door opened and Veronique crossed the room to place a tea tray on the table. Turning to Brigida she smiled, "Madame, Roland is running out of butter for the Hollandaise. I must go to the dairy. How many for dinner, madame, chef wishes to know?"

"Seven, tell Roland please, Veronique. Can't he wait for the milk wagon? Mr. Kier will be here any time."

"No, Roland cannot wait for the wagon, madame," Veronique said. "I'll return directly, madame. I give good service. You 'ave no reason to imply I go off on errands of my own, just because of . . . last night. I don't have a lover that I meet *en* secret. You are unjust."

"Veronique, I never said any such thing. I only thought . . ." but the maid was gone before Brigida's words were done.

"She was fabricating," Miri said softly. "Roland would not be preparing Hollandaise at ten in the morning for dinner at eight, would he? Who, besides Alain, heaven help him, and I, will be dining with you this evening?"

"The Carpenters, father and son, Ann Overton, Elizabeth . . ."

Miri was sipping her tea staring distractedly out into the garden. "You've snow trillium," she said. "That's lovely, darling. Oh, Brigida, come with me, please. We'll take a hansom and go to look for Alain."

"I'll come, Miri, but I think all this intrigue is telling on you. You should bring the baby and come to the country with me; Alain, too, and you'll all soon be happy again, I promise."

"Just hurry and dress, darling," was all Miri answered, and in a few minutes she and Brigida left the house and made their way across Washington Square toward the French Quarter, hoping to find Alain enjoying a pernod at Volet's, his adventure successfully completed and done with.

Broadway was crowded with laborers and merchants and well-wrapped and muffed ladies as Brigida and Miri walked quickly south. Amidst the noise of hammering and building that was everywhere in the city, they dodged vendors and shabby men with advertising placards and turned into Bleecker, passing a wizened old woman sitting bent in a chair, a basket of apples at her feet. Brigida purchased two and hurried on after Miri, who had gained entrance to Volet's and was halfway up the stairs, gesturing to Brigida to remain at the door. Biting into an apple, Brigida watched a butcher sweep the sidewalk in front of his shop opposite, heard the parrots' screams and the old woman's shout that silenced them, and moments later Miri appeared, looking more anxious than before.

"Darling," she said, grasping Brigida's arm and pulling her along, "we must find the *chinois* who was doing the deal. *Mon Dieu*, what has the fool done? Never again will I let him, never! Such an impossible romantic; anyone can draw him into the stupidest adventures. Never again, do you hear?"

"Of course I hear, Miri, but I'm not the one to tell.

Don't leap to terrible conclusions. What else did Madame DuBow tell you?" Arms linked, they hurried several blocks deeper into the French Quarter, past beggars and blind men and shouting peddlers—one offering dancing toy monkeys on India rubber strings. "Did her son return?"

"Non! He is not yet returned and that . . . that murderous boy always purchases the meat for the evening sitting at Volet's. The old crone is furious. There, across the street, is a hansom, darling," Miri declared, glancing about after dragging Brigida to a busy intersection. *"Regardez!* On the opposite side." There was a hack parked at the far curb, the horse's head buried in a nosebag. *"Vite, vite!* Hurry, Brigida."

"Miri, be careful—Miri, be careful! The drays and wagons . . . let's use the footbridge. It's the only way to safely cross here; that's why they built it, please. . . ."

"No, no, we will lose the cab. *Allez, ma petite.* I beg you." Miri stepped off the curb as a heavy black wagon, drawn by six steaming Clydesdales, came fast around a corner, bearing down on her. She froze, petrified, as the wagon careened wildly and the driver, his hat pulled low, shouted curses and cracked a heavy whip to urge his team to even greater speed.

"Miri!" Brigida screamed, the knuckles of her left hand crushed to her mouth. She stepped forward to pull Miri back out of the wagon's path just as a large form moved like a shadow to lift them both out of danger.

"Why are you here?" Levi Philips asked Brigida, calm as always. When he set them down, Miri slumped against him, quaking.

"Are you following me, Mr. Philips? I have had that feeling before. Why are you here, may I inquire?" Brigida bristled.

"Finding you where we did last night, I think you need someone to follow you, but it was Kier the milkman told us—me and Slade—that you were over in this part of town unescorted. A good thing we ran into him." Levi looked at Mireille.

"Yes, Levi . . . thank you." She smiled weakly. "Did Slade send you after Alain? Oh, I must have water."

"Come, my friend will give you drink." Levi led the two women about half a block along the street, then he stopped and rapped sharply in a precise staccato rhythm on a dark glass door. It swung open after a time, with a rattling of chains and sliding of bolts, and they followed Levi inside. The windows of the establishment were all of stained glass that barely lit the elaborately frescoed walls displaying elephants—white elephants—sporting in every conceivable manner.

"What is this place?" Brigida asked.

"Welcome, ladies, to the White Elephant Dance Hall." Under a painting of a larger-than-life voluptuous nude, someone leaned in shadow against a gleaming mahogany bar. A small, muscular, shaggy man with the face of a brawler and a boxer's large fists stepped forward. "Hello, Mireille," he said.

"*Bonjour*, Billy," Miri smiled, extending a gloved hand. "Brigida, my . . . old friend, Billy McGlory. Could I have some water, Billy, do you suppose?"

McGlory snorted. "You look like you're needin' somethin' stronger than water, Miri. You too?" he asked

271

Brigida. She nodded.

Carrying glasses, he led them to a table at the edge of a shining dance floor. "I brought you each an Irish whiskey, neat. Now tell me what you ladies are doin' here, Mireille. What happened, Levi?"

"Dray almost run them down. Black wagon, six Clydes, moving too fast." Levi downed a drink.

"That team was over to Lamm's warehouse earlier," McGlory said thoughtfully. "But what are these two ladies doin' in this neighborhood? I don't often see such quality in here, you know, Miri?"

"*C'est dommage.* I am so sorry to hear that, Billy," Miri smiled. "Madame Hawkes and I . . . we're looking for Alain and . . ."

"What's your Alain up to that you have to go out lookin' for 'im, Miri, like some drunkard's woman combing the bars?"

He swung about to address Brigida. "It was a gentleman she married, and now it seems he's a sot and a boozer."

"Alain doesn't drink, Billy. He's involved with the French and the Prussians and the war and . . ."

". . . yes, and the rifles, the very same Slade's been lookin' for so long," McGlory said with a shake of his large head. "You're all daft. Miri, you're too late." He moved behind the bar to pour out another drink for Levi and one for himself.

"Too . . . late?" Miri went pale, and Brigida rose from her chair.

"I only mean that your husband and that waiter were in the neighborhood hours ago. You best go to South

Street dock or, better yet, see the Chinee, Lamm."

"The ladies will take a hansom home. I will see to Lamm," Levi announced.

"The ladies will not take a hansom home," Brigida stated.

"Slade won't have you in such areas of the city. Dangerous." Levi answered. He poured his drink down his throat and pushed his glass forward for another refill.

"Come, Levi," Brigida smiled, "we would be perfectly safe with you, I know it, and Slade needn't even be told if that's what's worrying you. In San Francisco Mother's cook took me to Little China more than once."

"Around Mott Street and Pell, Mrs. Hawkes, is New York's Chinatown, and whatever you may hear about opium there and white slavery, it's only half true, ain't it so, Levi, my man?" McGlory's brown eyes took on a mischievous gleam. "These fine uptown women will sure be safe with a brute like you. No, there's no one there who doesn't know your husband's man, Mrs. Hawkes. He frequents the houses so regular. No one would lay a finger on you. But if you was to try goin' alone, I'd not give odds on how quick the pair of you'd disappear into the brothels. Happens all the time. Lamm's one of the biggest dealers in girls."

"Abductions here?" Brigida asked. "I can't believe . . ."

"Levi, take my rig," Billy offered.

Miri took the man's massive hand in both of hers. "Billy, thank you," she said quickly. "I'll . . . if ever I can repay your kindness . . ."

"Oh, go on now," he said brusquely, then turning to Brigida, smiled. "Get the captain to bring you back some night when we're open. We have some real fine times, real fine. Ask Slade, he knows."

Levi guided Billy McGlory's Narragansset Pacer toward a wood frame cottage a half block off Mott Street. Lin Kee Lamm glanced up from the newspaper he was reading and saw through his parlor window an Indian and two well-dressed women approaching his house, a most unusual sight.

Lamm rose and opened his door. Bowing to Levi, he asked, "What is it you require of me? I am at your service, sir. If you've come to sell your women . . . they're too costly for me, a glance tells."

Brigida and Mireille stood ignored at the entrance to the small, spartanly furnished room. Lamm occupied one of two chairs at a worn table, and Levi claimed the other as a silent girl placed a pot of tea and two cups before them and then withdrew.

Observing the faces of the two men, who were studying each other carefully, Brigida couldn't decide which of them was more an enigma, the Indian, with his cold eyes, or the diminutive Oriental, with a half smile frozen on thin, tight lips.

Brigida started when Levi's low voice broke the silence. "Billy McGlory told me you are the top man here. You know everything."

"Mr. McGlory flatters me," Lamm answered, still smiling.

"Billy tells me there was a large cache of Colt weapons stored here on Mott Street for many years." Levi gulped his tea.

"Yes? Did Mr. McGlory tell you that?" Lamm refilled Levi's cup.

"Stolen from the government."

"And . . . ?"

"A Frenchman purchased the Colts. For gold."

"Yes?"

"When he came to claim his purchase today, he and the gold disappeared. The weapons too."

"Yes? And what do you want me to do, Mr. . . . ?"

"Philips. Levi Philips. Tell me where the guns were stored on Mott Street." Levi had leaned forward in his chair, resting both heavy hands on the table, dwarfing the small teacup between them. "Tell me where the rifles and pistols are now."

Levi dipped his head forward and, for the first time since he had entered the house, offered a suggestion of a bow. "Slade Hawkes will make generous payment for your information."

Dipping his own head lower, Lamm said, "Tell Captain Hawkes the weapons were in my warehouse since some time in the year of eighteen sixty-four. Payment for storage was irregular but ample, made each time until last month by a countryman of mine who travels here from San Francisco every few years. The last payment, the final one, was made by a woman."

"What woman?" Levi's inflection never changed, the expression on his face didn't alter. "What woman? What was her speech?" he asked again.

"Tall, heavily veiled, Mr. Philips. She never spoke more than a word or two words. What further help may I be to you?" Another deeper bow went unacknowledged by Levi.

"Say what you know of Alain Manceaux." Levi proffered a hundred dollar bill.

The man's eyes opened wide for an instant. "Mr. Philips, there is a Chinese saying, 'Kill one to warn a hundred.'"

Mireille gasped, and Brigida took her hand.

"I can say no more," Lamm smiled.

"For ten of these you could say more." Levi counted out nine bills to add to the first that lay untouched on the table, and Lamm leaned forward. Quickly, quietly he whispered, "Behind the Atlantic Garden, the Prussian beer hall, if he is fortunate . . . if he is more fortunate than his young friend, who is dead and disposed of hours ago in the East River. Good day, Mr. Philips. Should you wish to purchase my services again, please be so discreet as to visit alone under cover of darkness."

Lamm was still bowing very low when Levi was urging Brigida and Miri toward the carriage tied at the curb.

"When word of the French defeat came," Miri said, shuddering as she entered the Atlantic Garden, "I am told a spontaneous cheer actually went up in this . . . this deathly place . . . Germans are such somber drinkers, not convivial at all like the French, just serious and steady, but when Alsace and Lorraine fell, they cheered. Here's the proprietor. You speak, Brigida, my accent . . ."

"Alain is all right, Miri, he must be. Try not to look so . . . is your back garden open, sir? We'd enjoy a hot chocolate out of doors," Brigida said to a fat, dour man in a white apron who came to seat them.

"Too cold for the garden, ya?" He eyed them suspiciously.

"A table at the back then, if you please, looking on the garden. That's almost as good," Brigida smiled.

They followed the lumbering figure the length of the dim, cavernous hall, and when they were seated they each ordered a hot chocolate and a piece of creamy pastry.

When the man had gone, Brigida whispered, "I'm going out back. When Levi comes, send him along." She stood and started to open the closest door.

"*Nein!* Do not go there! I told you once already it ain't yet open," the proprietor called, lurching toward them from the front of the hall.

"Sir, come please! My friend is faint and only needed a breath of fresh air. Hurry, water!" Brigida commanded. Levi slipped past into the back garden as the man stared unhappily at Brigida, who was frantically fanning Miri with a lace handkerchief.

"Ach! I'll call my *Frau* from the kitchen," he said unhappily, regarding Miri's ashen face. "Your friend, she is laced too tight, ya?" He hurried off.

At first glance the garden appeared deserted. Dusty chairs and tables were stacked along one wall under faded striped tenting, frayed and tattered by the winter wind. It flapped forlornly as Brigida tiptoed beneath thick tangles of bare vines that seemed to be holding up the weathered trellises arching down the center of the garden. When she had almost reached the back wall, Brigida saw the proprietor emerge from the kichen door, a heavy cleaver raised above his head.

"Don't!" she commanded. She held her small pistol straight out in front of her, and her hand wavered only slightly.

The man lowered the cleaver very slowly, walking toward her. "Take care, fraülein," he said, beads of sweat beginning to appear on his high forehead. "I was only protecting my property from prowlers. See? Look there."

In the fraction of the moment she took her eyes from the man's face, he was at her side, knocking the gun from her hand, raising his own weapon again, and then, as she screamed, Slade stepped from the shadows to bring the heavy figure down with two well-placed blows. Shaking, Brigida followed Slade to a wooden storage shack where she saw Levi crouched over Alain Manceaux, a dark, still bundle at his feet.

Dinner had been a somber affair, and Alain was silent throughout. Miri worried at him, asking repeatedly how he felt and, shaking her head, saying over and over, "You could have been dead now, Alain, think of that, you could have been. Look at him, *mes amis*, just look!" He had a black eye and a plaster on his left cheek.

"Damn it, Miri!" he exploded finally. "Don't you think I feel badly enough? They killed Jean Paul like that!" Alain snapped his fingers. His usually cherubic face was pained and very sad.

"Tell me again how . . . I can't understand it," Miri

shook her head.

"Someone betrayed us, there's no other answer. It happened after the wagon was loaded. Jean Paul . . . he never got his knife out of its sheath."

Del Carpenter clapped a hand on Alain's shoulder. "I admire your spirit and courage, sir. A man can only do his best."

"It wasn't good enough, my best." Alain rubbed his forehead.

"Are you quite sure you're safe, Alain?" Brigida asked.

"Of course, lovely Brigida. They've gotten everything they wanted, haven't they?" Alain shook his head again.

"What I don't understand, Alain," Ann Overton asked slowly, "is why you . . ." she paused. "To be blunt, why are you alive?"

"Ann, how could you ask such a thing?" Elizabeth was aghast.

"No, no, she is quite right to wonder. I have myself . . . all day waiting and waiting. What else could I think about? *Rien*, nothing, and I have no answer." Alain left the table, Mireille following after him, and the others found them later sitting silently in the drawing room.

Slade relaxed into a wing chair, stretching long legs toward the fire. Brigida sat on the rug, resting back against his knee. He lit a cigar and passed one to Ann. "Slade knows, don't you, Slade, why they let Alain go?" Ann said.

"What? What do you know, Slade?" Alain was on his feet. "If you gave us away for your own reasons . . ."

"You're an amateur, Alain. DuBow had been playing at this game a while. He knew the risks. He would have traded your life for his given any chance at all. Stay out of it now."

"You are of course just the one who would know about such things, Slade." Alain's round face was crimson with anger. "And I should, of course, acquiesce to your superior experience in matters of thievery and murder, but I'm afraid, *cher, cher ami,* I cannot! I will find the gold and the guns or die trying . . . it is the very least I can do for Jean Paul."

"Imbecile," Miri hissed, in tears. "Listen to what Slade tells you. Do you think I wish to be a widow so soon? Pardon, I must go. I am sad you all missed your ball because of us. *Bon soir, bon voyage*, Brigida; perhaps we shall visit you at Silver Hill, but I think not."

"Mireille, wait!" Alain called; then he rushed off after her, throwing a half-hearted goodnight to the assembled company.

"Ann, dear Ann, you're puffing like a chimney, and it is so unladylike to smoke . . . a cigar . . . in mixed company." Elizabeth coughed delicately.

"I don't enjoy domestic drama," Ann said shortly. "People should be emotional in the privacy of their own bedrooms, not in other people's drawing rooms."

"Mrs. Overton, sympathetic as always," Slade commented. "He was almost killed today."

"You of all people know better. You were seeing to his welfare from the first; I'd wager my life on that. He should understand, the fool, and be grateful." Ann tossed the cigar into the fire.

"That's all, Ann," Slade said evenly. "Are you packed, goddess?" he asked Brigida. She nodded.

"Go along to bed, then, like a good girl. I've some business to attend to now."

"Of course you have. But I'm not tired in the least. A game of hearts?" She smiled at Philip, who was ready, as always, to grant her least demand.

Fifteen

The black brougham, with Levi Philips up top and Slade's bay stallion at the rear, moved along South Street under the long bowsprits of docked sailing vessels, figureheads staring blindly across the busy roadway at sailmakers' lofts and nautical instrument houses.

"Are you sure you want to leave all this?" Slade asked. Brigida was silent beside him. "You won't see such a sight as that for a while." He pointed up with a bandaged hand at a pair of sailors dangling far above the street, securing a flying jib to a bowsprit.

"Oh yes, I'm sure, and you should come too," she answered petulantly, "at least until your hand heals and you're able to defend yourself."

Levi maneuvered the carriage onto a waiting ferry, and almost at once there was the thud of ramp and rattle of chains. "You must get down right now, Slade." Brigida stared at him as he sat unmoving, long legs stretched over the dog, his heels resting on the carriage seat opposite. With steam whistle blasting, the ferry pulled out into the rushing current of the East River, and speechless,

Brigida watched the city slip away, mansions and slums and houses of commerce thinning to the north where there were only scattered homes and farmsteads along the banks.

"Shall we get down and look from the deck?" Slade asked casually. "I enjoy this crossing."

They leaned at the rail with the wind full in their faces, and Levi joined them after he secured the horses. "The commodore's ferries will be out of business one of these days soon." Slade gestured toward the Brooklyn Bridge construction.

"Which commodore? Do you mean Vanderbilt?" Brigida asked, still startled, glancing at him quickly as if to be sure he was really there.

"Yes, Vanderbilt, the very same who now owns a few railroads, started life over there." He pointed south across the bustling harbor. "Richmond Town, Staten Island. He made his first dollar, as a boy, sailing people back and forth to Manhattan. Not long after, he had all the ferrying business hereabouts tied up tight. The bridge won't affect him; he's expanded his operations since those days, wouldn't you say, Levi?"

"Yes. Vanderbilt is like you, Slade; makes money easy. The old gent took to Slade the first time they met," Levi told Brigida. "The commodore had a granddaughter for him to marry. Slade wouldn't."

"Well, why ever not?" Brigida smiled archly. "How could you turn down an offer of marriage to a rich Vanderbilt?"

"Not because I was waiting only for you," Slade said coolly. "A tumble with one spoiled brat or other makes little difference to me. I'd have had to put up with the commodore. I don't admire the old man's manners."

Aggrieved by Slade's words, Brigida turned on him. "You go to blazing, bloody glory! What would you know about manners?" she glowered.

With turned-up collar and hands deep in his coat pockets, he stalked away along the crowded deck with Bran.

"I heard the commodore say to Slade once, 'Boy,' he said, 'we own America. I don't care how we got it, we're keepin' it!' I heard him myself. Slade doesn't like that sort of talk."

"What does Slade like, Levi? Not me, apparently," Brigida said miserably.

"He's angry now because we didn't find the guns last night, or the gold . . . We did find the drayman who took the guns, the same who almost ran you down. We convinced him to tell us a few things."

"That's how Slade hurt his hand?"

"Yeah, split the knuckles."

"And now he has to stay out of sight, that's why he's coming home to Silver Hill. Perhaps he'll be good at farming."

"He's good at everything he puts his mind to," Levi snorted a short laugh, "even if he's never content."

"Why not?" Brigida asked, glancing sidelong at the Indian's gaunt profile.

"Slade . . . he sailed the world hunting the largest beast on earth, risked his life in the war, had all the women he wanted, made a fortune that would satisfy any other man, races his horses and yachts and wins, and none of it satisfies him at all."

"But why not, Levi?" Brigida demanded again, turning up her small hands in a gesture of querying vexation, then smoothing her windblown hair with a gloved palm.

"Root," the Indian said. She understood at once and completely.

"Help me, Levi?" she asked. She rested a hand on the sleeve of the Indian's dark coat. "His hatred for Bluford Root touches everyone, turns everything to ash and dust in his hand."

Levi nodded. "But he does not hate you, Brigida." He used her given name for the first time, smiling. "How could he?"

She smiled back at him. "I'm sorry about . . . Lydia's," she said. "I was so . . . frightened I . . . I never thought, really, you were one of them."

"Don't be so sure of that," he grinned. "We've had some times at Lydia's, but that's done—for now."

When Slade came sauntering around the deck, he was interested to find Brigida and Levi standing shoulder to shoulder engrossed in conversation. He watched her place a hand on the Indian's sleeve and hold the man's usually impassive eyes with her sunlit smile.

"The fool must actually be taken with the little scapegrace," he thought, frowning. He observed the gesturings of her small, eloquent hands, the slight bend of her body toward her companion, all familiar, close, winning ways. "The sorceress will bewitch the poor savage if I don't protect him," Slade scowled to himself, moving to resume his place at the rail.

The flow of Brigida's words never stopped as he came

to her side. She just slipped her arm through his and rested her head against his shoulder for an instant by way of greeting. The easy intimacy of her motions touched something in Slade that he had to harden himself against. "The creature is soft as a kitten, she'd have me think," he mused, "and as much to be trusted as a wildcat in a cage."

There was an ear-splitting blast of a horn as the vessel made its landfall at Brooklyn Ferry.

The brougham reached Silver Hill gate long past midnight, when a half moon dappled the drive with shadows of budding oak boughs and the air was sweet with a touch of spring and the scent of the sea.

The next morning, Brigida slept until the sun had almost reached the noon mark, and when she descended for breakfast she learned that Slade had not only left her bed, as usual, but was gone from the house entirely. She surprised Martha and the Edwards girls polishing silver in the pantry and was greeted with happy exclamations of welcome.

"The place has been mostly shut up again in the time you've all been away. I opened the breakfast room for Slade early. Which others should be readied?" Martha asked. "Now Elizabeth has flown the coop, you are mistress here. Such decisions are for you to make."

"Well then, open everything, Martha!" Brigida decided. "Even though it's only Slade and me, I want Silver Hill lovely and alive in every corner. We shall all be working soon, did you know?''

"We do know about farmin' Silver Hill again; we've been knowin' since you left here. Levi had Johnny Hand and Robin workin' all this time you been gone, getting ready. The straw bedding and dung from the stables have been stacked against the barn to cure. Johnny is spreadin' the fields with it now, to richen the soil.''

"Before we left? Levi planned all this before we left? Oh, I can't believe it!'' Brigida exclaimed.

"You'd best believe it, missus. Even now he and Slade are out riding the land to decide what's to be put in where. The plowing will start soon's the ground is dry enough.'' Martha's round face was all smiles. "It is good to know the earth will be plowed again after all the years of it lying fallow.''

"Two cows have calved, missus,'' Nan announced, brushing a strayed lock of lank hair from her eyes with the back of her hand. "Kept Mary pretty busy.''

"How very nice. Squire's bull?'' Brigida gulped the tea Martha had placed on the kitchen table in front of her.

"Bubbles in your cup. Means someone will kiss you before too long,'' Martha predicted. There was a little silence as the three women regarded Brigida.

"Well, what is it?'' she asked. "Out with it now. You all look as if I'm holding back something you're owed.''

"We was just wonderin' if you and the captain . . . if you was expectin' yet, is all,'' Nan blurted.

"You were just wondering, were you?'' Brigida flushed. "We'll all just have to wait and see, I'm afraid.''

"You eat the very last egg ever laid by an old hen, on May Day, you'll give Slade the son he wants, and he'll be

content to stay home and be forever done with the past."
Martha set a plate before Brigida.

"You're certain of that, are you?" Brigida teased.
"How do you come to know so much about domestic
harmony and pagan spells, I wonder?"

"It's Slade I know about." The woman stood with her
arms folded over her bosom, the expression on her round
face adamant.

"It's being said about that Del Carpenter has taken
quite a fancy to Mrs. Hawkes again. Is it true?" Nan
asked eagerly.

"Mm hm, yes," Brigida nodded. "They will travel to
the Continent in summer, but that's a secret; she's not
yet mentioned it to Slade."

"Well, he won't care. He's always treated her so indifferent. No offense to your husband, missus, but I felt bad
for 'er."

"Mary, just hold that gossip's tongue of yours,"
Martha warned. "There's cause enough for distance
between mother and son."

"What cause, Martha?" Brigida asked. "Slade told me
a little but . . ."

"Well, he will just have to tell you more when he's
ready. You girls best be getting on with your chores,"
Martha instructed Mary and Nan. "Look at you two
straining your ears for any tidbit of tattle you can hear!"

"Martha, let them visit with me, please? I've been
away so long, we need a good talk." Brigida rested her
elbows on the table and propped her chin on her laced
hands, looking up appealingly.

"I'm off to the village. Mind, don't keep them too

long," Martha relented, and when she had gone, Brigida poured out three cups of tea, then wriggled back in her chair. Mary and Nan, who had been polishing at the far end of the table, brought their work closer.

"Is your young man ready yet, Mary, to work on my mill?" Brigida wanted to know first of all. "We shall want the mill turning before the harvest begins."

"Tom's been up to look over the thing, and 'tis certainly a job he'd like to do, with my brother Robin for helper. Shall he talk to you," the girl asked, "or to the captain about his fees and costs?"

"To me. This is my project. Now, Nan," she went on, "tell me what you've been at these weeks."

"Nanny," Mary giggled, "tell 'er about Johnny Hand!"

"Nothin' to tell," Nan answered, staring at the floor.

"She's sweet on 'im, but he's told Tom he's never seen another like you, missus. You spoiled 'im for ordinary girls. He hasn't even glanced at a one since he first laid eyes on you."

"But that's ridiculous, awful! We'll do something about it this very instant. We will make young John take notice of you, Nan. Hurry while we've the house to ourselves. Mary, heat water for a tub," she ordered. "Your sister will have admirers by the score when we've done with her."

"But I only want one, missus," Nan protested, following hesitantly after Brigida.

Seating the girl at the dressing table in her room, Brigida rolled up the sleeves of her gown and began at once to vigorously brush out Nan's dull hair.

"First I'm going to snip it all feathery about your face

290

so it won't keep dropping into your eyes like string. Then," Brigida went on, brushing, "we'll wash it— twice—with a concoction I made of crushed walnut leaves. That will make your hair glossy. A camomile rinse after will make the pale strands light and glowy. When you're done in the tub, I'll do your face. Your brows are much too dark; they dim your pretty eyes." Brigida brushed, pulling Nan's head back a little with each brisk stroke. "A new dress, a fresh apron . . . and then, my dear, you will just come right along with me to the Hands' cottage."

"Oh, I couldn't do it, I just couldn't go after him like that!" Nan looked petrified. "And I can't get home neither lookin' like a . . . a painted lady. Ain't it so, Mary?"

"Do I look like a painted woman, Nan?" Brigida asked, standing with her hands on her hips.

The girl shook her head no.

"Then stop worrying. A trace of beet juice or rose water on your cheek will give you a glow, that's all; you'll just look especially lovely and no one will ever know why except you, me, and Mary. Your tub's ready. Painted woman indeed!"

"Martha? Brigida? Damn, where the devil is everyone!" Slade called, taking the steps two at a time. "I need food and drink . . . where are you?"

He came striding through the door of Brigida's sunlit room to find her putting a finishing hand to Nan Edwards, who stood before the cheval glass regarding her own image with wonder. Mary, who had been reclining on the chaise, sprang to her feet at the sight of him, and Nan froze.

"The goddess Brigida and her Druids at play," he said. "This is not Miss Whats-its' classes for spoiled little girls; I pay these two good wages for honest work, not to waste their time entertaining my idle wife."

Brigida turned on him with murder in her eyes, but before she loosed a string of damning expletives, she thought better of it. "Captain Hawkes," she said, "meet the new Miss Edwards." Brigida half bowed, gesturing toward the girl with a flourish of her upturned hand, and Nan crimsoned under Slade's scrutiny.

After a long pause, he made a circling motion with an index finger, and the girl turned completely around, a solemn, expectant look in her eyes.

Her shining brown hair was streaked with lighter strands and fell in such a way over her brow as to make the shape of her face appear narrower than it had seemed before. Her cheeks were prettily pink, and her hazel eyes, which Slade had never really noticed, seemed large and lovely. She wore a high-buttoned, small-print blouse and matching skirt with a crisp, immaculate white apron tied about a defined, if not very small, waistline.

"Slade, say something, please," Brigida demanded.

"You're lovely, Nan. The lads will give you no peace until you choose one." He held the flustered girl's eyes with his and smiled into them in a way that set Brigida bristling. "Damn him!" she thought, "even here, even Nan."

"You're the sorceress, Brigida. Tell me how it was

done." The warming spring sun had already touched his skin, lending it a coppery cast, and his eyes were blue as cornflowers.

"Druids and dryads and sorceresses may never reveal their secrets lest their powers be taken from them," Brigida announced. "I only can say it was done with a touch of kohl and a snip or two of the scissor."

"Keep your secrets then, witch." Slade turned to Mary. "Run along, and take your pretty sister, too. You'd better be at work when Martha gets back from the village or there'll be the devil to pay."

"You are an enchantress, to work such a transformation in that girl. A dull, lusterless creature this morning, transfigured before midday to a blooming, muscular blonde. She'll well warm some lusty lad."

"Almost a blonde. Do you find her irresistible? Pity, you'd only frighten her. I've much to do. Why have you searched me out with such noise?" she asked.

"You've much to do? Here I've come away from my work to take you out riding, so you won't feel dull, and you tell me how busy you are, who've been playing about all morning keeping the servants from their chores."

"So considerate of you. How do you account for that all of a sudden?"

"I've an ulterior motive, of course."

"Of course," Brigida agreed. "And what might that be, pray tell?" She fussed with her hair and applied scent to her temples and wrists.

Slade relaxed in an armchair, tapping his riding crop against a boot top. "My real reason for seeking you out, goddess, was to abuse you. You're quite appealing when

293

you're piqued. It's exciting, I find."

Brigida turned on him, her fists clenched at her sides. He hadn't shaved, she noticed, and his lean cheeks were shadowed by a dark growth of rough beard. She found him extraordinarily handsome as he sat watching her with insolent eyes. She extended soft fingers to caress his face, following the faint in-curving beneath a high cheekbone, and he caught her hand to inhale the fragrance of roses.

"Soon you'll have roses from the gardens, baskets of them, all you could want," he said. "I came to ride with you. The first time you sit your new mare you might need me with you."

Hanging on one wall of the tack room were several types of headsets and a variety of leads and reins. Three new saddles rested on a trestle, and Brigida's eyes fixed on one that was light and small, of red Morocco leather and tooled in gold.

"Your choice," Slade said. "I didn't know which you'd like."

"So you bought them all? How extravagant. I'll ride astride in the western manner," she said. Her senses were intoxicated with the strong, sweet odors of the stable, and her heart soared at the sight of a beautiful, small, black mare.

"She is like you, goddess—well bred and beautiful, but overly spirited. She'll need a strong hand and a taste of the switch to keep her behaved."

"Oh no, you're wrong. She must be guided with a

velvet hand, given her head; that's the way to get the most from a sensitive lady."

The muscles and sinews in Slade's bared forearm stood flexed as he led the mare, dancing on delicate hoofs, into a small, white-fenced paddock, where he lengthened her lead and put her through her paces for Brigida's viewing. Called to a halt, the horse posed, absolutely still, in the spring sunshine, with her long neck arched and long tail high, appearing to Brigida as beautiful as a sculpture of onyx or of smooth black marble, perfect.

Slade helped Brigida up, and she and the mare trotted in the enclosure, getting the measure and feel of each other until he led out the stallion. Before he mounted, he adjusted the stirrups on Brigida's saddle and fingered her velvet riding skirt, his hand caressing up the length of her leg, his eyes continuing the climb to the swell of her breasts.

The horses walked sedately side by side out of the paddock to the long drive. They trotted under oaks that were young again in new leaf; then they turned to canter across an open, spring-green meadow. A dome of April sky was streaked with high bands of floating clouds.

With grudging pleasure, Slade had to admire the unwasted grace with which Brigida sat her mount. Like some mythic being, the beautiful lady and the dark, glossy-flanked mare seemed one elegant, flawless creature.

Brigida's skirt rode high, baring shapely legs in soft suede boots. As she put the horse into a gallop, Slade felt a cold ribbon of fear curl in his chest. The horse and rider approached a stone wall marking the edge of a field. His breath caught as the black mare lifted, as if on beating wild wings, legs neatly tucked, to clear the jump, Brigida's hair spreading out behind like a golden cloud.

When he reached them in the midst of a field bright with blue-eyed grass and meadow violets, the girl, with her head thrown back, was laughing aloud, her lips shining, sunlight dancing in her eyes. The mare pawed the ground, impatient to be off again. In the forge of his dreams, Slade knew then, he could not have created a more beautiful woman. The blazing disc of the sun hung suspended between them, gulls threaded the sky above.

"She will yield everything to me, no matter what it takes," he promised himself again, and the fierceness of his look dimmed the light of pleasure in Brigida's eyes. But only for a moment. Resolving to ignore his stormy moods, she blurted out, "Slade Hawkes, this mare is the most perfect animal that ever was, and she was born for me alone, I can tell. Thank you." She said the last quickly.

"Take care you don't injure her with your reckless ways," he said sternly, wanting to reach over and pull her to him and slide down, sinking into the soft grasses to capture the moment and to savour the wild sweetness of Brigida's body. An uncomfortable emotion simmering in him held him back from an action that at any time in his life before he would not have shied from. Wary of his own feelings, Slade went on in the vein of a displeased parent to a wayward child. "You are being willfully wild. You had no way of knowing the horse could clear the wall."

"I knew," Brigida answered, bright points of anger

showing in her eyes. "Some things one just knows, that's all! Besides, I had a very good teacher, a Spaniard from the California mountains, born on horseback."

"Another of your . . . lovers?" Slade asked coldly.

Brigida stared at him for a moment, then she wheeled the horse about to easily take the jump again. She turned to laugh over her shoulder before disappearing along the verdant forest path that led in the direction of the Hands' cottage.

Sixteen

"I know this mill, missus. I remember when the old captain's ox team drug it up this way, from the harbor. I was a little lad then, and the occurrence impressed itself on the mind."

Brigida sat behind Slade's desk in the small office very early in the morning, and Tom Sayre, carpenter and millwright, stood in the middle of the floor, facing her. He was a slim man, with brown hair and eyes and a shy manner. Attired in homespun shirt and carpenter's overalls, he clutched a cap in both hands, as if he would strangle it.

"Such a sight would impress any child." Brigida nodded him to a chair where he sat stiffly, cap still in hand.

"Most of the mills here have been moved once or twice, I've learned," she continued. "I've never before thought of such a large thing as a windmill as a portable object, but that does seem to be the way of it here."

"Yes, 'tis so, missus. They've no foundations. This one was restin' on rocks for level same way it is now.

299

Built in eighteen-twenty, she was, later than most of the others about. When she stood in the harbor on a high hill, she was called 'Flag on the Mill—Ship in the Bay.' Did you know that?"

Brigida shook her head. "No, I didn't, and it is such a wonderful name. How do you know so much about all this, Mr. Sayre?"

"Tom, please, missus." He nodded two or three times. "On my mother's side the family was millwrights going back a long time. My grandfather and his father, too, built most of the mills you'll see, wind and tide mills, both."

"But not this one. Its cap is different from the others. It's got no gables." Brigida poured two cups of coffee.

"It has got a Turk's head cap, missus, like those in Lincolnshire in England."

Tom Sayre's rigid manner eased somewhat. Placing his cap on the floor at the side of the chair, he grasped his knees tightly with large-knuckled hands. His expression became more open and his careful countryman's speech less formal.

"Now, when oncet I have got the Virginia creeper offn 'er, I'll know how many new shingles she'll need. The framin' tower is strong oak and the floors are pine. The tail beam and wind shaft are locust and seem sound."

"Is it cedar shingle you'll use, Tom?"

"Yes, missus, three-eighth-inch cedar with a nine-inch gauge."

"And have you inspected the brake and the cap circle and curb, Tom?"

"I have done that, yes." Tom Sayre extracted a meer-

300

schaum pipe from an overall pocket. He grasped it between his teeth, unfilled and unlit.

"Light your pipe, Tom, I don't mind," Brigida said. "What about the curb?" She took a sip of coffee. "Hot," she said.

"Some don't think it polite, smokin' indoors, with a lady," he answered. He patted his pockets until he located a match safe, struck a sulphurous light, and pulled at the pipe. "Wonderful invention, the lucifer. The captain, your husband, give me this box. Well, if the mill were mine, I'd give 'er an iron ring with iron rollers for the cap circle to rest upon. Easy to run, fast, modern, which Captain Hawkes is all for, I know. That way the cap will move with just a touch of the tail pole." A cloud of smoke from his pipe drifted toward the pull of the chimney flue.

"I learned about something better than a tail pole, I think." Brigida stood and came round from behind the desk to lean back against it. Gesturing with quick, graceful hands, she went on, "I heard of a fan tail that sits at an angle to the main sails and spins the cap to keep the mains full in the wind. It's an aiming device I have in mind. What do you think?"

"I think it will be a real pleasure doin' work for you, missus. I've seen diagrams for a fan tail I'd like to try."

"And I think it will be a pleasure doing business with you, Tom Sayre." Brigida clasped her hands. "How's the inside?"

"Floorboards will need replacing, stairs too, but her machinery is mostly sound and well made, very well made. Someday I'd give 'er iron gears, when the wood

301

goes. The stones—corn and wheat—are the finest I've seen. They'll do a hundred, maybe one hundred twenty turns a minute in a high wind."

"Why was such a fine machine allowed to go derelict, do you know, Tom?"

"There's always been talk, but I'd not care to be repeatin' what's tittle-tattle gossip. It's said she just upped one fine day when Captain Jarred was away to sea and sacked everyone—the miller, the overseer, gardeners, all the hands—and the whole place grew over weeds and fell to the wind. When Slade come back from the war . . . he never took no notice a'tall—before now."

Brigida had become pensive. "Why would Elizabeth let it go so to ruin?" she asked herself as much as Tom.

"'Tis said it was to spite 'im, her husband, but what he done to make 'er hate him so . . . well, Martha might tell you. I for one would not conjecture on it, missus." Tom Sayre clutched the bowl of his pipe, which had gone cold, and Brigida, ready to talk sums, went to resume her place behind the desk, feeling the barrier lent her some businesslike authority. She put a new nib in Slade's pen and dipped into India ink in a silver well.

"Now, Tom, tell me the costs of putting the mill right, and if we are in agreement, we'll seal the bargain."

Tom stuck the pipe in his teeth and began to rattle off a list of supplies, while Brigida wrote them out in a fast, scrawled hand. "Oak boards, two hundred feet or so, that's ten dollars, and five hundred feet of pine board for no more'n twelve dollars. I'll have to get a few replacement spindles from Norwich in Connecticut where a fella makes the good ones. I'll go, or send the lad,

Johnny, but either way it'll cost six dollars. I'll need fifty pounds of iron at twelve cents the pound, a half gallon of whale oil, two pounds of nails, ropes, lines, bolting cloth from New York City. That alone will be costing sixteen dollars, or thereabouts. There'll be my board and wages for three months, no more, two hundred fifty dollars, and board and wages for Rob and Tom, fifty dollars for the pair of 'em. That's it, missus."

Brigida began to add the long line of figures, but she had gotten only halfway down the column before Tom Sayre announced a total.

"Four hundred one dollars, half what a new mill would cost to be building now, and when you stop to think you'll be chargin' ten cent the bushel or a tenth the grain for grinding . . . good morning, Captain," Tom said, rising from his chair. "The lady and I have been talkin' a bit of business here."

Slade had entered the office through the garden door and crossed the room to rummage in one of the top compartments of his desk.

"Early in the day for you to be up and about, isn't it, Brigida? I'd not planned to interrupt, go on," he said, not finding what he sought, but Brigida waited patiently for him to be done.

"Oh, Slade, you've tracked mud half across the floor," she moaned. "Martha will be horrified!"

"I've been wading out in wet fields and marshes since sunup," he answered, standing over her. He glanced down at his jack boots, which were cuffed at the knee, and his eyes followed the trail they had left along the polished wood. "Nothing wrong with a little good dirt, is

303

there, Tom?" he asked, coming out from behind the desk to shake the man's hand. "How've you been? It's been a while since we talked."

"No complaints, Captain, none at all. I suppose you'd now be sayin' the same, well married again, as you are. The lady and I have been discussing business, as I said, and she knows a fair bit about the millwright's trade."

"She knows a fair bit about a number of things. She drives a hard bargain, watch yourself."

At midday, the long table in Silver Hill's kitchen was lined along both sides with the manor's growing staff. A new groom, the stable lad, and two gardeners sat on one side flanked by Brigida near Slade at the head and Martha near Levi at the foot. Opposite were Tom Sayre, Mary and Nan and their brother, Robin, and Johnny Hand. The board was stacked with baskets of hot breads and tubs of butter.

"Stir with your knife, there will be strife," Martha told the stable boy as she left the table. He looked about guiltily and removed the implement from his milk.

"I wasn't stirrin', just playin'," he said quickly.

"Looked like serious stirring to me," she grumbled, moving along the table, filling bowls.

Robin Edwards was as handsome as his sister Mary was pretty, and every bit as outspoken. He had placed himself to face Brigida across the table and turned his attentions to her.

"Tom says we are to begin on your mill soon. I am pleased enough," he said. "But not goin' to sea again, I will pine some for those fair isles of the Southern Pacific, beautiful as they are."

"We know what fair things you'll be missing most Robin, my dear," Mary scolded playfully, "but as you are no sailing man now you'd best settle down and marry, that's the way of it here, no matter what you got up to in the tropics."

"Me marry? Not yet by a score of years," Robin laughed, elbowing his sister as he lifted his spoon. "I'm too young to tie myself down to one, unless she's as lovely as the captain's lady there. Captain Hawkes, you are a man experienced in the ways of the world. Do you think my sister advises me right, to take a wife?"

Slade's eyes flitted over Brigida. "Take care. It's easy to be caught by a pretty face that hides a shrewish nature just until the vows are made."

"A pitfall you, Captain, have avoided," Robin flirted with Brigida.

"Your gallantry, Robin Edwards, is to be encouraged," she smiled.

"Late with your chores today, Mary?" Tom asked. "The milk's not even got a chill on it yet."

"You keep me out 'til all hours, Tom Sayre, and then Mother couldn't rouse me, and Dad would not wait, and I had to come up here all the way on my own two feet." Mary smiled at him.

"With all the work to be done now, Mary, wouldn't it be better for you and Nan to stay here at Silver Hill?" Brigida asked. "The millwright and his helpers will soon be living in the cabin near the stables."

"Well, Captain," Mary asked, "you want us here?"

"I've no objection. We'll be taking on hands and help for you in the dairy. I'm adding to the herd, and there'll be a full flock of Highland sheep besides the few we've always kept to crop the lawns."

"You'll be plowing in a few days, then?" Martha asked. "The corn should go in the ground when the new leaf on the oak is big as a mouse ear, that's the old way of it and the right way."

"Just so, you old heathen," Slade answered pleasantly. "All the acreage will be in corn, wheat, and potatoes, except the kitchen garden," he said, leaning back on the heels of his chair, hands behind his head. "It needs now a rake and a hoe," he told Brigida. "The top six inches of soil are already warm. Come with me; I'll show you the potato barn." He abruptly stood.

"You are not in the city now, man," Levi said. "You must move slower. If you'll be a farmer you need patience for growing things."

"I can't slow down the way you do, Indian. It takes me a lot longer to slow down," Slade said. "By the time I'm ready to leave, maybe then I might be at my ease here."

"Oh, John!" Brigida complained, "he's already talking about leaving. I really hate him, I swear it!"

"Call it that if you wish, pretty, but it is not the truth you're speaking. You're all wrathy and wrought up because you aren't mistress of your own heart or of his as you'd like to be. You'll never have Slade Hawkes on leading strings flinging himself at your feet, if that's what

306

you've in mind. You wouldn't want him that way." The old man shook his head and pushed wire-rimmed spectacles up higher on his nose.

John and Sarah were sitting together on a bench outside their open door when Brigida slid lightly from the mare's back. The blue bay was calm at low tide, undulant and glistening in the sun. "It'll not be easy with a man like Slade, but if you can stand some of the fleas that come with the dog, you might be surprised one day. Your husband isn't one to stint at anything. If once he decides to offer his affection to you, there'll be no end to it; it'll be like a dam breaking. He'll give you his love like no other man ever would."

"But he seems to hate me, really," Brigida said petulantly as the mare nudged her shoulder, and Sarah reached up to stroke the soft, dark nose.

"It's an odd fine gift for a man to give a woman he hates. What a beauty she is. Raven-black, and mild-tempered, she looks. I've a bit of a sugar cone left, on the mantel near the cozy. Get your fine mare a bit and then come take the sun with me," Sarah smiled.

The cottage was open all around to the spring sunlight, windows removed, shutters thrown wide. The first thing Brigida saw when she stepped inside was a new quilting frame standing in a corner.

"Oh, John! It's ready!" she called. "Can we begin now, Sari?"

She touched one of the smooth, blond wood pegs that held the rails and stretchers in place on a pair of slotted trestles.

"I thought you'd like it," John said, coming inside. "It's tulip wood I got special. Johnny carved the pegs for you."

"It is beautiful!" Brigida planted a kiss on the old man's cheek.

"It can be set up for any size work. I got to thinking that, when you finish the quilt for Slade, you'd be wantin' to start on a small one, a crib quilt, maybe."

"Not you, too!" Brigida snapped, turning on her heel and briskly striding out.

"Can we begin?" she asked Sarah shortly.

"What did that old man say now to upset you?" the startled woman asked. "Just pay him no mind and sit quiet for a time. We'll get to your quilting soon enough. This sun is good for my old bones. The first spring sun is always the most warming."

John came ambling out of the cottage and resettled himself on the bench.

"See the stream goin' inland from the bay?" he asked Brigida, pointing. "I been watching that stream all my life long. In February, the forsythia near it is already starting in to swell and, soon after, the swamp maples are all in a red haze of spring. Then the fisher hawks come and the peepers start in in the marsh. In May the wild rose will bud and there'll be a rush of spring along the shore so sweet and strong with life it can near take the breath from you with its promise."

Brigida watched a silver gull loop, flashing against blue heavens over landscape and water all shades of new green and bright blue, ribbons of white sand stretching off between. Unfastening her cloak, she rested her head back and closed her eyes, soothed by John's lulling voice.

"The pull of the moon and the tide, the sun dropping down the sky, that's what keeps the marsh and bay alive. This is a landscape for lovers, watery blue and rolling golden fields," he went on. "Before the autumn mists come again and the winter storms, I think you'll have what you're wishing for, Brigida. Just don't let any day pass unclaimed, nor lived any less than it might be. All will come round right, I promise."

Brigida opened her eyes to study the old man's profile, thin and gentle, closed eyelids fluttering. She saw him in that moment as an ancient oracular sage tucked away in a mystical corner of the world, possessor of all the secrets of time and life and love.

"It is right Slade's come home where he belongs and brought you with him to this place where the land touches the sea," the old man said. "You'll know the rightness of it, and so will he. Then he'll be happy, and so will you."

"John Hand, I just love you," Brigida said with a shining smile. "Now I'm going home."

"In San Francisco now the world is already abloom. Geraniums are as large as rhododendrons and there are masses of roses everywhere."

Brigida's eyes glinted as dark as her jet beads in candle-light. The sun had pinked her cheeks and scattered a spray of freckles over her fine nose.

"You'll have all that here, more roses than you've ever seen." Slade refilled her glass with champagne. They dined late, alone, and had dressed for dinner. He was in tweeds, she in a gray satin skirt beneath a black satin lace-trimmed tunic. There was a pleasant din of April rain at the windowpanes. "In a few days the rain will bring up the green hay. There'll be sparrows filching horse hairs for their nests, swallows and skylarks will be soaring and singing over the corn soon, blackbirds will be in the cherry trees, and you, goddess, will find yourself in paradise."

"You almost sound as you did long ago, talking about Silver Hill. And where will you be when this . . . this Garden of Eden is green and warm? I've been told you spend little enough of your time here."

"I've had other business to tend to," he said shortly, taking up his glass and hers. "Join me in the library," he ordered.

Slade sat and read the *New York Ledger*, which had arrived by post earlier in the day. Gusts of wind hurled raindrops against the window and set the fire dancing. Brigida stared at the flames a while, waiting for him to be done. She rose and began to browse the bookshelves, but nothing caught her interest. She sipped the last of her wine, petted Bran, who was sleeping at her feet, fidgeted with her jet beads, then cleared her throat.

"Why are you farming this year, after you let the land lie so long?" she asked.

"Damn, you're like a child, asking questions. You see I'm reading." He looked at her over his paper. "Sit still and hold your tongue."

They glared at each other until Brigida pranced from the room in a satiny rustle and flourish, slamming the door behind her. In a savage temper, Slade crumpled the paper and hurled it into the fire, where it took to flight in peeling sheets of ash. "Spoiled brat," he told the dog, who cocked his head first to one side, then to the other, listening intently. "You'd not put up with such trouble from any sleek, pretty bitch, would you?"

The big dog stretched and yawned while Slade stared moodily into the fire.

Up in her room, Brigida heard the heavy front door slam, echoing through the quiet household. She blew out her lamp and stepped onto the terrace.

The rain had turned to a fine mist and a haze-circled moon cast its light on Slade and Bran as they moved across the wide lawn toward the bay. Slade lifted a stick and sent it hurtling high in the air. The wolfhound disappeared into the fog and returned moments later to deposit the stick at his master's feet. Leaning to put all his strength into the next throw, Slade hurled again, this time like a primitive hunter loosing a javelin. The moon broke through fast sailing clouds as the returning animal crested the dune bluff and surged back over the lawn, streaking past Slade before slowing to a stop.

"Bran! Come!" Slade called. Turning, he saw Brigida then, motionless, enwrapped in moonglow, watching. "Damn," he whispered under his breath. Her spectacular beauty caught him again unawares, as it had so often before. He walked toward her, drawn as if by some sorcery that seemed to promise all the bliss of paradise. He wanted to possess the wild child, as she seemed at that instant, but he needed first to bend her to his will, to temper the independent spirit he saw shining in her moonlit eyes. A rush of desire flooded his loins as he remembered her perfect body—smooth as ivory spread naked beneath him—and its hungry passion belying any childlike innocence.

Brigida watched Slade's unhurried approach with a spreading ache of love and yearning that almost made her cry out. She gripped the rail, smiling a little, admiring the roll of his narrow hips and swing of his broad shoulders. She envisioned him looming above her, his hard maleness fusing with her ready softness as their bodies were hammered together in the heat of lust and loving.

"Walk with us." Slade looked up, tasting Brigida with his eyes. Her composure appeared to him perfect.

Not trusting herself to speak, and seeing Slade relentlessly self-assured as always, she nodded and left the terrace.

They came together with a gingerly caution. Their senses were intoxicated by each other and by the moist fragrance of the spring night redolent of damp earth and sea and dripping pines. In shimmering silence they walked through wet grasses to the water's edge. Whenever their hands brushed even lightly, Brigida moved off—willing her treasonous body not to betray her this time and send her flying into his arms as she longed to . . . as she had always done before.

Finally, exasperated by her remote silence, Slade stepped in front of her, placing his hands on her shoulders.

"You're not very nice to me," she said in a small, unsteady voice. Moonlight glistened on her pouted lips and wide eyes.

"Not nice, goddess? Don't I visit your bed often enough to suit you?"

"That is a matter of your convenience, as you tell me yourself. When you've no place else to . . . pour your seed."

"And as you tell me, that's all you want, besides the clothing and shelter I give you. Or have you changed your mind?"

She shook her head. "No, I've not changed."

They stood on the high bluff above the water with the bay, shrouded in mist, a dark cauldron below. As they listened to its lapping, an owl called in a distant stand of trees. "When I see how content John and Sarah are together . . . Johnny and Nan will be the same one day. I'm sorry I ever came here." Brigida was subdued.

"Why did you come to me at all? Speak the truth," Slade said.

"I thought . . . I really thought I'd be coming home to you . . . in a way. But I was wrong. You're changed."

"Nothing stays the same. . . ." His eyes were like hard blue stones. "Why else did you come?"

"You wouldn't believe me if I said I came for love, would you?"

"You're right, I wouldn't. Are you about to declare you've loved me all your life? You could as well tell me you've danced on the moon," Slade said with irritable quickness.

"I'm here because my mother wished it, but I think she would be persuaded, if she saw you now, of your unsuitability as a husband for me." Brigida's look was frosty.

"But you have fulfilled her wish, you are my wife for better or worse, as it's said. Does that content you at all?" he asked.

"Content me? How could I be content bound to a man who forced himself on me and hardened my heart? Content with a husband who thinks the sole purpose of a woman is to produce his children? You think a woman should be submissive, and gentle, and sentimental, even emotional perhaps, but certainly not clever, heaven forbid . . . I mean, content with a man who married me for some . . . some base motive of greed? Who wishes only to take his carnal pleasure of me, offering clothing and jewels as payment for services provided, as to some expensive whore, while he withholds the kindness and comfort and . . . love I might have found with some other? I am your wife, but not without sad regrets!" She turned her back on him and stalked off toward a wooded path that ran to the west of the manor house.

"Witch! Don't ever walk away from me like that," he called.

"Oh, you lean-minded, shortsighted, churlish . . ." Brigida's bluster was abruptly cut off when she faced him. There was something violent in his eyes when his arms enfolded her like steel wings and his open mouth came down on hers. She stood rigid, but only for seconds before her lips parted and her arms came slowly about his neck.

"In this I do content you, don't I," he said in a smoky voice. "This, at least, we share with equal pleasure."

"Slade Hawkes," Brigida's voice was unsteady as he lifted her and turned toward the house that was dark and

314

still under the misted moon. "Slade Hawkes, how do you know it's not all a sham? Proper girls don't have such . . . low feeling, do they? Your mother told me that. Your arrogance blinds you to the truth. . . ."

"Shut up your prattling, or you'll be damn sorry," he said, silencing her with a violent kiss that took away words and breath and all thoughts but one.

Seventeen

"Johnny Hand! Please tell your gram for me I'll not be down to her today!"

The boy, carrying a large spade, stopped and looked about until his eyes found Brigida in the kitchen garden. Her calico blouse was unbuttoned at the throat, its long puffy sleeves rolled to the elbow.

"She'll understand, missus." He came to look over the hedgerow and ribbon grass that bordered the garden. "You are lookin' busy." He leaned on his spade, studying a row of bamboo rakes and iron trowels, hoes, and filled watering cans.

"I'll want a pole fence. For tomatoes. Could you put it in for me, there? It will shelter my herbs from the sea breeze."

"I'll be glad to do your fence, missus," Johnny said, following one of the narrow walkways through the raised rectangular beds. He had become almost conversational, his shyness lessened, since he'd started working at Silver Hill. "Would you like some crushed clamshell to keep the club root off your cabbages?"

"Yes, and I will have clary and cress and sweet corn and cucumber. Today I'll do early lettuces and peas and leeks and onions, and if you'll dig me a trench later to blanch the celery . . ."

"Smellage, do you mean?" Johnny asked.

"That's what my mother called it, but I always thought it her quaint New England name for the vegetable," Brigida smiled.

"Well, my gram always calls it that. She likes to chew a stick before goin' into church, to sweeten her breath."

"Look, John. I'm going to mix flowers with herbs and fruits the way they used to do," Brigida announced, walking the rows in long strides with Johnny following. "The beans will climb the cornstalks, and I'll have peony and marigold with the sweet corn and violets and May flowers, if you'll get me some from the woods."

"Did you ever hear it said that rosemary flourishes in the gardens of the righteous? My gram told me it."

Brigida sank to her knees, mindless of the damp soil staining her skirt. "Then mine shall be luxuriant," she laughed, and Johnny was almost laughing with her, her delight was so infectious.

"Missus," the boy said, "seein' as you care so much for growin' things, you should know the orchard's been neglected awful and there's good fruit to be had from it yet, peaches 'specially."

"We'll see to it, if the trees are not beyond saving." She sat back on her heels.

"I can save them," Johnny said, drawing himself up tall. "I'll scrub the bark with whale oil soap to get quit of pests. You should plant you some tobacco, missus. Dried

318

and powdered it will keep crawling things out of your vegetables and flowers. Plant peppers, too, all over your garden, or make you a red pepper spray."

"But I am going to have enough for the worms and the bugs, besides all of us," Brigida announced, "though I do soak the seed in whale oil a day. It speeds growth and it's good against maggots, both. Oh, that's the bell!"

A cord ran from the handle of a brass bell mounted on a post in the garden to the kichen window. The string jumped as the bell sounded again.

"That's to warn off birds. Martha and I rigged it, but she must be signaling now it's noon. Run and see for me if that's what she wants, please Johnny, and check the stick at the kitchen door. If it is noon, I'm to be off."

"You'll be takin' the midday meal out to the captain in the field?"

"You guessed it. Is there a shadow?" Brigida called after the boy.

"Noon right now, missus. Hardly none."

Smiling to herself, Brigida paused on the kitchen step to look at Silver Hill Manor in the early spring sunshine. To the south and east were the carriage house and coops, stables and barns. Beyond were fields, then woods stretching as far as she could see. She made her way through the formal garden and along the azalea walk to the front of the house, struggling to understand how such love and dreams as she saw in the things about her could have so faded away. She thought of Elizabeth, years alone, a prisoner here of her own choosing, and of Slade, who had loved Silver Hill once and left it as his father had before . . . Slade! She'd be late if she didn't

319

hurry. Bubbling inside with the commotion she always felt at the thought of being with him, Brigida rushed indoors to scrub the earth from beneath her nails and touch rosewater to her wrists before riding out to join him.

"You'll have room, then, for pumpkins in the kitchen garden?" Slade lit a cigar. A breeze put out the first match and he leaned to another, cupped in sheltering hands.

"I'll have room. The garden's large and well laid out. Everything at Silver Hill shows the touch of an affectionate hand." Brigida shaded her eyes to look up at him. He helped her to her feet.

"My father did everything with exactitude."

"And love." Brigida brushed off her skirt.

"He had hopes of living out his days at Silver Hill. I'll put that in the wagon and bring it in later." Slade took the food basket from Brigida's arm. She folded the cloth.

"And you?" she asked.

"I'll see the place operating for profit again," he shrugged. "It's an investment to me, that's all."

"Oh? Like everything else you turn your hand to?" she asked with scorn. "You're just here now to gratify your . . . your greed, is that it?"

They stopped to face each other, she with hands on hips, the breeze loosing wisps of golden hair, and he with the basket on a shoulder.

"I can't let anything go idle when there's use to be made of it." Slade's smile was deviling.

320

"And everyone, everything is bent to your selfish purpose," Brigida said heatedly. "Tell me, why is it you want a son?" she demanded, thinking of the Slade inheritance Lydia Worsley had spoken of.

"Doesn't everyone?" he asked.

"I suppose, but why do you?"

"So all this won't go to waste," he said, "and . . . for other reasons."

"Is there nothing, no occupation, that pleases you for its own sake, no pursuit prompted by kindness . . . or affection?"

"My pleasure comes in the mastery—of ships, land, women, what you will—and I make good use of the riches of whatever kind they can be made to yield me."

The afternoon sun had given way to clouds, and a damp fog curled across the wide field as they walked in silence. A flock of crows, cawing, spread itself in the branches of a tree like a dark shroud. Brigida slapped agitatedly at her skirt with a willow switch.

"Slade Hawkes," her pretty chin set stubbornly, "I'll yield you no riches of any kind." Her tone was dispirited.

"I know that, but never once, Brigida, have you turned away from me in a blushing modesty, not from the very first. Admit we're two of a kind, goddess; we both take and use whatever suits us."

At his words, Brigida rushed at him in a frenzy with the willow switch upraised. He caught her slender wrist and shook the branch free of her grasp.

"Take care, pagan fury, lest I use that switch on you." He pulled her against him, her soft bosom heaving

321

against his chest as she fought to free herself.

"Oh, damn you, damn you! You torment my life with your dire plaguing words and endless provocations!" Her eyes swam with angry, hard-held tears that began to slip down her flushed cheeks.

"You'll unman me, strumpet, hold! I've a proposal to put to you. Listen to me!" When Slade bent her back and leaned to kiss her slim throat, the anger went out of her in a rush, and she hid her tear-stained face against his chest. He smoothed her flowing hair, making soothing sounds against her brow as if to calm a captive wild creature until she stood still, finally, in his arms. Holding fast to him, she watched Levi coming a long way off down the dirt path. He was leading a pair of massive, heavy horses that were drawing a flatbed wagon at a slow, steady walk.

"Well, make me your proposal, but be warned: if you try to honeyfoggle me with your glib liar's tongue, I'll have none of it."

"I've never lied to you, Brigida," he answered, toying with the gold band on her finger. "You may not like what you've heard, but it has been the truth. I've a truce to offer now. Just until the planting's done. There's too much at stake here, too many people around, too much work to tend to, for me to be distracted by your little moods and unpredictable tempers."

"What sort of truce?" She glanced at him sidelong.

Slade clenched a cigar in his teeth and his lips curled in a calculating half smile. "Despite your unflattering opinion of me, I'm willing to offer this: We'll playact . . . pretend we've a love match. We'll behave as if there actually might be some affection between us. It will be a challenge for you, I know, but it might occupy you so you won't be at me all the time."

They had moved apart and now they stared at each other, their looks unreadable, like a pair of gamblers concealing cards.

"Well, go on," Brigida prodded. "Tell me more before you ask for my decision."

"I will act the role of devoted husband with all the necessary ardor, and you, madame, will pretend to be the perfect loving helpmeet in all things; you will manage the house and servants, keep the paybooks and records. I'll need to have an accurate accounting of every pail of milk from every cow, the number of eggs collected every day, the weight of seed used, the quantities of food consumed by the hands at table. I'll want lists of new tack and harness purchased, horses shod, feet of rope bought, bales of hay put up—everything that enriches, every expense. The manor will run like an efficient business, down to the least spool of thread."

"You need an honest clerk, is all," Brigida answered, arch and aloof, restraining a growing excitement. "What's in this for me?"

Slade had paced off a little distance and was checking the strength of a stone wall with a booted toe.

"I've been expecting that question," he scowled. "I'll give you a percentage of the profit, if there is one, to do with as you will."

"As I will? There's no telling what I might do, is there, or where I might go, given a measure of independence."

"You're not going anywhere, money or not," he said, coldly confident. "Will you try it?"

Brigida tilted her head to one side, resting an elbow in a cupped hand at her waist. Then she gestured delicately with long fingers and upturned palm. "But pray, do tell me, Captain Hawkes, as loving man and wife in your little spoofery of wedded bliss, will there be other requirements that will call upon more than my ability to add and subtract? Shall we meet at breakfast to plan the day's work and at dinner to share the day's trifles? Will we walk out together in moonlight whispering love words under the stars? Are we to worry together over crops and blights and weather and then have the neighbors in to Sunday dinner? Do you really think, Slade Hawkes, that you and I will be able to persist in such a charade?"

"Anyone who can dissemble in bed as you tell me you do is a consummate actress," Slade leered at her. "Just take the role beyond your bedroom door."

"And you?" she asked, turning away. She waved to Levi, who had reached the crest of a low hill.

"I've been a spy, remember? We'll bring it off like that," Slade snapped his fingers, "if you're willing." He almost circled her waist with his strong brown hands and looked down into her now laughing eyes. "Well?"

"How long will this go on?"

"As long as I stay here. Until the planting's done."

"Oh? And will you stay the night at my side to comfort me in dreams? Will you smile at me in first dawn light?" she asked with ingenuous sweetness. "If I am really to live the part of loving wife you ask me to play . . . why, I've never even seen my husband's room and . . ."

"The door's not been locked to you, goddess. You'll have to come to me if you want to keep the game going all night long."

"No, I won't, but I will act in your drama. We'll start now. Here's Levi. If we can fool him, we'll gull the world."

"I've never had a secret from Levi," Slade said.

"Start now," Brigida directed.

Not wanting to interrupt what appeared to be a serious talk, Levi halted some yards from the couple and watched Slade lift Brigida from her feet, saw their lips brush lightly.

"What are you doing with those magnificent giants?" Brigida called after a moment. The big, patient horses were as large as Clydesdales, with bright eyes and feathered, light gray bracelets at thick fetlocks. "The great war-horses of noble knights. Perche-Normans, aren't they?" Brigida appraised the team as they came closer.

"We're going to clear stumps from an outlying field. Heavy beasts for heavy work," Slade explained.

"I'll not keep you longer from your task, lest you accuse me of distracting you." Brigida rose on tiptoe to lightly kiss Slade's throat above his open shirtband. His arms came about her like a sprung trap.

"That's only a requisite of the role I now play," she teased as he helped her to mount. "See you at dinner, love," she laughed over her shoulder, putting the mare into a canter. Brigida's golden mane, fluttering with red ribbons, flowed down her straight, proud back, and Slade watched until she disappeared into the leafy woods.

"Pretty, pretty," the Indian commented, leaning against the wagon.

"Yes, a little beauty, and clever, she thinks."

"I had in mind the mare," Levi said.

"So did I," Slade glared. "Come on, let's get that wagon into the field. You may have all night, but I don't."

When the mare, Raven, had turned onto the wooded path that led toward Sari's cottage, Brigida's laughter echoed like wild music through the woodland, blending with the low cooings of wrens and doves, the distant melodic song of a thrush. A cardinal seemed to lead her way, blazing like a red jewel among wavering boughs and branches. Wild cabbages raised bright green leaves against ghostly trunks of white oak and birch. A doe and her golden fawn stood still as statues in a stand of pines as Brigida passed.

"Oh, I will trap him now, Raven, I know I will," Brigida sighed, leaning forward over the mare's neck as they passed beneath a low bough. They crossed an open meadow at full gallop, and Brigida's heart was flooded with all the full promise of spring and the hope of love.

On a bright morning in May, Brigida was darning in the small sewing room tucked between her bed chamber and Slade's when Nan, carrying a pile of snowy linens, stuck her head in at the door.

"Missus," she said, "Johnny has asked me to marry!"

"Oh Nanny, when? We must have a party!"

"I named my bedpost for Johnny, did I tell you, and hugged it every night? That did it for a certainty. When Mary and Tom wed . . . with the end of harvestin'. I'll be off now, to lavender the sheets like you showed me."

When the girl had gone, Brigida dreamily wandered out onto the terrace. She watched large, furry bees move in the sunny air about full clusters of white blossoms raised by a billowing fruit tree. The bees hovered, she thought, like fish along a coral reef, wings treading air like gossamer fins in water. Gradually, through their low humming, she became aware of what had become an unfamiliar, disturbing sound—the tattoo of hoofbeats moving up the manor drive. Since their return, no outsider had intruded on the life at Silver Hill. That anyone dared to now seemed almost threatening.

When Brigida recognized Philip Carpenter and Hollis Stancel approaching, she rushed off with mixed feelings to greet them.

"You haven't truly become the farmer's wife, have you, Brigida darling? Yours is far too lovely a light to hide under any bushel. Just look at her, Hollis, the very picture of the country lass in calico and cotton and more beautiful and charming than ever! I'll take you away from all this at a moment's notice, you know."

"Not a chance, Philip. I couldn't leave before my leeks are trenched; even an indifferent country squire like you must know that. Do come in for some refreshment, and tell me what brings you to Silver Hill."

"I've a letter for Slade. From Elizabeth," Philip said. "I'll tell you the news, but you must let him read it for himself.''

''I can guess it!'' Brigida announced, clapping her hands once and bringing them loosely clasped to her lips. She led the way to the library where the windows were thrown wide to the spring day. Nan brought a pitcher of lemonade and glasses.

''The marriage was quietly done in New York several days ago. Only Ann and I were there.'' Phil sipped his cool drink. ''The happy couple will sail for the Continent early in July after a brief visit here and at Carpenter's Island. What do you suppose your husband will have to say?''

''We'll wait and see, shall we? Oh, there was a time he might have been . . . negative, but now, I doubt it.''

''Has life with you so mellowed Slade Hawkes, then?'' Hollis asked. He had swatted at a fly, damaging it, then watched the insect lurch across the table.

''Life with Brigida would mellow any man, Hollis,'' Phil offered. ''Tell me, lovely, what have you two really been up to here? No one's seen or heard from either of you in weeks.''

''We are working, Philip, honestly we are.'' Brigida was curled in her corner of the settee. ''The mill's rebuilding, the crops are nearly planted . . . I'll show you my garden if you ask me very nicely.''

''And where's Captain Hawkes, or is it Farmer Hawkes these days?'' Hollis wanted to know.

''Put that insect out of its agony, will you, Hollis?'' Brigida said, looking directly at him for the first time since he'd arrived, remembering their last meeting at Lydia's. She watched with distaste as he crushed the fly and flicked it onto the cold hearth.

"Slade is working the northeast pasture today. I'll be taking him the midday meal quite soon."

"The elegant Captain Hawkes up to his knees in mud and manure?"

"You forget, sir, my husband was harpooner on a whaling ship," Brigida said defensively. "For me to see him at real work doesn't seem at all a source of humor."

"You are well trained, hurrying out to the fields like a common laborer's woman," Hollis replied with an edge of irritation.

"You don't understand," Brigida answered coolly. "I want to see him. He's been gone since sunup nearly."

"A toast to the absent bride and groom." Slade tipsily raised a glass of champagne, and his dinner guests, equally unsteady, followed suit. Brigida looked on a trifle uneasily.

Dinner had been a sumptuous, noisy affair, and champagne flowed freely in celebration of the union of Elizabeth Slade Hawkes and Adelbert Carpenter. The camaraderie seemed warm and close, and even the usually taciturn Hollis had been drawn into conversation.

"Your little bull terrier bitch is growin' into a real beauty, ma'am; a waste not to breed her for blood sport. You surely duped me that time. She's no fit pet for a lady, no lapdog. You are wastin' good fightin' blood, ma'am, not raisin' her to the ring. It ain't right."

"Hollis," Slade interrupted, to all appearances good-natured and tipsy, "tell us about the Shenandoah."

329

Brigida saw Stancel's pale eyes narrow a fraction. "I never did go to sea, Captain," he drawled.

"I meant the Shenandoah Valley, friend. I told you, didn't I, that I . . . visited there once? The circumstances prevented much socializing."

"Hawkes," Stancel said coldly, "you surely must have been the perfect livin' image of the heroic soldier. Wouldn't you have liked to see him then, Brigida, those good looks even more strikin' than usual in Yankee blue? What do you say, Phil?"

"I didn't ride with Sheridan," Phil shrugged. "My father arranged for me to get a safe view of the war as a junior attaché at headquarters. I rarely heard a shot fired."

"I wish I could say the same, but it would be a lie if I did," Slade went on in drunken affability.

"We are all aware, Hawkes, of your heroics—burnin' women and children out of their homes, firing our whole green valley until you drove us to the edge of madness . . . and over," Stancel stated almost matter-of-factly, but the hate she saw in his face made Brigida shiver.

"Orders, Stancel, you know that." Slade's speech was suddenly precise, all signs of alcoholic conviviality vanished. "But tell me what you know about the other *Shenandoah*, that infernal pirate ship that should have been blown to hell and back with her crew hanged from the crosstrees."

Too late, Stancel realized he'd been purposefully provoked. He tried to back off and mask his exposed raw feelings with a strained smile.

"I . . . I won't argue with you, Captain, you are my host, and as you yourself said once before, the war is over."

"And as you said once before, Stancel, for some it will never be over." Slade leaned forward, eyes narrowed to lethal ice-blue slits, a muscle in his set jaw flexing. "For me, it will end when I've killed one Bluford Root. Is the name at all familiar to you? He was from Virginia, too, from the Shenandoah Valley, too. He murdered my father, Stancel, and all I could do then was watch it happen." There was a terrible silence.

"I didn't know any Bluford Root," Stancel whispered, shaking his head.

"He was cashiered out of the Confederate Navy in disgrace, Stancel, as a thief and a drunk. He was seen in Memphis, then laboring on the railroad after the war, near a place called Pit Hole, in Pennsylvania. It was a boom town then, full of gamblers and erring sisters, just the place for Bluford Root. He was in San Francisco until recently. He's in the East again now."

"I don't know any Root," Stancel insisted. "You are sniffin' up the wrong tree, Hawkes. I can't help you. But tell me, when and where did you do your spyin' if you were fightin' in the Valley?" Stancel leaned back in his chair as the dishes were cleared and settings laid for coffee and dessert.

"In Memphis, before I volunteered to ride with Sheridan, when the cotton speculators and flesh merchants were all there, too. I was looking for someone, you see, who'd likely be found in Sodom. I married his sister, did you know? More champagne, Hollis?"

The man remained strangely still as Slade refilled all the glasses. "Please bring the humidor from the library, love," he said to Brigida. "Our guests might enjoy a smoke with their port after dinner." There was a whisper of silk as she rose from the table.

"Where I come from, sir, gentlemen step out onto the veranda to smoke." Hollis's voice was sharp and mean. "No real lady would have a man smokin' in her house, where I come from. But then no real lady would ever be seen at Worsley's bordello, either."

"Phil, your friend is making a habit of this unmannerly behavior," Slade said in controlled fury. "For now, an apology will have to suffice."

"Don't, Slade, really," Brigida offered. "It's all right."

"It is not all right. Hold your tongue," Slade commanded, his fists slamming the table once, rattling the silver. "Well, Stancel?" he gritted.

"My apologies to your beautiful lady, Captain," Stancel said with exaggerated care. "Now I think I'd best retire. I've imbibed more than I should have again. I bid you goodnight."

"Tell me what you know about the man." Slade and Phil were in the library.

Brigida stood at the open window watching a sliver of moon in the May sky.

"Don't be cruel, Slade; he's lost all he cared for," she said.

"You try to be quiet. I need the information Phil can give me," Slade said. Brigida glowered over her shoulder.

Her eyes met Phil's. He smiled.

"Brigida is right; Hollis has lost a lot. He's angry and . . . oh, lonely, I guess. We read law together. I never knew much about him except that he could pull a good stroke oar in a race. Well, out of the blue, I got a letter from him a few months ago saying he was going to be in New York on business. He thought he'd have a good investment proposition for me. We met, he attached himself to me, and he hasn't let loose since. The investment . . . it's coming together, he says. At first, I thought he was after a free berth—you know, good company, pleasant surroundings. Father thought him a promising if not terribly ambitious boy of good family fallen on hard times, nothing unusual." Phil puffed thoughtfully. "But now . . . to be honest, Slade, something bothers me about him. He goes about with more folding money than I do, and for the life of me, I can't imagine where he gets it."

"Everyone has more cash than you do, Phil, that's nothing. What else?"

"It's you, Slade. He only loses control this way with you. Now, I know he had designs upon your lovely Brigida, but then, what man, thinking her free, would not?" Phil laughed self-consciously. "Hollis will be leaving in late summer. He's been offered a clerkship in an Atlanta law firm at eight thousand, which isn't at all bad. We'll be free of him soon, so why be unkind?"

"I agree," Brigida said. She had turned to find Slade's eyes on her, and she came to sit near him, moving across the room with her usual grace. Her wine silk gown set off to perfection the pink-gold hue of her sun-brushed cheeks and dark eyes. "And you, Phil? Will you go into some New York law firm?"

"Oh, no! It's such crushingly dull work, really. I'd never advise a client to go law, and that's the only way to fame and wealth in the profession. No, I shall have to marry a rich wife is all, that's the only hope for me, now I've lost you forever. For her," Phil told Slade with a comical shrug, "I would have done anything, even practice at law."

"Philip, really," Brigida scoffed, "you mustn't blame your lack of ambition on me." Though the hour had grown very late, there was about her still a rain-washed freshness and gentleness of manner that Philip, left alone with a decanter of port and a fresh cigar, found impossible to put out of his mind.

The visitors left early the next morning. Again the circle closed at Silver Hill. The days of June began to flame; sundrops unfolded large golden flowers in open meadows and fields. The wild rose bloomed, and a pair of great blue heron nested in the marsh.

For Brigida, it was a time of such fevered happiness that in quiet moments she secretly doubted her own sanity. She held nothing back from Slade day or night, she loved him without restraint, and her one greatest fear was that he would guess at her double duplicity and realize she played no actress's part.

In the fields with Levi and the hands, Slade would begin to look for Brigida before the sun stood noon high.

He'd watch her approach on the prancing black mare, her golden swirling hair undulant over her shoulders and held by a fillet of lace or ribbon circling her brow. When she reined in and stretched out her arms to him, he lifted her down feeling her soft breasts warm against his chest as she slid against him to the ground.

"Why are you late?" he asked on one such day as he led her a little away from the others to the shade of an oak. "I nearly starved waiting here for you."

"Then eat what I've brought," she said, "and stop pawing me in front of . . ." He pulled her to him.

"The queen and Missus Astor are a long way off from here, my love; there's no need for prudery before these rough lads. I'll paw as I please; I've the right." His hands wandered over her, and he pulled back with surprise. Brigida blushed, but her eyes glimmered provocatively.

"I put away my camisoles and hoops and stays and petticoats . . . I don't see why I must be shackled so, when I've much to do," she said, sinking into the grass and busily turning her attention to the basket of food. There was cold smoked fish and cold meats, bread still warm from the oven. "The queen, as you said, isn't anywhere near here and . . . why, what is it now?"

The severity of his look sent a quiver of fear through her. Her soft skirt of striped homespun and the white eyelet ruffle of the one petticoat she wore had slid well above her high-laced boot tops. Her small waist was sashed with a wide patchwork band of sewn quilting scraps, and when she slipped off her short jacket her breasts thrust temptingly free against the light fabric of a peasant blouse.

"It's the sort the Mexican girls in California prefer, to

work in the fields, or dance in the moonlight," Brigida smiled impishly, flicking a curl back over a bared shoulder. "Do you like it?" She was on her knees, and she leaned back to sit against her heels, resting her hands on her thighs.

"Queen or no, you shouldn't go about like that," Slade said finally. "If I'm to be a farmer and you a farmer's wife, you'll take care not to try and tempt me from my work in future, or you might be sorry. Today, it's already too late. Come."

"What will Levi and the others think if you hurry me off to the woods just after high noon?" Brigida smiled sweetly. "How will you explain it?"

"Witch, I need explain nothing, not to you, not to them." Slade rested on one knee, an arm across a flexed thigh. "And Levi will understand better than you think. There's nothing untoward about such a 'loving couple' as we are supposed to be slipping off for a bit, high noon or midnight," he said, offering his hand again.

She always had a tub ready for him in her room in the evening, steaming and fragrant with lime oil and spice. A new ironed shirt, still warm, would be spread on the bed, a comfortable suit of tweeds or corduroys hanging ready.

As the wildflowers had come, one after the other, to bloom, they appeared about Brigida's chamber and brought to Slade's mind the sweet thyme he found every morning, without fail, braided in his stallion's mane.

*   *   *

As the seeding was done, Slade came earlier in from the fields to find Brigida at her work in the garden or romping along the sand with the terrier pup. He'd wait at the top of the bluff until she looked up and called to him, and then they walked together at the water's edge, she with her skirt tucked up at the hips, he with breeches rolled calf-high, leaving their boots to be reclaimed later on the way home.

His tawny hair grew long and curled at the neck; hers turned a paler silvery gold, lightened by hours in the spring sun. Running together at the edge of the land, they seemed as perfect as a pair of golden eagles, regal and wild beyond all other creatures.

In her unbridled happiness, Brigida became a creature of pure emotion. Loosing all remnants of restraint as time passed, she let her love for him soar free. Though she knew she played dangerously, she was helpless to stop.

For his part, Slade was finding her mercurial, changeable as the light of day. His sense of her as an exotic deity of some vanished noble tribe grew, yet she was also very womanly, warm and practical.

The wild strawberries she gathered were quickly preserved, and her herbs hung drying with everlasting flowers—lunaria, larkspur and strawflowers—to brighten next winter's bouquets. Not a rose petal fell in her sight that she didn't save and add to her growing row of Limoge and Wedgewood boxes of potpourri, her own mixture of clove and clary and powdered orris root.

Slade was almost at his ease when she sat near after dinner, working some bit of embroidery for one of Sari Hand's quilts, her quick, long fingers moving steadily, a comfortable silence between them. But though her moments of passivity had a soothing quality, there was always something elusive about her, something hidden that kept him uneasy.

On one such seemingly peaceful evening, Slade gradually became aware of a certain gravity in her voice that usually so gently lulled him after the day's work.

"Why so solemn?" he asked edgily.

Brigida put down her needlework. "Squire's sow is due in a week. I want to buy a Cheshire piglet," she announced. "I'll have to have an enclosure built, at the back of the barn. What do you think?" She waited expectantly.

Suppressing an inclination to laugh, Slade looked grim, as if pondering the weightiest of matters. "How much will it cost to feed?" he demanded.

"It's a really good investment; I've worked it all out," Brigida bubbled. "I'll repay you myself for the feed, out of the mill profit, though the pig will get mostly food scraps and the whey left from cheese making," she blurted in a rush, afraid he'd interrupt.

There was a moment's silence. "Brigida," Slade began, "how much do you think it costs me to dress you for just one season? You've some idea, and you know what your emeralds would command on the open market. Why do you think I'd stint on a pig? Why do you want the damn thing anyway?" He saw a wistful look come into her dark eyes.

"We raised them, mother and I, on the deck of the *Emma*, along with the chickens and geraniums. Don't you remember? We had a goat too, once in a while. The men were pleased always to have the fresh meat after months to sea. Well, I promised myself then I'd have a farm one day. I always wanted a farm."

Feeling Slade's eyes on her, Brigida was suddenly aware she had revealed more than she meant to, that she'd bared a true secret of her heart. "Now don't mock me, you!" she added self-consciously, but when he spoke his voice drew her to him.

"I do remember your mother, hanging her washing on the spanker boom and baking apple pies that smelled of heaven. Those geraniums, goddess, held an eternity of spring in their roseate glow. They bespoke the comforts of home to lonely men long at sea. Those geraniums reminded us of the civility of gentlewomen and clean sheets and down pillows waiting in all the saltbox cottages in all the pretty petticoat towns we so yearned to see again."

"Were you lonely?" Brigida asked. "You never seemed to need . . . anything."

"I didn't need anything. I taught myself not to, but I took comfort where I found it."

Brigida traced a finger along Slade's tanned jawbone. With a swell of innate tenderness, unthinking, she took his hand to her parted lips. There was a little time of quiet, until she broke the mood.

"Your hands are getting stained and rough for such an elegant gentleman. You'd best let me see to them," she said.

"It's oxblood mixed with whey and lard they're soiled with. That's still best for painting barns." Her gesture of innocent intimacy made him uneasy. "My hands have been calloused before," he said. "They're sailor's hands and brawler's hands." He paused, watching her. "And lover's hands."

On a hazy, warm morning toward the end of June, Brigida came down to find that Slade hadn't gone out to the fields at all. He was taking breakfast in the garden, turning the pages of his paper. She joined him. He never looked up as she seated herself across the table.

It's over. The thought struck her like a blow. The planting is done and the act is over.

Slade glanced up, anticipating her usual smile, and was annoyed to find her out of humor, her look as threatening as the gray sky.

The show is over; the little witch is not acting her part, he thought, swept by a savagery of feelings that drove him from his place to stand over her.

Brigida just sat as if numb as the first drops of rain began to fall. When Slade ordered her into the study, she went passively, steeling herself against everything she expected to hear. She wondered in despair how she would ever go back to pretended indifference, and she raged at her own recklessness that had led her to this moment. She had gambled everything, and it hadn't worked at all. She should have seen the danger of the way she had let him lead her.

As they reached the door, a gust of wind came up through the pines with a rush, and there was a blue-white flash of lightning. Moments later, thunder rolled, and torrents of rain roared down through redolent green air, pouring noisily, flooding from the gables and running in deep rivulets along the ground down the hill toward the bay. They watched the display from the shelter of the open study window, and when the storm abated a little, Brigida's pride prompted her to speak first.

"It's over," she announced. "I'm no longer willing to play at this game."

A distant foghorn sounded, echoing mournfully, then sounded again.

"That's it then," was all Slade said with a casual shrug.

Soon after, draped in yellow oilskins, Brigida rode past the french windows where she was surprised to see Slade still leaning, watching the rain. She directed Raven down toward the water and was soon lost from his sight below the crest of the bluff.

Eighteen

Near the pavilion of the village green at twilight a cluster of farmgirls stood fluttering together like a mixed bouquet of flowers touched by a breeze.

Brigida had taken care to dress modestly for the country dance. Her frock was of plain white dimity cotton, the high collar and deep cuffs lace-trimmed. She wore no jewelry at all, not even her marriage band.

The men, those from Silver Hill among them, shuffled about impatiently as the musicians tuned. When the first reel began they quickly chose partners, and Robin Edwards led Brigida out first.

Children, simmering with excitement, and old people, smiling, surrounded the dancers, and ribbons and petticoats swirled to the tempo of the music. When she was returned after some rounds to Robin Edwards's arm, Brigida was flushed with pleasure, and he found her the most charming creature he'd ever seen.

"Slade Hawkes must be more a fool that I ever gave him credit for bein'," Robin said as he placed a hand at Brigida's waist, "to let such a lady as you out dancing without him. He's mad, that's the whole of it. Tell him I watched over his treasure, will you, missus?" Despite his stiffened leg, Robin moved with a fine, showy style. Brigida's tinkling laughter rose, and she looked straight into his smiling eyes.

"Slade didn't let me. He knows nothing of it. Robin, really, is that all you want to do, watch over me?" Furious at Slade, she flirted outrageously, enjoying the confusion on her partner's face as she skipped away to another man's arms.

With increasing urgency, Robin Edwards made claim to her hand again and again, until once, when she moved toward him, her prettiest smile beckoning, she felt her waist encircled as if by bands of steel. She looked over her shoulder, an indignant protest on her lips, into Slade's blue eyes, which were snapping with anger. A quick shaft of fear pierced her. "I thought you were otherwise engaged this evening," she said as coolly as she could manage. "You missed dinner."

"I was passing. On my way home. And who should I happen upon but my wife flaunting herself like the goddess Brigit among her wood nymphs. You enjoy inflaming these poor innocent youths. I've been watching you."

"I was keepin' my eye on the lady in your absence, Captain," Robin offered, moving off quickly.

"The girls . . . Mary and Nan, talked me into coming here with them. They thought I should after . . . oh, bother!" Brigida stamped her foot, pulling away irritably. "You said yourself our act is over. I wanted to dance and that's the whole of it. We did miss the Astor Ball, didn't we?"

"Will I spoil your pleasure by joining you?" He took her firmly about the waist again, and they moved together in perfect unison, as always. She turned her face, like a dew-dipped flower, toward his warmth, and his broad shoulders seemed to enfold her fragility.

The evening advanced, the music grew faster, and the dancers became more animated with pleasure. When it grew fully dark, reed torches were set to a bonfire near the green and, as the flames leaped, Brigida whirled in Slade's arms. He let no one take her from him.

At midnight the music ended. Breathless, they moved into shadows where Brigida, rising on tiptoe, folded her arms about Slade's neck, clinging.

"I am glad you found me," she whispered. "This was better than an Astor Ball, I'm sure of it."

Slade's icy smile flashed in the half dark where they stood. "We'll go home now," he said.

They rode together on the stallion through the summer night, which was lush and sweet, the darkness constellated with fireflies, a hot wind blowing as they rounded the last curve of Silver Hill drive. The oak trees hissed and flailed, waving frenzied limbs against a starry sky, and leaves fluttered like tethered wild night creatures caught in the shadow of the moon.

The house was deserted. Slade left Brigida at the door to tend to the stallion himself. On a silver tray on the table in the center of the great hall, a single lamp was burning. In its flickering light Brigida saw a buff envelope addressed in the precise, even hand she recognized at once.

"The damnable bitch!" she said aloud, gingerly fingering the envelope. She dropped it where she had found it and stalked to the kitchen to light a cooking fire for tea. "Oh, damn!" she exploded, when the flue wouldn't draw properly, and her eyes were blurred as much by angry tears as by the smoke that billowed into the room.

Slade, carrying a bottle of champagne and two glasses, found her in the rose garden.

"I thought you'd be waiting upstairs for me, goddess, with the wicks trimmed and the comforter turned back." His eyes ranged over her.

"Well, I'm not," she snapped.

He poured out two glasses.

"You are a creature of very small consistency," he said, unable to control his temper. "What the blazing hell has gotten into you now?"

There was no reply. "I want to talk to you. About extending the act just until Elizabeth has come and gone. It would please her to think you were happy here." Brigida downed her third champagne, seeking courage at the bottom of the glass.

"It's hard to pretend for so long," she said finally.

"Think about it, goddess. I'm going to the city—for a few days, two or three. When I return . . ."

"Will you take me with you?"

"Not this time, no. You don't want to be there now. There's no one in town, the season's over, it's hot. I will take you to Saratoga in late summer. There's a race . . . I have business in New York now."

"Oh? What business is that?" Brigida asked innocently. The wind had dropped, and in the night stillness they heard the distant, ominous rumble of the ocean at the peak tide of the year, pounding the shore of the barrier beach.

"I must see McGlory. Come to bed. I'm to leave early, and I want a full night's relaxation."

"McGlory is it? You liar!" she said furiously. "Miri told me all about that whoremaster and the soiled doves he harbors in his roaring den!"

"Hold your evil tongue," Slade commanded, wondering at that moment if he found Brigida more magnificent when she raged or loved. "The man's my friend. His habits don't concern you."

"And what of your habits?"

"They don't concern you either, as you yourself tell me often enough."

With an inarticulate exclamation, Brigida turned away and strode off, flinging her empty glass shattering against a tree. She rushed into the house and raced up the dim staircase, seeking the solace of privacy behind the locked doors of her chamber. She paced, alternately fuming and weeping, as she undressed, flinging discarded garments about carelessly until she heard Slade slamming about below, locking up, securing the house. She listened to his tread as he mounted the stairs, whistling between his teeth.

Brigida had pulled off her dress and flounced petticoats and was seated at the dressing table, violently brushing her hair, when Slade tried the door.

"Open it, Brigida." He slammed a fist against the wood.

"You go to glory! I'm ready for bed and not with you," she called. "Let me be."

She heard nothing more, only the door of his room open and slam shut. She was disappointed that he had given up so easily.

Now he was leaving, deserting her for that woman, and she had to vent her riotous emotions or explode. All the advice she'd followed, everything she'd done to try and hold him had come to nothing; nothing had worked—not her pretended disinterest nor her freest passion, neither her social success nor her dutiful devotion had any effect on Slade.

Well, now she'd be through with the devil for once and ever. No man, not even Slade Hawkes, would have her heartsick and weepy.

She jumped to her feet with a cry of alarm as the terrace doors crashed open and he came striding into the room, unbuttoning his silk shirt, pulling it free of close-fitting breeches. Brigida didn't dare move as he devoured her with darkened raging eyes. A muscle in his jaw jumped violently.

She took an aggressive stance, clenched fists on her hips, slim legs set wide. Defiantly, she tried to stare him down. The laces of her camisole were loosed, exposing the curves of her breasts. Silk pantalettes, lace-edged and flounced at the knee, fit smoothly over her rounded hips, white silk stockings, embroidered at the insteps with pale

pink rosebuds, outlined shapely calves that were
elongated by high-heeled, beribboned bedroom mules.

An unlit cigar clenched in his teeth, Slade mirrored
her stance, the muscles in his forearms flexing as his
hands closed in tight fists. "I'm waiting," his voice was
husky, "and the way you look . . . I won't wait long."

Deliberately, she turned her back on him to sit again at
the dressing table. "Oh yes, you damn well will. You'll
wait a very long time for me," she said with exaggerated
clarity. Slowly, lazily, she resumed brushing her hair,
pretending to ignore him as he paced the room, his every
gesture jarring, stoking her anger higher.

"If you persist in behaving like an unspanked child I'll
handle you as you deserve. I'd rather deal with the
woman you look to be. I've never laid eyes on one more
desirable, Brigida."

"Unprincipled scoundrel, flattery won't serve your
ends with me! There must be someone at McGlory's or
surely your broken blossom, Worsley, who will have
you. You'll not bed me tonight."

Slade stood leaning at the French doors looking out
and, watching him in the glass, Brigida saw his strong
back stiffen and the faint scars whiten. With an incredulous, chilling laugh he swung about to face her.

"You are pushing me too far, my provoking pretty
witch," he said, lowering himself into a chair.

"Adulterous whorehound! I'm in no mood for your
arrogance tonight." Brigida flung her brush across the
room, narrowly missing Slade as he ducked to one side.
He shot up, his tense body a long brown arc.

"Moderate your manner, witch, and get to bed." He

started toward her.

"I do nothing in moderation, you should know that much about me by now." Brigida rose slowly, glancing at the door, and backing away as Slade came on.

"We're alone here," he laughed coldly. "There'll be no one but me to hear your pleadings, my spoiled little brat. I remember you, Brigida, the petted pretty child surrounded by adoring brothers, doting father. You could twist them to your whim with all the skill of a princess of the blood royal. But never me, not then, not now. No one ever took you to task for anything, did they? Now I will."

He said the last with resolute slowness. There was a glimmer of panic in Brigida's eyes as her hand came to her lips.

"A little fear in one of the softer sex keeps her properly docile, I've found."

"Don't . . . don't you touch me." Brigida's voice wavered. "I remember you, too, you know, so serious, so arrogant and proud, besting everyone at everything. You were the ice prince, letting no one near enough to touch you ever, just because your mama didn't dote on your every word. Well, I'm done with you, now and forever. I've had enough! Stay away from me."

"Stay away? But I'm your husband, Brigida. That gives me certain privileges. You always wanted my touch before, from the very first time and every time after." His look had almost softened. Brigida fell back into the wing chair, trapped.

"You arrogant ass, that was all pretense," she lied furiously, wanting to wound him.

"All, Brigida? An act?" He leaned over her, grasping the arms of the chair, preventing her escape. "Granting you were capable of such double-heartedness, why would you . . . ?"

"To best you, you overly self-assured fool, as I said from the first day I would. Now let me be," she sulked, not meeting his look.

"I'd put such thoughts out of my mind in the ease and pleasure of our loving. Surely you don't expect I'll let you be. You should know that much about me by now."

To mask her thickening fear, Brigida spewed out a stream of expletives that would have done a deckhand proud. Slade stepped back with a startled expression, then he threw back his head and roared with hard laughter.

"This is going to be fun, lady, for me, if not for you." He moved toward Brigida again, and she struck out to tear at him with her long nails. Easily, he caught her hands, pulling her to her feet as she protested furiously. He pinioned her narrow wrists behind her, her thrusting breasts pressing to his naked chest. Then he lifted her with one arm about her small waist and carried her across the room where he hooked a booted toe on one leg of the velvet bench and pulled it away from the dressing table. Sitting, he turned Brigida over his knee and threw a booted calf over her kicking legs as first one, then the other of her slippers flew off, sailing to opposite corners of the room.

"You've been warned for the last time," he growled.

"You vile, bloody cur, let me go!" Brigida commanded, cursing him still.

"Give me a sailor's blessing, will you?" Easily, Slade undid the hook and tie at Brigida's waist and stripped away the silk. There was an explosion of sound, and Brigida's strident complaints became plaintive, and she writhed in a vain effort to escape his punishing hand.

"Don't, Slade, oh, do stop, please," she begged piteously. "I'll do whatever you ask, I swear I will," she promised. Her pleading had its effect.

She felt Slade's hand caressing where it had been hard, then he let go of her hands to cup a forward-spilling breast. "Such a lovely sight you are, goddess, I'm in no hurry to loose you," he said before letting her slide from his lap to the floor at his feet. She scrambled up and danced away, naked now but for white silk stockings, which she removed once she had gained what seemed a safe distance.

She had manipulated him quite easily, she decided. Now she determined to unman the bastard completely. Lifting a pink China silk bed gown from the chest, Brigida raised her arms and let it slither down, following the incurvings and swells of her lush body, while Slade watched her, waiting. With willowy grace, she paraded about the room, bending to retrieve her slippers and brush as the gown tightened provocatively. Seething with anger, her nerves taut, she went to the dressing table to apply scent to her temples and throat, then stood brushing her hair unhurriedly. She yawned daintily behind a fluttering hand, stretched languidly, piling a mass of curls atop her head, arching to thrust pink-tipped breasts against clinging silk. Slade got to his feet when, twinkling with impish charm, Brigida swayed toward him.

"Have you learned your lesson, goddess?" he asked in a low, smoky voice, moving to enfold her in his arms. Brigida let golden curls tumble down about her shoulders.

"Bullying tyrant!" she said, taking him by surprise. "You are wide of the mark if you think I'll ever learn anything from you. And now, sir," she airily dismissed him, "goodnight!"

On the instant, Slade's anger was awesome. The challenging glimmer of triumph he saw in Brigida's eyes snapped his calculating self-control and goaded him to action again. She moved to pass him, and with the instinctive swiftness of a striking bird of prey, he had her across his lap again before her indignant cry of complaint abruptly stopped. His hand ran fast down her lissome back and slim legs to the hem of her gown.

"I'll humble you this time, pagan fury. Those nocturnal eyes and trembling lips won't save you this time."

"Don't, Slade," Brigida implored with real alarm, struggling, almost wriggling free. He caught her and jiggled her forward.

"Morocco leather was made for you," he answered coldly, pulling his belt free of its loops with a snap. He held Brigida firmly with one hand at her narrow waist, and she heard a rush of air when he raised the belt, then brought it solidly down across the bare, upswelling curves displayed over his lap. The first stroke took Brigida's breath from her, the second wrenched a cry of surprise from her lips, the third brought a loud wail as she begged him for relief.

"Not so quick this time, witch!"

"Damn you, brutish lout! Barbarian! How can you? Stop!"

"First I'll put a touch of real fear into you. I'll have tears from you, and a few promises, besides."

"I won't . . . I won't ever cry . . . for you again," Brigida choked out, already weeping. "I'll promise you nothing!" she tried to rage.

"You will, and keep your word, besides," he growled, and in a very few moments Brigida's inarticulate exclamations turned to pleas that proved him right.

"Wait, Slade . . . leave off, please! Ask anything you want of me, but be done, damn you," she cried, fighting to staunch the tears flooding from her eyes.

"Swear, lady, never again to walk away from me in anger or to lock your door to me, ever, and then say you won't curse me again as long as you live. Will you promise, Brigida?"

"Yes," she whispered in a small voice. "Now will you free me?"

"One thing more, you sweet tormenting witch. Out dancing without me, teasing, bold as brass! You won't do it again."

He dragged her, protesting, to the bed, and forced her down. "Remember," he said, applying the belt again, using it until finally Brigida broke. She gave way completely, exploding into wild gasping sobs, and then she felt him looming over her, menacing and ominous, felt his powerful body cool against her heated flanks.

With deliberate brute force, with cold swiftness, he took her, and she knew, through her hurt and tears and shattered pride, that for him it was rape, nothing more—

or less. In his awesome anger he was mastering . . . breaching . . . forcing her body, which had always been, for him, so willing and so wanting before, and was even then, even after a time, just that way.

And he began to feel it, to know she wasn't fighting him anymore, to know she needed him. He stayed with her, cursing under his breath, holding back and waiting, then riding the slow tremors with her that were deeper and longer—and more than anything she had felt ever before.

When they had done, finally, and he was holding her hard, all she could do was cry again.

Slade tasted salt tears gushing from her eyes. "I didn't want to hurt you," he whispered in a gravelly undertone. "You goaded me to it." He was finding her tears intolerable. Used to commanding, to dominating, to having his way, he was irritated that her sobs could unsettle him. Her stubbornness, he knew, matched his own, her desire to bend everything to her whim and will was nearly equal to his. Seeing her so humbled pleased and bothered him both.

"I had to, Brigida," he insisted adamantly, "or else there would have been no peace between us ever. There can be only one captain, you know that, and underlings all must tread to the master's measure. Stop it now," he said with open annoyance, and he saw the apprehension in her limpid eyes when she looked up at him, biting her thrusting lower lip.

Brigida was feeling as she had never before—subdued and mastered completely. "I'm . . . trying to stop," she said between quieting sobs, moving away from him to the middle of the room, her lovely bosom rising and falling rapidly. She made a poignant effort to regain some measure of dignity.

With a smothered oath, Slade strode across the room to the armoire to find her a wrapper. Damn! The bitch cries as she does everything else, without restraint or moderation, he thought, sympathy swelling to temper his manner to her while she eyed the long muscles in his back rolling beneath tanned skin and saw the strength of his arms with a timorous shiver.

When he folded her in satin, his gentle touch loosed another shower of tears. She sniffed as he patted her eyes with his silk handkerchief. "Oh, Slade, it's just so . . . so lonely when you're angry with me." She looked up, tears clinging on long wet lashes that were dark rays about her darker eyes, and her words, her child-woman's beauty, took his breath away. "Stay with me now?" she asked in a tiny, unsteady voice. "Stay with me tonight before you go away? Hold me, please?"

He gathered her up in his arms and cradled her against him. In plaintive innocence she had turned to him, the cause of her unhappiness, for comfort. It was the first time she'd done that, and it touched a quickness in him.

"I'll send Levi this time; I won't go," he said. They sat in the rocking chair, he holding her curled in his lap. Her head rested against his shoulder, and she signed now and again until the rocking motion calmed her. By then Slade was finding his own emotions more unsettled. When she stretched like a kitten and curled back against him, he scowled and clenched his jaw.

356

"Maker of mischief, it was your own fault," he said. His voice was ragged.

"Will you just be quiet, Slade, and love me again now?" she asked, lifting her face to his angry eyes. All she wanted was to have him near her for whatever time she could hold him. "Just love me, please," she whispered against his tasting lips.

"Lady, that's all I intended doing when I came here tonight." His hands moved over her satin-sheathed form, and her arms went about his neck. Her breasts, in satin, were incredibly soft and warm against his bare chest. He kissed her eyes, her throat, and her elegant hands. He undid her robe and followed the same smooth lines again, tracing along skin smoother, softer than satin. His darting tongue was hot at the peaks as his caressing hands gathered up first one, then the other of her creamy breasts. Brigida felt the hardness of him beneath her questing fingers and when, sighing, she moved to him, over him, the chair rocked less slowly than it had before, the joining of their surging bodies setting the measure.

Blue dawn had come and long gone. The morning sun was full at the wide windows when Slade awoke, feeling Brigida's softness beside him. He studied her golden body touched by morning sunlight and brushed a hand to her cheek. She turned away in sleep. "I should have given her a taste of leather the first time she was unruly," he thought, pulling her to him, wanting her urgently, and her sinuous body was warm and ready when he loved her again with a deep tenderness he'd not felt ever before.

Brigida found Slade, later in the morning, in the rose garden, paging through a thick sheaf of legal-looking documents. When he looked up at her, his sun-washed eyes were incredibly blue. There was a momentary pause as each was captivated anew by the stunning comeliness of the other.

"You look busy and serious," she said, settling on the sun-warmed stone bench beside him.

"You don't." Slade put aside his papers and brushed her cheek with the back of his hand.

"Don't let me interrupt you." She leaned back, lifting her face to the sun and closed her eyes.

"I will let you if I choose to." His hand on her shoulder descended to her breast. "I should beat you every night; it agrees with you." He studied her profile against a backdrop of yellow rosebuds that climbed a trellised vine. The balmy air was aromatic with summer.

"What agrees with me is not waking lonely," Brigida said, tracing the soft petals of the rose he tucked at her throat. "This is one of your mother's Noisettes, this rose, a Mlle. Desprez, pollinated long ago, it's told, by an unknown yellow tea rose. Isn't that wicked?"

"With what result? That's all that matters."

"Oh, good result. That joining created the Souvenir de Malmaison, the oldest of the true Bourbon roses, which some prefer to all others. What were you doing?"

"Going over the bill of sale for the last of the ships."

"I miss the sea awfully, sometimes, don't you, Slade?

Answer truly . . . sun and sky rolling endless, forever. We were so free then, in our own small space. Our fathers were in command of their destinies. They knew what needed doing, and they knew exactly how to do it. A simple life, really."

"They lived at the mercy of wind and tide, with a yearning homeward, always. There is no better game anywhere than what we hunted. When a big bull whale would break, a few yards from the longboat, glistening black in the sun—that's a sight I'd not have wanted to miss. But it was only that single moment of truth that ever set fire to me. There are better ways to build a fortune than spending your life up to your knees in blubber."

"You'll always have whaling in your blood, Slade Hawkes, as I will, don't deny it. It made us . . . different." Brigida slipped the rose from her throat and lifted it to her lips.

"Stubborn you mean. Stubborn and strong. There are no rules for our kind; we make our own. Otherwise, I'd not have sent to you offering marriage sight unseen for ten years." Slade plucked another rose and planted it in the coil of Brigida's hair.

"And I'd not have accepted, if it were otherwise," she answered, her eyes bright as dusky diamonds. "I'd not have accepted if we didn't share that. I need someone to remember it with me."

"We're of a fierce race, Mrs. Hawkes, the same heated blood flows in us both. You'll see it doubled stronger in our sons."

Brigida turned away to look out over the bay. "Do you

really think there will be sons, or daughters, for that matter? We've been nearly six months together."

"You keep secrets, don't you? You hold distant from me. Not your ripe and lovely pleasure-seeking anatomy, that's easy for a woman like you to offer. It's an inner coldness you swore would never melt. No matter, I'll soften you one way or another," Slade said.

Brigida's smile disappeared like the sun shadowed by fast-flying clouds. "You're overly confident as usual." She sprang up and started toward the house. As she made to brush past him, he reached out and caught her about the waist, pulling her to stand before him.

"Stay, lady." His thick lashes fluttered against bright sunlight. "You gave your word you'd not turn away in anger."

Conflicting emotions caught Brigida as she stood, hands resting on Slade's wide shoulders. She feared she would laugh and cry all at once, as love and anger fought in her for an instant. She hesitated.

"Trust me a little." Slade's words came low.

"You, who trust no one, ask that of me? I did once," she said, distress changed to defiance, "and you used me meanly. Now let me go!" She twisted free and, scattering his papers over the grass, ran not toward the house but off across the lawn in the direction of the bay.

"The way you presented yourself, no man could have behaved otherwise! You wouldn't have wanted it otherwise!" Slade called after her in exasperation. "Stop, I have to speak to you, damn it. I'll tame you, pagan witch," he said under his breath. "I'll tame you if it takes the rest of my days."

Brigida stopped at the edge of the bluff above the bay beach. A band of gulls on the water below undulated on full swells like a silken scarf in a breeze. She glanced back to see Slade coming after her, running fast and easy, wide shoulders shifting, tawny hair wild, his lips pulled back in a grimacing grin.

Laughing, she slid down the side of the bluff to the sand below and landed running, petticoats flying. Slade reached the dune crest in time to see a flash of lace and loosed curls disappear into the boathouse. Unhurriedly he descended a long row of wooden steps to the beach, then sauntered along the shore, whistling through his teeth. He skipped stones across the placid surface of the bay, sending the gulls farther offshore, rescued the rose fallen from Brigida's hair and, coming abreast of the boathouse, tried the door. Inside, Brigida held her breath, watching the handle jiggle. She had thrown the bolt and it held.

"Are your promises worth nothing, goddess?" Slade called and got a girlish giggle in response.

"Now, Captain, do you think me a fool? I shall just outwait you. I've far more patience than you do."

The door gave way to one blow that separated rusted hinges from gray, weathered timbers, and Slade stood silhouetted against the sky. He came toward Brigida with a slight roll of narrow hips, and she saw his eyes ablaze beneath his disordered hair, backlit by summer sun.

"I was only toying with you, Slade; don't look that way," she laughed nervously, the back of her left hand flying to her lips.

"Will you never learn? Come here," he demanded,

finding her extraordinarily beautiful, her black eyes wide, darting like those of some feral woodland animal, caught.

On the palm of an extended hand, he proffered the fallen yellow rose, and Brigida knew then that what she saw in his eyes wasn't what she had supposed at all. She smiled.

"I thought you really were angry with me again," she breathed with soft relief, bending toward him. They moved to each other in the half gloom of the boathouse warily, like two cautious wild creatures, and when they met, caught together in a netting shaft of dancing golden sunlight, his arms came strong about her narrow waist and hers enfolded his neck, her fingers raking his hair as he lifted her from the ground.

His lips never left her moist, eager mouth as he worked at her hooks and ties until the fragile fabric of her dress gave way. His dark strength enfolded her and they sank down together into a deep bower of faded, wind-softened sails.

They remained entwined a long while, Brigida's head resting on Slade's shoulder as he held her.

"We have a compact, then," he said, breaking the silence. Brigida raised on an elbow to look puzzled at him, until understanding brightened her eyes.

"Yes, I'd say we have, the act will continue. Just until Elizabeth and Del have come and gone, remember," she added, almost as an afterthought.

362

Nineteen

The Fourth of July was hot, the thrumming air slow and heavy with languorous perfumes of summer. Brigida was up early seeing to the day's preparations.

She milked with Mary and Nan, directed the setting out of long tables and benches on the great lawn above the bay, sent the stable hands clamming with old John, and the housemaids to the fields to heap baskets with new potatoes. Bread was baking, strawberry and rhubarb pies were cooling, pitchers of creamy milk and lemonade— covered with weighted cheesecloths—stood near rows of watermelons and kegs of beer and ale in the icehouse.

Just after noon Brigida came to the wide front veranda of Silver Hill. Rounding a corner of the house, Slade saw her there, beautiful in a gown of palest pink faille with puffed sleeves and an apron of a sheer fragile fabric. Crystal beads glinted at the shell curves of her ears, her eyes glimmered with happiness, and she seemed aglisten as with dew and spangles.

"Slade, do you think it's Elizabeth?" she asked, catching sight of him and an arriving carriage at the same moment. Her lovely mouth seemed to him inviting as roses and snow.

"That's Roland and the footman from Washington Square come on early. Sit with me now in the garden or you'll be spent before any of your guests arrive."

"But I can't!" she exclaimed with a kick at the pleated frill of pink fringe at her hem. "I'm too excited. I want it all to go perfectly, and I'm afraid I've forgotten something, or it will be too hot, or it will rain, or people will forget and not come and . . ." She stopped speaking to watch Johnny and Robin carry two bushels of clams across the lawn.

"Hello, missus! Captain!" Robin sang out. "This will be the best clambake in these parts in many a year!"

Brigida nodded. "You're not forgetting the chickens? Good fat ones?"

"We won't be forgettin' anythin' a'tall," Robin said, laughing, then paused to watch as first Roland, then his companion alighted from the coach at the manor door.

"Oh, Slade, how could you?" Brigida giggled, seeing the French chef in his starched stand-up collar strutting about with stiff, high-kneed steps like a rooster. "How could you put him and Martha in the same kitchen? It is mad!"

"They're both professionals. They'll do fine." Slade started toward the new arrivals, who were looking about.

"*Bonjour*, Captain. If you will show me to the kitchens, *s'il vous plaît* . . . ? Madame," Roland bowed a greeting to Brigida. "*Votre château est très magnifique.*"

"Do you think so, Roland?" Brigida asked, coming to stand at his side and look up at the house with him. Every door and window was open to the summer day, with curtains fluttering, and there were roses everywhere. Brigida felt that Silver Hill Manor had really become, at least for a day, a hospitable place open to all the world.

"Your room is there," Brigida pointed to the third floor. "Here's Mary; she'll show you up."

When she and Slade were alone again, she resumed her pacing. "Do you think Elizabeth will be pleased by all this fuss and frummery? I mean, perhaps she—they—would have preferred to visit quietly and talk."

"My mother has never been noticeably interested in conversing with me. Why begin now?" he answered, frowning.

"People do change," Brigida offered quietly.

There was a marble hardness in Slade's face. "It's too late, the damage is done."

"Must you look that way?"

"She drove my father away from this place. I've told you before. She sat up there cold and silent the day he left Silver Hill for the last time."

Slade was pacing now, and Brigida followed his movement with worried eyes. "The irony is that after that day when he went forever from this place he loved, she hardly ever left it again, until you came and freed her from her . . . prison."

"He must have done something. There must have been a reason," Brigida said vehemently, her heart twisting at the anguish and rage she saw in Slade's eyes.

"He might be alive still if she hadn't driven him off."

"Oh, Slade, please, not today," Brigida implored. "Today . . . today try to be . . . oh, kind, that's all."

When she took a step toward him, he rested his arms on her shoulders, and she clasped him about the waist.

"Walk down the hill with me? They should be here anytime." She stretched on tiptoe to brush a kiss at his throat. "We'll meet them at the gate." She enticed him with a smile.

". . . and I have never seen my son more relaxed and handsome. Everything about him signifies contentment." Elizabeth was at the dressing table in her room, smoothing her hair. "Are you as happy here as I expected you would be, as I promised? That pleases me more than I can express. Silver Hill harbored only sadness for so very long. Come in!" Elizabeth answered to a soft knock, and Martha, carrying a sweating pitcher of cold lemonade on a tray with glasses, was followed by Johnny Hand laden with boxes and cases.

"I'll be needing just the one, Johnny, thank you," Elizabeth said, making a selection. "We will only stay the night. Take the others back out like a good lad, yes? Martha, wait!" she commanded. The Indian woman raised her pudgy hands.

"We will visit later, Elizabeth, but I must tell you one thing now. This child," Martha glanced at Brigida, "brings the same light you had years ago when love was still whispering in your heart. Now, I have work. A chowder is steaming," Martha said, "and I don't think that man can watch it right."

"Roland?" Elizabeth asked. "He is one of the best cooks in all of New York City. Surely he can watch your

366

chowder. We've not talked in so long a time."

"I see you are well; I hear you are happy. That is enough," Martha smiled. "I am told you are going away?"

"My dearest angel!" Elizabeth said with great feeling. "Can you ever forgive me for leaving? It's you who should have been free, so long ago."

"But I never cared to be," Martha said softly, leaving the room.

"Will you be going to Paris, too, Elizabeth?" Brigida, puzzled by the exchange she had just witnessed, filled two glasses with the chilled beverage and handed one to Elizabeth, who carried it as she wandered about the room, caressing small objects fondly.

"Later perhaps. There was a horrible bloodbath there when the Commune fell, and that was only little more than a month ago. We'll be staying abroad until we've wearied of traveling, so we'll see Paris later on. Your French friends, will they be here today?"

"Miri and Alain? Yes, of course, everyone will celebrate Independence and wish you bon voyage. The Hands and the Edwards, the Squires and all the Carpenters, of course, Ann and . . ."

"And Lydia Worsley. We trained out with her, and I must say I was a bit surprised. Philip and that friend of his," Elizabeth said the last with a touch of distaste, "took her off to Carpenter's Island. They'll be along later."

"Worsley?" Brigida's face lost its color. "I wasn't told she'd been invited, but then she and Slade are such old friends."

"Lydia is as much Slade's business associate as anything else. During the war, you know, she and Slade . . . oh, my dear, forgive me. I didn't realize. Seeing you and Slade so happy," Elizabeth shook her head. "I never thought . . . tactless of me, of course, to speak of Lydia, but it is over between them, surely."

"Then why would he invite her here?" Brigida stood at the open window, her back to the room. Elizabeth placed a light hand on her shoulder.

"June is the month of roses. Was it beautiful here?" she asked.

Brigida nodded.

"Brigida, do you know how the rose got its color? I shall tell you. When the goddess Aphrodite rushed to the defense of her lover Adonis, she pricked her foot on the thorn of a rose. She stained the white flower with her blood, and the rose has forever after been red. So you see, even for the goddess of love, the path wasn't smooth. My dear, no matter what I may have said to you, I longed to be in love once more, just once more. I'm a dreadful romantic really; I couldn't believe I would never feel that way again. In some small, secret place I never stopped wishing. I think that's true of us all, no matter how resigned we may seem to a lonely, loveless life. Del has given me another chance, my last, and this time . . . I'm going to tell you something—listen to me carefully, Brigida," Elizabeth went on, almost angrily. "Jealousy will erode even the brightest jewel of love. I know too well what I say to you. Has Slade told you about . . . his father?"

Brigida nodded. "A little."

"I will tell you more," Elizabeth said in a determined manner. She moved to the mantel and, hands clasped, head high, she went on in a clipped, tense voice. "I refused to go to sea. Your mother went with your father, she insisted on going, but I was too frail, I thought, for such a life, too refined."

Elizabeth roamed the room and then settled at the edge of a chair, folding her small hands in her lap.

"Slade's grandfather founded the first real Hawkes fortune. His wealth built part of this manor house. Jarred, his son, my husband, never had to go to sea at all, but the Hawkes men have a sense of . . . of a glorious destiny." Elizabeth's inflection was scornful. "And a mad desire, bred into them, it seems, to outdo each other and everyone else. Jarred never had to go to sea, but he went, he went and increased his wealth many times over with whale oil and bone. He added the large new wings to this house for me, but I never forgave him for leaving me here alone. Your mother knew nothing of what I am about to tell you. Understand?"

Brigida nodded.

"Slade is like his father and his grandfather; he has spent his life doing better, getting more." Elizabeth sighed deeply. She pulled a fine lace handkerchief from her sleeve and dabbed at her brow. "I drove Jarred Hawkes away from me, from Silver Hill. My pride and unforgiving nature drove him off this land, and he loved the dark plowed earth so, more than any sailor had a right to, really."

"But why?" Brigida demanded. "What happened? You loved him, I can hear in your voice you did."

"Yes. And hated him, too." Elizabeth shielded her face with her hands. "The whalers' mailbox on Morgan Island? You know of it, of course. Men on passing ships stop to find letters from home left by vessels lately out, and ships turned homeward carry messages to the northeastern towns. I got a letter. In the middle of what was to have been Jarred's last voyage . . . he promised, he promised. A letter came from a missionary wife, well intentioned perhaps. . . ." Elizabeth's hands were clenched and the knuckles were white. "Slade's father, Brigida, had . . . another wife. Not a legal one; an Island woman he returned to faithfully every voyage out as regularly as he came home to me."

"Elizabeth, I . . . it isn't . . . unusual. Men alone at sea for years . . . ?"

Elizabeth shook her head to silence Brigida.

"I know that. I even thought then that woman was relieving me of his . . . lustful domination. My dear, I've lately learned that my own . . . appetites are not so different. There was only one real difference between us, that woman and me. She had given Jarred the son he so longed for. I had not, after years."

Brigida, not able to summon any word of comfort that seemed equal to the moment, held silent.

"The woman who wrote to me?" Elizabeth went on.

Brigida nodded, seeing the anguish and anger in Elizabeth's raging blue eyes so like her son's.

"She felt I must know and, childless as I was, should agree to raise Jarred's boy here at Silver Hill. She may have been well intentioned, trying to save us all, but the damage was done. . . . Well, a year after that terrible

370

letter, Jarred's voyage ended—such a long time to let injured pride and jealousy fester like a disease in my heart. He had given some other woman the child I should have had, and I couldn't . . . I couldn't bear it. I waited, I schemed against him and I was ready to use anything, anyone to hurt him.

"Oh, Brigida! I can hardly speak of it yet, and one would think, after all these years, that time would have swallowed up the shame and hurt as mere drops of water in the sea."

Elizabeth rose, crossed the room, then wilted onto the chaise longue near the bed. With a fluttering hand she waved Brigida to a chair. "Do you want to hear more? All of it?"

"Unless it's too painful for you," Brigida answered. She rolled a sweating cold glass against her temple and waited.

"Jarred had always been . . . drawn to Martha, always, from the first day we took her in. I knew that, I saw the way he looked at her; she was so soft and warm, open like his Island girls.

"I'd been careful, before the letter, not to place temptation in his way, but after?" Elizabeth laughed cruelly. "I saw to it that he was alone with her, here. I went off to the city, or visited at Carpenter's Island for weeks on end. I denied Jarred my bed on one pretext or other until . . . it was inevitable. I used her to entrap him and it worked, it worked very well." Elizabeth began to shiver a little in the heat of the July day.

"I let them be—for a time," she continued very slowly, as if a great weariness had come over her. "I let them be and watched and waited and she—Martha really loved him, she does still, and that may be the saddest part, though it's all so grievous it's hard to know.

"Well, when I finally 'discovered' them together, they were desolate, abject with guilt and regret at wronging me as they had, and they swore never again. When I had heard them out, I calmly suggested that the three of us could be tolerably happy at Silver Hill, bound by an entirely unholy affection, he pleasuring us both in the most interesting ways. Oh, I was very descriptive, very . . . graphic. I was made wonderfully imaginative and eloquent by meanness and rage. But Jarred? He was sickened to despair by what I asked of him. I mean, it was one thing, in his view, for a man to engage in immoral behavior, but for a woman, a respectable woman, his wife to even think such things? Jarred was . . . crazed. He . . . violated me. He almost killed me, Brigida, and then—he went away. Slade was born . . . after that."

For some moments, nothing stirred in the room but the light summer curtains touched by a hot breeze. When Elizabeth spoke again, her voice was barely audible. "I let Silver Hill fall to ruin—the mill crumbled, the fields went to seed—all to hurt Jarred. I think I conceived Slade out of spite after all the barren years."

"What a cruel thing to say." Brigida was stone still, her eyes unbelieving. "That can't be possible."

"I've come to believe it is possible. I never gave Jarred a child before because I begrudged him . . . everything. Then, when I was desperate, when I knew there was no other way to hold him . . . but it was too late. I realized that, too, after time, but by then Madame Restell refused to . . . help me. I was past the time for treatment, and that's the one saving miracle of this sordid story.

"So, when Jarred next returned, Slade was three years old. The father had never had a single word from me of his son's existence. Understandable, isn't it, that Jarred denied the boy was his? Well, his visits here were brief and few after that. He was cold to the child, and I saw the father clear as day in the son and was bitter toward them both. I blamed Slade, I think, for what his father had done to me."

Brigida's question came in a pained whisper. "How could you?"

"I tried, I swear to you, I tried not to visit my resentment on that fierce, proud child prowling these silent halls and rooms; I did try, but not hard enough. While I wasn't watching, it seems, Slade grew up, and I hardly even noticed. He grew into the very image of Jarred. The configuration of form and face, gestures . . . all, all except the eyes. Only his eyes are mine."

Elizabeth stood and went to the window. "Your guests begin to arrive, my dear," she said softly.

"It doesn't matter. Go on, please." Brigida came to stand beside her.

"When Slade returned from his voyage with you, Jarred saw himself finally in that gallant young man, and then they went to sea together, father and son. A first frail affection was beginning to bind them and—you know what happened: Jarred was killed, murdered, and Slade was unable to save him. Slade blames me, I know; the accusation is always there in his eyes, there in all my direful dreams. Help him, Brigida, don't turn him from

373

you as I did his father. Don't let wasted years pile up about you as I did, please!"

Carriages and wagons had been rolling up the long drive all the time Elizabeth had spoken, and voices now sounded about the house and gardens and in the hallways as guests were shown their rooms.

"Brigida, where the devil are you?" Slade called up the stairs. "You've all night to gossip."

"Brigida, wait," Elizabeth said urgently. "There's one thing more I want you to know, only you. Levi, too, was born after Jarred left Silver Hill that terrible time. Levi and Slade, Brigida, are both Jarred Hawkes's sons. Until this moment, only Martha and I have ever known that."

Brigida, wordless, hugged Elizabeth quickly and rushed from the room. She raced downstairs and flung herself into Slade's arms. At one end of the wide entrance hall the doors were open to the green lawns and blue bay and, at the opposite end, to a luxuriant garden, a mass of color with larkspur and phlox and black-eyed Susan. The summer wind wafted thick with the scent of roses and new-cut hay.

"Are you all right?" Slade studied her face. "I thought the hounds of hell were after you, the way you came down those steps."

"Do I overplay my part, do you think?" Brigida asked in an oddly impassioned tone, much affected by Elizabeth's words, which had made Slade seem less the unreadable puzzle than he had before. "I wouldn't want to tip my hand, being too strong in the role, especially now I've learned you invited your Miss Worsley."

Slade held her at arms' length. "Who the mischief told

you that?" he asked.

"You didn't invite her here? But she came out on the train with Elizabeth and the others."

"Don't trouble about it, goddess, it's not anything to do with you, and in answer to your first question, the character you are supposed to be acting can't be over-played." He bent to her lips, drawing her to him, their bodies close, fingers twined. Neither turned to a rustle of satin until a sharp, dry cough intruded to capture their attention.

Lydia Worsley, elegantly gowned, her angular face cold and haughty, swept toward them with Hollis Stancel in her wake. There was a small, awkward silence until Brigida disengaged herself from Slade's arms and extended her hand. "Welcome to Silver Hill, Miss Worsley. Do let me send for a cooling lemonade. The day is so warm and you so sumptuously attired."

"Mistress Hawkes, you've lost all your pale, delicate looks. You are nearly brown as a field hand, and that cunning little dress is reminiscent of a milkmaid's attire. No lemonade, thank you. Your husband knows exactly what I like." The woman's crimsoned lips curled in a forced smile.

Slade nodded. "And for you, Stancel? Phil with you?"

"I'll get myself an ale, Captain," Stancel responded. "Phil's settin' up that camera of his out on the grounds somewhere, and the beauteous Brigida," he turned a tight smile in her direction, "is to be the first to stand or sit, as the case may be, for a photograph." He offered Brigida a crooked arm. "Philip insists."

Philip's dark tent was set up under the pines, and the

375

large camera on its heavy wooden tripod was gathering a crowd as Brigida moved in its direction, greeting guests, directing some to refreshments, others to comfortable chairs in shady corners. Like the most beautiful blossom in a wind-scattered bouquet of wildflowers, she went gracefully among country girls in calico and cotton, city ladies in linen, in muslin, in pineapple cloth of saffron yellow, fringed parasols up, shielding them from the sun's touch. Farmers in brogans passed the time of day with gentlemen in Prince Alberts and dark cutaways. A group of children in a game of tag chirruped like a flock of starlings swooping a cornfield. Firecrackers snapped and popped, and the acrid smell of powder hung with puffs of smoke in the July air.

When Brigida finally reached him, Phil's head was hidden beneath a dark cloth as he made some adjustment to his camera. It stood on its tripod, grand and imposing, taller than Brigida, a large wooden box with telescoping bellows and a brass protrusion at the front.

"Philip, do a photograph of Ann Overton," Brigida asked. "She always looks so elegant."

"No, no, darling, you first, absolutely," he responded, pulling his head from beneath the cover to take Brigida's hand. Then he caught a glimpse of Ann.

"Ann, Ann, here!" Phil called waving. "I'll do you both together. Ann Overton, you are ravishing," he gushed, taking her extended hand to his lips. "Stand with Brigida for the camera, please, there in the sun while I fix the plate." He disappeared into his tent.

"You are looking happy, Brigida; Slade as well. I'm pleased for you both," Ann said in her slow, throaty voice, eyes weary as always, mouth down-curved at the corners until a flash of smile lit her face for a brief instant.

"And you look fine! I hear the salon is prospering. Tell me what else you've been about?" Brigida was pleasured to see her friend again after so long.

"This dress suits you. I knew it would." With a proprietary gesture, Ann straightened the edge of Brigida's apron. "Don't bruit this about now, but I actually fell in love with another man," she said matter-of-factly with an arched brow and the faintest shrug.

"Oh? Anyone I know?" Brigida mimicked Ann's casual manner, barely restraining her almost irrepressible vivacity and excitement.

"Billy McGlory. As a matter of fact, you did meet him at the White Elephant in New York. Whatever is Phil doing in there? I'm getting dreadfully warm," Ann complained.

"An ale, Ann? It will cool you some." Brigida filled a mug from a cold, foaming pitcher Nan had just brought out and set on a near table. The girl was on her way back to the icehouse when Ann stopped her.

"Why Nanny, what's come over you?"

"The missus cut my hair and all. Now I'm marryin' up with Johnny Hand." Nan flushed almost scarlet. "I must go, they are wantin' another lemonade in the side garden."

"You've a real talent, 'missus,'" Ann nodded to Brigida. "I've a job for you at my salon, as I've mentioned before. I've some customers who would benefit from your attentions as much as Nan has. There's Billy."

377

Ann lifted her chin toward the house where Slade and McGlory stood talking at the front portico.

"It is so exhausting, being in love, but now I don't know how I lived not being. I was taken with him right away." Ann's features were almost animated as she watched Billy gesturing grandly. "He brought a girl to me to be properly outfitted. He said she was his niece, and of course I credited that as much as I believe the sky could fall, but as it turns out Caitlin really is his brother's girl, an orphan. Billy wants her to get a respectable rich husband, and he's got her working as a barmaid in that dance hall of his. I told him she'd get a proper husband that way soon as she would walking the streets. She is such a little jewel, I offered to take her on as a manne-quin, but I told him first to bring her out here to you and Slade in the country to get her away from some tough she's got bothering her."

"That's fine, really, Ann, but tell me about you and Billy. How . . . ?"

"Oh, Billy," Ann almost sighed. "Billy . . . he's a lover, Brigida, and a dreamer, like no one I ever knew before . . . a scrapper and a brawler, too. He's the bras-siest dresser, the loudest, the most flamboyant . . . Lydia says he's the most uncouth man she has ever met. I think he's perfect. For me."

"Opposites being drawn, you mean?" Brigida's lilting laugh rose. "Well, Miri Manceaux didn't think Billy uncouth. It sounds wonderful!"

"Don't move!" Philip rushed from the tent carrying a wet silvery plate of glass, which he slipped into the camera. "Ready?" His voice came muffled from beneath the cloth as he angled the machine a little to please him. "Don't move 'til I say." He pressed a bulbous tube and held it for what seemed an eternity while Brigida smiled and Ann stood casually, her downturned mouth pursed, the expression on her face one of bemused boredom.

"Now!" Philip exclaimed. Quickly, he extracted the glass from the camera and was gone into the tent again immediately.

"Billy once adored your friend Miri, even wanted to marry her. I'll be back to see what Phil's done." Ann sauntered off, and Brigida moved toward Slade, drawn to him as always, but she stopped to talk as she went. Lydia Worsley was nowhere to be seen, and she didn't hurry.

As the leisurely afternoon wore on, some visitors sailed the bay before a light wind; there were croquet and badminton on the lawns, ambling walks to kennels and stable, quiet talks in leafy, shaded gardens lit and perfumed by the irridescent belled blossoms of aromatic summer lilies.

When it grew near time to eat, Slade and Levi began to fill the waiting cauldrons, and Brigida observed them together, seeing the resemblance clearly now, wondering that she hadn't before. There was the same hard leanness about them. The severe, handsome faces, fine proud carriage of head, a grace and nobility of movement and gesture were the same, or nearly so. The differences were of degree and shading: one tawny, the other dark; Levi's sharp, aquiline features chiseled finer in Slade's face. But there was one real difference, Brigida realized. The fierce bitterness she knew in Slade was lacking entirely in Levi, who looked at the world armored in calm, his impassive eyes showing nothing.

Over stones in the bottom of the kettles, potatoes were layered, then chickens, lobsters, and then corn, beneath mounding heaps of clams at the top, each layer separated from the one below by spread strips of seaweed and eel grass. People came drifting together from all corners of Silver Hill when the clambake was ready to be served with chilled kegs of beer carried from the icehouse, with cases of champagne, pitchers of milk and lemonade and, later, pyramids of new-made ice cream. The meal lasted a long time.

Before the day had almost imperceptibly slipped away between the trees, Philip had photographed everyone. Family groupings and clusters of friends sitting or standing, rigid and businesslike, all stared into the camera with serious faces. A special portrait was done of John Hand and Sari. The warmth and kindness of their worn old faces was captured to be held forever, Philip promised, on a piece of silvered glass.

The jeweled hues of evening began to come down and the moon to rise over the southern horizon. The wind fell away, the darkening waters were mirror-smooth, and the green twilight seemed to last forever.

Sitting beside Slade, Brigida knew, no matter what might happen later, that she was home. The harmony, the rightness of it all almost frightened her. It seemed too perfect to last. Slade, as if sensing her mood, brought his hand to the back of her neck and, passing it round, caressed the lovely line of her throat. His fingers set the crystal trembling at her ear, and where his touch went, his eyes followed. Taken by an unfamiliar look about her, he stood and pulled her with him to lead her from the table.

Each passing day of late had disclosed to him another of her moods, a new shade of her disposition, and as her rampant beauty had always, from the first and ever after, caught him by surprise, so too, now, the quicksilver emotions that bubbled in her arrested his attention. They threaded the pines, distancing themselves from the others until they were aware only of faint laughter drifting on the summer night.

"When your eyes are polished by moonlight, I'll brighten the sky for you, goddess. Will you like that?" Slade asked.

"Flares? Yes, I've always loved the pyrotechnics best. Will there be many?" There was such contagious delight in Brigida's manner that Slade lifted her with his hands about her waist, and when she placed a slim hand on each of his shoulders, swung her about.

"So many you'll be amused 'til moonset." Still holding her, he looked up into happy dark eyes until her arms twined around his neck and her mouth came slowly down to his.

There was a rustling sound, the murmur of satin close by, and Slade and Brigida moved apart to observe Lydia Worsley emerge from a wooded copse and hurry along the path toward them. She appeared preoccupied and almost rushed into them before she became aware of their presence. With a stifled gasp, Lydia came up short.

"Ah, the charming newlyweds, though not that newly,

is it? This does seem to be my day for interrupting your play. Phil's been showing me the grounds. It is a fine estate, Slade, but so very rustic. How do you keep amused in such surroundings? I mean, there is only so much fondling even the warmest pair can abide." Lydia had regained her composure and placed a pale hand on Slade's arm. "If your little bride can bear to part with you briefly, I've some business to discuss—privately."

Slade's expression went blank.

"Really, Miss Worsley," Brigida purred, stepping in front of him, "this is no time for business; this is a party. You must amuse yourself, I insist." She moved back against Slade in a possessive manner, gratified to see Lydia's haughty smile turn to a grimace. The woman stalked off down the path toward the manor house, then paused as a sudden loud yapping erupted from the kennels. Without turning, she continued quickly on her way.

Bran, who had been nosing about in the ferns and brambles, crashed onto the path and flew off to investigate.

"What do you suppose that's about?" Brigida asked Slade as they turned to follow Lydia back to the gathered company.

"A squabble. They're a scrappy lot, terriers; some upstart is always trying his strength against the top dog. Now I've something more important to talk to you about. Billy McGlory's brought his niece, did you see her? Beautiful."

"Robin Edwards thinks so too," Brigida answered. "Billy wants to leave her here. Ann told me."

"She can be helpful in the dairy, unless you've somewhere else you'd prefer to place her."

"Mary can use an extra pair of hands. It's a good place . . . look there who's finally arrived!"

Gathering up her petticoats, Brigida ran to meet the carriage coming to a stop at the top of Silver Hill drive. Miri and Alain alighted.

"If I hadn't secreted away your plates," Brigida scolded, "you'd neither one have anything to eat. Where on earth were you?" she demanded, stamping her foot and shaking her head.

"How fearsome she is, Slade, your *petite beauté*, when her ire is roused," Alain laughed. "We . . . I rather, was delayed."

"Delayed! His difficulty, darlings," Miri scoffed, "is that he lost his pocket watch, and his purse, and even all his papers. So careless," she clucked.

"Miri, didn't I tell you a thousand times already I didn't lose anything? They were stolen, that's it!" Alain was exasperated. "I stopped last evening," he went on, addressing Slade, "at Volet's for a glass of wine, that is all. I paid the *addition*, but when I got in the carriage, my pockets were empty. Ask Stancel, Miri. I ran into him at Volet's. We had a drink together. When I let him off at Lydia's . . ."

"You let him off where?" Slade asked, his eyes narrowing.

"At Lydia Worsley's, darling," Miri laughed. "The man's often been a guest there. Did you want Lydia to pine for you forever? Pardon, Brigida, I don't mean to be indelicate, but really!"

Brigida waited for Slade's answer, and when he made no response she laughed derisively. "Well, you've arrived just in time for the fireworks, but first you must have something to eat." She slipped her arm through Miri's and drew her off a little distance.

"Brigida, you should be over all that about Lydia," Miri admonished.

"Did you see his face when you mentioned Hollis and that woman?" Brigida demanded. "I took all your advice, Miri. I took everyone's advice, and don't think there wasn't a lot of it. Every woman he's ever met had something to say, and most of them act as if they really know him, as if he's been a lover, even you."

Miri smiled. "In some cases, darling," she said, "it is just wishful thinking, I'm sure."

Brigida laughed. "I tried to be perfect, as you advised, and never show the least jealousy, but I think now it's time to speak the truth and . . ."

"Too perfect can be tiresome. Now *petite*, I've more to tell you. Love, in its immaturity, may be sweetest, but until you've given Slade a child, you won't really know the true beauty of it. You will soon. One glance at you and Slade together, darling, is all one needs to know that. You are being silly."

"What you see is only an act," Brigida snapped.

"*Très drôle*, darling girl, to talk so! No one, not even Slade Hawkes, is so good an actor as you would have me think. Now, you are being inhospitable. I must have sustenance, darling. We will have time to talk later. Alain and I plan to stay on some days, if you will have us. *Mon mari* withdrew himself from all that stupid spy business, so there is no need for us to hurry. It just was not right for Alain. He's not devious enough. Ah, how beautiful Silver Hill is again, thanks to you, Brigida, no doubt!"

They approached the house, which was lit now in every room and still open to the evening air. They paused in a rainbow spread of columbine and English daisies in a lantern-lit side garden.

"Not devious enough?" Brigida asked almost wistfully. "Not like my husband, you mean?"

"Slade? *Un beau sauvage*, darling. There is nothing Slade can't handle, except you, perhaps? Oh, see!" Miri pointed. There was a low whine, a loud pop. A puff of light flowered against dark heavens and blazed, reflecting in the darker bay, then fell, a sparkling and hissing shower of light along the night sky.

Miri and Brigida went to join the others gathered at the dune bluff. The flares came quickly, one after another, to sighs and applause, as smiling upturned faces were tinted by the soaring colored lights.

Brigida came behind Slade and passed her arms about him, resting her head against his back as if sheltering from a coming storm, feeling firm muscles through silk. Without pausing in his talk, he reached to draw her forward into the curve of his arm. It was then Brigida met Lydia Worsley's malevolent look with a complacent little taunting smile. I'll strangle the bitch, I swear it, if she interferes another time, Brigida thought, even as her smile sweetened.

"I will strangle the witch. I myself will turn assassin, I swear it to you, my friend," Brigida was startled to hear Alain whisper furiously. "That perverted pair she has employed? They are as responsible as she for Jean Paul's death. And the girl's. That procuress Restell provided them the terrible means to extract information from Janine D'Arcy before they killed her. They are evil, Slade, evil."

"Alain, I'll take care of it. Don't you involve . . . Brigida," Slade turned to her, "will you go to Mrs. Huntting, please? She and the reverend are ready to leave, it seems."

"And you, it seems, are trying to be rid of me," she protested. "Who is Alain talking about?"

"Will you never learn? There are some questions you don't ask. Go on!"

With obvious reluctance, Brigida moved away.

Only then did Slade continue. "Don't involve yourself, Alain; you don't know the half of it."

"Don't involve?" Alain interrupted. "I know she works with you a long time, but people change, believe me."

"So I've been told once before today."

"Slade, she will betray you, too, if you give her the chance. Take care." Alain's tone was anxious, almost pleading. "Don't be sentimental; in your trade you cannot afford to be."

Later, when guests and drowsing children had taken their leave or been settled in rooms upstairs, Brigida was passing Slade's study door on her way to the kitchen when his insistent voice halted her.

"I've told you before to stay away from Stancel," she

heard him say, "and leave Philip alone, too."

"But Hollis has been most useful to me," came Lydia Worsley's clipped reply. "And you've not been so available of late as I should have liked."

"I've been otherwise engaged, Lydia. You're being unreasonable."

"So engaged with your little bride that you can't attend to me? Really, Slade, you are a grown man, as I know better than anyone. How can you be so distracted by that child, winsome though she may be? I know you need more."

"Do I see a touch of green in your eye after all this time?" Slade taunted. "Leave off, Lydia. I'm not distracted. I'm putting this estate on a profitable footing. It's time consuming. I always come when you need me, even so."

"Almost always," was Lydia's crisp retort as Brigida stepped into the room. The woman stood with her hand on Slade's shoulder, and there was an unmistakable look of triumph on her arrogant face when her eyes met Brigida's. "I'll leave you for now to your wife, Slade. It is a ride to Carpenter's Island, and Mr. Stancel is waiting for me. Goodnight, Brigida, such a lovely rustic party," she offered patronizingly.

"I know the level of entertainment isn't up to what you provide, but we enjoy ourselves," Brigida smiled.

"You will come to see me, Slade, now I'll be so close for a time," Lydia threw over her shoulder before disappearing toward the front door.

*   *   *

"I'm sorry about the pit bull. I brought you this. It might help." Levi extended a massive hand that barely contained a wriggling pup of a soft, silvery gray. "He's Bran's, whelped at nearly two pounds. He'll be big as his sire."

"How was the bull terrier killed?" Slade asked. It was very early the morning after the party. He was at the desk in the library, and Brigida sat curled on the settee. She reached for the wolfhound puppy Levi offered, her emotions plain in her stricken eyes.

"Skull crushed. Rock, some heavy thing," Levi said. "I buried her."

"It was all so lovely yesterday. Silver Hill is such a sanctuary from the world. Who could be so cruel?" Brigida sighed.

"Even with so many people here, it's hard to think of anyone who . . ." Abruptly Slade walked to the windows that streamed with an almost tropical summer rain. The boughs of the pines were billowing in the wind, like a wall of green wild water.

"Would you like to have that whelp for your own?" he asked, changing the subject. "There probably isn't another like him, except his litter mates, this side of the Atlantic."

Mireille and Alain stayed on for several days and were much interested in the work of the manor. They came out to the fields with Brigida to watch the haymaking, arriving to find Slade shirtless and tanned, a scarf tied about his throat, standing knee deep in yellow hay atop an overflowing wagon. The large muscles in his upper arms bulged as he forked the sweet grasses tossed up by the farmhands below, with whom he kept up a steady banter as they worked.

"What a delicious animal your husband is, darling," Miri whispered to Brigida. "He is *un force de nature, vraiment.*" Brigida felt a fast streak of possessive jealousy, then she smiled, nodding agreement.

"And happy with this work, and content. He is a country boy, *en vérité*, darling; he belongs here, but what of his investments and real estate and so on?"

"His clerks come out on the train with papers."

"Excellent. Then you will be able to keep him here, if you want to."

"Do you really think so, Miri?" Brigida asked, starting toward Slade, who had jumped from the wagon and beckoned with a cool smile.

During the next few days, Slade, with Miri and Alain, would come looking for Brigida in the dairy or the cheese loft where she'd be finishing up before dinner. Once, they came upon her showering golden corn from a basket to a flock of white geese. The upraised, knobbed yellow beaks clacked impatiently, and the tall birds with their long, serpentine necks surrounded Brigida as she stood barefooted, in a cotton work dress, hair loose and catching the long rays of sunlight that streamed through an overhang of green.

"She is enchanting Slade, *non*? Some fairy-tale princess in disguise, I think," Alain had murmured. Slade's only response was to cock an eyebrow and smile just the least bit.

The day's work done, the four dressed for dinner and ate and drank with pleasure and good conversation. Miri and Alain had gossipy tales to tell of the latest doings of New York society, polite and otherwise, scattered in summer from Long Branch to Newport and beyond.

Without either one of them having to say a word, Slade and Brigida extended their charade for the benefit of their guests and, since the first time he had stayed the night with her, he was always there when her eyes flickered open to the morning light.

The lofts and storehouses of Silver Hill were filling. Brigida had already put peppers and beans to hang with pickling tomatoes in the root cellar. The early corn was stacked in shocks, and the mill, only weeks from completion, would be ready to grind the first wheat harvested at Silver Hill in many years. Brigida found an ever deepening pleasure in walking the blooming gardens and rugged pastures, at seeing the crops standing green in the fields, the orchards bearing, cheeses ripening in the dairy. Peering into the sheds and barns, watching the work of the manor going forward, made her happier than she could ever remember being, but mostly it was Slade; he was always there. She could just stretch out her hand and touch him whenever she chose.

Twenty

The day after Miri and Alain had gone, Brigida, watering sunflowers taller than she, saw a horse and rider approaching along the drive. The advancing figure had almost reached the front of the manor house when Slade, on Blackhawk, intercepted him. A buff envelope was handed over, opened, glanced at quickly and slipped into a shirt pocket. Unseen at the corner of the house, Brigida felt her heart twist with desperation.

"He won't do it," she insisted. "He can't leave me after all this; he can't go to her. I have to tell him now, how I feel, whatever happens. I can't contain it, and if he laughs at me, I'll do him injury, I swear!"

She startled the stable boy out of a drowsy reverie with her brusque demand for Raven. When the mare was saddled Brigida rode out fast along the beach to seek comfort in the seclusion of the Hands' cottage.

On this day she found no easing of her mood, even there, and by the time she returned to Silver Hill in the evening, her state was worse than ever. Angry resentment swelled and thickened as she imagined Slade and

Lydia together, touching, kissing, locked in every fanciable embrace . . . laughing together—at her! In thwarted fury, Brigida had screamed back at the hovering gulls and urged Raven up the incline from the shore, right into the stable paddock at full gallop.

"I missed you at midday, goddess. They told me you went out of here like a shooting star." Slade's sharp flash of smile greeted Brigida as she dismounted and began to cool out the foaming mare. She barely responded with a half shrug, and he climbed up to straddle the fence and watch her walk, his look darkening as the silence between them grew weighty. "I'll do that for you," he offered gruffly when she decided that the horse was ready at last to be stabled.

"Never mind. I'll do it myself," she almost snarled. "Where's the boy?" She glanced about.

"I sent him to help Levi bring in the Percherons. We're leaving the wagon in the field. It's only half filled. You're not playing your part. Why not?"

"There's no need. Miri and Alain are gone; who's to see us?"

Slade was silent, slim and dark in the shadowy light, watching Brigida all the time she tended the mare. Finished finally, she made for the stable door. "Coming?" she demanded over her shoulder.

The hurled word was a goad that brought the old taunting smile to his lips. "Not just yet," he said.

The light fabric of Brigida's dress, sun-shot as she stood in the doorway, revealed the shadowings of her long, slender legs.

"Hold still." Slade spoke again, and then she felt his

arms encircle her waist, his lips hot at her ear. His mouth went to her throat, and when she lifted embracing arms to reach back and twine around his neck, his hands caught her raised breasts, then slid to press her hips hard against his firmness. Brigida was breathless in his hands, twisting to face him, her parted lips seeking his, rage and love and desire vying in her when he crushed her against him, his mouth wide and brutal. She pulled away with a gasp and led him by the hand to the back of the stable, the air redolent of soaped leathers and new-cut hay.

Brigida exclaimed at a strong slap on her buttocks. "You pagan witch," he hissed. "You'll do as I say and be as I want you, understand, act or no." He fell with her, over her onto a low couch of baled hay that pricked the skin of her back through the fine fabric of her dress, which slid up to her hips when she took his hard body hungrily, rising to meet it. Her hands were light on the knotting muscles of his waist and hips, playing across the plain of his broad back until she gripped him hard, and her eyes opened wide, holding his even as a deep surging tremor shook them both, and then she was sobbing against his chest while he held her, amazed at her unexpected display of emotion.

Masses of scattered clouds caught fire in the slanting rays of the evening summer sun and pollen motes danced in lower beams. They walked through a field of uncut hay, and grasshoppers, green as jade, flashed in the knee-high juicy grasses, landing and holding for long moments to Brigida's white dress like brilliant, living jewels. She

393

nibbled a long shaft of hay as they went, the apprehensions of the day nearly dispelled. It was time to tell him. She was ready. She stopped to brush a snail from the greened hem of her skirt and, to her mild surprise, Slade lit a cigar, something he'd done lately only after dinner. The blue skeins of smoke floated away on the slow-moving air as she started to speak.

"Well, here they be comin' in now, Martha!" Nan sat on a stool in the kitchen yard snapping beans. "Such a handsome couple they are," she smiled. "What fine babies they'll be makin'." Nan watched Slade and Brigida pause as his arm slid about her waist and her lovely face uplifted, a breeze holding back her flowing hair. The wide blue band that had held it, the startled girl observed, was now about Slade's brow. Brigida's blue sash was pulled through the loops of his breeches, and she wore his broad leather belt low on her hips.

"Oh, Martha! Oh, dear!" The girl stood, spilling beans from her apron about her feet. "Just like that, so quick," Nan whispered, watching Brigida pull violently away from Slade and stand glaring at him, her fists clenched. Martha and Mary came out of the kitchen, Caitlin McGlory followed, and all four gasped as the master and mistress of Silver Hill raged stamping and gesturing furiously in a half-grown field of green summer hay.

Mary exclaimed and started forward when she saw Brigida stand unflinching and Slade raise his riding crop. After interminable, endless seconds, he hurled the object away with all his strength, sending it turning end over end against the sky. Then he stalked off toward the water, and Brigida stood statuesque until he was gone from sight.

By the time she reached the kitchen garden, Nan was back at work and the others had withdrawn inside.

"Can I get you a cup of somethin' missus?" Nan asked diffidently, avoiding Brigida's eyes.

"No, Nan, but I will need a bath, if you please," Brigida called, already halfway up the back stairs. Then they all heard the slam of her door reverberate in the evening stillness.

"The arrogant fool! The bloody, contentious, hot-tempered fool! He can go straight to the devil for all I'll care!" Brigida paced her room, brushing her hair with hard, long strokes, fuming, brooding over the explosive quarrel that had flared like wildfire to confirm the worries that had been plaguing her all day long.

Halfway across the last field, when the kitchen garden came into sight and when Brigida had knelt to brush a snail from her skirt, she had looked up with pursed lips and direct candid dark eyes. She waited as he had lit a cigar.

"Slade," she started, "now we're alone here again . . . with no outsiders, I mean, it's time really to end this pretense. I must say something to you and if you don't want . . ."

"Not yet," he said with a sudden dark scowl. Then he caught her to him and kissed her roughly. "Not yet," he repeated. "I'll be taking you to Saratoga soon, right after I get back."

"Back from where? New York? Carpenter's Island?"

Brigida wrenched out of his arms. "Why are you going?"

"I've business," he said.

"With Lydia Worsley?" she demanded curtly. "I've had enough of your business and your game, I assure you. If you go off, I shall do just the same. The sham is over; it's done!"

"I have other interests to look after from time to time," he rumbled. "It is too much to ask, I realize now, for you to give even a little of the softness a man wants in a woman; even the pretense of it is more than you can manage. I had supposed, well paid as you are for your services, grasping witch, you'd manage to play along a while yet."

On the brink of proclaiming love, Brigida was struck speechless, and when tears of righteous anger glistened in her eyes, Slade turned away from her passionate distress.

"What more could I give you?" he demanded. "I have put all my goods and lands at your disposal, dressed you in the finest stuffs, adorned you with jewels . . . you are well mounted . . . all my servants are at your command, and even so, you everlastingly threaten desertion. What will content you, lady? I have given you more than most women dream of, any other woman would be . . ."

"I am not any other woman," Brigida choked out. "You give nothing I ever wanted!"

"And you?" he asked coldly. "What do you give me? Not comfort or amusement or ease of mind, nor gentle company either, not wealth or dower, not even the sons I want." Clutching the riding crop in a clenched fist, he turned to her again and saw her bright young beauty tinged with flickerings of pain and stubborn pride. She shook her head, unable to speak, and with calculated heartlessness he said, "Any farmer's daughter or shop-girl would quicker breed than you, and I'd not be bothered with fancy tempers."

The silence between them was filled by the lonely, bittersweet warblings of a thrush, and Brigida listened until some spirit rose in her again.

"Slade Hawkes, this is a pairing that serves no comforting purpose." Her face was pale. "I'll tell you again what I told you from the first; I'll give you nothing."

He had raised the crop then, and she hadn't moved but stood still, sun-gilded tears sliding down her flawless face.

"What the bloody hell do you want, witch?" Slade had demanded. Then, with an oath, he turned, hurled away the crop, and stalked off.

The heat that settled the day Slade left Silver Hill thickened and swelled over the countryside. Through long, slow fiery days and simmering nights, no breath of air, no sea breeze came to cool even the dark hours that were filled for Brigida with dolorous dreams.

In the terrible, desperate time before first light, her fevered imagination was haunted by demons that terrified her. Throwing off the dampened sheets and piling up her strangling tresses, she went to stand on the terrace and beseech the distant moon with unformed, forlorn yearnings. Then she spoke aloud the words Slade never had heard pass her lips. "I love you," she whispered, "I love you, now—forever. Come back to me; I'll tell you so, please come back."

The days were better, but just a little. Cicadas thrummed without ceasing, black flies in the barn and stable were lazy and slow, and the cabbages went limp in the hot glare of midday sun. The horses were short-tempered, and Bran and the growing pup lolled listlessly together, prostrate on the stone step at the icehouse door enjoying the cool draughts that flowed beneath it.

A week passed and then another, and the pain in Brigida's heart became a longing ache that never left her, though she worked from first light to last.

Despite the heat, kettles hung on cranes and crossbars over the kitchen fire, crocks steamed, beans and corn were set to dry in the ovens with peeled and sliced ripened tomatoes. With their sleeves rolled up, hair pulled back tight, Brigida and Martha worked in silence, dabbing often at their brows and throats with dampened cloths, the Indian woman doing more than she would have in the heat to keep the unhappy girl distracted.

When they had dried and potted and stored all the herbs that were ready, they thinned the onion beds, hung strings in the cellar and mounded more under boards and earth for winter.

They set casks of brown sugar, yeast and water out in the sun. Covered with cheesecloth to keep off the flies, the mixture would turn, in the weeks before the first chill of fall, to vinegar. Afterwards, they set mealy potatoes bubbling to make more yeast. Brigida gathered ferns and mosses from the woods for the parlor greenhouse Levi had built for her, careful to keep the seeds of wild flowers that clung to the roots. She put up jars of sorrel leaf bleach for Slade's stained hands, made a syrup of horehound for cough drops.

"You'll have more rosewater and rose lotion and rose conserve than we could use in three winters," Martha said, watching Brigida crush rose petals in a mortar, adding sugar and honey to make a paste.

"It is good for whatever ails you, Martha," Brigida answered dully, "almost everything—chapped hands and burns and chilblains . . . and the attar of roses?" She sighed, "Oh, attar of roses—the most beautiful scent of all."

"Is that what you're making in the crock you put up in my chimney cabinet?" Martha was picking over peas.

"Yes. The young petals will give up their oil in the warmth. It takes long, and you get very little each time, but by summer's end . . ." Brigida's voice trailed off wistfully, and the Indian woman shook her head and sighed.

Meals at the kitchen table were somber. Brigida ate little. When the others tried to cheer her, Martha went about preparing the finest delicacies she could think of to tempt Brigida's palate. None did. Levi and Tom Sayre exchanged troubled looks, and Mary insisted Brigida take lavender tea for the nerves and dried dandelion root to purify her blood. Spiritless, Brigida did everything they suggested.

After the evening meal, in the blue and gold stillness of twilights, heavy with sorrow and longing she walked the shore, Bran at her side, the majestic protector, the gangling pup clowning in his sire's long shadow. When they passed out of sight of the manor house, Brigida would undress, leaving her gown crumpled on the sand, and plunge into the warm water. She swam with knifing, fast strokes, courting the exhaustion she hoped would bring escape in sleep. It didn't, and when her desperation was at its worst, she passed long hours, the slumbering house silent behind her, leaning at the terrace balustrade, listening to the distant crash of the surf and the million sounds of the throbbing summer nights. The stars whirled above, and she felt small and lost and lonely beneath the spreading immensity of the endless sparkling heavens.

The long, sad howl of a hound drifted up from the kennel one tantalizing hot night when a crescent moon was on the wane and pools of mist floated over the dark bay. A red point of light moving at the far edge of the lawn caught Brigida's eye as it glowed brighter, dulled, then flew off in a long arc and was gone. She stared, but where she thought to find the ember again, only fireflies darted, yet the illusory fragrance of Slade's cigar, strong and rich, seemed to engulf her, and the emptiness in her heart again became a pain of terrible longing. She was trembling when she fled the terrace with a cry and, grabbing up a wrapper, raced from the house and took to the woodlands.

She was a pale wraith, wild and beautiful, more akin to the mythic unicorn than to any mortal, to the white devil deer of Silver Hill, poor Jerusha Hawkes, hanged for a witch when she only longed, Brigida knew, for her true love lost. An owl belled again and again in the cathedral beauty of the midnight moonlit woods.

Before dawn, her mind was made up; she would leave Silver Hill as soon as the first wheat was ground at the mill.

Mary and Nan exchanged relieved glances when Brigida came to sit with them after the midday meal next day to drink lemonade in the shade of an ancient oak near the kitchen dooryard.

"It is good to see you sittin' a bit. He will be back, you know," Mary said, wiping her brow with the back of her hand. "If you doubt that, you are a fool, pardon me." Mary never looked up from her stitchery. Nan nodded in silent agreement. "We saw his eyes when he looked at you," Mary pronounced with finality.

"Oh, Mary!" Brigida shook her head and fluttered a pretty pleated oriental fan.

Nan nodded again, agreeing with her sister. "That vain pride you two share, missus, will do you both harm one day, though I'm not wishin' it on you."

Brigida lay back, stretched full length on the grass, and hid her face behind the spread fan.

Martha, who had been listening at the kitchen window, came out wiping floured hands on a white apron. "A man is some part boy all his days," she offered with conviction, hovering like a hen over a brood of chicks. "I'll tell you some ways to know if he loves you, if that would make you easier in your mind; count apple seeds, count bluebirds. For luck, always look at the new moon over your right shoulder, wish on a wet moon and on a piebald horse, look for your initials in a spider web—that's the best luck. If you'd only do what I tell you . . ."

"Oh Martha, please! Next you'll be having me run round the holly bush and jumping May Day fires." Brigida was gently indignant. "But . . . what about bluebirds?" she asked a little sheepishly.

"One for sorrow, two for joy, three take a journey, four get a boy, five is silver, six is gold, seven's a secret that can't be told, eight . . . eight? I can't recall eight, but nine means your true love loves you. If you ever see nine, well, there you'll be, and then you won't mock me, miss, with your independent, modern ways."

"Did any of it work for you?"

"I saw four," Martha answered, "that's all."

Brigida blinked up over the edge of the fan into Martha's serious round face. "I can't wait for him forever, can I?" she sighed. Martha withdrew to her tranquil kitchen.

Brigida stopped at the mill on her way to the fields. She heard the steady tapping of hammers from some distance off and saw the raw patches of new shingling, like healing wounds among the weathered old gray boards. Coming nearer, she heard Robin Edwards's lilting tenor voice and Tom's warbling whistle. She paused to listen, with an ache in her heart, to plaintive words of love lost and betrayed.

"Early one morning, just as the sun was rising
I heard a fair maid singing in the valley below.

402

Oh, never leave me, oh, don't deceive me,
How could you use a poor maiden so?"

"Hello, missus!" Robin called. The tapping and the melody stopped. "We are hurrying right on with the job. The work is complete but for the hanging of one sail."

"I see that," she said, staring up at the men on the scaffolding. "Robin, do you know any happy love songs?"

"No such a thing comes quick to my mind, missus, but I'll try to think of one for you, for another day," he said, climbing down after Tom.

With modest, self-effacing pride, Tom led Brigida through the mill, and Robin, chattering a bit boastfully, followed after. They climbed past the stones and the great spur wheel, up along the mill shaft with its nuts and cogs and ropes, into the cap at the very top.

Following the narrow open stairs, Brigida hugged the wall and kept her eyes high, never glancing down, a trick she had first learned during a moment of weakness at the top of a swaying mast.

"Be careful, missus, them's the brake ropes you're holdin' to. They are drawn taut through the pulley there," Robin explained. "When the miller wants to free the wheel, he takes off the ropes and hooks them careful through one of the holes cut special down below in the floor so they don't get loose and flail about."

"Don't trouble the lady with trade talk today, Rob. I don't think she's of a mind for it," Tom said softly.

"Mary is lucky to have such a feeling man as you, Tom," Brigida sighed.

She looked out over the drowsing green and blue countryside far below, wondering where Slade was at that moment on such a beautiful summer day.

"We'll be ready for your wheat before this fine day is out, missus; all that will be wantin' is a wind."

"There's not been much of that these past weeks," Brigida answered, her eyes scanning the horizon as if for distant ships, a sailor's habit. "Tom, where will you go now? Have you other work?"

"No, missus, and it ain't good times. Machinists' wages are falling, I've heard, but I'll get something. I always do."

"Stay on here." Brigida turned to the millwright. "I need a miller, and Mary will feel happy."

Tom clenched the cold stem of his pipe in his teeth and nodded. "I will, 'til fall, and when there's no wind I don't mind workin' on the land; it's what I prefer to all other work."

"Good, that's settled," she said briskly. "I'm riding out with Levi now. He thinks it is time for the wheat. And Tom? There's already corn waiting for you soon as you've tentered your stones."

Levi took off his deep-brimmed dark hat. He extracted a few kernels of wheat from the husk and crushed them in his heavy, calloused hand. Then he split a single kernel between his teeth to see if it was dry enough to store.

"Good," he said, watching Brigida imitate his actions. "'Put ye in the sickle for the harvest is ripe,' so saith the prophet Joel," he recited.

In the blue morning, stooped figures at the edges of the field began to move in the sweeping, rhythmic motions of the harvest dance, timeless and ancient, almost unchanged over centuries. Now, Brigida mused—with the new reaper—it will all be different.

Levi adjusted the handles of his scythe, then stopped to grasp a handful of wheat stalks just below the heads. With a long swing he brought the curve of the tool to encircle the grain and slice the stalks just above the ground. He and the others, in long sleeves and heavy gloves in the summer heat, worked until a swathe had been cut all round the field just wide enough for the mechanical reaper to follow. They ceased their labors to watch the machine clank in ever narrowing spirals, leaving dark swarms of gnats in its wake—grasshoppers, crickets and field mice driven deeper into the shrinking stand of yellow grain.

The work went on for long, hot days. Brigida, with the others, labored in the sun and dust and chaff, feeding the stationary thresher that winnowed, too. It beat the grain from the husks, then blew off the chaff—chaff that hung in the still air and filtered into clothes to scratch and grate against the skin.

Halfway through the first day Brigida was sure she wouldn't last to the next. Her muscles spasmed, and in her heavy linen dress and bonnet the blaze of the sun seemed fire-fierce. Perspiration trickled tickling between her breasts and soaked her back. When it flooded her eyes, she wiped them with her heavy cuff, pulled her bonnet a fraction lower and persisted, her scraped, sensitive skin a torment until she reached her room and tore off her work clothes.

From first light until full dark when the dew came down, the work continued. Then, sometimes too exhausted to eat, Brigida bathed and fell thankfully into a deep, dreamless sleep that seemed but minutes long when Martha came to rouse her in the morning. With little time and no energy for anything beyond the harvest, Brigida found some measure of relief from her loneliness for Slade.

"You need rest," Levi said, coming to sit by her one day during the short noon pause. "You are thin."

She gulped icy spring water from a cup he handed her, and when her parched throat was soothed some, she answered him. "I need this work, Levi. Don't bother about me. In a few more days, we can all rest for a bit. By the way, foreman," she swept off her wide-brimmed straw hat, "there's spillage."

Levi gave her a surprised, almost righteous look. "What spillage do you mean?"

"If you lose even so few as six grains a square foot, that's a bushel an acre, and I promised Slade . . . well, why am I counting eggs if I'm to lose on grain?" She pulled on one heavy leather glove.

"You're a tough boss, just like he is," Levi grumbled a little. "Rob!" he called, and the men sprawled under a near tree lifted their heads. "Boss here says we been spilling. Go back over where we been and glean every grain you're able."

*   *   *

The fat filled sacks of wheat were piled up on the dirt floor of the mill until no room remained, and then the granary filled, too, yet no wind came, only little puffs of air that were gone before Tom undid the brake ropes of the mill. The wheat harvest was done and the days continued heavy and still, the skies were overcast, and everything at Silver Hill seemed to be waiting expectantly, tensely, for the wind.

"I have come to photograph you at last! Besides, I heard Slade was . . . away," Philip grinned down at Brigida from his wagon seat. "Isn't this the perfect time to make my play?"

"There couldn't be a worse, Philip Carpenter; there's nothing to do here but hard physical work, and that's not exactly to your taste, is it?" Brigida frowned, though she was almost pleased, really, to see Phil. Sorrowing, she dreaded an empty hour. With the wheat harvested she was again finding herself at a terrible loss. Filling her time with Phil would be a not unpleasant diversion, she decided on the spot, and for the next days she let him follow her everywhere. He was amusing and chatty as he lugged his camera out of the wagon at the least provocation to capture Brigida in every outfit she wore, at every activity that engaged her.

"Darling, you must make a resolution of this . . . this situation, all this. It's bad for you," he said late on the third night of his visit. They were on the porch swing, Brigida curled in a corner, Phil barely moving it with the tip of a toe. "This place will swallow you up as it did Elizabeth, you know." His outstretched hand rested over Brigida's. "If you remain alone here . . ."

"Don't you think Slade will ever come back to me?" she asked quietly.

"He may, but he'll do the same again, believe me. Come to my island, Brigida, there'll be no one but me to bother you, now father and the girls are away. You can think in peace. Silver Hill must plague you with dark thoughts of its . . . blighted history."

"I'm leaving here, Philip, I've already decided that. I can't wait for Slade forever, but I cannot come with you, either. Philip? Thank you. You're . . . kind." She saw fine droplets of sweat on his brow.

"Kind? Self-serving, perhaps. Where will you go?"

"To New York, San Francisco eventually. I wrote to Ann a few days ago. She did offer me a position once, and now . . . you will have to tell Slade for me, one day, that I tried to wait; I did try but I . . . oh God, I sound like Elizabeth! History does repeat itself, it seems." Brigida's lower lip quivered. "Oh, why is it so damn bloody hot! Will it never end?" She stood and lifted her hair to hold it piled atop her head. Her eyes were closed. "Let's swim," she sighed. "Come with me?"

The sky was low and the air heavy as the two rode along the shore to a secluded stretch of bay beach halfway to the Hand cottage. When he helped Brigida to dismount Raven, Philip's hand grazed her breast. She pulled away, pretending not to notice.

"You're very unhappy," he said.

She nodded. They watched distant heat lightning fork

against the sky, imprinting itself for seconds after in their eyes.

"Let me help you, Brigida. I want to."

"But you can't. Keep your eyes closed." She shed her clothes and plunged into the ink-dark cooling water, then called to Philip. He splashed in after her.

"Divorce him. It's possible, you can. Captain Barrat's wife divorced him for adultery. Slade's always been reckless, a terrible heartbreaker. He picks up and discards women like . . . like cigars. You'd have no trouble getting rid of him. I'd give you all I had, I would . . ."

"Stop, please, Phil. I could never." Brigida's weary voice was pained. She hurried out of the water and up the beach and was only half dressed when Philip followed. She turned away from the dim sight of his pale nakedness. He pulled on his breeches, then he was at her side.

"I love you, Brigida, I love you. Please!" Ever the gentleman, he did no more than take her hand to his lips, and even in the throes of her own agitation Brigida reached out to comfort him.

"Oh, poor Philip! I am sorry, I'm so sorry." She cupped his face in her hands and saw his usually boyish-bright eyes all at once become aged with sadness. "You're like a brother to me, Philip; that way I love you. Do you think I would be here with you in this . . . this state of undress if my feelings were otherwise? I love Slade, and you must tell him so for me one day after I've gone and . . . Philip, hold me, I need someone to just hold me."

"I can't trust myself to just . . ." His arms came tentatively about her. "I will love you always, Brigida, remember it. There will never be any other. If you need . . . anything, ever . . ."

"Oh, this is too awfully, awfully sad! You will find someone else, I promise." Brigida leaned to place a kiss on Philip's brow, and the two met in a woeful chaste embrace. A splatter of moonlight fell through parting clouds, blue-white lightning forked again. Approaching thunder rumbled distantly, and Brigida thought she heard her name sounding on its fading roll.

"Brigida, you faithless Druid witch, what are you doing? Brigida!" It was Slade's voice wild on the rising wind. The embracing couple leaped apart.

"Oh, Slade, you left me so long, you left me too long alone!" Brigida said tearfully, and then the back of her hand came to her lips. She heard her own words as they must sound to Slade advancing toward her out of the darkness. Her heart stumbled with joy at the sight of his hard, handsome face, gone almost pale now under his dark tan. She was ready to hurl herself into his arms, but the strange look in his frightening eyes made her hang back.

"It's not as it seems," she whispered, but a glance at her own half-clad form and Philip's silenced her.

"Too long? You didn't wait long at all, deceiver." Slade's terrible eyes never left Brigida's face.

"Let Phil be," she said, stricken.

"Cross-tempered little bitch, I'm bound in honor, now, to kill him, though you're really the one at fault with your giving whore's body."

She watched him with distrustful eyes. "Listen, please," she asked, "or are you afraid of what I might say

410

to you?"

"Do you really think anything you could say would matter to me now? Turn your cheating eyes away. Now, at least, show a trace of modesty."

There was, unexpectedly, a note of desperation in Slade's ragged voice, and Brigida thought she could feel a dark wind from out of the past swirling about them.

Oh God, she thought, it's happening again, the jealousy and misunderstanding and pain that Elizabeth . . . "Slade, listen."

"Go home. I'll see to you later." His gripping fingers bruised the soft skin of her shoulders.

"Slade, this once, doubt what your eyes seem to show you. I'll never ask anything of you again if you grant me this."

"Go home or I'll . . ." Slade roughly pushed Phil aside when he tried to intervene, and then he froze, staring off at a point in the dark. Brigida whirled about to see Levi emerge from the shadows.

"Leave off," he said to Slade. "You're wrong this time. I'll take her away now, until you're . . ."

"One step more and I'll level you. I know how long you've lusted for her. Since Lydia's, isn't it? Hell, I wouldn't turn my back on you and this . . ."

"Loved," Levi said. "Since the first day. You never knew what to do with her. I would have."

"Do with her?" Slade asked with a furious, rueful laugh. "We both know how to do her right, same as all the other cheap whores we've shared. I'll take seconds, you heathen, or maybe it's thirds, if she and Phil already . . ."

411

Levi swung out, catching Slade off balance, sending him staggering back. Slade didn't lose his footing, just looked at Levi with cold eyes. He rubbed his chin almost casually, then drew back, putting all his weight into a blow that struck Levi under the right eye. The Indian stood his ground.

"I know how you fight, man," Levi said. "I know every swing, every feint and dodge you'll make. I can take you. Try me."

They circled each other guardedly, fists clenched, wide shoulders rolling, then stood face to face, breathing hard, the same mean grimness in their eyes. They began to trade blow for blow in turn, their strong, stationary bodies reeling and recoiling again and again. Through the dust and sweat and sand on their faces, cuts began to ooze red and then blood to flow, after a time nearly blinding them both. There were agonized explosions of breath and the harsh, terrible impact of bone on bone as they began to falter and stagger. Almost imperceptibly, Levi drove Slade back inch by inch toward the water, and the blows came, still in turn, but a little slower, a little less sure, until, with one wide swing, Levi brought Slade to his knees. It was only for an instant, but it was enough. The pattern changed; the two closed in a wrestler's crouching, circling dance until they fell together in water that covered first one raging face, then the other. They rolled, grunting curses, spitting and flinging water from their blazing eyes that were nearly blinded with blood and salt.

It seemed interminable, and Brigida, silent, shaking, thought of the dog fight, the two perfect, perfectly matched animals, bred to kill, who slowly, surely, inexorably had fought to the death.

When the two massive men in front of her, gasping, on their knees in the water, grasped for each other's throats, she began to scream, threw her head back and screamed a long, despairing, angry wail. Levi stopped and stood and stared, dripping, knee-deep in water now as she paced the shoreline, weeping, flinging a silk scarf about her throat, then undoing it, again and again, swinging her long mane of wet, wild hair.

"You damn stupid fools, you stupid idiot bastards," she shrieked. "Leave off before you kill each other! You get away from me," she snapped at Phil who was dogging her steps, trying to quiet her. "Look at them, look at them," she demanded. "They're brothers, they're brothers, and they are going to kill each other like a pair of damn pit dogs, like . . . damn you both, damn you both to bloody hell!"

Slade, still on his knees, recoiled at her words as if struck again. Levi staggered a few steps, his large fists opening, his eyes, moonlit, confused for an instant as they met Slade's steady, guarded stare. Then a twitch of a smile touched the Indian's lips.

"Get up," he said. "No brother of mine should be crawling on his knees in the mud."

Slade accepted Levi's extended hand. "Surprised . . . brother? I'm not," he said, standing, returning Levi's spreading grin. "Brother," he said again as if testing the word, enjoying the sound of it. "Brother, there's one thing you better keep in mind. She's mine."

Later, Brigida would remember the look of disbelief in Levi's distracted eyes as he went down, and the look of triumph in Slade's as he delivered the finishing blow.

Slade's knuckles that had healed were cracked and split again, Brigida saw, when he lifted her to the mare's back. Lace and curls flying in the risen wind, sobbing aloud, she raced off down the beach toward Silver Hill.

The landing clock was striking two when she reached the manor. The whole house was lit and in something of an uproar. She caught Nan at the bottom of the back stairs. The sleepy girl, her hair knotted in cloths, pulled a wrapper close and, yawning, answered Brigida's urgent question.

"It is the wind, missus, the wind come up! We're all goin' to the mill now to see Tom workin'. 'Tis good luck, the first grinding, Martha says. Hurry!"

Watching with the others in the misty-white floury air as the mill wheels turned, Brigida shivered beneath a shawl, despite the heat of the summer night. The occasion was such a celebratory one that no one, not even the usually vigilant Martha, noticed her agitated state.

Johnny Hand had tapped a keg of ale and was solemnly passing about filled mugs. Brigida was standing a little apart, watching golden grain from an open bag trickle through her fingers—like all the dreams, she thought, she had brought to Silver Hill and lost now forever.

"Aye, Captain! You come back at a good time," Robin's jaunty greeting sounded. "Can I get you a mug, to celebrate with us now your lady's mill is turnin'? Captain, what happened to you?"

There was silence, no talk, just the steady grinding and thumping of the great wheels and stones and the creakings of the windshaft high above. Slade stood framed in the low doorway in his wet, tattered clothes, his face bruised and bloody. Brigida hesitated uncertainly, then, catching up a lantern, began to climb.

She was standing with her back to the small window in the cap of the mill when Slade reached the top of the stairs, and over the rising whine of wind and the noisy workings of the great machine she hurled a question at him. "You've done Philip harm, too, haven't you?" She was shivering violently and her half-mad eyes were wide, he thought, as the gates of Hell.

"I've seen to him and sent him home, and now I've come to deal with you as I should have long ago." When Slade started toward her, Brigida withdrew a hand from beneath her shawl. Unsteadily, she raised her small pistol in his direction.

"You couldn't if you wanted to, which you don't," Slade said evenly. "Put it down."

"Damn you!" Brigida cried out, bursting into tears. "But I so wish . . . I so wish I could. Keep off!" She waved the Colt. There was a small report, a low pop—a champagne cork flying, no more, she would later remember thinking—and then an agonizing sound of splintering wood as the brakes jumped to the great main wheel. The mill came to a slow, grating stop as shards of glass filled the air with flying points of light. In a terrible confusion of squealing brakes, shouts from below, and loosed, wildly flailing ropes, Brigida, as if in a dream, heard a wild scream tear from her own throat, heard

Slade cry out . . . watched him throw up his arms. In the endless nightmare moment before he fell, she saw that his luminous eyes were fraught with disbelief and his hands were filled with freshets of wildflowers and strands of diamonds.

The doctor from the village had come and gone and another, much touted, sent for from New York. Dosed with laudanum, Slade slept. Brigida and Levi sat on the terrace outside his door, each wanting to comfort the other but finding easing words only with difficulty.

"I didn't mean to, Levi. I wouldn't ever . . ."

"I know. He will know, too."

"I didn't mean to speak, either, about your . . . father."

"We've always lived as brothers, Slade and me. Nothing will change."

"If I come between you?" she asked, studying his bruised face.

"You won't again," Levi said.

"I shouldn't have taken the Colt, but I was half mad with missing him. And fearing him." Circles had darkened about Brigida's eyes and her cheeks seemed hollowed.

"When the bullet struck the rope, it snapped, the loose end came whipping. A freak accident that it caught his eyes when the beam struck." The Indian sipped from a jug of rum and offered it to Brigida.

She shook her head no. Numb with sadness, she dug her knuckles hard against her own eyes, but no tears came. "Head injuries are so . . . dangerous, and he could be blind, Levi. His eyes . . . so beautiful."

"If you think the worst, you will call up the devil, like Martha says. Go rest."

"How can I?" Brigida stood and stretched, and hearing sounds within, hurried to the door. Bran lay at the foot of the bed. Slade seemed deep in sleep, the bandage over his eyes horribly white against his tan skin. Martha was grimly padding about and fluffing pillows, folding and refolding a summer coverlet helplessly. "It had to come to harm, so fierce and wild you both are together, ill fated as this marriage was," she whispered. "I told you the day you were wed, demons are everywhere, waiting. You didn't . . ."

"One would think hell was empty of devils, listening to you! One would think they were all right here!" Brigida hissed furiously, fleeing the room.

Slade slept fitfully through the day that had been washed cool and fresh, finally, by summer rain, and Brigida filled his room with fragrant flowers to scent the air with summer sweetness. Whenever she felt that she couldn't be still another second, she rushed to the garden—only to return soon again with more baskets and bowls of blossoms.

At early evening when she and Levi stood at the fluttering curtains, watching the sun set, Brigida became intensely aware of life going on as usual along the bay and in the gardens, aware of the wafted sweetness of the orchards, of the fields throbbing, of everything waiting for moonrise. Her senses were so sharpened, her nerves so taut that she seemed to hear the sap moving in the maples, to see the waves of air that carried the gulls over the bay. The whole world outside was vibrant with life. Inside, the pulse of time had stopped.

"It was wrong, this marriage." Brigida, wan and tired, looked up at Martha when the Indian woman brought her a tray. "It could have been different perhaps if . . . if I had spoken the truth and let our lives take their course. But I set myself against him like a child playing a game. So foolish!" Brigida said, shaking her head.

"I am at fault." Levi's deep voice startled her. "I should have told him how it was with you when he was gone, but . . . I wanted him gone, I think." He draped himself over a chair and shook his head.

"This is his fault too, and don't forget it," Brigida said in a strident whisper. "Only he can know his own heart, unless he speaks what's in it, and he never does that, ever. Go away and rest, both of you, please. I need to be alone."

When Brigida awoke it took a few moments for the events of the last days to come back in a rush like a bad dream remembered. The heavy quality of the darkness told her it was very early morning.

Slade was still asleep, but barely. His breathing was light and shallow, as it always was just before his eyes flicked open to reveal an unguarded fragment of feeling, just for a small moment.

When this morning came, she wouldn't see his eyes

open. Nor would he see daylight touch the window. Her own eyes flooded with tears, deep, silent sobs wracked her and she felt that she wept for every pained and lonely being on the face of the earth who waited, as she did, for the dawn.

Drained finally, Brigida was calmer. Sitting at Slade's bedside, she silently bargained with the fates, with the heavens, with all the powers of the universe she could think to summon, dark or glimmering, and she made a pact that she meant to keep. "If he sees," she swore, "I'll never want anything again, never. I'll go away from here and be content with nothing, the barest life, the loneliest life, if only . . ."

"I love you," Slade said.

"Don't!" Brigida whispered, horrified. "Don't say to me now what you never would before, now I've . . . caused you such hurt. I could have killed you."

His hand seemed very dark at his bandaged eyes, then it brushed Brigida's face, caressing, touching tears. "Brigida, I loved you before, from the first. I came home to tell you so. Everything before you dulls and loses its gloss, only you shine for me now. I'll be content with you forever, no matter . . ."

"You've had a terrible blow on the head, that's why you're saying these things. Ssh, you must be still, your head . . ."

"I'll be still only if you listen." He had risen on one elbow and groped for her hand.

"Lie still!" she pleaded. "I'll stay here if you promise to be still." She climbed up on the bed and sat cross-legged studying his battered face anxiously.

419

"You were a beautiful figment of my dreams, standing in the high road that first day. You had all the grace and carnal glow of the Island girls who always had pleased me best. I stretched out my hand and took you, and I never meant to love you, but I did, right then. Say something."

"I can't say . . . I don't know what to say. Why were you so hard if . . ."

"I didn't want to be without you ever again. I thought if you knew you'd maneuver against me; if you knew, the challenge would be gone. I needed to hurt you, to deny what I felt." Slade brought his bandaged right hand to his brow. "Whenever I was gone from you those slumberous, dark eyes of yours haunted me every hour. Where are you going? Stay with me, Brigida."

"Yes," she answered softly, and she never went beyond the reach of his voice during the days that followed.

A week later, Slade was up in a chaise on the terrace where Brigida had led him. She sat near, reading aloud from a *New York Ledger*, until he stopped her.

"I need to see you. When will you take these damn things off?" he grumbled, gesturing at the gauze about his head.

"Just a little longer. You heard the doctor. There could be scarring in the eye. You'll only heal properly if you don't blink even once. Oh, please be still! Are you tired? Can I bring you anything? You're too warm, I'll get a cool cloth and . . ."

"I crave the sight of you as the fiend his opium. Be

calm, Brigida, don't worry so about me." He reached for her hand and she gave it.

"I can't be calm, I can't! What if your eyes don't heal? What if your sight is . . . damaged? What then?" Brigida tried to pull away, but he held her hand fast.

"If I can't see, goddess, will you be my eyes?" He raised her fingers to his lips. "Why won't you answer?"

"I can't," she sobbed.

"You can't? Here I am blind and helpless and all I ask is that you love me a little." He pulled her to him, felt her silken hair against his cheek, her breast soft against his chest and the fragrance of roses everywhere. "It's been so long," he rasped.

"Let me free, Slade, don't touch me that way—I . . . we're dangerous together, to each other. Look what I've done to you! I was provoked to a violence that leaves me in total despair. As soon as you're well . . ."

His grip tightened. "You love me."

Brigida held still in distressful silence, until he thrust her from him. "Help me inside. Send for Levi. These damn wraps have to come off. I'll see your face and read the truth in your eyes—now."

Twenty-One

John and Sarah were at supper when Brigida crossed the doorstep of the cottage. Neither questioned her as she filled a bowl from the chowder kettle and came to the table. Her wicker case, which she deposited near the door, held the peasant skirts and blouses and the few dresses she had brought from California. All the gowns and wraps and jewels she had left at Silver Hill.

In their unself-conscious, kindly manner, the old couple let Brigida feel that their simple home was hers. They shared its comforts without reservation and tried to soothe the troubled young woman who had come to them in need.

They performed the homely tasks of their days with a simple nobility that Brigida came to prize more and more as time passed, and she entered into the routine of life at the gatherer's cottage.

The old couple garnered the offerings of the uncultivated bayshore and woods. A goose or wild turkey often hung in the chimney, smoking over green oak logs and aromatic laurel, and old John always smoked some of the fish and eel he pulled in each day.

Sarah taught Brigida to spin and card wool and to weave. They picked red currants and blackberries, wild leek and wild carrots growing below undulating canopies of Queen Ann's lace.

Brigida's days gradually became attuned to tide and sun, the noon stick's lengthening shadow, the call of geese overhead at dawn. So determined was she not to see Slade again that, though her heart never stopped aching, he and Silver Hill began to seem part of another world she had visited only in dreams.

"I am takin' this girl out gatherin' acorns, old man, while you're catchin' supper," Sari announced one slow and lazy pastel afternoon. Promptly, she tied a scarf about her head, took a calico drawstring bag from a peg near the door and beckoned Brigida to follow. They walked in silence a good distance from home, inland along sun-shot wooded paths. When they came to the bank of a crystalline brook, Brigida, who always went unshod now, gathered up her skirt and tiptoed in, lifting her knees high with each icy step like a lovely long-legged sea bird wading. Sarah began gathering some of the herbs that infused the air with pungent odor.

"Your heart is gone out of your own keeping I know," the old woman began a bit hesitantly, "but I think you'd best talk about it. If it is truly over between you and Slade Hawkes, then at least you'll neither of you know that other sadness, of love that binds too long and chills."

"It's said that love found and lost is more hurtful than

never finding any at all. I think that's so," Brigida answered.

"If you love Slade, go the way your heart takes you," Sarah said with determination. "Love may not come to either of you ever again." The old woman kneeling in the green glade looked a gentle witch instructing the glittering nymph beside her in the secrets of some timeless spell.

"Sari, it is done with . . . Slade and me," Brigida barely whispered.

"You seem certain, so be it then," Sari said, shaking her head. "And now 'tis time for us to move on our way. I promised John roasted acorns for his sup and he will be wantin' them soon now. Come along, the white oaks are just up the path a little from here."

Brigida didn't turn when she heard the jingle of bridle, not even when the sound grew louder, blending the muffled thud of hoofs on sand. She stood rigid, breathing deep, her eyes clenched tight until the stallion snorted close behind her. Then she broke into a panicked wild run, darting among the reeds and cattails growing on the muddy riverbank, and she screamed, hearing the horse bear down just before she reached the refuge of the woods. She was caught about the waist, lifted, held as if she were of no more substance than a cloud, and carried off some distance down the beach, struggling furiously like a wild creature clasped in the talons of a swooping bird of prey.

"Hold, wild witch! Hold or I'll beat you and it might

not be near so much fun as last time." Slade reined in and, securing Brigida in front of him, swung both legs to one side of the saddle and slid off, landing lightly, keeping her toes just above the ground as she struggled against him.

"Will you behave if I set you free? Will you walk my way a little and talk with me, Brigida?" he asked in the rough-edged, smoky voice that always touched her heart. She nodded, swept by relief that he seemed, still, just the same, unchanged.

"Say it," he demanded, shaking her.

"I will, yes! Now let me go, please." His closeness sent a torrent through her remembering body. She couldn't stand the strong arms about her, the voice so close, the azure eyes, blue as cornflowers, as . . .

Brigida pranced out of the circle of Slade's arms, then turned to look up at him. As his lightning grin flashed, her left hand flew to her lips, and the sky seemed to reel above her. "Your eyes!" she barely breathed, suddenly weak, and Slade moved to steady her as she swayed.

"The dark spectacles frighten you, goddess? Levi had them made for me. Bright light pains me and there's some blurring on the left, but you did me no permanent damage." He removed the glasses and she looked into caressing, depthless blue eyes. Recovered from her vertigo, she let his arm stay at her waist for a moment before she pulled away.

"I am . . . glad you're well, Slade." He was studying her intently, and she felt a slow warmth wherever his eyes touched. Her Spanish blouse had slipped from one smooth shoulder. The deep-laced corsalette at her narrow waist drew his look from her round hips to her high breasts, floating free beneath the soft fabric. He blinked and shaded his brow with a hand.

"You are so beautiful you stagger me," he said very slowly. "Come home." His rough tone was wooing, beseeching. "It's been so damn long since I touched you. I love you, Brigida, come with me now." The special urgency was there in the low tones, and she responded to it in every inch of her being, his words touching her soft skin like caressing fingers.

"I won't!" she said, near tears, taking a step back.

"You won't?" He slipped the dark glasses on and waited, his jaw clenched. "I'll fill a drunkard's grave, witch, if you won't have me. Why?"

"I'm afraid."

"I won't hurt you, I swear it."

". . . of myself as much as of you. I could have killed you."

"But you didn't. I won't even touch you . . . until you ask. Come home with me now."

A great white heron, wings spread in a wide span, rowed the clear, luminous air and gliding, landed in shallows left by low tide. As it fished, they watched in silence, until the bird, polished by midday sun, rose and sailed off, a flashing silver silhouette against the blue sky.

"I can't ever come with you, Slade," Brigida said firmly. "This was wrong. From the very start."

"We'll begin again; I'll put it right." Slade reached for her hand. She withheld it.

"We've too much anger and contention between us. Even you, Captain Hawkes, can't reverse the passage of time or undo what has gone before. You said to me that there could be one master—you—and I must march to your measure. Once, I might have . . . now I choose no measure but my own."

"I am master, sweet, but you are my guiding star. I'll love you better than I used to, Brigida."

A long-fought desire to trace the curve of his jaw almost mastered her, and she went off a way to sit on a bleached log of driftwood near the edge of the water.

"You won't ever get over me." Slade followed, then placed a foot on the log beside her and leaned down over her.

She shrugged a little. "Perhaps not. The attraction between us . . . the bonds of passion are . . . were strong, too strong, but there was nothing else. All good sense and judgment are lost in such heat. I must leave, you see."

"But the bonds of passion . . . they're all entwined now with tethers of love that are even stronger, Brigida, and to have both together, love and desire . . . you can't just walk away, I won't let you." Slade's words were said with a disquieting cold certainty.

He fingered a twining curl, then straddled the log and examined Brigida's profile, perfect small nose and pouted lips like peonies, the flutter of her heavy long lashes as she closed her eyes.

"You raise up dreams with your smile. Will you deprive me of it forever?" Brigida was quiet. "There are times now, goddess," he went on, "I can't sleep. I walk the shore for hours and when I come home to Silver Hill at dawn with the memory of you all green in my heart, I imagine I hear the rustle of silk on the stair. I look up, expecting to find you in all your outrageous beauty, smiling down on me as you used to do. Will I wait for you forever?"

"I waited for you. Every interminable day I waited, expecting . . . something. You were never out of my mind, never, and I'll never let myself feel that way again; so unarmored and vulnerable. Leave me in peace, please," she asked.

He rested a hand on her bared, sun-warmed shoulder. "How can I? No woman ever pleased me in all things as you do, Brigida. In that first moment I felt the future stirring. I knew it then, but I didn't want to give you a hold in my life, I didn't want to be responsible for you then, for anyone. Now, you are my lady, truly."

The back of his hand was gentle against Brigida's cheek, and she brushed it away, fearing to be tempted by the immeasurable longing she heard in his voice and felt in her own heart. Conflicting emotions reduced her to a state of near yielding meekness that she struggled to hide.

"Without benefit of ceremony, Captain, with barely a greeting, you forced yourself upon me, though I protested. Without the growing, comforting affection of courtship, without even close acquaintance, you made me your wife in every way and contrary to the usual order of such things." Brigida turned to face Slade, her eyes accusing. "I trusted you to care for me, but I know now it is best to do as others do in matters of the heart and proceed with utmost slowness and caution."

Slade removed his dark glasses. "You agreed to it all. With your first kiss you showed desire so sweet and strong I judged you above the trifling conventions that lesser women hide behind."

"I did think, that day in the carriage that . . . I was in love with you. But I was wrong. It was only a . . . an attraction of the body, that and false memories of a boy who long ago had promised to take me home to an enchanted place called Silver Hill."

"I did take you home, you did love me then, on sight. I know it, but if it's courting you want, now you'll have it. You will be wooed with diffident caution, slowly, with care, in the most conventional manner until you tire of my overfaithful, polite attentions and come to me of your own choosing, in your own time. You will, you know."

Brigida looked at him askance. "Sure of yourself as ever. You've not the dogged patience to win me." She almost smiled. Slade threw back his head and laughed and leaped to his feet.

"May I have the honor of this waltz, madame? 'Tisn't right that such a pretty flower, no matter how shy and innocent, cling the wall, as you do."

As always, Brigida found him completely winning, and a hint of her former vivacity glinted in her eyes. She rested a hand on his shoulder, and he placed a hand at her waist, keeping the other at his side as she did, and they waltzed, barely touching, while Brigida's skirt belled like the loveliest ballgown. They whirled round on the damp sand, her lilting laugh floating about them until, quite breathless, she pulled away and retreated to her safe perch on the driftwood log.

"You'll let me come courting you, then?" Slade had replaced the dark glasses and stood holding Blackhawk's reins, casting a shadow over Brigida where she waited.

"I . . . it is only fair to warn you I've already made up my mind. I've a whim of steel, Father used to say. Your efforts will avail you nothing, though they may prove diverting for me."

"Your steely whim will bend this time. I've made up my mind, and nothing diverts me once I've set myself to something." He seemed in deadly earnest. "I will háve you back." He swung up onto the stallion and the animal danced a little.

"I'll not be listening to your nonsense all day; I've work to do," she snapped and hurried off toward the cottage with a quick, buoyant step.

Slade watched until her slim, swaying figure disappeared behind a hillock. Then, whistling one of Robin Edwards's ballads, he turned the stallion toward Silver Hill, and Blackhawk's hooves sent rainbowed droplets of spray rising into the sunlit air.

Early the next morning, as the sun was rising and the cottage was stirring awake, Brigida, in her nightdress, stepped outside to appraise the day. On the doorsill, beneath overhanging eaves, she found a basket filled with pale pink rosebuds loosely tied in white satin, and despite her best effort at indifference, she had to smile.

Slade came back to the cottage at sunset bearing a basket of ripe peaches from the orchard, and he brought the dogs.

Brigida was knitting—settled on the bench at the cottage door enjoying the cooling evening air with John and Sarah—and though she barely glanced up from her work, her heart quickened as Slade dismounted and came toward them. His manner, she perceived quickly, was reserved.

"I've come to call on Mistress Hawkes," he addressed John. "I'll join you for a bit."

He had dressed, Brigida saw, as if for an occasion, in silk and linen and polished boots. Sarah and John moved closer together to make a place for him, and he passed pleasantries with the old couple, frequently glancing over the tops of their heads at Brigida, who sat silently knitting at the opposite end of the bench.

"I'm considering grapes for next spring," Slade told John. "What do you think?" He lit a cigar and passed one to John.

"Grapes growin' wild all over hereabouts, so you might just as well cultivate. Pick your placement real careful for sun and wind. How'd you do with your wheat and oats?"

"Best yield ever from Silver Hill fields. I'll be sending you our own ground flour this winter, and for that you may thank the lady there. She insisted the mill be set to rights. Your income from the mill will be a pleasant surprise, Brigida."

"I don't want it," she said.

"What about your kitchen garden? It needs a knowing hand about now and you'll have to be thinking about next spring if you'll . . ."

"Someone else will have to be thinking about your kitchen garden next spring, Captain," she blurted.

"No, love, you're wrong," he answered. Turning to Sarah he begged some pennyroyal to treat the dogs' fleas.

When it grew full dark he took his leave, insisting that the pup remain at the cottage with Brigida. When he had gone, she had to fight a chill of loneliness, and she was glad to have the dog there to distract her.

The following morning there were daisies and marigolds on the doorsill; the morning after, phlox and honey bells; then blue lace and bittersweet and baby's tears. Slade came down to the cottage earlier each afternoon. One day, he was leading Raven. "She was a gift to my wife," he explained to Sarah. "I want Brigida to have her. Perhaps she will consent to a ride with me."

"You tryin' to get the girl off by herself, Slade?" Sarah winked. "Well, you just let 'er be like you promised."

"You keep your own council. Here, meddler, this is for you." He offered a large piece of deep plum velvet and several smaller squares of silk in purple shadings.

"Slade! How do you always bring just what I'm wantin'? It will make a rich quilt, this fine stuff, won't it Brigida?" Sarah smiled. "My fingers are just itchin' to work it."

"It is lovely, Sari," came the gentle response. Brigida had just come up from the water, drawn by a distant glimpse of Slade approaching from the land side along the crest of the bluff above the beach. She greeted him now with a sedate nod. "You shouldn't have brought the mare. I'll be going off soon and . . ."

"Enjoy her while you are here. She's yours, you know," Slade answered, then quickly strode from the cottage to help John at some bayman's task.

"He's so kind to you, you could at least give him a smile now and again, even if you are leavin'. It never does to be over-hard for no reason." Sarah watched Brigida's nervous gestures and pacings.

"During all those months, Sari, when we were together?" Brigida paused and the old woman nodded.

"Every time I thought I saw a lovelight in his blasted blue eyes, I did soften to him, and it was just then, when I was sure he'd never ever be able to leave me alone again, that off he'd go. How could I have been so wrong?"

"You weren't wrong at all. He went before because he was feelin' and carin' for you more than he wanted, but now he's spoke his love, what do you ask of him?"

"I've made up my mind, Sarah, and don't you try to talk me out of it!"

"Well, suit your own fancy, miss, but don't say I didn't council you otherwise."

That evening, Sarah and John withdrew early, before full dark, and when Brigida made to follow, Slade caught her wrist. "Walk with me a little, goddess? I won't bite you, I promise," and his smile was so imploring she relented, but with a complaint.

"Oh, don't smile and taunt me, you. There's nothing of a jocular nature here," she said grimly.

"It's not the end of the world either, no need to be so staunch. You want to leave here? Fine, I won't interfere with your plans."

"You won't?" she asked suspiciously, surprised and annoyed at his indifference.

She had let him take her hand and lead her toward the riverbank, where a wooden swing hung from a high branch of an oak. "I'll push," he offered.

When she was settled, she felt his hands at her hips as he lifted the swing back, then set it flying into the perfect blue summer evening. Each time the swing crested its arc and stopped, hanging in space for a tiny fraction of time before falling back to Slade's waiting arms, Brigida's heart caught in her throat, and her spirit soared with the circling gulls above.

"No, don't! You promised," she protested when Slade's arms enfolded her waist and he pulled her back off the swing that went flying without her. The fragrance of spice and lime, the feel of his arms and lean body set her struggling against him until he set her on the ground.

"You are too tight-strung, sweet, ease up. I'm a man of my word. Or is it yourself you're fighting?"

Brigida smoothed her neat coil of hair, then fussed with the cuffs of her gown in frosty silence.

"Why won't you speak to me, Brigida?" The moon was risen and it shone full in Slade's eyes as he stood looking down at her.

"I've nothing to say to you." She turned away. "I was perfectly peaceful in this place until you came to disturb me. There is only harmony and order here and the turn of time and season. Sometimes you can hear the music of the stars if you listen."

He slid down slowly against the tree to sit on his heels and watch her. She sat beside him.

"One day, when you're ready, I'll take you to a place where life is simpler even than here," he said.

They were still, embroidered in moonlight. A tense silence between them lengthened as the sky swung low overhead, heavy with stars.

"I . . . I'll go in, Slade," Brigida said after a while, when she knew she had to get away from him or lose control. "It's very late I think, past twelve by now . . . and . . ."

"Will you send me off alone again?" he demanded. "You promised me!"

"I want you now." His voice took on the familiar smoky, rough edge. "And you want me, don't lie. You can't fool me; I've been loving you too long for that."

She scrambled to her feet and he stood and grasped her arm. "Oh, this is madness. Let me go!"

Slade backed away. "Love that isn't madness isn't love, a poet once said. I'll go now, so as not to tempt you more, sweet. Till tomorrow, then."

Some time in the dark of every night, Slade gifted Brigida with a lovely thing, and each morning she softened just a little as she imagined him riding out alone in the predawn shadows to leave a treasure on her doorstep while she slept curled just beyond his reach within the still cottage.

Before the noon stick lost its shadow, Slade was there again, bringing other gifts—fresh-picked corn, tomatoes from the garden, baskets of eggs, tobacco for John's pipe, bright bits of oriental silks for Sarah's quilt—and he stayed and worked.

He mended John's nets with clever hands, helped with the old man's crab traps, repaired the thatching on the cottage roof, started stacking logs against the coming autumn chill and winter cold.

Brigida, determined to avoid him—however rarely that was possible now that he spent his days at the cottage—went diligently about her own work; but all her impulses seemed to drive her to his side. Her veneer of frosty self control was, she knew, almost transparently thin, and her inner agitation became daily more difficult to conceal.

Slade made no demands on her, but he was relentless, always there wherever she was to help pull a full pail from the well, to carry a bushel of mussels up from the shore, to spread laundry to dry, to help her mount Raven who, Brigida explained, really did need the exercise.

"Not that I want to do this," she protested as Slade wove his fingers to form a step, "but she will get fat and lazy if I don't ride her, isn't it so?"

"It is," Slade would answer pleasantly, a hand lingering just a moment on Brigida's small browned bare foot before she slipped away. His touch seemed always accidental—a brush of hands as they walked, or his thigh against hers, he reaching his arms around her, grazing her breast, as they leaned at the well to pull up the dripping bucket. At those moments, when she felt her hard-held reserve about to shatter, Brigida fled.

One day he brought a goose for dinner from Silver Hill. He roasted it over a wood fire out of doors to save them all the heat in the cottage. The fowl cooked dripping and hissing fat into the flames. Slade and Brigida, working at separate tasks close by, took turns rotating the spit. When it was nearly done to a crisp golden brown, Brigida, a bit late for her turn, burst through the cottage door into

Slade's arms, and he held her fast just long enough to se
her temper flaring.

"Fool! Watch where you walk," she spat.

"Here I was about to do your work and what thanks do
I get?" he grinned down, feeling her begin to tremble in
his arms. Slowly he released her and they stood still
suffused by a flash of passion.

"If you don't tend to your business now, your goose
will be better cooked than you'd like," Slade said huskily
turning away.

"I'd walk out with Brigida now, if she's of a mind to go
with me," Slade announced.

"You'll not keep her too long away, will you, Slade?"
John asked with a quick wink. Dinner was done, the
goose food for the gods, the old man had pronounced, and
the dishes were all cleared away.

"We are retirin' now. Just stay right here," Sarah
ordered. "'Tis past our bedtime, what with all this eatin'
and sippin'. Come on, old man, and leave the young ones
to themselves."

"Sari, don't go off. Anything we have to say can be said
in your hearing. More blackberry cordial, Sari?" Brigida
offered.

"You'll not detain me longer, young lady, with your
drinkin' and eatin'. I need my rest. Come, old man, or
you'll get nothing done at all on the morrow."

When Brigida and Slade were alone, he extracted
something from his shirt pocket. Wordlessly, he handed
it to her. She opened a little round basket to find a golden

438

chain coiled inside, its linkings double eights—the lover's knots all sailors knew.

"What's this for?" she asked warily.

"In some places in the world, a man gives a linked chain to a woman instead of a ring. Will you wear it? I've had it a long time. It was always meant for you."

"If I wear your chain, will it mean I've agreed to become your property again?"

"It will mean whatever you want it to, Brigida, no more. Think of it as a pretty trifle, is all, or a parting gift, if you prefer." He took the golden strand to coil about Brigida's throat, and the scent of woodsmoke was in his hair when he leaned to barely brush his lips to hers, his hand tracing the gold chain's flow over the curve of her breast. "You'd best go in now," he whispered. "You make it very hard for me, you know that."

Brigida nodded, fingering the delicate chain. "It can't be helped," she answered unsteadily. "A parting gift, I'll accept it only as that."

But she made no preparations for departure, and Slade came daily to the cottage. His patience seemed endless, and she began to grow easy in his company, smiling and chattering almost as before. Only when he tried to touch her did she stiffen and a glacial coldness come back into her eyes.

"Brigida, you belong at Silver Hill, no other place on earth." Despite the light late summer rain that pattered against the cottage, Sarah and John had gone off, he to fish, she to the woods to gather bait, a task made easier by the wet weather.

Slade roamed restlessly about the cottage, fingering the finials of a chair, lifting and replacing a cup, a candle snuffer, opening and closing the pie cabinet. His prowling charged the atmosphere and made Brigida edgy, too. "I'm not going back to Silver Hill; that's final," she pronounced.

"You still don't trust me, do you? What's this?" He held up a letter, still sealed. "Are you going to read it?"

"I know what it says. Ann wants me to come to work in her salon. I will. I'll use the money I earn to get back home again, to California. Whatever is the matter, Captain? You look . . . odd. You're wearying of this chaste, quiet life, as I knew you would. Look at you pacing and scowling."

"There aren't many men who'd put up with you as patiently as I have, goddess." There was a bitterness in his tone.

"Consider yourself quite free to go back to your Miss Worsley, or whomever. You are not here at my request, you know." Brigida was rocking quite fast in Sarah's chair near the cold hearth, her starched apron very white against a saffron, lace-edged dress.

"You're gorgeous, you know, however much trouble you give me," he said.

"Oh, you just stop it. Why don't you run off to her now, as you did before? Try now coming to me reeking of her scent. I saw those little notes. That's all it ever took for her to claim your undivided attention."

"We worked together during the war, Brigida, you knew that. Lydia was well connected in certain English circles that were supplying the Confederacy. She was a good spy. Because of her, tons of supplies were intercepted. Countless lives were saved on both sides as a consequence." Slade sat opposite Brigida, pulling on a cigar. "I owed her a lot."

"Such a long time to pay a debt? You were still sending her gifts after you and I were wed. I saw that incredible dress, the beautiful red and black, on Ann's sketch pad when I first arrived." Brigida closed her eyes. "I would never expect fidelity just for its own sake, only out of love. You kept going to her, and now you try to say you loved me from the first." She shook her head.

"We've still some unfinished business, Lydia and I, but anything else was over between us the day you came to Silver Hill. The dress was a parting gift of sorts, like your chain."

"She wore it when she came to call on me at Washington Square, did she tell you? No? That's when she told me you'd do anything she asked. Then she delivered your invitation to that . . . that gathering." Brigida waited, her hands folded in her lap.

Slade smiled a little and shook his head.

"She had no right to say anything to you. I never told her to invite you anywhere, you know that."

"Oh, I heard you myself, after the party, promise to come anytime she sent to you. Really, Slade, it is over between us now; you don't have to fabricate, not now."

"If you sneak about in shadows like a thief, you'll likely hear what you shouldn't and not understand half.

But that's all water under the bridge, isn't it? As it is over between us, there's no need for me to explain, is there? But I will anyway, just to leave things right, you understand?" He was prowling the cottage again, his cigar gripped tight in his teeth. "Lydia and I had . . . have one last assignment to complete, that's all. You never had cause for jealousy, not of Lydia or any other woman. That's truth. Does it ease your mind? Tell me, if you had known that before, would you have stayed with me? Will you now?"

"I can't, Slade, I can't," Brigida said in a choked whisper. "I . . . I need time to be free, don't you understand?"

"Free? I have to be the only one. No, I don't understand. I think you're hiding something, but it doesn't matter now," he said bitterly. "I know you love me, I know it." His eyes darkened with anger.

"But why couldn't you have told me sooner, instead of going on with your playacting and your vile tempers?"

"I always knew how to touch you, goddess, but not really how to love you, not until I realized one day I wasn't acting a part at all. I never wanted anything as much as I did you, not wealth or pleasure, nor any woman, and not just your body, either. You've a whole secret life in that golden head that you wouldn't share with me, would you? Now, it's too late. Now I'll set you free, if you'll do one thing only that I ask."

"You damn fool! It could have been perfect, it really could have!" Brigida had jumped up, leaving her chair rocking violently and fled the cottage to pause irresolute before plunging off into the misty rain. Slade found her

442

under the oak near the brook, protected by a canopy of leaves.

"There should always be lace and roses about you, you know, and skylarks," he said softly. He sat on the swing and pulled her to him. She rested against his shoulder, the rough fabric of his work shirt chafing her cheek. His touch was tender. Having her in his arms after so long nearly overwhelmed him. He set the swing in slow motion. Neither of them spoke until Sarah came hurrying out of the woods with tendrils of white hair damp about her smiling face.

"You'll be suppin' with us, Slade, of course," she called. "I've mushrooms."

Reluctantly he let Brigida loose.

"What is it you want to ask of me?" she queried sadly. "What proposal will you offer me now?"

"Help finish the harvest at Silver Hill. I'll give you the percentage I promised. It will be more than enough to take you back to California. It's a business arrangement, good for us both."

"I ... I'll think on it," Brigida flung over her shoulder as she followed after Sarah to help with the supper.

It was a quiet meal, and Slade rose to leave as soon as it was done.

"Come home, come home with me now!" He grasped Brigida's hand as they stood together near the shed where the horses were sheltered. "Let me love you now, just tonight."

"Tonight?" she smiled ironically. "Just tonight?"

"In all seasons and weathers I would love you, goddess, in all times and places, now and always, if only you'll let me. The way it was with us . . . for some it's that way only in dreams."

The words came thick and smoky, and Brigida hid her feelings in the sheltering darkness.

"No, no, not tonight," she said hastily. "I can't. Oh, Slade, you promised!"

"When? When will you let me hold you? Once more isn't much to ask," he pressed.

"I don't know! Perhaps . . . never. I'll go in now."

"Why? Do you think any other man could please you as well as I have? I know you better than you know yourself."

"Do stop!" she implored, tears glistening in her eyes. "We're too alike, you and I. I fear a union that is all tempestuous storm and no steadying balast. That is why."

"But your impetuousness is so unlike mine, goddess; you twinkle and glimmer with a luminescence that lights my darkest mood. Haven't I been steady these weeks and wooed you well? Don't cry now."

She nodded, twisting a handkerchief in trembling hands. "You have been, yes. I'll think longer on your offer." She slipped away in the dark and Slade waited until he heard the cottage door close softly after her.

Brigida was wide awake suddenly as if something had

come on the soft air to rouse her. A full moon rode high, lighting the room, and she listened a moment to the rush and splash of the rising tide before going to the door. Careful, trying not to waken John and Sarah asleep in the small bed chamber, Brigida lifted the latch and stepped into the warm, misty night.

In the depths of her dreams she had wanted Slade urgently. Now, with purpose, she rode the mare along the shore toward Silver Hill, the near-grown pup gliding with her. When she had passed the boathouse and the manor was in sight, she reined in. The house was dark, the curtains of her room fluttering out over the terrace in misted moonglow, and she stood still for a time while conflicting emotions worked in her. "No!" she said aloud finally, swinging the mare back the way they had come, and the animal, so close to home, nickered a soft complaint as they went.

In the moist perfume of the spray-blown summer night, Slade stirred restlessly in a shallow sleep and then woke to an ache of need so strong he groaned aloud. He rose, stepped out onto the terrace, and in hay-gold misty moonlight thought he saw a fading glimpse of the slender form that so haunted his dreams. He thought he heard a horse neigh not far off, and an owl, hunting, call in the still pines.

"Damn the witch, she's got me imagining, wide awake. This will stop now."

As Brigida was slipping back into her narrow bed at the cottage, Slade was turning the stallion onto the high road at the foot of Silver Hill drive. He put Blackhawk into full gallop toward the sunrise that was a scant hour away.

In the morning, no gift waited on the cottage door-step. By noon there was not a sign of Slade. Brigida went about in silence, doubts flourishing, quiverings of the heart alternating with flares of hot pride as she went repeatedly to the door to peer out along the beach. She saw nothing, only kelp and eel grass wrapped at low tide about scattered rocks, and mussel shoals glistening darkly.

"Maybe he will be comin' and maybe he won't, the way you been actin' to him. Either way it is no use to be moonin' about. Here, I'll fill the iron for you." Sarah lifted hot coals from the hearth with tongs and sent them rattling down the spout of a heavy iron.

"She's frettin' terrible. See if you can cheer her, old man, like usual," she said to John, who had just come up from the bay for his midday meal.

"I saw he wasn't here soon as I come off the water. Well, darlin', perchance he needs a rest. T'ain't easy on a man, such waitin', and he been so patient and steady."

"I always said a girl must know her own mind. Fickleness is nothing but terrible." Sarah shook her head. "I told you once, love's plan is not for you two to fathom. If you love him, say it. I told you before, he's a good lad, a touch of temper sure, but you wouldn't be wantin' any jellyfish, not a spirted thing like you. More chowder? No? Such a strapping fine-made man, hand-some as Adonis, some girls would not have toyed with him so."

"And him tryin' so hard to please you," old John took up. "Well, darlin', there's just a very few human stories, and you must live the right one, for you, or be sorry ever after. It don't do to be too cagey and cunning. Outsmart your own self sometimes at that game."

Brigida, who had been glancing from one to the other, burst into tears. "I don't want him," she sobbed.

"Well, that's an end to it then, isn't it? So why weep? Now dry your pretty eyes and get ready. We are goin' to the harbor to stay the night with our Joan. You're to come along." Sarah patted Brigida's hair.

"No, but say thanks for me, please, Sari." She took a long breath. "I'll finish the washing and ironing, then pack my things. Say goodbye to me now. I'll be gone tomorrow morning before you come home."

Slade saw the quick-moving figure from a long way off, dressed in faded overalls, shirtless, bare arms and shoulders sun-touched gold. A basket was braced on one hip, a hand secured a wide-brimmed straw hat against a light breeze. A scarf-wrapped cable of braided hair bounced almost to the narrow, loosely belted waist, and it took only seconds for Slade to recognize the graceful strides as Brigida's.

He put Blackhawk into a canter and overtook her before she reached the river's edge. "Carry the basket for you?" he offered, dismounting at a run. Brigida slowly turned to face him.

"The rear view was enticing, but this vantage is irresistible," he smiled. The narrow bib of Brigida's overalls, scantily covering the peaks of her breasts, exposed the full outer curvings to either side.

Brigida had resigned herself to thinking he had gone away for good and all, and his unexpected nearness made her giddy with a flooding weakness. As he came closer she began to tremble a little, her heart to pound violently. Her yearning senses filled with the sight of him, the sound of his voice, the rich aroma of spice and leather. Her tongue flicked over her lips, and she craved the taste of him, wanted his hard body against hers, once more, just once more.

"I'm going away tomorrow," she said.

"Are you?" He paused. "So am I. We have to talk about that, about your future, I mean. I have a responsibility; I have to know your plans before . . . I'll let Levi bring in the harvest and then close Silver Hill for good this time; what with Elizabeth gone . . . I've put the land up for sale. I'll give half the money to Levi. It's rightfully his."

"Oh, but you can't; it's your home, and Levi's and Martha's."

"And yours."

"NO!"

"You made it home for me. Without you there, Silver Hill is no more than my prison. I won't stay there without you. It's to be broken up and the land sold off."

His words caught at Brigida's heart like a cry and, watching her, seeing the pain in her eyes, Slade was struck nearly dumb with loss and regret.

"Where . . . where will you go, Slade?"

"To Africa. For diamonds. There's been a strike that will dazzle the world, I'm told. Robin's to go with me. We'll be at opposite ends of the earth, goddess, you and I . . . Brigida, what is it?"

She was trembling violently now, and her dark eyes burned. "I . . . want . . . you to touch me—Slade, touch me one last time," she pleaded, and then she saw the awesome need come into his eyes.

"What are you doing in these?" he asked huskily, reaching out, slowly tracing down along the straps of the overalls. He placed cupping hands at the bare sides of her breasts and felt the peaks rise to his thumbs' pressure through the worn fabric covering them. "Are you ready for me now, love?" he asked.

"Don't!" she gasped, suddenly fearful. "I'd given you up; it's so late in the day. Had I known you'd come, I would have hidden myself away in the gloomiest glade, be sure of it! It's the washing. I must do the washing all at once, so I borrowed Johnny's old . . . don't, oh, you promised." Brigida's feeble entreaty was uttered in breathy little whispers, and she made no move to resist when Slade slid his hands inside the overalls, slowly lowering them to the small of her back, then to the soft curves below, pressing her forward against him.

"You know where my mind has been every moment, every second of these past months," he growled. "You'll not take me this far and back off. I will beat you, if you try." She yielded then with a trembling cry of submission, her hands on his shoulders . . . then threading his hair that smelled of the wind and the sea . . . her mouth wide and seeking as she clung to him, hovering somewhere between laughter and tears. Then his breath rasped raw in her ear.

"We surely will leave our glow in the sky, goddess, if nothing else," he whispered, touching, tasting. "I had in mind to leave you today without goodbye, but I couldn't. I went as far as the harbor before turning back. It's well I did, even if this is the last time for us." While he spoke his hands were filled with her softnesses, his mouth and hard body moved and caressed and, roused, Brigida melted into his embrace without restraint.

"Sarah and John?" Slade questioned, lifting her.

"Gone," she answered, her arms tightly encircling his neck, their eager mouths joining again and again. "Hurry," she sighed against his lips as he started toward the cottage.

Brigida heard Slade moving about, securing the cottage. She waited where he had placed her, curled on the Hands' four-poster bed. She traced the lines of the rolling star on the quilt beneath her and felt shy . . . almost frightened of him as she had the first time. Now, though, she knew what was coming—the touch of his lover's hands on her skin, of his lips and teeth moving over her swelled breasts . . . down along her ribs and hips to the inner curves of her thighs, to touch and incite her until she couldn't exist another instant, until she would whimper for him to stop . . . and beg him not to, ever. Anticipation sent a stab of heat surging up through her loins. She rolled onto her back, hands resting palms up at her sides, one leg raised slightly, bent at the knee. She breathed deeply, waiting.

Undoing his shirt, Slade stooped through the low door of the slant-ceilinged bed chamber. "Take your hair down," he ordered, his dark blue eyes going over Brigida thoroughly. Sitting up, silent, she obeyed, and he came and kissed her lips, but only lightly, as he pressed her down again. He undid her overall straps and lowered the bib to her waist. He slid his hands up along her ribs to her breasts and barely touched her hard nipples with his tongue. Slowly, he slid the overalls down over her hips to expose the flat plain of her belly, which he brushed with a familiar hand before he finished undressing her and removing his own clothes.

"I've waited this long time," he said in a strangely even tone, "and now you're ready for me, are you?"

Brigida's eyes were wide, the pupils dilated. She only nodded, lying back, watching him. Then she turned away, cradling her face against a crooked arm, shivering when he traced his hand down along the channel of her spine and deftly slid his finger between her giving thighs. She moaned softly.

"You are ready for me, lady," he whispered, his eyes glowing, she saw, looking back over her shoulder, seeing him ready, too, and smiling a little odd, cool smile.

Without warning, his hand came down, the ringing slap driving her instinctively up onto her knees with a cry. He caught her loosed golden hair in a tight coil, holding her rigid.

"Witch, you deserve any punishment I could devise, don't you? For leaving me now when I want you with me? What do you think I should do to you, Brigida, answer me!"

"Slade, I . . . do whatever you will because I want it all, anything you . . ." She choked off her words, biting her lower lip hard, grasping the bedstead with both hands. She was still on her knees, held in place by his grasp on her hair, when Slade came behind her, kneeling over her. Loosing her hair, he pulled her knees wide. She felt his lightest touch between her open thighs, his fingers moving gently, steadily, brushing and teasing until he began to probe in a slow, excruciating invasion that set her whimpering and writhing with her terrible need of him.

"Oh, Slade . . . please, now, please! I want . . ."

"You'll soon get it all, goddess," he hissed, "enough to remember for a lifetime."

His hands were at her hips, holding her still, and she arched back, clutching the bedstead when he plunged— filling her with his first thrust as she begged him to, as he had so many nights in her lonely, fevered dreams. His fine hands were working her, playing her body expertly while his lunges deepened and strengthened until her throbbing, luminous, rainbow wave spread and shattered about her in a million points of dancing colored light. Sobbing with relief and pleasure, she sank slowly, her knees sliding, giving beneath Slade's weight. He rolled to his side, still a solid flame inside her. He held her against his chest, his arm a band about her waist, and then he was on his back, forcing her up until she was sitting astride him, twisting to look at him over her shoulder—her breasts thrust high. His face was savage, his lips parted and twisted a little, his eyes mere slits of blue fire when they met hers.

"Damn you, Lucifer!" she whispered.

At his muttered command, she began to move, riding high, feeling him go deeper and deeper inside her. Again, his hands were manipulating the places he knew so well how to touch. Then he was breaching a new path.

"Slade!" Brigida screamed once. All sensation focused only where Slade exquisitely touched and invaded; she existed now, it seemed, only because he was using her body—totally.

"Love, when you've had everything you can take . . . all you think you can take of me, when you think I've loved you all I can . . . then we're going to start again." Slade's voice was caressing and warm, and a sob broke from Brigida's throat. She couldn't speak. She didn't want to. Her arms enfolded his neck as she buried her face against his throat, pressing her breasts to his dark chest. Then she was up crouching beside him, wildly kissing his eyes and his throat, the broad expanse of his chest, her hungry mouth going everywhere. He moaned with pleasure while she seemed ready to devour him, and his touch again went to her soft, enfolding depths. When

453

he raised her chin to look into her glazed eyes, his wide mouth, hot and hard, found hers. When he took her again, she knew a stunning reverence for the absolute power of his virility, for his generous, giving lover's body, which presented hers with feelings so endlessly, exquisitely perfect.

The old four-poster bedstead in the bayman's cottage could as well have been a gold-leafed bower in Eden for all they knew of the world that day. Nothing else existed . . . just the two of them and the long pent-up desires that flowed in cresting, sensuous surges through the slow hours of purpling dusk and deep into the night . . . until the morning star rose.

Brigida entered the library at Silver Hill, aware all at once of many familiar things—Slade's papers on the desk, the slant of sunlight on gold-tooled bindings, the scent on the morning air drifting from the kitchen of fresh-baked bread and coffee. There was a distant yapping from the kennels, the lowing of cows, the slam of a door far away upstairs.

With a deep sigh, she sank on the sofa and closed her eyes. She didn't move when Slade entered and crossed to kneel over her, a knee to either side of her hips. He kissed her, and she began to stir with a moist, sensual softening. She let his low voice caress her. "You, goddess, are my only obsession now . . . my pact with life and love and the devil all at once. You're my vision of romance come true. Say you'll stay with me always."

Opening her eyes, she said, "No, I can't say it, and I'm not a romantic vision, only weak flesh and blood, is all, else I wouldn't be here with you now. . . . What do you mean about the devil?"

"Flesh and blood, of course, but such an extraordinary arrangement of such ordinary substances," he smiled. "I'm ready. Just get a few things. You won't need much where I'm taking you. Just a figure of speech, about the devil."

"Well, I've my own pact, and he's more than a figure of speech to me, I'll tell you," Brigida said on her way from the library, wondering at herself for having let him convince her to take this excursion. But he was persuasive, particularly when she was in his arms.

"Give me just a few days' undisturbed possession of you," he had asked, and it had seemed an irresistible request early that morning as they lay together, limbs woven, in a moment of ebbed passion. They'd have each other in the way that most pleased them both, he had said, and that would be an end to it: no ties, no bad feelings. She had agreed. Now, she wondered if he really would just set her free as he'd promised. And what she'd do when he did.

Some hours later they rode across a narrow wooden bridge from the mainland to the outer strip of the barrier beach. The horses plodded up a dune, and there, stretched below, was the sea, the gray-blue ocean under blue sky, white sand meeting white foam, breakers coming in in layer after layer piled high, roaring at the sky, hissing along the edge of the land. Rolling dunes were tufted with beach grass and decorated with wild rose and wild plum, with bayberry and small twisted pines. Salt spray flew against their faces as they turned to ride along the firm, damp sand at the ocean's edge.

"You asked me once," Slade said after a time, "where I was at home." The sun was high and getting hot when Brigida saw the cabin set atop a dune amidst wavering tan rushes and tendrils of beach grass. "I've never brought anyone but Levi here," Slade said when they stood at the top of the dune, entranced by the hot day, the sparkle of sea and sand. When they turned to each other, Slade's voice became smoky. "We'll be starting where we left off this morning, lady."

"Really, sir, I must protest," Brigida teased, a wave of desire beginning to uncurl deep inside her. "If you think I came all this way to be debauched by a perverted, unmannerly ruffian . . . oh!" she giggled, "stop or I'll cry out. Put me down. Whatever will the neighbors think, you treating a poor, defenseless . . ."

With a growl Slade had gathered her up. He kicked open the door and strode inside. "Well, will you like it here?" he asked.

The peaked roof of the cabin soared high. Its skylight sent patters of brightness through horizontal beams. A sleeping loft, accessible only by narrow open steps, was tucked up against the slant of the roof. A trestle table and slat-back chairs were placed under windows that looked on the sea. A jelly cabinet held shelves of cobalt glass, stoneware pitchers and pewter flat plates. Cheese baskets hung from pegs, a copper kettle from a fireplace crane, and a tin coffee pot, painted with coiled fruits and flowers sat on the hearth.

"There's spareness here that soothes," Brigida said.

"'Whatever is fashioned, let it be plain and simple, unembellished by superfluities which add nothing to its goodness and durability.' One of the Shakers' rules of life from their *Laws of the Millenium*."

"And you've the sky and the sea. It's like a shipboard cabin. I could stay in this place forever if . . ."

Near the north window on the bay side of the cabin, white China-headed nails tacked a row of sketches to the wall. Two shelves were laden with carvings of waterfowl and birds—ducks, geese, cranes, herons, slender-legged tern, old gulls and young ones in juvenile plummage. "Do you do these?" Brigida looked at Slade with wonder. "Why didn't you ever tell me?"

"It didn't seem of pressing importance, in our particular circumstance. I learned the craft from the Indians, from Levi's people. I use more detail than the Shinnecocks do. They prefer unpainted decoys. Levi—he uses live ones. There's water in the rain barrels, tea in the cabinet. You'll be wanting dinner. I'd best be catching it."

When Slade returned to the cabin later, the windows

were wide, inviting the shining day to fill it. There were baskets about of yellow beach heather and silvery wormwood and jars filled with sprays of flowering sea lavender that grew in the bayside marsh behind the cabin.

"You make every place you are in homelike and lovely. You've been busy," he said.

"So have you," Brigida answered, studying him bemusedly as he deposited a dozen cleaned snapper at the center of the table. "Or did those just leap out of the water for you? Everything does seem to come so easily to you; I'd not be surprised."

"Everything but you," he agreed, "but there's still time."

"Now I've rejected the adventurer, the speculator, the manipulator, the roguish rake and wild ladies' man, the gentleman farmer, the society dandy who goes from the heights of Mrs. Astor's ballrom to the seamy French Quarter where cutthroats and thieves are thick—now I've rejected you in all your many other guises, do you think to win me in your new role of simple woodcarver—alone in his sea-bound cabin?" Brigida stood, hands on her hips, head high, waiting an answer.

"Surely the lady doth protest too much, sweet," Slade scowled. "Be easy, Brigida, the contest is over between us, remember? We're just spending a few . . . pleasured hours together before we go our separate ways, though if you change your mind and want to stay, I'll keep you."

"Impossible," she answered. "Before, when I did everything I knew to try and make you love me, nothing worked, nothing."

"Everything did, everything worked."

"But you left me alone."

"You were with me on every summer breeze and in every troubled dream until I had to tell you. I couldn't deny it any longer. You know, no one could have hallucinated you, goddess, beautiful as you are beyond any dream."

"I was not the witch you thought me at first, and now I'm not anything like the divinity you would pretend I am," Brigida said quietly.

"But you are both, Brigida, goddess and witch and more, warm and lovely woman. I'll love all three in you if you'll let me." His eyes lingered on her troubled face.

"Too late," she said, flinging her hair back from her brow. "Any regrets?"

"No regrets. I wouldn't take back one instant spent with you. I wouldn't have missed you for the world," Slade grinned, his mood suddenly light again. "Come on, we won't linger in the past if we've just a little time left together. Have you seen the bed loft? We'll be lingering there a good bit. After you." He bowed her to the ladder and sent her scurrying up before him with a deft slap.

Above there was a four-poster bed, a mirrored iron washstand and a pine sailor's chest. A telescope stood on a tripod at one end of the loft.

Slade lifted a wooden trap that hooked open against the slant of the roof. Together they watched a silver gull flash above low, lazy waves, barely managing now to break. The wind had dropped. The sand was tinged pale rose-pink by the low sun.

"I've another view," Slade said, leading Brigida to a window at the opposite side. He swung the telescope to face it. "There's Silver Hill. Have a look."

She peered through the glass. "Oh, it is wonderful. You can see . . . everything! The terrace, the beach, even the Hands' chimney top." After a moment she whirled on Slade with a mixture of disbelief and consternation in her face. He shrugged, turning his palms up in a gesture of resignation.

"You saw!" she accused.

"Yes, I saw. I saw all your comings and goings and pacings, Brigida, in daylight . . . in moonlight. I saw you roam the beach with your skirts caught up looking like a woodland nymph come to try the water; I watched you raise your fist to the heavens and when you swam alone, love, in moonlight I watched. I was moved near to madness then wanting you."

With a gasp Brigida flung herself to him, all the lonely longings of those sultry nights returning strong in memory. "Spy!" she breathed against his lips. "Deceiver, pretender, untruther—to let me think you were far away so long."

"I came some nights to walk through the gardens like a ghost beneath your window, and your perfume came wafting down to heighten my agony. I did think then that you really were a devil-sent witch come to plague me for some evil I'd done. Now I've got you trapped," he leered, his mood changing again with disarming quickness. "I'll take my revenge on your delectable person."

"Really?" Brigida asked. "Tell me all about it."

"Clearly, I am the overlord here and you, sorceress,

are my captive. You will indulge my every wish, else I'll beat you, I promise. I intend to keep you prisoner here forever in my secret lair. I intend to have my way with you whenever I choose. What do you think of that?''

She had crossed to him, smiling a little, stretching extravagantly, undoing her shirt, and then she began on his, curling against him, nuzzling, almost purring. "You bore me, liege lord, with all your talk," she sighed, mouthing his lips. "Make me weak and helpless now, Lucifer, with your devilish, perverted misuse of me. I dare you. Shall we see whose strength fades first?''

"And you'll love every moment of it, heathen, won't you?'' With a deep, growling laugh, Slade tumbled her onto the bed, pinning her beneath him. "Still challenging me, goddess?'' he said. "Well, this is one contest I just might let you win.''

"You won't need that here.'' Slade watched lazily from the bed later while Brigida tied a narrow floral scarf about her bosom, knotting it between her high breasts. Then she proceeded to drape another about her hips.

"No?''

"No. Take two lengths of toweling from the chest. There's no one here to see you, except me. I intend to see as much of you as I can.'' He stood, stretching and moving languorously, to undo her flimsy drapings. "You're more beautiful every time I look at you. You'll always belong to me, no matter where you go, Brigida.''

"Don't, Slade, please don't.'' She was in an instant near tears. "What do you want of me? I told you . . .''

"I only want a promise you'll stay with me forever, or else a smile." He brought a hand to her cheek, and she inclined her head to it.

"A smile? You ask that who did nothing but glower at me for months?"

"People change, you were the one who liked to tell me so. Come, don't ruin the day. Let's go."

Slade followed Brigida prancing and plunging into the surf, which was calm and warm on their sun-warmed skin. They played, swimming about each other, diving beneath the surface, racing with long strokes. Slade's hair, wet, washed straight back from his brow; his face glistened dark tan. The warm water, the touch of sun on salty skin, flashing glimpses of Slade's rippling back and arms made Brigida soft with slow-rising desire. When the length of their slick bodies brushed, Slade stopped. Treading the deep water, he coiled a hand in Brigida's hair and pulled it back from her glowing face, his tongue tracing her salty lips. An encircling arm came about her waist, locking their undulating bodies close, and their mouths met. Brigida's hands slid down Slade's back, her smooth breasts pressed against his chest, their slippery hips and thighs, working gently as they floated together, brushing. They broke apart and, laughing, she pushed off against him to swim away, but he grasped a slim ankle to pull her back to him—his hands on her hips securing her against him. "Where do you think you're going?" His whisper was smoky in her ear. "Get that body up to the cabin now."

"That's exactly where I was going, liege lord," she smiled back at him over her shoulder.

Slade hoisted a rain barrel onto an overhead frame and opened the spout. They stood close under the warm flow, washing the brine from each other's body, hands lingering and caressing. Slade toweled Brigida briskly, bringing a pink warmth to her golden skin, and she slowly polished all the flat planes and swells of his hard body with a smooth, fragrant cream. He took her hand to lead her to the loft again.

Next morning they cantered the horses along the sand, swam, gathered driftwood for the evening fire and loved under the afternoon sky with only the gulls to see them. At night, their passion was slow and gentle, bittersweet for the knowledge that their time together would soon end.

It did, before either would have ever wished. They awoke the second morning to find Levi waiting patiently, leaning against the cabin, scanning the horizon.

Brigida prepared the fresh eggs and sliced the bread he had brought from Silver Hill, and when they had eaten and sat over coffee, the Indian addressed Slade pointedly. "When will you be coming back?" he asked.

"We may never," Slade said, looking at Brigida, who had risen to clear away the plates and take them out to wash. When she returned, there was a hardness about him she hadn't seen in a while, and a distracted inward manner that always before had told her he was going away.

"Now it is over," she thought, the awful realization tightening her throat. She took up a book and strip of toweling and left.

Slade found her propped on her elbows, staring vacantly out to sea, the unread book open before her. There was a ship off the coast moving eastward. "A Liverpool packet," Slade said. Brigida felt his shadow on her bare back.

"I guess," she answered dully.

"He's left. Levi's gone back to Silver Hill." Slade stripped off his clothes to lie on his back beside her, looking up at her delicate profile.

"It's time for us to leave here, too," Brigida stated flatly.

"I'll bring you back again, if you'll let me, goddess." Brigida rolled onto her back, her hair fanning out over the toweling, draping Slade's near shoulder. Behind closed lids, she saw sun spots dance in colors, felt Slade's shadow over her again, and she moved a silky limb against his hard thigh, tasted his lips, arched to his hand at her breasts, the crests firming in his long fingers that moved then down over her to her parted thighs.

"I'll bring you back here," he said against her throat. Brigida caressed his tanned shoulder, followed the smooth, hard line of his body, and his mouth covered hers again. He whispered her name as he moved above her, and sunlight flaked in her eyes, the air about them seeming to dance with shards of silver and spangles of gold.

"You won't," Brigida said softly.

"I won't what?" Slade rose on an elbow to smile down

at her.

"You won't bring me back here ever. There's no returning to paradise, no matter how hard you try, and if you ever do get back, it's ruined."

A cooling came at sundown. Slade built a fire after they finished supper, and he piled down pillows to make a nest near the hearth. He lay back, puffing a cigar, watching the stars through the skylight. The moon rose as Brigida sank down beside him.

"Prisoners and dreamers love the moon, Brigida," Slade said. "And lovers." He kissed her. "I've something to tell you. Blueford Root will be at Saratoga Springs next week."

"So that is why we're leaving, and you professing such love for me. You can't love me so very much if . . . let Root go, Slade. It's been so long."

"There's no measure of love, Brigida. I love you as my life," he said. "I'd stay here with you forever in this place that's scrubbed clean by the wind and sea. It's always the same," he said, leaning back to watch the stars, "timeless and changing, no two days alike, colors that shift and blend so you never tire of what's before your eyes, and with you here . . . I would give up Root . . . for you, but there's another reason now I have to find him." Brigida, who had been listening dreamfully was taken by the urgency of Slade's manner.

"What reason?" she asked with apprehension.

He stood to pace the room, his shadow thrown long up the walls by leaping firelight.

"I never saw my father until he came stamping into my room in the middle of a winter night and scared the devil out of me. I was three years old, and I'd never seen him before." The hard edge in Slade's voice kept Brigida silent.

"I have a son, Brigida . . . a son I've never seen. I must find him now. Will you help me? No, don't get up, hear me out."

"Whose?" she barely managed to whisper.

"Bonnie's. I never knew. No one at Silver Hill knew. Levi just told me; that's why he came here today. Billy McGlory was out to fetch his girl home. He's the one who heard Root will be at Saratoga. He's the one who says Root has Bonnie's child, my child . . . Root's nephew. McGlory has ways of knowing. He's always been right. Brigida, listen. I brought Bonnie to Silver Hill and left her. That killed her just the same as if I'd lifted my own hand and crushed her." Slade stood leaning at the mantel, staring into the fire.

"Why did you go?" Brigida asked in a small voice.

"To look for Root in the Falkland Islands, I told you."

"No, really why?"

Slade lifted his head and rolled his shoulders as though they were suddenly stiff. He raked a hand through his hair, then looked full into Brigida's eyes. "I'll tell you now what I've never said before. I made Bonnie mad, drove her insane. I had to keep her with me after that. She seemed my own crazed image in a broken glass. I saw my own demons in her restless eyes. I married her out of pity. She hated me for it, for not really loving her, for destroying her home, for being . . . the enemy. When I realized what I'd done, I escaped to sea as my father did before," he finished quickly.

"Pity, it's been said, is the straightest path to love. Oh, it can take so long a time to understand some things," Brigida offered.

"My father didn't help me to understand anything," Slade said in a tone heavy with bitterness. "He didn't even own me as his until I was almost grown. Elizabeth? At least she was there, wasn't she?"

"I'm sorry, truly," Brigida said, coming to stand against him. "Elizabeth told me some of it. Slade," she said, "I'll help you find your son and then . . . then, I'll go home to California."

Twenty-Two

The tracks of the Hudson River Line hugged the base of rising hills and outcroppings of rock, and ran sometimes along man-built embankments. There were boats on the river all along the way—ferries, rafts, canoes, barges pulled by tugs. On the banks, houses and summer villas were tucked against the hills, small cities and villages were set in a landscape that changed with every curve as the soaring cliffs of the Palisades gave way to the successive ridges of the Catskill range. The glaring day was hazy with late summer heat. Smoke from the engine drifted back into the open windows of the cars where fashionably dressed ladies, tight-laced, buttoned and bonneted, fluttered fans and made frequent trips to the cooler for cups of iced water, while gentlemen pulled at starched collars and mopped their brows.

"Them's icehouses, miss." Brigida had hardly taken her eyes from the window. Slade, next to her, was engrossed with business papers. The voice came from the seat behind them. She glanced back into a flushed, ruddy old face. The eyes, under snowy, plumed brows, were

469

bright. "They cut it all winter, then iceboats take it down to the city all summer. How be you folks? I'm Captain Jesse Leathers, bound to rejoin my ferry up to Albany."

"You're a river captain, sir?" Slade asked.

"I am. I mastered a Hudson sloop before the war, took bricks and butter to the city, Miss . . . ?"

"Hawkes, Mrs. Hawkes. This is Captain Hawkes, whaling."

"Whaling is it? Well, we was heroes of a sort, too, all up the Hudson. Real lovely, the sloops were, a hundred foot long and flyin' five thousand feet of sail. Doin' a Hudson Rive jibe, there's nothin' to compare, I'll tell you, boy, whales or no, swinging that seventy-foot boom. Maybe roundin' the Cape comes close, but you'd know more about that than I would."

"How do you happen to be traveling by train?" Slade inquired.

"Here, we are comin' up on West Point opposite, Mrs. Hawkes," Leathers pointed. "A fella chartered my ferry, takin' a party and a horse up to Saratoga for one of them new stakes races. They didn't want no outsiders with 'em. They give me a good price, and I got kin all the way upriver, watchin' out for my vessel. Oh, I see I put the lady to sleep with my talkin'. Ain't she the prettiest thing, though?" Jesse Leathers smiled.

Brigida had removed her straw bonnet and her golden head was resting against the window post.

Slade shifted her so that she leaned on his shoulder.

"Yes, she is the prettiest thing," he said. "Tell me, Jesse, about this party that took your ferry. I've some friends due up from Virginia for the races. It would be just like Brad Rand to slip into Saratoga on the sly and surprise his old buddies."

Slade had arranged for a carriage to take them to the Clarendon, one of the older hotels in Saratoga—patronized, he explained, by sportsmen, millionaires, an occasional politician . . . and their ladies. "Vanderbilt, Belmont, that sort stay at the Clarendon," he told Brigida, guiding her through the crush at the station.

"All the idle rich, you mean? Who else comes to Saratoga?" Brigida quipped snappishly as the carriage moved into the flow with many others crowding the street and raising clouds of dust in the hot afternoon.

"Don't be irritable, pet, you can soon have your bath. Not only the idle rich come here. Look around you. Saratoga is a cradle of fashion and intrigue. It's been the site of many an illicit rendezvous."

"As you no doubt can well attest." She scowled. He grinned.

"But that was before you, goddess. On this trip, I suppose," he sighed dramatically, "I'll have to settle for the French cuisine and fast horses Saratoga is famous for. And its mint juleps." The traffic was barely moving, and Slade nodded, grinning broadly at a bevy of fancy ladies in an adjacent open carriage.

"And who are they, pray tell?" Brigida sniffed, feeling wilted in the gown she'd worn since early morning.

"Grace Sinclair and Hattie Adams. City madames putting their best goods on exhibit."

"In broad daylight?" Brigida gasped, only half jesting.

"Where have you brought me, sir?"

"There's no business done here. The ladies vacation at rented mansions on the lake and the madames leave their city addresses with interested gentlemen from Philadelphia and New York."

"Still the flirt you always were, I see," Brigida complained.

"Don't pout. Now that you're leaving me, I'll need some companionship with the softer sex. Don't do that," Slade laughed, fending off her piercing elbow. "Look, you're attracting even more attention than you usually do. Smile, now. That's Jim Morrisey, an old friend. He's looking you over. Do you want him to think I've married a shrew?" Slade raised a hand in greeting, and a burly, dark-bearded man three carriages away broke into a big grin.

"Will I be seeing you later, Slade?" Morrisey bellowed across the busy street. "Everything always on the house for you, remember!"

"Jim opened the gaming house here summer before last, and the gamblers have come in from everywhere— for that and the racing. The Thoroughbreds, of course, have been running here nearly twenty years."

Slade turned the carriage onto Broadway, a triple-width dirt street shaded by graceful giant elms.

"That's the Union Hotel on our left. They seat a thousand for dinner most summer nights. Opposite is the Congress." He raised the buggy whip toward a turreted building with towers, cupolas and bays. Gingerbread fretwork ran along a veranda where hundreds of people sat watching the passing parade, rocking in their chairs, diamonds glinting in the sun.

"Diamonds in the afternoon? Do they come here to do nothing but dress and display?"

"Saratoga is a great spectacle; enjoy it, pet. Some of the more flamboyant spenders are loud and their tastes run to the gaudy when they put their ladies on display. Now you, love, will be better dressed and jeweled and more proudly displayed than any. You will sit on your veranda with the others, your pretty hands folded in your silken lap, and Blueford Root will find you."

"Me?" Brigida looked at Slade quizzically.

"Yes. He'll try to get at me through you. You did bring your infamous little Colt?" Slade's raffish smile earned him a look of shock from Brigida, and a tremor passed through her. "I'm sorry," he said quickly.

"I could have killed you, and you jest." She shook her head. "Yes, I brought it, reluctantly though. So I'm to be the bait to lure your prey? Now you're involving me in your plot, you'd best tell me about Mr. Root, so I can be on my guard."

"Root? Pretends he's a fine southern gentleman. He was a horse trader of some repute before the war. The one thing on earth he cares for now is this stallion he's running. It's his only tie to a glorious past. The man's a thief with a larcenous soul and no human feeling at all, no better than a serpent consumed with malice." A muscle flexed in Slade's jaw. And his eyes went flat and cold.

"Don't look that way, you frighten me," Brigida said as the carriage came to a stop at the Clarendon. Slade lifted Brigida down, and they collected the curious glances of guests seated in groupings of twos and threes beneath the front portico.

"Smile, pet, you're center stage again. There's just time for a julep while the maid unpacks your things. She'll be right along with the luggage. There's an iron bench at the end of the back garden placed so you can see the shade of the mountains to the north. The view is pleasing after a journey. Brigida?" He looked at her with a sudden brimming of concern. "I'd not ask this of you, with Root, if it weren't for the boy."

"And I'd not be here if it weren't for the boy, you know that. Even if we had our own baby, I would feel just the same about your son. Come," she sighed, "show me about, don't stand there looking so . . . odd. Whatever will people think? What are you thinking, for goodness sake?"

"About making babies with you. It's not too late, Brigida." Slade flashed a wicked smile at an elderly gentleman passing through the quiet piazza where they stood. He raised an ear trumpet and stared before continuing on his way. When they were alone again, Brigida turned to Slade with a wistful smile.

"Captain, it is too late; it's over. And if ever I was going to have your child, I surely would know by now. It just wasn't meant to be, that's all. Where is this view you spoke so highly of, and the mint julep you offered? I feel in need now of some soothing refreshment."

"When will you require me, madame?" The new maid was at the sitting room door of their well-appointed suite when Slade and Brigida arrived. She had unpacked

Brigida's gowns and placed out her brushes and scents. Slade's clothes also were hanging in the armoire, and his pewter brushes and straight razor were on the washstand.

"The lady won't be needing you again tonight, Betty," he said. "I'll tend to her hooks and fasteners, thanks. Have they shown you your place?"

"Yes, Captain, up at the top of the hotel. I share a room with Angel, Miss Worsley's maid."

"What's Miss Worsley doing here?" Slade asked sharply. "She usually stays at the Congress."

"I don't know, Captain. She is here in this hotel. She came yesterday with Mr. Stancel and Mr. Carpenter."

The girl slipped away and Slade turned the key in the lock after her. "Come here," he said, beckoning Brigida with his eyes. "If I'm to do up your fastenings, I'll have to undo some first, won't I?"

"We'll miss dinner." Brigida attempted a prim look, but as her unbound coil of hair fell loose, her eyes began to shine.

"We already have. I've ordered a supper sent up to us. Later." He dropped his jacket on a chair. "Don't make a liar of me, goddess. I told Betty I'd do that."

Brigida rested her hands on his shoulders as he undid the row of tiny mother-of-pearl buttons on her bodice.

"You could take employment as a dresser, should your fortunes ever founder," she teased, offering him the buttoned cuff of her silk sleeve with a limp, imperious hand.

"Your servant, madame," he half bowed, bringing her tapered fingers to his lips. "But I think the position of undresser suits me better."

"No servant, sir, would dare what you do," she sighed as his hand slid inside her dress.

"Any servant presented such a view would do exactly as I intend," he smiled.

Brigida turned her best smile to Slade as they entered the well-lit anteroom of the casino, and he rested a guiding hand at the small of her back.

He was sleek in dark evening clothes, and Brigida was in a dusky rose satin gown, the décolletage low, her bosom ablaze with diamonds. A white feather boa of whispery marabou, draped over one shoulder, reached almost to the floor.

Swinging heavy fists and grinning through his full black beard, Jim Morrisey came striding across the floor to grasp Slade's hand. "Captain, have you come to leave some more of your gold in my coffers?" The man thumped Slade's back with a heavy paw. "I heard you've come up to run a two-year-old on Saturday. Did I hear right?"

"You did, Jim, a promising one. Brigida, love, allow me to introduce Jim Morrisey. Jim, my wife," Slade watched the man's eyes light with pleasure.

"A delight, Mrs. Hawkes, and how nice it is to say those words—Mrs. Hawkes. I worried about my friend here and his wild ways. There comes a time when a man needs to settle his life. I'm sure you'll help do that for Slade, as my Sue has for me."

"How's business, Jim?" Slade was guiding Brigida toward the gaming room.

"Couldn't be better. There's a lot of money around, a

lot of money, some western gold and . . . oh, you'll be interested in this. I took in a stone for chips last week, big as your fist, and perfect. The diamond strike in South Africa is the gold rush all over again, but bigger. Have you heard?"

Slade nodded. "I'm going to see for myself. Prospecting is something I never have done."

"There's not much you haven't tried, I know, but now you are so well favored in a lady," the man smiled on Brigida, "I'm sure you'll give up that scheme. I'm sure she'd rather you were here with her than have the biggest diamond under the sun."

Brigida looked away.

"She could always come with me, Jim," Slade said, "wherever I go; she knows that."

They had reached the double doors of the public gaming room on the main floor. There was a fragment of silence and the usual admiring stares as heads turned toward Brigida.

"I don't allow ladies in there. It seems an especially wise restriction just now. You'd no doubt disrupt all play, Mrs. Hawkes, and walk out winning my entire faro bank," Morrisey laughed.

"Mr. Morrisey, how do ladies amuse themselves while gentlemen are losing money at your tables?" Brigida returned his smile.

"I've a fine dining salon that welcomes members of the fair sex, and if you'll come with me now, Suzie and I will pour champagne to toast your future full of happiness."

The low hum of voices and the click of the turning wheel resumed behind them as Slade led Brigida toward a wide, red-carpeted staircase. "Don't let him fool you. There are private rooms upstairs where the real money's played. Jim will take it from whomever has it to lose, won't you, Jim?"

"Sure I will," Morrisey grinned, "but no credit though, you know me, Slade. By the way, Lydia Worsley was here last evening with two young men. They didn't have five dollars between them by the time they left. She was playing with Carpenter's money, lost a lot . . . even a ring he was wearing. She said you'd cover her losses if I let them sit in one more time. I wouldn't do it without your word on the matter. I hope I did the right thing."

"You did exactly the right thing. I'm not paying Lydia's bills anymore, but I will buy Carpenter's ring from you. I . . . look here—Suzie!" Slade said with genuine warmth to a queenly figure bearing down on them like a racing train. Before he could say more, the generously proportioned woman hurled herself against him and set a kiss full on his mouth.

"My wife," Morrisey informed Brigida proudly.

"I don't know what we'd have done without your husband, Brigida. Black Friday cleaned us out; we almost lost it all." Suzie Morrisey and Brigida were alone. The men had gone off to the game room. "Jim had a real insider's tip, from old Vanderbilt, no less, and would you believe? That bit of information right from the source himself cost Jim eight hundred thousand dollars, like that, lost on New York Central stock!"

"And Slade, how did he . . . ?"

"He picked up most of our debt, kept us afloat 'til Jim got back on his feet. Slade financed this place. Your husband is such a gentleman, he even bought my jewelry back." Suzie Morrisey fluttered a dimpled hand at a diamond star set in her dark hair, and the rows of diamond bracelets climbing her arm clinked pleasantly. "You are a very lucky woman to have got Slade Hawkes for a husband. How did you do it? How did you and Slade find each other? I so enjoy a sweet love story." Suzie rested her chin on the heel of her hand, leaning forward over the table expectantly.

"Well," Brigida started, "we knew each other first a long time ago, as children. He was a cabin boy on my father's ship and I . . ."

"How criminally romantic! More champagne? Jack!" Suzie commandeered a passing waiter. "This is a champagne story, Brigida, isn't it? I can tell already. Slade was your true love, but he left you for a southern belle. Then, when she died, he realized he had loved you all along, but you had run off to the Continent, and he searched the wide world over to find you, and he did, he did, he rescued you from the clutches of an old man, a count with a penchant for small blondes, who would have given you wealth and position but no love, no children, no happiness. Oh, what a wonderful story! Can I tell it to Jim? He's a very sentimental Irishman under all his whiskers."

"Absolutely," Brigida laughed, throwing up her hands in amused dismay just as Slade came to her rescue.

"What's funny?" he asked, planting a quick kiss on her ear.

"I know all about your wife now, Slade. We have no secrets, she and I . . . and I think she is perfect for you. There," Suzie pronounced.

"I agree," Slade added. "Jim's waiting for you, Mrs. M., so we'll bid you goodnight. See you at the races."

"There's no one in town who doesn't know you're here. You made a spectacular entrance this evening, goddess. You always do, you know."

"Yes, I know. You do rather well yourself. I see the way women look at you." Brigida's words dripped honey.

"I don't notice a one of them anymore, only you. Believe me?"

Brigida looked up into prankish eyes and her heart surged. "No," she told him, "but it doesn't matter now." She buried her chin deep in floating feathers and held silent the rest of the way to the Clarendon.

Slade and Brigida fell into the rhythm of the late summer days at Saratoga Spa, driving out to take the waters early at High Rock. The springs were housed under pagodas, gazebos, or pillared domes, where waiters in bowlers and dark suits ladled out cups and glasses of the fizzy mineral waters that came cold from the ground. Then the ladies, in starched cambric morning dresses, and the gentlemen, in broadcloth suits and straw boaters, returned to their hotels for breakfast—cereal, fish, omelets, griddle cakes, a cutlet or chop, cold ham or beef, and potatoes, all washed down with chocolate, coffee or tea. At noon everyone took the waters again. Dinner served at two, was eight courses and lasted for hours.

In the heavy heat of the afternoons, logy guests lingered on shady lawns listening to hotel bands, or drove out to Moon's Lake House, where they nibbled Saratoga chips—crisp fried potato slices—played on the swing boats, rowed on the lake, and returned to their rooms to rest before dressing for supper and an evening at the casino or dancing on airy pavilions under the stars.

Throughout all, Brigida was endlessly amused by Slade's terse biographies of the other guests.

"Brilliantly witty," he would nod in the direction of a man at the punchbowl. "Rolf Gwynne, banking. Unfortunately, Rolf's wife is a bit *floue*, as Miri would say—vague."

"I see." Brigida watched an amber-haired young woman with vacant blue eyes drift past. "Who is this coming to greet you now?"

"In the dark gown? Ida Brisbane. Don't be fooled; she's reliably indiscreet, despite her severe appearance. Ida's husband is in coal. Behind her is Tedrow Gilchrist, a very dull man with few friends, no enemies, and a splendidly spoiled wife, a bad combination."

"Like us, you mean?" Brigida couldn't resist.

"You may be splendidly spoiled, but I'm not dull, you'll grant. We are perfectly suited, no one doubts it, but you."

"We're too well suited, I've told you," she answered flippantly, with a false laugh. "Who is that unfortunate-looking fellow? He's staring at me," she whispered behind a raised hand.

"Someone's always staring at you." Slade studied a figure leaning against a fluted pilaster. "He could be one of Root's people, but I think he's a man crossed in love. I think he's a man of many secret flaming passions, a man who will commit murder if his lady persists in putting him off. Now you'd best waltz with me before I commit murder over your incessant questions," he said in exasperation, leading her by the hand onto the floor.

Women changed their costumes four or five times a day, and kept their maids very busy. Brigida did, too, though she drew the line at sweltering in dark silks and bent brimmed bonnets during afternoons at the track, preferring light cotton lawns of pale lime or soft blue.

Coaches and carriages, aflutter with raised parasols, flowed out along the wide-treed streets of Saratoga to the grandstand twenty minutes distant from town. Slade and Brigida went every day, watched every race, checked every card. They endlessly walked the paddocks, almost oblivious to the noise and flying flags, to the liveried outriders and the splendid, colorful equipage of the racers. Slade's growing impatience showed in the hard set of his jaw, in a flickering muscle along the hollow of his cheek, in the dark, sinister intensity of restless, searching eyes.

Brigida did what she could to calm him, but when Lydia Worsley attached herself with apparent permanence to their party, her own nerves, already on edge, began to fray. One night, she mentioned this to Slade.

"We'll be here only a day or two more. Can you put up with her just that long, goddess, show her nothing but smiles?" He gently clipped Brigida's chin with a clenched fist.

"Why does she follow me about? Obviously, we detest each other equally. If she's helping you find your boy, I suppose . . ."

"The race we've come for is day after tomorrow. Root will show; we'll find my son."

It was late after an evening at the casino. Watching Slade move about their rooms, Brigida realized that they had lived more closely the past week than in all the months that had gone before. "A day or two longer," she repeated to herself, unbelieving. She had known him now in private moments of unguarded ease, late, when sleep had almost come, in the early morning before he had steeled himself for the business of the day. She smiled a little, watching him undo his shirt and casually drop it over the arm of a chair, stretch, run a brush through his tousled hair, then glance fleetingly at his image in the glass before donning the dressing gown she had left for him on the edge of the bed.

With a sad presentiment of loneliness, she drifted away to stand on the small balcony outside their sitting room. Silently she cursed the horned moon in a starless sky.

"If you don't wear a bonnet and carry a parasolette you will ruin your complexion," Lydia Worsley said, admiring the long fingernails on her left hand. She and Brigida waited together on the iron bench at the foot of the Clarendon's garden for Slade. Finding herself burdened with the woman, Brigida gazed off toward the distant mountains.

"But I like the sun," she said, yawning.

"People will think you odd even here in Saratoga, which is far from being a center of the true *haute monde*, such as Newport. Newport is civilized, compared with this circus. One must put up with all sorts here, dreadful, vulgar people. I prefer the aristocratic tone at Newport to this commingling of classes." Brigida met a gray reptilian stare when she turned to the woman seated next to her. She felt compelled to disagree.

"Saratoga is a lovely place, very gay and festive. My only complaint is that it's a touch too formal."

"People will be forgiving of your shortcomings, Brigida, for a while, knowing you're a Westerner, but the things you talk about don't help you at all. I hope you don't mind my saying this, but I'm only trying to make it easier for you. After the . . . mistake of our previous meeting, I feel I owe you something. The count convinced me of that." Lydia was now peering at the nails of her other hand and didn't notice Brigida's eyes. Taking silence for acquiescence, she went on lecturing.

"Polite young women never mention politics or business or anything else controversial. Men don't like it; men don't like overly clever women."

"Oh? If that is so, you should be constantly surrounded by admirers, which is not the circumstance." Brigida's tone was honey-sweet. In turn, Lydia fixed her with an icy, venomous look.

"If you could dispatch me to glory with a glance, I'd be gone!" Brigida laughed. "My husband actually prefers clever women, didn't you know that?" Brigida stood. "If you'll excuse me, Lydia, I'm off to find him now. We're invited to Frank Leslie's for tea. Have you ever been? I'm told the house is lovely, very grand for a summer cottage. Miriam Squirer is hostess there these days."

"Miriam adores being rich. She'll prove exceedingly costly to Frank with her taste for Worths and diamonds. He's divorcing for her, did you know? It's all scandalous, of course." Lydia was adjusting a wide gold link bracelet that had become twisted. "Miriam is one of those women who always gets exactly what she wants. Miriam is rather like me in that. There is nothing we won't do to obtain our ends." Lydia smiled a little and began pulling on a glove.

"You'd better change into something more . . . sophisticated, more showy for such company, hadn't you? Your innocent air may be charming at first, but it becomes tiresome."

"More showy?" Brigida echoed, doing a dainty curtsy, then turning full circle. She wore an ecru piqué dress entirely trimmed in ecru lace. The flounced skirt was done all over with embroidered pink May rosebuds touched with pale apple green.

"In her innocent simplicity, Mrs. Hawkes is quite compelling, completely charming, Miss Worsley, you should agree. Hers is that rare beauty that needs no embellishment to enhance the abundant gifts bestowed by nature."

Brigida looked into a pair of watery, pale eyes, and, despite the addition of a full beard, she instantly recognized the speaker.

"Mr. Rand! My husband has been trying for months

with no success at all to contact you in San Francisco about the settlement of my estate. What a coincidence to find you here in the East."

"Not really such a coincidence, my dear. Saratoga is where fashionable people are at present for the waters, you know, very healthful." The man had taken a place on the iron bench and mopped his brow with a pocket handkerchief. "Anyone seriously interested in Thoroughbred racing in America would not miss tomorrow's event for two-year-olds, would they, Miss Worsley?"

"You have some previous acquaintance with Mrs. Hawkes?" Lydia asked the man, getting to her feet and moving to the back of the lacy bench.

"I have indeed," he answered with a weak smile. "I had the great pleasure of a too brief acquaintance with Mrs. Hawkes, Miss Lydon then, in San Francisco. She slipped away before we could become really good friends." He, too, stood and, taking Brigida's hand, brought it to his damp lips. She recalled his hot, heavy hands shaded with dark hair, and the blunt fingers encrusted with jeweled rings. She pulled away, at some pains to hide her distaste.

"Mr. Rand was legal counsel to my father, Lydia. He handled the estate as executor."

"Oh, was he? I didn't know you were a lawyer, Mr. Rand." The woman's normally pallid face now had a chalky quality, and she swayed a little, clutching the bench back.

"There is much you don't know, Miss Worsley." The man turned to Brigida. "You, dear child, appear to have done quite well for yourself, despite your recent impoverishment. How very nice for you, to be well married to a man of such means as Slade Hawkes. Now you will excuse us. Miss Worsley and I have business elsewhere. Do give my assurances to your husband, the captain, that I will seek him out quite soon."

"Do wait, Mr. Rand, Slade will be joining us in a moment, and I wouldn't want to lose you again," Brigida half smiled.

"Have no fear of that, Mrs. Hawkes, but now we must be off." The man gripped Lydia's arm, his blunt fingers digging into her soft flesh below the loose, short sleeve of her summer dress, and Brigida watched Rand guide the woman across the lawn toward the hotel. She hurried off, bursting to tell Slade the news that Bradford Rand was in Saratoga Springs.

"Levi Philips! Why, I thought you'd quite deserted us," Brigida exclaimed in pure delight as she burst into the sitting room to find the Indian sprawled comfortably on a settee, a cigar in one hand, a glass in the other, and Bran on the rug at his feet. The big dog lumbered up and came wagging toward her. "Slade, I must tell you who . . . oh, sorry," she said, noticing the look of indulgent irritation on his face. "I'm interrupting."

"Root's horse was brought into Saratoga this morning," he said, gesturing her to a seat at his side. "Levi's been watching the animal these past days at a farm outside Albany. Now sit and be quiet. Finish," he said to Levi.

"The horse is in good condition but of uncertain temperament, wild. He started out as a promising yearling, then got wild, the trainer told me, a real rowdy, burns out early in a race. I know horses like that," Levi smiled, sipping. "You get nasty with 'em, they get nasty right back. You got to sweet talk 'em out of it. This trainer, he knows it, but his orders have been to push the stallion for this race. He really likes the horse, wants to buy him. The owner says he won't sell. But it seems there's a woman, too, owns a share of the horse, who'd like nothing better."

"Papers on the horse?"

"I didn't see them, Slade," Levi said, nodding his thanks to Brigida who had refilled his glass. "Virginia-bred, the trainer says."

"And the boy?" The question was asked in a controlled voice.

Levi shook his head. "Nothing."

"But we are getting closer to the child, aren't we?" Brigida asked. "This woman . . . if Root doesn't come, we'll have the woman to tell us," she offered hopefully.

"We have her now, have for some time," Slade said. Levi brought his long body to an upright position.

"Lydia!" Brigida became agitated. "And there's a man with her, Slade. It's that Rand, my father's lawyer from San Francisco."

"You saw him?" Slade's eyes were points of blue ice. "Heavy man, thick hands with rings on every finger? The bastard never was your father's executor. The man you've just seen, Brigida, is Blueford Root."

"Root?" Brigida echoed. "He's got a beard now, is the only change since . . . but why is Lydia with him?"

"The stolen shipment of Colts. She and I never stopped searching for them, she for the money . . ."

"And you for Root?"

"Yes, for Root." Slade stood at the mantel fondling Bran's ear. He began pacing, the big dog at his side. "We knew he'd sell, sooner or later. It was Madame Restell who came to Lydia with the news that the guns were on the market and that the Commune was trying to buy them. That was before Alain told us."

"Did Lydia kill that boy from Volet's?"

"There's someone else involved, too, the other buyer, remember? The fact is, Lydia is into something messy and dangerous. For the money, always for the money. She never is satisfied, no matter how much she's got. Hell, I'd always have given her more than even she'd have been able to squander, but it wouldn't have mattered. Am I right, Levi?"

"She wants you, not your money," the Indian answered.

There was a silence as a tall clock counted out the hour.

"We'll go to Leslie's now. In the morning we'll watch the regatta before we go out to the grandstand. I knew Root wouldn't be able to miss this race, I knew it." As Slade's fist struck his palm repeatedly with a full thud, Brigida could imagine Rand's face crumbling with each heavy blow.

By eleven the next morning, Moon's Lake House was filled with summer socialites in full, colorful dress. The day was already fiercely hot, the air thick with choking dust—though water wagons had sprinkled the grounds only shortly before.

The far side of the lake, opposite Moon's verandas and porticos, was crowded with the carts and hay wagons of New England farm families, come over during the night to be sure of a good vantage point from which to watch the boat clubs launch their racing shells.

"Smile, goddess, and stay close." Slade guided Brigida's arm through his. They moved through the festive crowd in Moon's out onto the shore—the heat and glare so intense, even Brigida put up a parasol.

"Lydia took it upon herself to lecture me yesterday, did I tell you, about wearing a bonnet? I haven't seen a glimpse of her yet, or of him, have you, Slade?" She looked eagerly about like a child at a party.

Moon's was draped in bright bunting. Flags fluttered everywhere in the hot wind as they threaded great parterres of red, white, and blue flowers that spelled out the team names and "God Bless America." It was the last regatta of the season, and the mood of the crowd was festive.

"Lydia knows how these games are played. She'll be here." Slade loosed his tie and undid the shirt stud at his throat. "And so will Root. Come on, we'll make ourselves obvious. They'll find us." He directed Brigida toward a small rocky promontory that extended out over the water to where a group of children were undoing high-laced boots and rolling down their stockings.

"Shall I dangle my legs, too? It looks so cool, and it will attract a certain amount of attention." Brigida skipped ahead of Slade, then stopped abruptly. The four or five children were now ranged in a row at the rocky edge.

"Look there." A little girl pointed, her ribboned straw bonnet slipping, falling forward to float like a lily pad on the lake surface. "There's a lady under the water," the child announced with wonder.

Brigida's left hand was at her lips and her eyes were wide when Slade passed her, moving quickly. She was at his side when he dove, and she hurried the children away before turning back to help him pull Lydia Worsley's limp form from the depths of Saratoga Lake. The woman was clothed as Brigida had last seen her the day before, the rich gown now tattered, the heavy dark hair wet and wild, clinging in snaking strands to a bruised and swollen face.

"It's the first time I've ever seen her hair undone," Brigida said softly, studying the distorted features for a moment before turning away. "Slade, she didn't drown, did she?"

He lifted the dead woman's hand in what appeared to Brigida a gesture of sad affection, until she saw him pry something from the clenched fingers. "Keep this," he said, passing her an object that she concealed in a tightly closed fist, just as Lydia had done. "Her skull's been crushed. Tell that to the police when I send them up," Slade said to the staring crowd of farmers who were the first to converge on the promontory.

"She sat just where you are, only yesterday. Why would he kill her?" Brigida asked. "She was working with him."

Levi and Brigida waited for Slade at the iron bench. "Root has been known to kill for pleasure," Levi said, and Brigida shivered in the summer heat, "but I think she crossed him."

"Now it will be more difficult to find Slade's son, won't it? He'll never have a moment's peace until he does, you know. There he is now."

They both turned to watch Slade's progress toward them. His eyes narrowed a little against the midday glare. He had changed from his wet clothes, but his hair was still water-darkened and slicked straight back.

"It will be more difficult to find the boy," Levi said, "if Root was warned off by something Lydia did."

"You should wear your dark spectacles, really," Brigida smiled up as Slade approached. "Do you know who . . ."

"It could have been any number of people. You, goddess, Levi, me—we all had our motives. Alain Manceaux had a better one, I think—Jean-Paul. I just took Alain's papers and watch from Lydia's room, by the way, left there to implicate him, I'm sure. Since she helped your friend Phil lose what was left of his inheritance at Morrisey's casino, Mr. Carpenter isn't above suspicion either. My money's on Root. He's gone. His groom came looking for Levi while I was changing. He'd heard about Lydia, but not until after Root paid him to ship the horse West. I know the destination."

"You'll want this now," Brigida said, holding forward the match safe. The little box was black enamel and silver with a gold plate monogrammed "LW." It was warm from

Brigida's grasp when Slade fingered it.

"I gave this to her a long while ago," he said, pressing a corner of the lid to release it. When he pressed again, a concealed compartment in the base sprang open, and from it he took a thin sheet of flimsy paper, folded carefully many times over. When he had smoothed it flat, the tiny even script that covered the page was just legible. "Read it," he said, handing the sheet to Brigida, then moving off a little distance, hands in his pockets, to look out at the mountains.

"What if there are things I shouldn't . . . private words meant only for you?" Brigida held the document gingerly between her forefinger and thumb.

"I have no concealments from you. Read it."

There was no salutation; the message began abruptly. " 'Before I knew for a certainty I had lost you forever and still thought to win you back to me, I intervened in the sale of the Colts. I have the Commune's gold and Root's guns. I knew Root would come after them. I put it about the right circles that I would deal with him without your interference. Besides the Commune, I had another buyer. Price was no object. I wanted Root to dispose of your wife in exchange for double payment for his goods. Then I was going to deliver the guns and Root, dead, as a gift to you. I know now,' " Brigida's voice faltered a little, but when she looked up at Slade he nodded for her to go on, " 'I know now you will never love me,' " she rushed on. " 'and so I would disengage from the plot while I've a vestige of decency left. I fear Root will not release me, though I have offered him the guns and the gold. He wants you dead, as you know, but I now know he wants

Brigida very much alive. In the likely event something happens to me—I am, after all, playing loose and free with madmen, the other buyer still is pressing for the guns—you should know these things: The Colts are at Lamm's warehouse, where they always have remained, recrated in crockery boxes. The French gold is buried in your Washington Square garden. Bonnie's child is, for the moment at least, in some utopian settlement in Indiana or Ohio. Forgive me.'"

It was raining over the mountains when Brigida finished; a cool breeze was blowing down. "I feel awful," she murmured. "Do you, Slade?"

He took her hand. "Get ready. We're going to Indiana, Levi and I. We'll be taking you part of your way home to San Francisco. We'll leave as soon as you're packed."

Twenty-Three

"I cabled ahead to arrange space for you on a Pullman Palace out of Chicago, Brigida. This day coach that far isn't ideal, but it's the best that could be done on short notice. Pullman would have sent a car to pick us up if we could have waited." Brigida stared out the window at the heat-faded countryside flowing by. She had raised the Venetian blind and was settled deep in plush upholstery.

"I don't mind this," she sighed, feeling with each passing mile her final separation from Slade grow nearer. "We'll be in Chicago by tomorrow afternoon?"

He nodded and took her hand.

The train was jammed, the aisles cluttered with trunks and bonnet boxes and ladies' parasols. Gentlemen didn't have easy passage of the aisles as they made their way to the rear platform for a cigar or a pull on a flask.

At every stop there would be a crushing stampede to the doors, and passengers would swarm to grab and gulp down what sustenance they could before the whistle blew. As the train rocked along again, young boys made laborious progress through the crowded cars selling fruit and nuts and lemonade for the ladies and children, cigars for the men, garish novels, penny dreadfuls, and picture postcards of wild red Indians and mountain peaks.

Brigida purchased something from every boy who passed, building up a good supply of apples and maple sugar candy.

"Expecting to starve?" Levi inquired. Slade had gone for a smoke and the Indian moved over from across the aisle to sit with Brigida.

"I just like to talk with them. They are so serious, they hardly seem like children at all under those dusty caps. It's the braces and round shirt collars, I guess, makes them seem so sweet."

"Some of these train butches make near eighty dollars a month. Engineers get sixty. Don't feel bad for the little imps."

"But I keep thinking of . . ."

"Jude. Slade's son is called Jude, I think. Bonnie said once that would be the name she would want. He is younger than these boys on the trains."

"Will you find him?" Brigida's dark eyes searched Levi's face eagerly. He nodded.

"The village where Bonnie went when she ran off, a man by the name of Robert Owens built it. He came from the West. He had followers in a settlement he called Utopia, a commune with a sawmill on a lake, it was said. We'll find Slade's son there, I think."

Later that night, in a narrow bunk made up from the day coach seats, Brigida stretched out next to Slade.

When he extinguished the oil lamp overhead, they watched the dreamlike, moonlit landscape flow past. Brigida was soon lulled to sleep by the clicking of the wheels and ceaseless rocking as the train moved through dark little towns and farm fields tall in late corn. Slade remained awake, holding her against him, her deep breaths passing through half-parted lips. "Stay with me," he whispered against her brow. Her eyes fluttered open.

In the quieted railroad car they heard only an occasional sigh or half-spoken phrase uttered from the depths of dreams. Slade's hands began to move over the curvings of her soft body curled to his. "Here?" she whispered with a smothered giggle. "Now? Respectable women don't even half undress in such close proximity to strangers."

"Here," he answered. "And yes, now. Because it could be our last time together. It's not meant to be wasted." There was a long, sad, wailing whistle as the train approached a deserted country crossing, and then all was quiet once more.

"A man come and took 'im just yesterday. He been with me near two years, Jude, such a proudling. I don't know where that come from, his high-blown way."

George Pullman had located Robert Owens's daughter Ellen Coles at a settlement south of Chicago and had put his carriage at Slade's disposal. The plain, large-boned woman stood now in the doorway of a sodded log house and wiped rough hands on a threadbare apron. A small boy in ragged pants secured by homemade knitted suspenders clung to her knees, then moved off to sit on a rusting iron pot that lay overturned in the muddy dooryard.

"My father left the child here for our carin'. We take in all that's needful; it is part of our belief. T'ain't easy, but we manage. We live like one family here. We share the land, the work, whatever we have. It has been tried in other places. It has not often worked out real good." The woman looked anxiously from one to the other of the stony faces before her. "Can I get you a dipper of water? It's been a awful dry, hot summer, you know, it's been lean times. I've got nothin' else to offer, but the water is cold from the well, and you are lookin' terrible warm, ma'am." Her hand lifted tentatively to touch the lace collar of Brigida's dress.

"But why did you let him go, Mrs. Coles? How could you?" Brigida turned away.

"Don't, Brigida," Slade ordered as the woman's worn, worried face took on a pained expression.

"I couldn't help it. The man knew the child's name and where he come from, even the mother's name. He told me he was a relative. He come in a carriage like you folks and dressed like a gentleman, even if there was somethin' odd in his eyes, I said so to myself, and my oldest boy saw it, too. But I couldn't prevent him takin' Jude, could I? I felt it was wrong, and now you tell me this here is the boy's own natural father. No doubt of it. One look is all anyone would need to know that for a truth, and the poor little lad thinkin' himself a orphan and not even knowin' his family name." Ellen Coles's agitation increased as she talked, and now tears stood in her distraught eyes as she wrung her big hands helplessly.

"You did all you could have, Mrs. Coles; don't blame yourself for anything," Slade said. "Did the man give you any idea of where he would take the boy?"

"To the western ocean. On a train. It was the steam engine tempted the child, and the sea voyage after, got 'im all excited. You know the way little ones are. Before Jude heard tell about the train, he was skittish of going, clung to my skirts, which ain't a'tall like him. This was his home, you see, the only one he knew. He didn't remember much about before he come to us, or he didn't feel like sayin'. He was real quiet at first and turned inward-like, but he came round. Well, I gave the little chap a penny for his pocket, and off he went. I wish I could help you more, I do so wish it."

Brigida took the woman's hand. "My husband will never be able to repay you for your kindness to Jude, Mrs. Coles," she said. "Thank you."

The woman smiled for the first time since her visitors had come, and years seemed to fall from her weary face. "I know you will find that child, ma'am, I feel it, just like I know by the look of you you'll be a fine mother to 'im and love 'im like he was your own. Now you tell Jude we miss him, hear? Don't forget. Promise?"

As they stood in the cabin dooryard, the hot red ball of the sun hung suspended among reddened clouds that billowed in high mounds and streaked across the wide prairie sky. The evening spread slowly to the west over a vast, endless flatness that seemed to go on forever.

*　　　*　　　*

"There is a telegrapher with his own box relay on every train out. They can hook in and be in contact with my office here in Chicago in minutes. Every station-master between here and California has Root's description, and the boy's." George Pullman had come to the station to see Slade and Brigida off. "I still would prefer to get you a private car, if you and the lady will wait overnight, Captain," Pullman offered. He was a round-faced, boyish-looking man of fastidious appearance. His manner was reserved, formal, almost shy.

"We won't wait, but thanks for the offer, sir." Slade's restless eyes studied the figures passing outside along the length of the train.

"All eight cars of this train are Pullman made, Mrs. Hawkes. You will be treated like royalty all the way, my boys have been told."

"It is a rolling palace, as we've heard, Mr. Pullman," Brigida said, fanning herself with a wide-brimmed straw hat while she studied the marquetry, inlaid woods, and gilded glass that surrounded her.

"We are introducing elegance to the prairie, Mrs. Hawkes, and a taste for good food and fine wine. We have already convinced some of the rich stockmen to remove their boots before retiring."

"Take off their boots? You mean they didn't . . . don't?" Brigida laughed, with a little spice of mischief in her dark eyes. "I think you're a jollyer, Mr. Pullman." He blushed.

"I'd never be that, Mrs. Hawkes," he answered quickly. "Most of them still wear boots to bed, they are that rough and ready, but don't worry. As a rule, they only shoot their friends and acquaintances," Pullman jested shyly.

"By the way, Captain, where is your man Philips? Indians are not allowed aboard usually, except with the baggage, though some of the chiefs further West ride the immigrant trains. I've taken care of it for your Indian this time."

"Damn good of you," Slade said coolly. "He'll be right along. Show us your wares before the whistle blows."

"You are riding the best rolling stock there is. This train makes it coast to coast in eight days. It's a special express, of course; it won't get shunted off on any sidings like some of the others," Pullman said with obvious pride.

"Eight? It took me one hundred and eighteen days round the Horn," Brigida marveled, "though it was certainly a lot cooler that way."

"This heat can't last forever, nor the dry spell," Pullman said. "I can't recall when it rained last."

They had come to a hotel car, where the floor was covered in rich Brussels carpet and the furnishings and carpentry were of inlaid and filigreed black walnut. Purple velvet portieres and crystal chandeliers graced the social areas and oil lamps lit the private sleeping cabins, which were hung with silk curtains and decorated with bevel-edged French mirrors and frosted etched transoms.

"I never cut fares as some of my competitors do, but I never cut services, either," Pullman pronounced. "Americans, I firmly believe, will always be willing to pay for quality."

The train was beginning to fill, and there was a growing excitement of departure in the air as passengers boarded, trailed by porters carting mountains of luggage.

"There is hot and cold running water and flushers." Pullman demonstrated hurriedly while Brigida peered out the window of their cabin. "There'll be daily papers, local ones, in the library forward; there's a barber for Slade, always a game of cards—euchre, whist—running in the smoker, and for the ladies," he turned to Brigida, "a hairdresser at your disposal."

"Oh, yes! Ann Overton told me, Slade, about a woman who actually had her hair crimped going along at forty miles an hour, and I hardly believed her. Oh, listen, the conductors are calling now. Where is Levi?"

She glanced anxiously out of the window again and answered her own question. "There!" she pointed.

The Indian, in his neat black suit, was making his way through the crowd along the length of the train, glancing up at a window now and again. He saw Brigida and his face lit, though he didn't actually smile. He climbed aboard at the next stair.

"I thought you were going to miss the train, Mr. Philips. Where were you?" Brigida demanded.

"Doing a little something for Mrs. Coles. This looks fine," he said, nodding to George Pullman.

"Pleased you are impressed, Mr. Philips," Pullman answered stiffly. "Well, I'll be leaving you now," he said, shaking Slade's hand. "I'll be in contact; we'll find your boy, I'm confident of it."

"I so hope you're right, Mr. Pullman," Brigida said, extending a small, white-gloved hand. "There's such a vast space out there. One man and a little boy . . . they could . . . disappear; it could take three lifetimes to find them, I think."

"Don't worry, Mrs. Hawkes. The smallest things become conspicuous in big empty spaces. We are watching every town, every water tower, every livery stable and boardinghouse along the line. This man Root has only had a half day's lead on you. Don't worry, Mrs. Hawkes; try to enjoy your journey. It is the most magnificent country in the world you'll be passing through. Slade, dinner's on me tonight. Allow yourselves ample time; the wine list just might be better than Lorenzo Delmonico's. The food is easily as good. Mountain brook trout à la Normandie, leg of mutton with caper sauce, quail on toast, buffalo tongue, braised bear in port wine, antelope in sauce Bigarde, grouse in Madeira, teal duck à la royale, even escalloped oysters, escalloped Long Island oysters. Good luck. See all of you and the boy on the return."

"I hope you're right, Mr. Pullman." Slade darted a glance at Brigida. "I hope you're right."

The flatness of Illinois disappeared behind the racing train that moved out onto the immensity of the western plains where the ceaseless wind agitated tumbleweed and prairie flowers and set sweeping endless grassland undulating—wild and beautiful as the sea. Grass fires sent smoke swirling about the train, crickets swarmed as darkly as biblical plagues. Farther West, thunderheads ominously clouded the sky, turning noon dark as midnight. Wind whistled, hail rattled maddeningly loud against the steel cars, and the travelers watched tornados twist off in the distance.

The sound of steel wheels on steel rails and the long, hollow calling of the whistle came, after the first day and night, to define the whole world and, needing human warmth amidst the close swirl of wild nature all about them, passengers gathered in the evenings after dinner. A pretty Boston matron settled at the organ in one of the hotel cars to play and sing a selection of hymns and popular tunes. While the music echoed out across the empty prairie night and the train sped on through the darkness, Brigida sat close to Slade and listened, sighing, to sad songs. "Was My Brother In The Battle?" with its desperate hopes, "Darling Nellie Gray," with the moon climbing the mountains while angels cleared Nellie's way to heaven. Most touching of all was "Those Wedding Bells Shall Not Ring Out."

". . . She shall not break her vow to me,
She's mine through all eternity,
She's mine 'til death shall set her free. . . ."

Every time she heard it, Brigida would flee to the cabin to hide the tears that swam in her dark eyes.

From every water tower, every station and town, Slade's messages went out on lengthening telegraph lines to Chicago, but the replies from Pullman that waited at the next stop offered nothing. Slade grew restless, and

Brigida became more fearful for the child's safety. Only Levi didn't seem to doubt, and only his confidence kept his companions hopeful.

After the express moved out of Omaha, the roadbeds became more uneven than before. Sometimes the train moved tediously along at barely ten miles an hour; at other times it flew at thirty-five. Later, in the far distance, the towering mountains seemed almost sinister in the wild prairie sunset. They crossed the Wyoming barrens in the night. Moonlit sagebrush was all there was to see, as Brigida lay awake watching.

She was still wide-eyed at dawn. She touched Slade's shoulder, and he came awake with a questioning look, then reached to enwrap her in his arms, waiting for her to speak. That was best, he had learned, when she was troubled.

"How do you know we haven't passed them?" she asked.

"I know Root's heading for San Francisco. That's where the horse is being delivered. If we don't find Root there . . . well, then we might . . . I might have to chase him farther."

"But they could be out in some wilderness living on the land, hiding. How do you know they aren't?" Brigida had risen and was trying to pace the tiny space between the bunk and the door, pivoting every second step.

"Root is a helpless greenhorn. He wouldn't last two nights in this country. He's on a train ahead of us or, more likely, one just behind that was pulled off to let us pass. I expect to be there to greet him when he steps down in Sacramento."

"I'm glad you're so damn sure of yourself, as usual," Brigida almost growled. "Once we get to San Francisco, I'll have more to do, you know, than continue on this bootless quest of yours."

The closer they got to their journey's end, the more changeable Brigida became.

"You promised to help me find my son, but if you want to quit on me now, I won't stop you. When we reach San Francisco, I'll say goodbye," Slade blandly lied, "if that's what you want." He had mounded pillows behind him and leaned casually back, smiling a little, his wide shoulders dark against the white linen, to watch her with unreadable blue eyes. He had decided not to ask her again to stay with him, not even to act as if he much cared. It was the only possible way to break down her resistance, he had decided.

Brigida continued to pace like a caged cat, his indifference galling her to anger and sad regret.

"What are you smiling about?" she whirled on him. "You're chasing across the country after a madman who's got your son who you've never even seen with a wife who's leaving you first chance she gets. What's that to smile at?"

"Not much, I admit, goddess, but if there's one thing I've learned from you, it's to try and see the bright side. I've still got you to play with for a few days more at least, haven't I?"

"Yes, and you damn well better make the most of

that!" she said, flinging herself into his arms.

Humming quietly and putting a finishing touch to her hair before going to the dining car for breakfast, Brigida peered into the glass while Slade leaned impatiently at the door, trying to hurry her along. "You're beautiful, as always, pet. Every man on this train envies my nights in this cabin with you, but I need to stretch my legs. Come on, we're late every morning. The other passengers are ready for the midday meal before we start breakfast."

"Sinful, isn't it," Brigida laughed. "Now I am ready. It isn't my fault you don't let me out of bed before . . . why are we stopping?" She tucked a handkerchief into her sleeve, and Slade pulled open the door.

"Loose rail, Captain," the porter explained. "You all go along to your breakfast. I'll have your stateroom done up 'fore you're done eatin'."

"Where are we?" Slade asked.

"Wasatch, just over the Wyoming border in the mountains of Utah," the porter said. "Oh, Captain, your man says he done got off to see about the telegraph. You'll be findin' him at the stationhouse."

"Zulu train out there, he says," Levi greeted Slade and Brigida as they entered the small railroad shack.

"What? What does that mean?" Brigida asked the telegrapher as his machine began to click.

"Lady, that's foreigners and orphans, everyone knows

507

that. They been pulled off the track for hours waitin' for your train to pass. Happens all a'the time. They shippin' them people out here just like they move cattle East. Ain't you seen the handbills? There's a old one tacked over there."

While Slade waited for the man to decode a message from Pullman, Brigida went to read a tattered yellow poster.

> To the West. Land of the Free.
> Emigrants to the West.
> Leave for Lincoln Nebraska and West
> Wednesday, June 28, 1871
> Workers, Farmers, Craftsmen ONLY
> NO clerks, lawyers, professors wanted.

"The railroads own the land, millions of acres all across the country," Slade explained, showing Brigida out of the hot little stationhouse to stand in the shade of its overhang with other passengers who were grumbling at the delay. "They've sent hundreds of recruiters to Europe to bring in settlers. Whole colonies of people are being brought here to farm the land. They will plant and raise up crops and one day they'll have a surplus to sell. And they'll have to sell where the people are, back East. They'll ship by rail, of course."

Brigida took Slade's arm and they walked across the dusty space toward the halted express to watch the repair work on the loosed rails with Levi and Bran. "But why the orphan trains?" she asked, troubled.

"Cheap farmhands," Slade said.

"Captain Hawkes! Hey, Captain," the telegraph operator shouted. "Got somethin' about to come in for you. I'll write it out when I'm done receivin'," the man said.

Levi waited outside with Brigida, who was too nervous to watch the slow decoding, and when Slade came out to crush a sheet of paper into her hand, his face was dark and his eyes narrowed slits of fury.

"Man of B. Root description reported seen at St. Lou with B. Hogan. No Child. Repeat, No Child. Keep looking. GP."

"I said we could have passed them! Oh, Slade, I'm so sorry. Please, Levi, say something to him," she appealed. "Who is B. Hogan? Perhaps he will know about . . ."

"Hogan?" Slade spat with contempt. "Hogan's 'the wickedest man in the world,' self-described. He ran French Kate's place in Pit Hole. They branched out, he and Kate, had a chain of Hogan's Lager Beer Parlors and Sporting Houses, gymnasiums, he called them, where, I quote, 'both sexes enjoy wholesome exercise using the body in such a way as to bring all the muscles into play,' end quote."

"Perhaps he'd help us," Brigida said. "He may know something about Jude and we could . . ."

"Hogan help us?" Slade looked at her coldly. "What do you mean 'us'? You're getting out." His eyes were raging. He stuck a cigar in his teeth, then turned away and began patting his pockets for his match safe.

"Yes, I am getting out. Now, if you're so ready to be rid of me!" In tears, Brigida rushed away to climb a little rise above the station, where she sank into the tall grass and, tightly clasping her legs, rested her forehead on her knees. Bran had followed her and he nuzzled her cheek now and again until she looked up tearily and patted his head.

"Nothing is coming round right, old Bran; everything is terrible, and soon I won't even have you to talk to, will I?" She sniffed, and taking the handkerchief from her cuff, patted her eyes and looked about.

On a siding waiting for the Pullman Special to pass, the three-car Zulu train sat baking in the sun. Weary-looking men in soiled shirts and shabby, wrinkled suits stood about in small groups, infrequently exchanging words in a language Brigida didn't recognize or begin to understand at all.

"He's so anxious to be rid of me, I'll train West with them and not trouble him longer," Brigida told the dog, who looked at her dolefully. She stood and moved with her usual unself-conscious grace toward the group of men, who regarded her with some alarm as she approached the door of the first car. When she placed a foot on the bottom rung of the ladder a man rushed forward to stop her.

"Not go in, lady," he said in some alarm in heavily accented English. "Too hot for lady."

"Don't be silly. Your women are in there, aren't they? Besides, I'm looking for someone. I'm looking for a boy," Brigida said to an uncomprehending stare. When the man moved again to stop her, Bran growled low in his throat.

"Boy, child, *kinder, petit garcon?* Please, let me look."

With a fearful glance at the huge dog and a quick shrug, the man pushed his hat to the back of his head.

"So," he said, stepping aside.

Bare wooden bunks and slatted benches bolted to the dirty wooden floor were packed with women and children, their flushed faces wet with sweat, tired eyes darkly circled as they leaned at all angles against one another, not awake, but not really sleeping either. Appalled by the contrast with the elegant accommodations she had just left, Brigida watched a thin young woman propped near the door. She was trying to take advantage of the hot breeze that gusted past as she nursed her baby.

"But why don't you go out?" Brigida asked, gesturing. "Cooler, much cooler out."

"Train leave us," the girl said.

"No, no. Didn't anyone tell you? It will be a long time, hours before the track is replaced.

"Train leave us," the girl insisted, pushing a lank band of hair off her forehead.

Her eyes grew better adjusted to the dimness, and Brigida looked about again. Children lay curled sleeping everywhere—on the floor, in corners, and near the pot-bellied stove meant to provide heat, if any coal or wood was supplied, when the train crossed the cold, high mountains. At the moment the sweltering air was fetid.

"I'm looking for a boy," Brigida said loudly, gesturing in an effort to make someone understand. "A little boy, about six years, blond, blue eyes?"

"Blond? Flax like you?" the woman asked. "So fair?"

"I don't . . . a little darker perhaps . . . amber and gold like honey, and eyes blue as larkspur," Brigida said softly. She knelt to look into the girl's thin face. "Jude.

He's called Jude," she whispered as the woman shifted the baby to her other breast and glanced at a dirty bundle curled in a corner.

"Jude, ah! But not fair. Hair dark like night. Jude, Jude, up," she called.

There was a muffled yawn, a low curse, then a ragged bundle took the form of a child, who sat up, rubbing his eyes.

After another stretch, the figure turned toward the woman with a wide grin, and Brigida's heart seemed to stop, as azure eyes, clear as summer skies, looked into hers and widened with surprise.

"Yeah, what you want Molly, wakin' me early. I ain't had half a hour yet to rest," he said to the girl while Brigida stood transfixed by the upturned dirty little face. The features were chiseled—cheekbones high, nose narrow and straight—and though a baby roundness softened the jaw and chin, it was Slade she saw in that face, beyond any doubt, Slade's face beneath a tangle of hair blue-black as midnight.

"Stand. Pretty lady looks for Jude." The girl buttoned her blouse while the contented baby, smacking its lips, dozed in her arms. The boy scrambled to his feet.

"No lady like this would come lookin' for me, Molly," he said, then waited to see what would happen next.

"Will you come with me now, Jude? There's someone who would like to see you," Brigida requested with her most dazzling smile.

"Yeah? Who?" the child asked distrustfully. "I ain't going."

"But why not?" Brigida countered with some surprise.

"Last time, I went off with some lackwit who said he was my uncle. Now I got to be careful. He's lookin' for me, I know. He was going to sell me to someone name of Hogan, I heard him say, so I run off, and Molly taken me along with her and the baby. Molly been nice. I don't see why I should leave her like I done Mrs. Coles. I ain't coming." The child had jammed his fists into the pockets of his patched overalls, and with apparent disinterest leaned casually against the iron stove in a manner Brigida found all too familiar.

"Jude Hawkes, you come with me this very instant!" She stepped toward the boy, her manner pleasantly menacing. "Your father is waiting, and don't you say ain't again, understand?"

"Jude . . . Hawkes?" the boy repeated almost dreamily, and then his composure gave way to a conflicting rush of emotions that passed quickly over his expressive little face.

"I ain't got a father, nor a mother neither, and you've no call to be giving orders to me." His hands were clenched in small, tight fists at his sides, his cheeks flamed, and his chest rose and fell faster. "It ain't kind of you to be funnin' with me," he said imploringly. The bright blue eyes grew dark, then softened, then glistened with a sparkle of tears. He kicked furiously at the pot-bellied stove and abruptly sat down to cry in earnest over his paining toe.

"I'm sorry, oh Jude, really, I am. I should have given you some warning." Brigida rushed forward. The drowsing figures about them stirred to full wakefulness when she dropped to her knees and folded the weeping

513

child in her arms. "It is true, really it is. Just come look for yourself. I'll bring you right back here to Molly, I swear, if you don't find what I promise. Here, wipe your eyes. You don't want to look like a crybaby, do you, when you meet your father?" Brigida handed Jude her lace handkerchief, and he struck at his grimy, tear-streaked cheeks.

"I don't never cry, it's only a cinder in my eye," Jude said, sniffling, and wiping his nose with the back of his hand.

Brigida dampened the handkerchief and scrubbed at the child's dirty cheeks. "That's better. Come now? Please?" She held out her hand. Jude put his small one in it.

Slade's back was to them as Brigida and Jude came hand in hand along the track toward the small station where he and Levi stood talking. The Indian saw the two figures advancing and began to shake his head in disbelief before his somber features cracked into a slow, spreading smile. Slade didn't turn.

"You don't ever look at anyone that way, man, except my wife. What's she done now?" he asked. Stubbornly, he refused to follow Levi's gaze. "She's just coming to get her things, is all; you'd best get used to it."

"You won't believe it, you won't believe this," Levi said, starting forward, his smile widening, before he broke into a full, wild, triumphant laugh that made Slade, too curious to resist, slowly turn.

He stood stock still as Levi started into a long, loping trot, then went to his knees to grasp the child's shoulders in his massive hands while Brigida danced about, her dress stained, her hair loose and floating in the hot wind, her beautiful face radiant.

Slade saw Levi gesture toward him and watched the child's eyes follow. Seeing Slade, the boy grasped Brigida's hand to pull her along until the two stood looking up into Slade's grin, the little boy grinning back, no one saying a word, not knowing how, not needing to. Slade ruffled the dark head once, then, laughing, he lifted the small figure in one arm and passed the other about Brigida, whispering to her, "I love you, Brigida, I really love you, you know."

Before the Pullman Special pulled, hooting and hissing, out of Wasatch, the three-car train of immigrants and orphans had been provisioned with the best that could be found or hunted or bought for miles around—buffalo steaks and antelope, sweet potatoes and new picked corn, fried eggs and chicken stew, hominy, iced milk, cornbread and coffee all prepared by George Pullman's chefs, spread on linen-covered trestle tables under the Utah sky. Brigida saw that food and blankets and wood were placed in each car before long farewells were made, and she left Slade's address with Molly, just in case the girl needed for anything, ever.

Twenty=Four

"Jude will stay with me and Bran across the hall," Levi announced after the party had checked into the Occidental Hotel in San Francisco. "I've the space for him. You two have business, don't you?" Slade and Brigida both looked at him coldly. The awkward silence was broken by Jude.

"I'll go with you if you tell me about Silver Hill again," he said to Levi, "and about John Tabor, the whaling man . . . John Tabor's ride on the whale with Neptune of the briny deep. Will you?" He pulled at Levi's hand, looking up.

"Again?" Levi pushed his hat back and scowled.

"Again," Jude said, not at all intimidated.

"If you take a tub, I'll tell you again."

"Mrs. Coles said it was bad to get wet all over." The little boy stood stubbornly with hands on his hips.

"Jude, that's only in the winter in a draughty cabin on some windy plain," Brigida said. "Even Mrs. Coles would love to wash all over in a big warm tub like the ones here. Now, be a good boy. Tomorrow we'll get you some proper

517

clothes and I'll take you to Cliff House to see the sea lions."

"Proper clothes? These are proper clothes, ain't they, Levi?" Jude examined his round-collared shirt and faded pants held by someone's cut-down braces. "What sea lions?"

"The sea lions that bray and snuff and snort like this!" Brigida gathered the child up in a rush, swinging him about, then nuzzled against his neck, tickling him until he laughed wildly. She let him loose. "Then they bake in the sun until they get so hot they need a dip. After we see that, I'll show you where I used to live."

"And then will we go home to Silver Hill, Brigida?" Jude asked, following Levi toward the door.

"Yes, then your father will take you home to Silver Hill," she said.

When Slade crossed the room to pick up the child, Brigida studied the matched profiles of father and son— small dark head against the other's tawny hair. An expression of wonder came into Slade's face as he looked at the boy. With sadness, she regretted that this child Slade cherished so would not be hers to love, too.

"I've business in San Francisco," Slade said. "We'll leave here when I'm damn good and ready, understand? Now go on and close the door after you."

The little boy scurried after Levi.

"Brigida, you listen to what . . . what is it now?" Slade roared at the door.

It opened again and a robust man with curly gray hair, a full, bushy gray mustache and gracefully fluttering necktie advanced on Slade with an outstretched hand.

"Slade Hawkes, by God, it is good to lay my eyes on you again, you wild devil, after all this time! How the hell are you, boy, since . . . ? Oh, beg pardon ma'am, my language isn't suitable, I know, for a lady's company, but I haven't seen the captain here in a lot of years. You, of course, are Brigida Lydon—Mrs. Hawkes—I take it?"

"Mrs. Hawkes, yes and your enthusiasm, sir, doesn't surprise me at all. My husband never lacks for friends, no matter where he goes, Mr. . . . ?"

"Bruff, Anson Bruff, Brigida," Slade said, warmly shaking the man's hand. "He practices at law from time to time when he's not looking after my western interests. Anson, my wife."

"A pleasure, ma'am," Bruff said with a smile—his brown eyes twinkling. "California ladies, you know, Slade, enjoy a reputation for rare beauty and charm. There's something special about them, a certain ease . . . graceful bearing . . . a self-possession. No one could mistake Mrs. Hawkes for anything but a San Francisco girl. Looking at you, ma'am, no one would doubt the truth of what I say."

"Don't ogle my girl, Bruff," Slade laughed. "Don't try your silver tongue on this lady, or it's me you'll answer to—not some stockbroker in Philadelphia, too busy counting his money to notice you making free with his young wife."

"Don't believe a word he says, ma'am. The man's a natural liar, though he's the best spy the Union had, I'll admit. Talk about making free with other men's wives— the last time we were together, in Philadelphia it was, during the war . . ."

"Whiskey, Bruff?" Slade interrupted. "Ring for the attendant, please, Brigida. We'll want a bottle of their best whiskey for my so-called friend here, the usual for me."

"I'll just go along to find the bellman. That will give you two a chance to talk over the good old days quite privately," Brigida sniffed. Flinging back a curl, she left the room.

"So, you old law merchant," she heard Slade saying as she closed the door behind her, "tell me what you've found out."

She moved away down the corridor, and when she had given the order for drinks, she tapped at Levi's door.

"Where's Jude?" she asked brusquely when, barefooted and in shirt sleeves, he admitted her.

"Tubbing. In there," the Indian gestured. "What brings you?"

"Nothing. Well, something. I want to say goodbye to you now. I'll be gone in the morning."

Levi took a tailor-made cigarette from a pack, struck a light and inhaled deeply before he spoke. "I'll get Jude."

"No, no, don't! I couldn't . . . you'll tell him, after I've gone."

"You're not just a fool, you're a coward, deserting a poor motherless waif." he dropped into a chair and slid down, hunching his shoulders. "Why are you leaving? I don't understand. You love Slade. You came East because you did. I know it."

"You look exhausted." Brigida studied Levi's angular face. There were dark circles beneath his eyes and the lines on his leather skin seemed more deeply etched.

"I don't rest easy on a train," he said. "Trains make my belly heave. Don't laugh. I'd take two years at sea to two days on the iron road. Why are you leaving us?"

"Why? You should know, you were the one who told me once that nothing is a challenge to Slade, that no victory really satisfies him. I'm going to be the exception; I'm leaving . . . before he's had a chance to tire of me."

"You are lying," the Indian said. "Slade won't tire of you in less than a century. You fill every corner of his life now. You took him home, to Silver Hill. You are punishing yourself for the accident at the mill. He forgave you long ago."

"You know about Jerusha Hawkes, don't you Levi? Burned for a witch with a curse on her lips for all who came after to try and make a life at Silver Hill. Sari told me."

"Well? You don't abide such thoughts."

"I know, but what else could have . . . Levi, I made a pact . . . I promised, I swore beneath the moon . . ." Brigida threw herself into a chair and buried her face in her hands. ". . . if his eyes . . . if he could see again, I swore I'd go away and never come back—ever. If I don't keep the vow, something terrible will happen, I know, I feel it. I called up the devil and the devil will always have his due." She rose in suppressed agitation to sit against the sofa arm, her back to Levi, not able to meet his eyes. "Now do you understand?" she barely whispered.

"Is that all?" she was amazed to hear the Indian ask. A smoke ring floated above her to the high ceiling, and she turned to face him. "And you were the one who disbelieved in luck and fate. Listen," he went on, "don't be a damn fool. You've made a bad bargain. You can't be called in the light of day on a terrible promise given in dark, desperate hours. No one knows more about dealing with the devil than I do, Mrs. Hawkes. Martha taught me. She's the expert. I'll take him on for you. I'll take over your debt. We'll get this figured out together, if it really worries you. Just do the things I tell you. While I'm thinking on this problem, you do exactly what I tell you, for luck. Look at the new moon tonight over your right shoulder and curtsy to it three times. Get out of bed tomorrow on the same side you got in. Be sure to hang an acron at your window to keep the lightning away and throw a pinch of salt in the fire. You know, what to do. Martha taught you, too. Didn't she?"

Brigida nodded like an obedient child. "She told me fringe keeps off the evil eye. Oh, Levi, are you laughing at me?" she asked shakily.

"I would never laugh at you," he smiled. "None of us may ever laugh again if you leave us now. Brigida, you must not turn away from love. You must not waste happiness. To do that is worse than breaking a promise wrenched from you by . . . by mind demons, when you were too weak to resist them. Brigida, do you know that all the treasures wasted on the earth—all misspent time, all broken vows, and fruitless tears—find their way to the nimbus of the moon? Do you know that?" Brigida shook her head no. "If you break your love vow there'll be bitter tears, there'll be a gauze about the moon for a long while. We may never see it shine clear again." He took her hand. "This will be our secret. We will fix it, and put

Jerusha to rest forever. Now go back to your husband and let me and the child rest. Brigida?"

"What now?" She looked up into Levi's eyes.

"Did you ever read your initials in a spider web? If you did, that would give you luck to last forever. All dark deals would be off."

"But I never did."

"Well, then wear your fringed Russian cape with the scarlet ribbons and the Zodiac necklace Elizabeth gave you."

"Yes, I will. Levi . . . Levi, do you think I'm foolish for having these thoughts? I feel such a child, but I was really afraid, until now."

"I've always thought you a lady of uncommon good sense. Everyone has fear, a dark magic buried deep. Don't ever believe otherwise, no matter who denies it. Go now."

"But what if I've lost him, being so hard when he offered all I ever wanted, said all the words I'd have him speak? Oh, Levi, what if I've thrown it all away, wasted it?" She stood irresolute, the back of her hand to her lips. "I'll go to him now, and if he doesn't want me . . . well, at least once I will have said 'I love you.' Levi, I love you, too."

"I've news for you, Brigida," Slade greeted her when she burst into his rooms in a rush and flurry of silk.

"No, wait, I must tell you first. I . . . oh, Mr. Bruff."

"Sit down, Brigida," Slade said. "It's Anson, actually, who has news for you. Tell her, Anson, will you?" Seeing a dark, fatal cast in Slade's eye and the muscles in his jaw flex repeatedly, she looked to Anson Bruff with apprehension. It is too late, she thought, something terrible already . . . Levi can't help and . . ."

"Blueford Root, or Bradford Rand, whichever you like, swindled you out of your fortune, Mrs. Hawkes," Bruff announced.

"But I already know that," Brigida answered impatiently, looking inquiringly at Slade. "When I stopped at Boston I learned that . . ."

"Be still for once in your life and listen," Slade shrugged.

"I got some of it back for you," Bruff went on. "The deed to your house and some mining shares, worth a lot. They were in a bank vault Root couldn't locate. I'm sorry, ma'am, I couldn't find your horses or the jewelry. I tried, because Slade wrote saying how much they meant to you. Root sold what he could for cash to gamble in stock on California Street. He failed. He lost it all. Every little housemaid in this city is speculating her month's wages there now, but it's mostly the brokers who are making money. Whoever bought your stock originally, ma'am, did real well. You are now a very wealthy young woman in your own right. Well, say something, Mrs. Hawkes. It's not every day . . ."

Brigida glanced repeatedly at Slade, who was silent, smoking, an arctic coldness in his eyes.

"I'm sorry, Mr. Bruff, it's just that I wanted to tell Slade something. But it can wait. Thank you for your trouble. What has happened to Root, do you know?" she asked.

"The word is he's back in San Francisco, came over the mountains on the same train you folks did. He hasn't been seen in town, but we're looking."

"He couldn't have been on our train, could he Slade?" Brigida was appalled. "Then he knows we found Jude."

"He could have been, if he never left his cabin. Don't worry, Brigida, Levi and I will take good care of the boy." Slade crushed out his cigar and refilled the glasses, putting a small amount of whiskey in a tumbler for her. "Congratulations, madame. Now I've a beautiful and wealthy wife." He showed her a bitter, one-sided smile.

Trying to ignore him, she raised her glass to the lawyer. "Thank you again, Mr. Bruff. I was dreadfully stupid, wasn't I, to have let that swindler gull me as he did?"

"Root has bilked a lot of folks more worldly-wise than you. So don't feel too bad, you were young and inexperienced. His specialty, by the way, is bereaved widows and orphans of seamen. The cur's got no real sand in him. He's a coward. We'll get him." Bruff began gathering up his papers and placing them with meticulous care in a smart leather case.

"Here is the deed to your house, ma'am. The place is bare as a picked bone, but it's there for you if you want it. I'll be going now . . . leave you two to discuss your good fortune, but I'll be back to take you to dinner. Slade hasn't spent much time in San Francisco; you and I will have to show him around. You'll love this town, Slade. It really lights up at night like a fine jewel. There are the usual birds of prey and passage, of course. It's a city full of fortune hunters and professional pioneers who date the Creation from the gold strike at Sutter's in forty-nine." Bruff savored the last drop of whiskey in his glass.

"Maison Dorée at nine. Best restaurant in town."

Left alone, Brigida and Slade sat at opposite ends of a long divan, he grimly smoking, she starchy with growing agitation at his coldness. She turned to him after a while, her heart beating wildly, but before a syllable could pass her lips, he stood, and pressed the deed to the house into her hands.

"Now you've got your comfortable fortune almost intact, you'll not be needing me. Feel free to leave whenever you wish," he said with remorseless irony.

"Now I'm a woman of some means, you're afraid of me, I think. Now you've got the son you want and Elizabeth's inheritance is secured, you'll not be needing me, will you?" she exploded.

"But I will, Brigida, be needing you. I do need you," he answered. "I love you, you see."

"Oh, really? Do you indeed? How much do you love me, and for how long will you love me, do you suppose?" She was trying to keep her tone indifferent.

"I've told you before—there's no measure to it, a lifetime won't be long enough. I waited so long for you, Brigida, I'll love you forever." Slade slid into a chair, trying to fathom her true feelings. When Brigida began to walk the floor, he eyed her with heart-swelling tenderness. Her determined little chin quivered, and her eyes were bright. "What is it?" he asked. "Tell me."

"What is it?" she parroted incredulously, with a catch in her throat. She rounded on him like a fury, eyes flashing gold. "You dismiss me as though I were some . . . some paramour you've wearied of, and in the next breath you think to wrench my heart with protestations of endless love. How can you?" she demanded, but she wouldn't hear his answer. "You still don't know me after all these months, if you think I came to you for . . . for your money. I traveled halfway round the world to you, Slade Hawkes, when I could have had my pick of husbands—rich husbands—right here in San Francisco! And never mind that, I could have taken care of my own self quite well, thanks, if I'd chosen to. No, no, don't dare to interrupt me, damn you!" She brandished a small fist when Slade stood and started toward her. "No, no, I've not finished. I've not yet made you understand. I've always been provided for. Mother had property in Boston. I learned that before I ever reached Silver Hill. I didn't marry you for wealth or social position or power or . . . heirs. None of that mattered to me . . . because I loved you always." Brigida said the last very slowly, emphasizing each word separately. "But you!" she glowered. "You sent for me only because your mother wished it, and you deigned to treat me as one of your concubines, no better, coming to me reeking of that woman's perfume. When I didn't start right in breeding for you, you dismissed me like that!" She snapped her fingers, turned away, and started to cry. "I hope you enjoy Jude's money," she sobbed, "because I'm going to enjoy mine now and . . . oh, don't touch me!"

With a low, inarticulate roar, Slade was at her side, looming over her. With a gentle violence, he propelled her to a chair and planted her firmly in its cushioned depths. Frightened, she sat quite still. "Now you listen," he ordered fiercely. "You announced you weren't interested in me, only in my money. When I asked for your understanding, you withheld it. When I offered you my heart, you left me. Please, don't take amiss what I say now," he scoffed in a voice thick with sarcasm. "I don't blame you, goddess, perfect as you are in all things, for what is doubtless a lack in me, but I wonder—couldn't you have been just a little softer, just a little kinder? You shut me out and kept your secrets, and if I'd known you could have loved me . . . that would have eased my ragings and sooner freed me of the pains and angers of the past. It did gravel me so, Brigida, that you needed to be perfect at everything, needed to compete with me whenever you could at whatever you could." She shrank back in her chair, watching him stride the room as he ranted, slamming a fist into the palm of his hand over and over.

In a very little voice she whispered, "You never said you loved me . . . until it was too late. You were just going to let me walk right away, today, with the deed to the house and . . . it was only lust . . . you said so."

"NO!" he exploded. "You're wrong! It was never just that, and I'd never have let you go, not if I had to hold you captive until the end of time. It was a ruse to shake you out of your stubborn idiot pretense. I've had enough of that, so you'd best behave, understood? And another thing—Jude's so-called inheritance? It was not much more than a pittance from Elizabeth's grandmother, and it was lost on Black Friday in the gold crash. That was two years ago, long before I ever sent for you. Who told you that old tale?"

"Lost?" Brigida echoed. "But Lydia said . . . it was her perfume, you were always going off to her. I could tell."

"Not always, not for long. It didn't take much time for

me to realize she was using one pretense after another to lure me away to her. You know, we really were trying to find the weapons, there really were people to see, information to pay for, informers to be . . . handled, but when Lydia kept offering old information, I soon stopped going to her. I took you home to Silver Hill, didn't I? She always greeted me . . . warmly, always tucked one of her damn gardenias in my lapel." Slade stood before Brigida, smiling a little, shrugging, feeling helpless at the sight of her tears. "I didn't want to love you, but I always did, always. Do you really think I've ever done anything only because Elizabeth wanted it? Do you?" he demanded. Now it was Brigida's turn to feel helpless. She shook her head and accepted his handkerchief.

"Gardenias" she sniffed. "I never saw . . ."

"I threw them away once I was out of her sight. Goddess, I never wanted anything from her once I had you, and if I lose you now . . ." He wanted to kiss away her tears and hold her but he made no move. Instead, he crossed the room to lean at the window, feeling the Pacific breeze cool on his face. "Men have been known to sell their souls for just one breath of such ecstasy as we've known," he said. He heard a small cry and turned to Brigida. She seemed to glide toward him with infinite grace—her dazzling, boisterous beauty a golden vision. He held his breath, and his entreating eyes were brimming with love when she reached him and rose on tiptoes to place her hands on his wide shoulders. She pressed to him, her moist lips parted, glistening in the evening sunlight. His arms came strong about her and he swept her up, holding her cradled against him. Their lips met with a raw hunger born of long pent-up love and rising passion.

"I will say to you now what I swore I would never."
Brigida spoke against his lips, his throat, his tawny hair.

"You don't have to say anything now." His mouth
silenced hers, but she pulled away.

"Yes! I have to. Let me. Slade Hawkes, I really love
you," Brigida said. "You are my one true love, and were
always, from the first, and will be forever."

"I know," he said huskily. "'Whoever loved that
loved not at first sight?' the poets asked, long before you
and me." His open mouth found hers again, and she
caught his lips gently in her small teeth. Her hands were
in his breeze-blown hair, and she kissed his eyelids softly.

"I love you so, it nearly breaks my heart with the
strength of it, and that is the only secret I ever kept from
you, I swear it!"

"I know," he said again. "I know now you were giving
me everything, from the very first time." He crossed the
room to set her down before the cheval glass near the bed.

She waited impatiently for him to undo the row of
buttons down her back. He worked with a tantalizing
slowness, the faintest hint of a teasing smile on his
handsome face as she watched him in the glass. When he
had done finally, she slipped her arms from the banded
sleeves of the gown and stepped from it. Slade kissed her
shoulder, coiled her long mane in his hand, and the peaks
of her high breasts rose in dainty shadows against the
creamy satin long-shift that was all she had worn beneath
her gown. He smiled at her sudden intake of breath, and
discarded his clothes while she pulled the shift over her
head. There was that instant of wonder, of surprise, as

always, when they viewed each other anew, and then she was in his waiting arms, pressing to him hungrily. His hands held her hips locked to his while his eager mouth tasted sweetness, then his tongue worked at nipples budded to advertise her desire.

"Look how beautiful you are," he whispered hoarsely, turning her to the glass. His hands slid down between her slim thighs, caressing, and then her softness parted to the surge of his thrust. Hesitantly at first, then with proud wonder, Brigida watched in the glass as their lithe bodies curled and moved together, Slade's broad shoulders and muscled arms enfolding her satin smoothness, his darker hair falling forward, swirling with hers, golden and glimmering. His tongue flicked over his lips. She met his eyes, which were almost savage, and she was fired by the pure male strength of him, by the almost brutal beauty of his chiseled face, of his lean body, the full hard-edged muscles working.

They broke apart and turned to join again, sinking onto the bed, together riding a swell, a tidal surge that crested in wave after wave of pure crystalline pleasure that dazzled their senses and left them clinging, drifting breathless in a rainbow wash of love.

"I used to think," Brigida whispered, drowsy and sighing in Slade's arms, "I used to think that it couldn't be any . . . more, or . . . any better. And then . . . it is."

Night shadows danced the walls when they woke. Slade's voice in Brigida's ear was rough and soft and loving all at once.

"If ever again you threaten to leave me, I'll beat you," he graveled. With a tiny tingle of fear she looked into his face expecting to find the familiar steely, blue-eyed anger, and discovered instead, love.

"Never," she said, clinging to him. "I never will want to leave you. Besides, if I tried you'd hold me captive 'til the end of time, you promised." She rested her chin in the palm of her hand and sent silken curls flooding over his chest when she leaned to his lips. "I will ever be subject to your governance, sir," she smiled.

"I'm as much a prisoner as you," he said, caressing her face. "And ravishers have been known to fall in love with their victims before, you know."

"I love you," Brigida said smiling, "and that's only the third time I've told you that—ever."

"Tell me often as you like, Brigida, my sun-drenched Druidess escaped from some wind row, some sea margin of the past, to bewitch my heart. Sloe-eyed lady huntress, you've rendered me helpless in your well-set snare."

"Oh, Slade!" Brigida's happy, burbling laughter floated like the tinkle of a pretty bell. "You aren't exactly helpless, thank heaven, and I set no snare, I just loved you, always. Even when I was a little girl. Mother called it calf love then, but I was heartbroken when you went away from us. Truly, I was."

"Wouldn't she be amazed to see you now?"

Brigida had risen and, wrapped in a sheet, moved about the room lighting the lamps. "Mother? She wouldn't be at all amazed. This marriage was her idea. You know, Slade, it never was my way to be calculating or . . . or deceptive, but I tried to follow everyone's advice about you . . . Phil's and Elizabeth's and Miri's and . . . they were wrong, all of them. Mother told me once my own instincts would always lead me right, but I forgot. For a while. Mother thought there wasn't a man alive who wouldn't be on his knees to me in minutes, except you."

"Wise woman. She understood her daughter almost as well as I do. Now you're so properly behaved, love," Slade said rising, "I've something to give you." He crossed the room, took a small object from his jacket pocket. Brigida caught a glint of gold when he held aloft a dark stone, hanging from a fine chain. "Tiger eye, almost as beautiful as yours. If I could, I'd carry you away now to a place of endless summer where the moon is always full and the tides forever high."

"You, love, are sun and stars and tide enough. This is forever. Just carry us home to Silver Hill. That's all I want."

"Evening tomorrow soon enough to leave?" Slade slipped the chain about Brigida's neck and lifted her long hair over it.

"This . . . I'll never take it off . . . ever in my life," she said as the smooth stone glowed against her golden skin like a dark star. "I've something for you, too, I was saving for a parting gift, but now you must have it, this very instant." She pulled open her large trunk and flung things wildly about while Slade watched, laughing, until she located a good-sized wrapped parcel almost at the bottom. When he had undone the cord and folded back the paper Brigida helped him spread the quilt on the bed.

"It's the finest gift I've ever had," he said, kissing her.

"It's Silver Hill."

"Of course. It's perfect."

At the center of the blue cotton quilt with its border of multicolored stripes and gingham dots, was the manor house, pieced and appliqued, surrounded by roses. It was flanked left and right by ribbon trees, birds perched at the top of each, great wolfhounds at the bottom. Every window of the house was open wide. There was a smiling face at each, and chains of laughing children going in and out at every door. "There's another thing now, I'd give you." Brigida was suddenly serious. "But I'm afraid I never will. At first I was so . . . so hurt and angry at you, I didn't want to have any baby of yours, and later, when it was all so perfect, that lovely springtime at Silver Hill, I was loving you so I was afraid to let anything come between us, not even our own baby. But now . . ."

"Now, it will be all right, I know, I've always known, but Brigida, it doesn't make a difference between us, understand?"

"Well, there's Jude of course, so if there aren't any more, at least . . ."

"Now there's Jude, yes, but if there weren't . . . it never would have mattered with you and me. Believe me?"

"I believe you," Brigida nodded seriously. They were curled together in bed, under the quilt, she fingering the warm stone at her throat, he fondling her almost absently, as if unaware of the effect.

"But Slade," Brigida breathed, "what about Root? Will you give up . . . ?"

"I'm not bound any longer by old rages, love, you've freed me of them. I've wasted too many years already on that bastard. We've other things to be thinking of now, you and I."

"Yes, right now," Brigida sighed, "before that impish child and his uncle, the tall Indian, fall upon us." Her breath was sweet and warm at his lips, her slim hands caressing, moving.

"I promised you'd beg, didn't I?" he laughed low, fending off a barrage of flying pillows before he pulled her beneath him.

The San Francisco night was a celebration. Anson Bruff arrived at the hotel in a caleche drawn by a flawlessly groomed, lightly blanketed gelding. And, as Martha had told her so many times to do, Brigida made a wish on the piebald horse. She gathered her crimson skirt close and held the fringed long shawl on her lap as the gentlemen climbed in on either side of her. The evening was warm and the carriage hood was down, affording a view of the brightly lit fruit stands, peddlers' handcarts, and many jugglers that crowded the corners.

"Every vegetable woman and baker has a horse and buggy in this town, Slade. No one walks here. Am I right, Mrs. Hawkes?" Bruff enjoyed showing off the city.

Brigida smiled, nodding, holding fast to Slade's hand.

"It is certainly a rich town, Mr. Bruff. I've heard that every ounce of gold or silver unearthed from Alaska to Arizona finds its way here to be spent—one way or another. Though it does seem love and gluttony are the primary businesses. I'd almost forgotten."

"There may be no end to bordellos and gambling parlors ma'am, but sailors long at sea need certain distractions. Am I right, Slade?"

"Anson, I know you can buy anything in San Francisco, even China dolls at open auction, live ones."

"I incline to the Barbary Coast myself, stay out of Little China and let the tongs run things," Bruff said.

"Our Chinese cook used to take me through Little China" Brigida offered, "on the way to those pretty tea and silk shops, you know, with the bright pendants on the fronts? I looked into the basements when we passed— they wash and iron and barber and twist cigars and live all packed together. It was awful."

She was thoughtful for a moment. "It seems so much a matter of pure chance that some spend all their days in misery and others . . . are so happy." She looked up at Slade, holding fast to his hand, and he returned the pressure.

"Accept your own fate, love, that's all you can do."

"Yes, but it's times like this you should touch wood, Martha says so." Brigida leaned forward and tapped the paneling of the carriage.

"That old woman will have you bedeviled as she is, if I don't take you in hand." Slade brought an arm about her shoulders to pull her closer to him. "Nothing will ever harm you, I promise." And looking up into his eyes, Brigida couldn't have doubted him if she tried.

"The weather's more changeable here than any place else I know. There can be clear skies, then torrents in a matter of minutes, so don't get too far from the hotel, my friends," Anson Bruff cautioned, bidding Slade and

Brigida goodnight after a long, and very expensive meal.

"It's still fair, Anson," Brigida offered her hand. "We need to walk and talk, some. We've plans to make for the future. Don't worry about us. We'll be fine."

"I'd not doubt that for a minute," Bruff said, grinning. "'Til tomorrow then," he called as the carriage pulled away.

"What plans?" Slade asked. He lit a cigar as they strolled along a quiet street.

"Oh, plans for Silver Hill, whether to live there and farm it or . . ."

"That's the one place in the world we really belong. You know, domesticity didn't come easy to me. I resisted, but now I want nothing else. We'll work the land."

"But don't you have to be in the city to see to your investments?" A little wind came up, and Slade draped her fringed wrap about her bare shoulders.

"Only some of the time. We'll give the Washington Square house to Elizabeth and Del and we'll build a new one on the Fifth Avenue land. I want Jude to be at ease in both places . . . look there." Slade pointed across the bay. There was a great burst of steam whistles and suddenly the sea was lit for miles. Boats were putting out from all directions, heading toward a large vessel just entering the Golden Gate.

"It's the fortnightly steamer bringing the mail! Oh, Slade, it's always an event here. Let's go down to the docks, please?"

Brigida had led Slade a shortcut through a maze of narrow back alleys where painted women, scantily clad, leaned at windows, calling out and posing, dangling slippered feet and half-bared legs, making it obvious they wore nothing beneath flimsy kimonos. They were ready for business and advertising their goods. A heavy-breasted small, dark girl made so bold as to accost Slade on the street and, though Brigida held fast to his arm, to describe her services in some detail. "Come back later on, mister, when you've got free of little missy there," the woman concluded. "You're one I'd wait for for a while."

Slade's face was lit in the glow of a gas lamp, and Brigida studied him as if appraising his appearance for the first time.

"Mm, he is quite perfect, no doubt of it," she mused aloud, "but I'm afraid," she said to the woman with a sweet smile, "you'll wait an awfully long time for him, dear. He has all that and better at home."

"Pure-minded nice girls ain't supposed to have nasty thoughts," the woman said, stepping closer out of the shadows. She was very pale, her skin almost blue-white against black hair, her eyelids, like parchment, fluttering. She seemed ill and weak.

"I'm sorry," Brigida said. "I couldn't see . . . I didn't mean to make sport of you."

"Sporting's my trade," the girl said calmly. "Never mind, I don't want your charity."

"Get some food and get off the street." Slade placed a fold of bills in her hand. "This will cover your night," he said to the girl as he guided Brigida away.

When they rounded a corner, a balding paunchy figure, puffing with the effort of the climb up from the bay, stepped into the street to watch them pass. Blueford Root wiped his pate with a soiled handkerchief, then hurried into a gaming hall close by, glancing about with quick, shifting eyes. The faro dealer, in shirt sleeves, his back to the wall as usual, looked up through a thick haze of cigar smoke and nodded to Root, who made his way through the crowd to the table. "My associates . . . have they arrived, my man?" Root queried.

The dealer nodded. "Back room. Out here was a little too rank for your high-toned Eastern gents," he said with disgust. "Where'd you find them, Root? What you plannin' to do with 'em?"

"Patience. In good time, my man, it will out. Drinks all round gratis, on me," Root said loudly. Then he made for a door at the back of the room.

Twenty-Five

Wrapped in a vast blanket of fog that had floated up from the Pacific during the night, the deserted street was silent at midmorning when Brigida and Jude climbed down from a hack. She asked the driver to wait. "About ten minutes, we'll be, no more; then we'll go on to the wharf."

"What wharf?" Jude asked as he and Brigida mounted a long flight of steps toward a house tucked up against a hill. A three-story, turreted tower rose high. Limp curtains hung at dark leaded windows.

"We're meeting your father at a sailmaker's loft. Then we'll all go to Mr. Bruff's for a meal before we get the train. He wants us to see a Mr. Hallidie. Slade may invest in the man's cable cars. I think it's a fine idea, if it works. They're going to build a model first."

"Levi told about the inventors—the paper bag man and Mr. Pullman and . . . Brigida, did you live here once?" the little boy asked.

"Yes, but nobody does now. We'll leave a caretaker in it . . . our old cook. That way, if my brothers ever . . .

my brothers went on foot across the ice when the whale boats were caught. I still think, sometimes, they'll find their way back home again," she sighed. "Look the door's ajar. Run ahead, Jude, and tell me what you see," Brigida smiled.

She stopped to watch the small figure, dressed this morning as his father had been, in buckskin and boots, the fringe on his leather jacket swinging as he climbed, and then she stood a moment on the porch, worrying over the paint that flaked from the carved railing, sad to see the house fallen into disrepair. "We'll fix it," she said resolutely, turning to follow the child inside.

"We've only a few minutes, Jude, don't play at hide and seek with me now!" she called into the silent house.

When the door clicked shut behind her, Brigida began to move through the bare and echoing rooms. Memory welled like distant music, growing stronger with each step. The parlor doors squeaked open at her cautious touch. Hesitantly, she crossed the room to pull aside the dusty draperies. In the dim, fogged light, she curled on the bay-window seat, as she used to. She recalled the room as it had been when last she saw it—round marble table at the center, India rugs beneath the settee, ship models on the mantel amidst a clutter of figurines and paper weights and oriental vases. She remembered her brothers poring over a game at the hearth, imagined her mother and father as they had sat of an evening, the captain calm and distinguished, his diminutive wife at his side, as they enjoyed a rare time together in their parlor ashore.

"You'd be so pleased, all of you, to see us now," she

whispered, closing the parlor door behind her. She went toward the kitchen at the back of the house, touching the carved balustrade as she passed the stairs, absently opening the door of the cabinet tucked beneath them. "Oh," she sighed. "Lurinda!" The doll was crumpled in a corner where Brigida herself had placed it long ago, cast off after many companionable years at sea. "Lurinda, you have traveled almost as many nautical miles as I have, I think. Not many can say that, you know, and you're as pretty as ever." The doll had come from France, Brigida remembered. When she lifted it, the smooth, white-kid body was familiarly weighty in her hands. The head and face were of unblemished Bisque porcelain, the large brown eyes were paperweight glass. The doll had a flaxen blond wig and tiny pierced ears, and she was dressed in a yellowing lace gown with a silk and ribbon bonnet.

"A new dress does wonders for a lady, you'll feel worlds better soon." Brigida laughed at herself as she tucked the doll under her arm and moved toward the kitchen. The late September sun was burning off the fog. In the pale light a single strand of silver spider silk stretched across the kitchen doorway, glistening. At the sight of it Brigida felt a rush of loneliness in the terrible silence of the empty house.

"Jude, where are you?" she called. "We must leave this instant! I shouldn't have come, I never should have come here," she said softly to herself, reaching up to break the spider's thread with a slender finger.

"You are quite right, my dear. You should not have returned to this empty mansion," a voice spoke close to her, and Brigida screamed as Blueford Root stepped into her path. "But I guessed that you would, I planned accordingly. I've dismissed the hack, don't look for help from that quarter," Root grimaced. "And I've rendered your young charge silent for the time."

"What did you do to him? What do you want with us?" Brigida asked coldly, her tone heavy with contempt. "Haven't you done enough to us already without continuing to—we're leaving San Francisco in a few hours. We want nothing more to do with you."

"Your husband, the captain, has hounded me through all these many years, my dear. Even if it were true that he loses interest and now gives up the chase, which I don't for a moment believe, I would have to have my revenge, wouldn't I?" The sickly smile vanished from Root's sweating face and a cruel scowl replaced it. "Hawkes destroyed my home. He carried off my sister to lure me out of hiding. He drove her mad in so doing. Well, he shall never see Bonnie's son again. You I may send back to him, after a time. What good is revenge, if no one sees it? I doubt he'll want you then, my dear, when I've done."

"Slade won't let you harm us," she said. Her heartbeat was loud and hollow.

"Won't let me?" Root laughed. "My dear, I've fooled him before at his own game. Whyever do you think he went off to the Falklands? Whyever do you think Bonnie left him?"

"You?" Brigida was stunned for a moment. Then, eyes flashing, she faced Root squarely. "Stop lying to me and to yourself. I think your sister was quite mad always, even before the war. Admit you caused her death by luring her away from Silver Hill and poisoning her fragile mind against Slade; admit you murdered Slade's father, you odious fraud, and then . . ."

The back of Root's hand caught Brigida a glancing blow and a heavy ring tore the soft skin of her cheek. She reeled back, gasping with pain.

"Murder? It was war, dear child. We'll not speak of it again as murder."

"You did murder Lydia Worsley. There's no other word for it, is there?" she goaded him, speaking very precisely to mask her thickening fear. Root's agitated, watery eyes flicked rapidly from side to side. He mopped his brow, then dabbed at a trickle of blood on Brigida's face. She flinched away.

"Miss Worsley was going to betray me, you see. She promised never to let slip about our deal. But I couldn't believe her, could I? No, no," he answered his own question. "I wasn't quite done with her just yet. She could have been helpful, just a little longer. I killed her rather by mistake. You see, my dear, I've a temper."

"You swindled me out of my inheritance, Mr. Root. I'd not ever done anything to you. That was simply the action of a common thief." She brought tentative fingers to the throbbing place on her cheek and winced.

"It will swell, my dear, but probably there won't be a scar," he said condescendingly, and then continued, "I was forced into this life of treachery by Hawkes's incessant hounding. It is his fault, all of it and it is simply one of those strange and wonderful accidents of fate that you now provide me the perfect means to destroy him. Come along, dear child. That little urchin Jude is waiting. If he's to remain unharmed, for now, you'll do as I tell you with alacrity."

"Slade will kill you if you hurt his son. Or me." Brigida studied Root's sweating, leering face with obvious loathing, then stopped herself from saying more, for Jude's sake.

"Wake up, girl, come on, you can't sleep forever. Lord, they did a job on you. I've never seen any poor thing so drugged up as this. Did you give them a fight?"

Vague shapes drifted past Brigida's paining eyes. She closed them tight when a candle was lit.

"Where's the child," she asked.

"This is no place for a child," the calm voice went on. "Here, I've brought you some coffee. Sit up, that's it and . . . ah, you!"

On hearing the exclamation, Brigida made an effort to open her eyes, and the pale, haunting face she saw teased her fogged memory until the girl spoke again.

"The money your man gave me the other night? It would have taken me a week to earn that much. I sent some of it home to my sister so she won't . . ."

"Where . . . how long have I been in this place?" Brigida looked about a small, narrow room, empty but for a rumpled bed and a cracked wash basin. The door was barred, like a jail cell.

"You're in a crib at Mrs. Mohl's. Don't look so stupid. Don't you know what I'm talking about? Fifty-cent girls in these cowyard cribs. Thirty men a day at fifty cent a roll. A fellow pays downstairs for the key, gets his wick dipped, and it's over in less than five minutes, that's it."

Brigida got unsteadily to her feet to peer through the window at the deserted street three floors below. "What will they do with me now?" she asked softly.

"First, they'll get you broken in, like they do all the new stock so you are properly . . . accommodating. You won't work here, though, you're far too young and pretty. They'll probably sell you at auction. You'll end up in the Orient, I'd guess. That's the best market for blondes. One perfect as you will bring a great price."

"That's . . . that's slavery, they can't. Damn you, where's my little boy, I must see him."

Brigida's head was clearing, and she began to understand the horror of her predicament.

"He's here. They'll sell him, too. There's a demand, in some parts of the world, for little boys. White slavery it is, you're right, and who's to stop it?"

"Go to Slade Hawkes at the Occidental Hotel. Tell him where we are. He'll help you, I swear it, and so will I. Please." Brigida extended her hands, imploring.

"Harriet Glover, help you? Not likely."

The girl's detached calm was maddening.

"Why not? How can you live this way? I don't understand."

"I've no self-respect left at all, they tell me, that's how. None of us have, whether we came to the life voluntarily or not. They have ways of breaking your will and your courage . . . if you ever had any to start with." Harriet Glover smiled a little. "Even yours," she added.

"If you escape . . . I mean, they let you out to walk the

547

street. Someone will help you if you tell your story."

"Escape? Where to?" Harriet demanded. "My family won't have me back, after what I've been. I've no money, no friends, and the police are on the bribe. Go to them and they'll bring you right back here to be beat or cut. Look, fine lady, the madame is my friend, and so are the girls. I belong here."

"No one belongs here," Brigida snapped, beginning to pace.

"No? Is that so? Don't you see us as a necessary evil to save you from love's baser passions? After all, we . . ."

"Did you come by your calling naturally, Miss Glover? Were you born a cowardly whore, or did you learn the trade at your mama's knee, or was it later that . . . ?" Brigida choked off her angry words, appalled at her own cruelty as she watched the girl's eyes fill with tears. "I'm sorry, I'm sorry," she said quickly, extending her hand again. "We'll help you, I swear it. Let us take you away from the Barbary Coast and help you live decently. Go to my husband and tell . . ."

The expression on Harriet's wraithlike face went from sadness to interest to abject fear, and Brigida looked up to see Root's sharp, restless little eyes peering in at the door. The key grated in the lock and he entered the room.

"Recovered nicely, I see, and you've actually been attempting to get Miss Glover to do something other than lie on her back. Pity you've wasted your efforts on such an empty husk. Anything she ever hoped for in her shabby little life was destined not to be. Now, she doesn't hope any more, do you Harriet? Tell Lady Hawkes how right I always am, about everything."

"You dunghill braggart, let me alone," Harriet hissed. "Filth of the earth, selling girls into slavery."

"Did the eloquent Miss Glover tell you her own tragic tale, my dear? The wretched girl was a runaway from the family farm, where they used her like an animal in more ways than one. Her uncle loved underfed little girls, didn't he Harriet? Harriet went away to Chicago, answered an employment agency ad for a domestic, and wound up some rich woman's kitchen slave. Only there was more to it. For her meager pittance of three dollars a week, she was expected to serve her employer's husband in various ways. Am I correct, Miss Glover?"

"Bloat-bellied sot, you get yours for free," Harriet said.

"All their stories are so pathetic—runaways, delinquents, charity ward cases, dance hall tarts, foreigners who can't understand a word one says." Root smiled.

"Yes, you pimp," Harriet smiled back. "And if a girl protests, her clothes are stripped off and hidden and she is raped again and again and beaten and starved until she comes round. And do you know why we all come round sooner or later? Because, deep down, we believe we deserve our fate, our punishment. We sinfully crave luxury, and romance, and an easy life, and we all have nasty, evil cravings that have caused our downfall."

"A whore is a whore," Root said indifferently. "You, my dear, are an exception," he told Brigida.

"How?" she asked suspiciously.

"You'll bring me a fortune in the Orient, fair and perfect as you are, and dark eyed. I'm taking you myself. To entrust such a treasure to an agent, I've decided, would be foolish, and Hawkes is already breathing down my neck. Here." He tossed her a dark, threadbare cloak. "We're leaving now."

There was a clanking as a lock slipped, and then the door creaked open. Brigida and Jude blinked in the unaccustomed brightness, and Blueford Root, a handkerchief held delicately to his nose, descended a few steps and peered into the forecastle. The reek of sea water, sewage, and rancid bits of whale meat was choking.

"The accommodations are not what you're accustomed to, dear lady? You and the brat will come up on deck now we're a way out of San Francisco. There's a good wind. Hawkes couldn't find you now if he had wings. Here, you," he commanded someone out of Brigida's line of sight. "Bring our little friends up now for a bit of fun."

It took two burly men to handle Jude, who kicked and fought, while a third hauled Brigida out of the dank hold into the bright sunlight above decks. She took several deep breaths of the sea air, as if drawing strength from the wind after the interminable hours in the hold, which had been almost like her worst nightmare come true. She looked about. "I'd expect you to sail in a wreck like this," she told Root archly. "Who is master of this rotting, rat-infested hulk? No self-respecting captain would have anything to do with it." The vessel was covered with grime and filth, the decks slick with oil and rancid blubber, the paint peeling, sails ragged. Turning full circle to count the crew, Brigida's eyes went up to the quarterdeck. Hollis Stancel, watching the scene being played out below, nodded and raised a hand that shook with the drinker's tremor.

"Y'all join us, Miss Brigida, in the captain's cabin for a pleasant meal?" he slurred.

She spat in his direction and turned away in wordless contempt while the assembled hands hooted with laughter.

"Tie the dear girl to the foremast," Root ordered. "A few hours there will teach her to graciously accept whatever is thrown her way." He ripped her lace blouse and tore away her skirt, leaving her in her camisole and petticoats.

"Hollis Stancel, you've been a guest at my table! How can a so-called gentleman like you, Hollis, be party to this?" Brigida furiously raised a small fist.

"You try my patience, my dear, and you agitate poor Mr. Stancel overmuch. His nerves are not steady, but then, when we've done with you, yours shan't be either. You'll crawl on your knees begging deliverance. Take her away."

In the midday sun that beat down like fire, Brigida's eyes burned. Her lips were dry and caked from the saltwater dowsings her captors delivered each time her wet, clinging garments dried. "We're all to have our chance with you, when Root's got his fill," one of them moronically repeated again and again, his bloodshot eyes touching her revealed shapely body slowly.

"My husband will kill you," she answered each time, "you'll see."

"Yeah? How you think he'll find us? There's the whole

blasted Pacific to hide in, ain't there?" her guard whined, but Brigida heard a hint of uncertainty begin to come into the thick voice as the hours wore on.

By late afternoon when Root cut her bonds, Brigida was only vaguely aware of the hard, desolate splendor of the sinking sun glaring from beneath a low bank of red clouds, its reflection staining the water like blood. Her arms pained horribly, her thirst was unbearable.

"Dear girl, is it water you desire?" Root smiled. "The barrel is amidships. Take my arm?"

Scorning him and weakly clutching the rail, Brigida moved slowly, painfully, as circulation began to return to her prickling, stiff arms and legs. Nothing mattered but reaching the water, feeling it cool on her dry lips, on her parched, thick tongue. After, she'd try to think, afterwards she'd decide what to do—but now . . . reaching the barrel, she peered in to find it barely a quarter full. She looked about frantically for the dipper.

"Up, dear girl," Root directed, and when she raised her eyes, she saw it. The dipper was swinging freely as the ship rolled, hung high in the cross trees that seemed miles above the slanting deck. When Brigida wearily reached for a line, Jude broke free of the man holding him and began to climb, moving from spar to boom with the agility of a young monkey.

"Oh, Jude, don't look down, don't ever look down," Brigida tried to tell him, but her voice was barely a whisper.

"Don't worry, Brigida, don't worry! I've almost got it," Jude called with a fearless laugh, and Brigida, afraid to watch, whispered to herself, "Don't look down, just

lon't look down," over and over until the boy was
ooking up at her, a dripping dipper of cool water held
orward in his outstretched hands.

Hollis Stancel swallowed two tumblers of dark rum
quickly, one after the other, then passed the bottle out to
the crew and turned to Brigida standing unsteadily with
her back to the cabin door. A threadbare, soiled blanket
was thrown over her shoulders, and Jude clung close at
her side.

"Are you really so startled to see me here, Miz
Hawkes?" he asked.

"The most despicable people often do hide behind a
screen of false propriety," she snapped. "And you
wouldn't smoke in a lady's parlor! Will you tell me what
you're doing with this . . . this villain?"

"Blueford and I, we go back a long way together. We're
cousins some little distance removed, and if it hadn't
been for the war . . ." Stancel's right eye jumped con-
vulsively, "Bonnie Root would have been my wife. I'd of
wed her, for all her drifting and weakness of mind. Hell, if
it came down to it, I always could have chained her in the
barn like they did the old man, the grandfather. Fed him
regular, no complaints. Well, it is all in the past, the war
is over, and now we are turnin' our attentions to other
affairs."

"I thought for you, sir, the war would never be over."
Brigida smiled coldly, echoing words they'd both heard
before.

"Yes, ma'am, that's why we're all here. Now, I'm

representin' certain interests in the South that are working to retain what remnants exist of our prewar ways. Eventually, we will restore the South to her full glory, but for the time bein' we've found a way to keep order and make sure, damn sure, no interlopers arouse the local population to aspirations more lofty than they rightly should have. Do you understand?"

Stancel opened another bottle of rum and, not bothering with a glass, pulled a long swallow from it.

"I understand more than I care to Hollis. You are a disgrace to the Confederacy. You're one of those outlaw scum terrorizing and killing all over the South."

Stancel moved menacingly toward Brigida. Jude, rushing at him head on, would have bowled the man over if Brigida hadn't intervened.

"Jude, please," she whispered, "don't make it worse."

"Jude, you little brat," Root hissed, "I'll throw you back in the hold and you'll not see the light of day until you're an old, old man."

Exhausted and frightened, Brigida sank into a chair and pulled the child close against her. "Let them talk. Your father won't let them harm us," she whispered in Jude's ear, with more conviction than she was feeling. How on earth, she wondered, would Slade find them once they were well out to sea, with the whole Pacific to hide in?

"Mr. Root, I learned some months ago," Stancel went on, "had weapons for sale. My people want them."

"What's this to do with the boy and me?" In the brief ominous silence that followed her question, Brigida watched Root light a lamp, and she took note of the compass, showing a southerly course.

"Things were going well until Lydia tried to back out at the last minute, some sop about loyalty and love, just take the money and the guns and forget all about her, she said, she wanted nothin'." Stancel's bony fingers twirled his watch fob quickly as he talked. Root sat smiling and smug, heavy hands folded across his belly.

"Mr. Root here didn't believe the harlot for a moment, did you Blueford? The bitch was too clever for her own good. I'm sure you'll agree Mrs. Hawkes, ma'am. Rum?" Stancel shoved the bottle under Brigida's nose. She pulled away, gagged by the smell and, unable to control herself, began to laugh wildly.

"Lydia crossed both you fools in your own game, didn't she? Now you've got nothing—no gold, no guns—nothing. How stupid of you to have killed her a bit prematurely, Mr. Root."

"Oh no, not at all. Everything has come out better than I could have planned, dear girl," Root sneered, lumbering from his chair. Methodically, he wiped his profusely sweating face and neck and came toward Brigida and Jude. "Better than I ever could have planned, because now I have you. You know where my gold and my guns are, don't you?"

"Why would I know?" Brigida asked, with a sickening twist in the pit of her stomach. "We weren't exactly confidants, Lydia Worsley and I, were we, Mr. Root?"

He pulled up a chair and sat facing Brigida, his knees grazing hers. "I will be delighted to describe my dear, the lengths to which I will go to determine whether or not you do know. You'd be well advised to save yourself a frightful ordeal, if you have the information I want. I'll be absolutely certain you do not, you see, before I'm done and it would be a pity to ruin such lovely soft skin needlessly. It would diminish your value on the market. You'll do better for yourself if you're not marred." He extended blunt, ringed fingers toward Brigida's face and, before she could stop him, Jude was out of her grasp, sailing into the bloated figure, sinking small sharp teeth into Root's offending hand.

Root cuffed the boy off with a heavy blow, and in a high-pitched shriek ordered him removed from the cabin. "Throw the little brat back in the hold," Root screamed, folding a cloth about his injured hand. The moment the cabin door was closed and locked, while Jude's furious oaths still hung in the air, he turned on Brigida and pushed her onto the bunk, where she rolled out of his reach and landed a low kick that set him sprawling back, gasping. Then she got to her knees and crouched like a cornered wildcat as Stancel took unsteady steps toward her.

"Now, ma'am, ah would never be one myself to take a lady by force, but I'd be pleased to hold you for my friend Blueford here if he can't handle you alone." Stancel's drawl was very slow, his speech badly slurred. "Later, when she's a mite more willin', I'll have at her, Blueford."

The heavy man, recovering his breath, removed his jacket, flicking a bit of lint from the lapel, then both men turned to the slender girl, who had clambered out of the bunk and stood braced against the locked door, her pale curls in wild disarray, petticoats ripped to expose one slim leg to the thigh, camisole slipped from a shoulder.

Her hours in the sun had turned her skin a gleaming deeper gold, and her dark eyes were feverishly bright.

The two men looked at her with awe. "Such a prize is not easily lost. Slade Hawkes will spend the rest of his days searching for you, my dear," Root wheezed. "For a while you will be mine, to use as I will. Some of my tastes may not be much to your liking at first, but you will accommodate me, I know."

The two men advanced cautiously, and with difficulty wrestled Brigida down onto a leather settee battened near the bunk. Feeling Root's hot breath at her neck and his groping hands at her petticoats, Brigida was goaded by revulsion and rage to greater strength than she knew she possessed. She freed herself again and, snatching up a sextant to brandish it like a dagger, violently pushed him away from her.

"The bitch will have to be tied," Stancel snapped.

"A touch of the cat will render her more pliant, I trust." Root's voice was thin. "Of course, the cat is a bit crude for so elegant a creature. Did I tell you, Hollis?" he asked, turning away from Brigida, "what I discovered in Mexico? At a bull baiting? A very rare refinement, a scorpion's tail lash. Of course, I had to have one, it drove the beasts quite mad. I'm told the pain is exquisite as it flays the skin to slivers. I've not seen it used on anything soft and fine as you, my dear," he told Brigida. She returned his leering look with one of indifferent contempt, though she was cold with fear. "Then, too, Madame Restell taught me some very persuasive tricks," Root smiled.

"Slade Hawkes will kill you," Brigida said. "Very slowly."

"Get her out of here," Stancel ordered the deck hand

who had been summoned to lead Brigida away.

"If you was a man, you'd be strung up by your thumbs," a voice wheezed in Brigida's ear. A pinched-faced man with a shuffling gait stood before her. He and his mates had bound her wrists, and now she waited, arms stretched taut above her, feet barely touching the deck.

"If you were a man, you'd have no part in this," she answered hotly.

"I'll take my part with pleasure in bringing you down," the sailor whined. He cut the lacy straps of Brigida's camisole, and it fell, leaving her body bare above the waist but for masses of curls spilling forward to hide her breasts from the circle of eyes surrounding her.

"Veronique!" Root shouted as he slowly circled about Brigida, "Do up your mistress's hair for the occasion."

It had grown dark, and lanterns sent shadows playing over evil-hued faces, exaggerating lecherous grins. Into this devil's ring Veronique came like a dark witch to her coven.

"You! I'm not surprised," Brigida said with loathing. "The captain will find you, Veronique, you know I speak the truth, don't you?"

"But *non*, madame, he will never find me. Monsieur Carpentier has promised." Veronique licked at her lips nervously and came closer.

"Phil? What do you mean? He's not part of this."

"*Oui*, madame, he is. He is to bring Monsieur Root's stallion from the train to the ship. Then he is to have you and some money. He said your husband would never find you. Or me. He promised."

"That poor fool can't promise you anything, Veronique. Stay away from me!" Brigida kicked out and the maid fell sprawling on the deck.

"I'll tend to her myself," Root pronounced as Veronique fled to the quarterdeck, where Stancel leaned drunkenly. Root wrapped his hand in Brigida's hair and twisted it back so tightly her eyes stung with tears. Breathing heavily, he touched the bared tips of her breasts with trembling fingers. "Oh, very lovely indeed, but, sadly, not to remain so longer. Captain Hawkes will never look upon this perfect body again, without thinking of me, my dear, if he finds you. My man will begin with the black snake. Now," Root commanded, stepping back.

Brigida heard his words as if from the depths of a horrible dream. "Please, no," she said softly to the burly man who drew near flicking a long-handled braided whip along the deck. He brandished the weapon, and cracked the sliver of rawhide at the tip with a sound like a rifle shot in the still night. Then he stepped back and sent the lash snaking through the air like something alive.

"*Mon Dieu, non!* Stay your hand!" Veronique screamed out. "Hawkes—he will kill us all, I know it, I know it!"

Startled, the man checked his swing. "Blast you Root, is this Hawkes's woman then? I'll not do this bloody thing. It will kill her sure."

"Cowards! I'll have to do it, though I prefer to watch." Root grabbed the whip, sending it out with all his strength against Brigida's frail form, and it snapped, coiling full circle about her narrow waist. Biting her lips, she kept silent as Root's terrible laughter echoed over the sea. The others were absolutely still. In the lonely circle of flickering light, Brigida tried to concentrate on distant things—the low wind moaning in the riggings, the creakings of beams and boards, a sail flapping, the familiar soft sound of the sea lapping at the bow, and something else, too, something not quite . . . the back snap of the whip recalled her to reality, and she screamed, every nerve in her body anticipating the next cruel cut. It never came.

There was a confusion of muffled sounds, a shuffle of feet, blows, curses. She felt herself being lifted, her wrists cut free, strong arms came about her, and then she saw his eyes, dark blue and deep, saw them turn wild with demonic fury. Gently wrapping her in his jacket, Slade set Brigida beside Levi. Then, taking up the black snake whip that lay at his feet, he turned on Blueford Root, who now brandished another of his own. Sweat poured from the heavy man's face, and his shirt clung in sticky, damp patches to his soft chest and protruding stomach.

"I've killed a rattlesnake at twelve feet with this, Hawkes," Root croaked, rocking from foot to foot as he shifted his massive weight. There was a loud crack, and at a wide rent in Slade's shirt, blood oozed down his arm. Then thick braided leather curled around his throat.

"Now I can break your neck with one good twist, Hawkes." Root took up some slack.

Slade's eyes went blank just for an instant. Suddenly, with a flick of the whip in his hand, he ripped Root's heavy cheek below the right eye. The man screamed and fell back, pulling the noose tighter, and Slade, his lips curled in a grimace of hate and rage, came on lashing out furiously, shredding Root's shirt and flaying the skin beneath it, drawing new blood with each slice, until the man was at the rail and had to stand. With one perfect curl, Slade snapped the fat man's wrist and the useless weapon fell from Root's limp hand.

"I can take a cigar out of a man's teeth at five paces, Root," Slade said, almost conversationally. There was a loud crack as he snapped the whip within inches of Root's shifting, pale eyes. "And I know how to kill a man with a few well-placed cuts."

Another snap sounded, rawhide danced, and the braided length of leather left a bloody swath across Root's thighs. He sank on the deck at Slade's feet, blubbering and begging. The relentless blows bit into his bloodied back until his quivering form was splayed out and still.

Slade, breathing deeply, flung away his weapon in disgust and turned to Brigida, who started toward him with a cry before the world began to spin and suddenly everything went black around her.

Brigida saw, through the porthole above her bunk, a blaze leaping against the sky. She looked about for Slade, and he came to her as soon as he saw her eyes open. "Jude, Jude was below decks," she moaned, "and . . ."

"He's fine, goddess, we're all fine, only worried about you. Can you sit up?"

"Of course. Why not?" Brigida gasped as she struggled

to one elbow.

Every muscle in her body complained when she tried to move, and she sank back against her pillows with a sigh. Slade lifted her, blanket and all, and held her close against him gently, as though she were a fragile bit of rare porcelain liable to crumble in his hands. He carried her to a large, deep chair, and in silence they watched the last flares of a dying fire off in the distance.

"How did you find us, love?" Brigida asked after a while. "Root never expected . . ."

"A girl came to see me, Harriet Glover, and then there was Carpenter. He came for Root's horse. I was waiting. Phil swore he thought his part in the scheme was to exchange the stallion for your freedom at Baja.

"Veronique told me Phil wanted . . . me." Brigida shivered and Slade held her closer. "Whom do you believe?"

"Phil's always been . . . easily led, and he did want you, but Root was lying to him, using him. They'd have killed Phil without a thought. He's gone away. For a long time. On an excursion down the Colorado, for starters. Before he went he told me that Root's ship wasn't provisioned, there wasn't even water. Root had to run along the coast to Baja. It was easy to overtake you in the *Indian*. The navy is just done fitting her for steam and her captain welcomed the chance to take her out with me aboard. We were just over the horizon for hours, but I had to wait until dark. I know Root would . . . he'd have killed you and Jude if he saw us."

There was a rumbling deep in the heart of the ship as

562

engines turned and built up speed.

"Root?" Brigida asked shuddering. She began to tremble as if with violent chilblains. "You . . . killed him."

"He won't ever trouble you again," Slade said, his arms tightening about her. "Don't worry."

"I'll be fine if you just stay with me a little," Brigida said, snuggling against him.

"I'm staying with you forever," he said.

There was a tap at the door, and then Jude, washed and dressed in a sailor's shirt and too-large breeches, bounded into the cabin, pulling Levi after him.

"Are you better, Brigida?" Jude asked. "My father saved us like you said . . . and Levi and Bran. They killed them mostly, and captured some. Right, Levi?"

"Veronique?" Brigida looked at Slade. "How . . . did Veronique die?"

"Stancel . . . she tried to save her own neck by accusing him of abducting her. He hurled a whaling iron. She upset a lamp when she went down, and Stancel took to the riggings with Bran snarling at his heels."

"Levi hit Stancel with a blade, ain't I right, Levi?" Jude's blue eyes were wide.

"Jude," Brigida sighed, "I've told you; don't say ain't; it isn't right."

"But you sure ain't wrong, boy." Levi smiled, ruffling the boy's dark hair, and Brigida laughed.

"And then we had to get off. The fire was spreading, and . . ."

"And it's over, once and forever, and now we can all go

563

home to Silver Hill—together!" Brigida said.

Sitting low in the water of San Francisco Bay like a curved sliver of sickle moon, a trim white ketch rode at anchor on a rising tide, her Blue Peter up and snapping in a brisk blow.

"She's yours," Slade said quietly, handing Brigida aboard.

"Mine? But . . . look, her signal's flying, she's about to put out. How . . . ?" Brigida said haltingly.

"It's all taken care of."

"But the train, Chicago, we . . ."

"Seems all of Chicago's in flames. Pullman wired. We'll give it a wide circle," Slade grinned, "very wide. Don't you like my gift, love?"

"Oh, Slade, she's the most beautiful craft, but I don't understand."

"You told me once, you wanted all your sons to be sailors, remember? They can learn on the *Whitehawk*, we named her that. Come, look around."

Slade watched Brigida as she inspected the exterior of the trim, polished vessel, and her face was a study in delight. "Perfect, Captain, she's perfect," Brigida repeated over and over as they circled the deck.

"Teak plank, bronze riveted on oak frames and keel. The spars are spruce, the sails are of the finest Egyptian cotton, vertical cut," Slade explained. "Come, lady, you'll want to see the quarters." He led her through a low portal.

The interior of the *Whitehawk* was mahogany and teak with brightly polished brass hardware on doors and abin panels.

"She's built on Puget Sound by an apprentice of
Donald McKay come out from the East."

"The Boston shipwright, McKay?" Brigida asked,
running a finger along the edge of a polished table. "He's
a master, I know, but Slade, it will take us months to sail
her home, and I so long to see Silver Hill before the turn
of the year, before the wedding."

"We'll stay with the *Whitehawk* only so far as the
isthmus, and then train across. Levi and his crew will
bring her round the Horn. We'll run before a lover's
wind, I promise, and you'll see Silver Hill again under the
hunter's moon. Does that suit?"

"It does, you know it does. Show me the rest of this
craft, Captain? If we're about to sail in her, I'll need to
know where things are, won't I?

"Perfect, perfectly done," Brigida said as they went
from galley to pantry to crew's quarters, where they
found Levi and Jude. "Slade, she'll sleep eight comfortably, not even counting . . . oh, my!" They had entered
the aft chamber that spanned the width of the boat. A
Morocco carpet covered the floor, a pretty blaze burned
in a blue-tiled fireplace, and a large bed was set right into
the curved oak hull of the graceful craft.

"Our cabin, Mrs. Hawkes. The sea will sing in our ears
here, when we're loving."

The look in Brigida's eyes was almost solemn when she
came into Slade's waiting arms. As they enfolded her, his
lips traced the curve of her neck, lovely as a flower stem
above her creamy lace collar, and their senses dulled to
everything but each other.

"Love me here, Slade, now?" Brigida whispered, their

bodies bending, pressing close. "Will you, will you?" she sighed.

"I've loved you every place else I can think of, why not here?"

Their lips met, softly at first, tasting, then parted and shifted, and an urgency came into each kiss.

"I'm going to sleep forward in a hammock like Levi and Sam Smith," a clear voice piped at the half-open door and Slade and Brigida pulled apart.

"Is that so?" Slade asked in a strained tone as he moved to lean at the mantel.

"Yes," Jude answered. "Nice," he said, coming into the room and looking about. "Sam Smith sailed in the *Whitehawk* before, did you know? Only then she was named something else. Sam Smith says she's crazy to windward and reaches as good as you could want. Harriet Glover is cooking supper, now. She's coming home with us. See you two later," the boy concluded and was gone.

"Your sons will all be sailors I think, Captain Hawkes, by the sound of that one."

"And my daughters, lady, will be sailors, too, like you love, their minds filled with sea lore and dreams of tall galleons and far-off places."

"If you don't lock the door, you may never have any more sons, or daughters, either," Brigida laughed, loosing her hair.

They heard the *Whitehawk*'s anchor chain rumble and clank as it rose, heard the call of gulls soaring over the bay, and then the sighs of the sea and the whispers of love were all and everything.

Epilogue

Early on a dewy July Fourth morning, a year after they had left, Elizabeth Carpenter and her husband, Adelbert, returned to Silver Hill. It was a bright day. The sky was pastel blue. Pink ribbons of cloud were caught in the top branches of oaks and maples, green in summer leaf.

The refurbished gatehouse at the entrance to the manor estate was the first sign the visitors saw of the change, and Elizabeth had the carriage stopped when Nan appeared on the doorstep.

"But Nanny, dear," Elizabeth said with concern after warm greetings, "why so early to work, and in your condition? When is your baby due, child?" Elizabeth's blue eyes were smiling.

"I'm thinkin' it will be before the first grain is ready or harvestin'. And I ain't at work a'tall, Mrs. Carpenter. The captain and his lady, they give us the carriage house, a marriage gift, it was, and we fixed it. My Johnny does a good lot on the place now," Nan said proudly. "He's at the mill already this day. Mrs. Carpenter? We was all real pleased to hear you and the mister was comin' home!"

When the carriage passed close to the tall mill, the sails were spinning in a morning breeze. A curl of smoke rose behind the mill, and when Elizabeth had the driver turn off that way, she discovered a neat new thatched cottage. Inside, she found Tom and Mary Sayre, she with an infant at her breast. After the first exclamations—Del's booming voice blending with Elizabeth's excited expressions of delight—the four sat at the kitchen table for a visit.

"Well, my little Mary," Elizabeth said, shaking her head, "I remember when you were no bigger than your pretty daughter there, and now you and Nanny will be raising up young ones together. If only Slade and Brigida . . ." Elizabeth stopped herself at a look from Del. "Who's seeing to the milking, Mary, now you've other calls on you?" she asked.

"I'm still dairy maid, Mrs. Carpenter. I just take Emily along. Tom's miller, and more than that, overseer like. Manager, Slade calls him. The captain and Brigida gave us two fields back of the mill when we wed, to farm for ourselves, so we are well pleased, very well pleased. Did anyone of 'em write to you about my brother Robin?"

"They did little enough writing, I'll tell you," Del huffed. "Phil dropped a note from California to say he was off to photograph the Wild West, and that was the last we heard, almost a year ago, but he said he'd be gone a long while. Well, what about Robin?"

"Robin Edwards up and run away with pretty Caitlin McGlory," Tom announced. "It was months 'afore they sent any word, and that was from Chicago a long while ago now, when the fire was. They were heading to a place he called the Sacramento Valley, to farm, can you imagine? They could just as well have stayed right here at home."

"Well, so you say, Tommy, but Cate's uncle would not have her marryin' up with a half-lame ordinary out-of-work seaman claiming no land or wealth. What did he bother comin' away here from Ireland for, Billy asks, and been slavin' ever since, if the girl's to end up like her mother and father in the old country, marryin' for love at seventeen and cold in a grave by thirty? So Caitlin and Rob run off. Broke Billy's heart, he says. Only, he looks healthy enough to me. Cate never sent her uncle a word, that flighty girl, but Robin, he wrote us, like Tom told you."

"Robin always had the wanderlust, didn't he Mary?" Elizabeth mused. "But they're a clever pair, and pretty as pictures, both of them. They'll do very well, I'd bet on it."

"You've not been to the manor house yet, have you Mrs. Carpenter?" Mary asked in a way that made Elizabeth a little uneasy.

"No, but we should go at once, Lizzy," Del said, standing and extending a hand to Tom.

"Just take me for a ride once around the manor, Del, before we go up? It is still so very early. We don't want to wake them, do we, dear?" Elizabeth looked up at her husband and, as always, it wasn't in him to deny her anything.

The red barns of Silver Hill were all freshly painted. The fields were green and gold, with young corn standing tall. The peach trees were bent heavy with ripening fruit.

Cows gathered along the fence rail at the barn, lowing softly in the feathery shade beneath the trees, waiting, Elizabeth knew, for Mary and the other girls. The air was filled with morning trillings and the calls of birds.

"They must be aging cheese, don't you suppose, Del? Why else have a goat?" Elizabeth puzzled.

"And ponies?" Del answered. "And a trap? I must remember to ask Slade. If he's breeding ponies, there is sure to be a very good reason, my dear."

A three-wheeled velocipede stood down the drive from the manor house, under the silver linden tree. There was a red India rubber ball in the cropped grass. A carved wooden cow on wheels, painted black and white, like Slade's herd, rested on the porch.

"What on earth is that, do you suppose?" Elizabeth pointed at what appeared to be a wooden birdcage hanging from a beam above the porch.

"I've not seen the like," Del said, helping her from the carriage. There are figures inside."

The manor house door swung open as they mounted the veranda steps. Elizabeth, bursting into tears at the sight that greeted her there on the sill, brought Levi and Martha hurrying out from the kitchen, Slade from above. And Brigida found them all gathered there when she tripped down the wide center stairs looking, Del remarked later, like a child herself, fresh as a spring day.

"My father says he'll be down directly," Jude had stated, "and you are to please come in now," and Elizabeth had looked down into smiling eyes blue as cornflowers, azure clear as the summer sky.

"How could you? How could the two of you do such a

thing to me?" she asked, laughing and crying at once while Del stood helpless, grinning broadly over her shoulder as she knelt to clasp the squirming little boy in her arms.

"It's a surprise, Mother, don't take on so," Slade said by way of comfort.

"What a fool I am not to have guessed! I mean the pony, the tricycle . . . I just . . . but what is that thing over the door?"

"You'll have to ask Levi. He and my wife set great store by it. These heathens have won Brigida over completely."

"It's a man, and a wife, in a house. To fool evil spirits," Levi said, glancing at Brigida. "It's done what it was meant to."

"And he's convinced me to keep a reaping hook at my window, a fishhook in the door jamb . . . all for luck," Brigida said, with a wink back at Levi.

"I might have expected this . . . this surprise of my son, but not of you Brigida," Elizabeth scoffed, releasing Jude to embrace her daughter-in-law, who smiled, lovelier than ever in saffron silk and white lace, golden hair flowing, dark eyes bright with a little hint of mischief.

"We didn't want you to think you had to come back before you were really ready to, Elizabeth," Brigida explained, leading them all to the library. By the time they were comfortably settled with tea and coffee, Martha, who had slipped off unnoticed, returned and presented Elizabeth with another surprise. The two women, friends for so long, were too filled with happy feelings even to speak at first as they looked into each other's face over a tiny newborn with smoky blue eyes.

There was a bright red ribbon round one fat dimpled wrist.

"To keep off the evil eye, red is best," Martha said finally, as Elizabeth began to laugh with delight.

"Lord in heaven, have you any more hidden away?" she asked, looking at the smiling faces around her. "And who, may I inquire, is this?"

"That's my brother, Jarred. There's no more," Jude said. "I'm going to teach him to talk, ain't that so Brigida? Isn't it so?" he amended with a grin, and everyone laughed.

"Grand times these are, grand times, Lizzy!" Del boomed, taking his wife's hand.

"Now that we're home at last, I'll do the portrait, the family portrait," Elizabeth announced, "and we'll all be in it, even Bran, for the whole world to see and admire."

"And Phil will do his photographs when he comes home," Brigida added. "Then our great-great-grandchildren, and everyone, forever after, will know us, and know the promise that was in this house this beautiful summer day."

Slade's eyes met Brigida's then and, in the midst of all the bubbling life about them, they were alone together for an instant—their hearts lit with the wonder of love.